OUT OF SIGHT

OUT OF SIGHT

MARTIN GRANGER

Red Door

Published by RedDoor
www.reddoorpress.co.uk

© 2021 Martin Granger

The right of Martin Granger to be identified as author of this Work has been
asserted by him in accordance with sections 77 and 78 of the Copyright, Designs
and Patents Act 1988

ISBN 978-1-913062-61-3

A CIP catalogue record for this book is available from the British Library

Cover design: Megan Sheer

Typesetting: Jen Parker, Fuzzy Flamingo
www.fuzzyflamingo.co.uk

Printed in Great Britain by TJ Books limited

One

The Leong family had no idea that their favourite game show, *Challenge the Leader*, was being transmitted from 22000 miles above their heads. They had stumbled across the programme a few months back when channel-hopping and had become addicted to the Friday-night show. It was an obscure channel, and the programme probably an old rerun, but the amiable host and the childlike graphics appealed to them more than the slick American mainstream networks. They were also unaware that they were one of only a few hundred families in Penang who could receive the programme. It was a remnant of television's distant past. Someone had signed a contract promising years of broadcasting only to find that modern transmission space was at a premium. In the last few months the corporate lawyers had found a loophole. There was no mention of how the programme was to be broadcast and so they simply moved the station. Its new home became an old, partially defunct, satellite that was launched in the early 1990s, only months after the Malaysian government sanctioned its private space program. The game show had been merrily flying through the ether ever since.

The satellite was nearing its twenty-five-year decommissioning status, a promise the operators had made to one of the many organisations around the world trying to make sense of this space-age chaos. But the original operators were long gone and the control of the satellite had passed through many hands, until today it was just a minor annex to one of the major Malaysian satellite companies. As a result, in an isolated featureless concrete building in the middle of Kazakhstan, an unmanned machine was sending old-fashioned radio waves to keep the thing on course.

'On course' was a high-level orbit around the Earth at a speed of seven thousand miles an hour. In the early days not a problem, but recently the space around it was getting rather crowded. The passage of some newer satellites was now within a tenth of a degree longitude, the closest under a hundred miles away. And that was only the beginning of the worry. The Earth's atmosphere is a rather congested place. At the last count, half a million pieces of space junk are flying around at speeds of 18000 miles an hour. At that speed even small flecks of paint will make a colander out of your satellite. Fortunately there's an organisation looking at this stuff and, while the Leongs were shouting out the answer to the last quiz question, on the other side of the planet Ralph Mears noticed a spike of concern on his monitor.

'Haven't seen that one before; it's big too, possibly about ten centimetres diam.'

His colleague leaned over and checked the data. 'Probably some of that South American telecoms satellite that ruptured its fuel tanks back in 2017. They had explosions during ground testing – still launched the damn thing. Fucking idiots. Now we've got another few thousand bits of crap flying around up there like some crazy race circuit.'

Ralph ignored Carl's expletives. 'Well I've not seen this piece before. Could be that some junk has collided with other junk and made more mess. Check out its trajectory, let's see if it's going to hit something important.' Ralph moved out of his chair and made towards the kitchen. 'Coffee?'

Carl slipped into his position behind the monitors. 'Fresh one, none of that stewed stuff.' He bent over the computer and started to tap the keys. 'Okay cutie, let's see where you're going.'

The flat scrubland near Baikonur in Kazakhstan was devoid of population apart from the few waterbirds that inhabited the low marshlands that encroached into the desert. With a good pair of binoculars, the single-storey building surrounded by the rusting wire fence could be seen from miles away. The road leading to this structure was unmade and a long way from the nearest highway, and few people had the need or inclination to visit it. Fifty miles away the Cosmodrome was another matter entirely. The place was heaving with visitors. The world's largest space launch facility, despite being located away from large centres of population, can be accessed by a network of modern rail services and motorways and the hotels were full. The launches were more discreet twenty years ago, when the rocket carrying a satellite bus and its *PhreeSat* payload soared into the cloudless sky. The Malaysian operators were new to the game and settled on a primitive control centre in the barren outlands to guide their spacecraft. The land was cheap, their Kazakhstan landlords experienced, and the satellite needed minimal attention. At the time everything could be controlled from a small office in downtown Singapore. Since the takeover this had been wrapped up in some vast administration office in Kuala Lumpur. Ironically, linking the satellite to the sophisticated computers at their HQ was the worst thing the latest operatives could have done.

The two birdwatchers parked their car about half a mile down the unmade track. The concrete hut looked like the perfect hide in this flat, treeless landscape but the ruts and potholes were getting too deep to drive any further. As they approached on foot they were dismayed to see the barbed-wire surround but, as they had come this far, they walked around the perimeter to see if there were any points of access. The wire was old and unattended and it didn't take them long to find an opening, probably torn by some feral animal. The two men pushed their backpacks through before crawling under the fence. The building was a flat-roofed structure made of unrendered breeze blocks, crudely slapped together by unpointed cement. There was one metal door and one small frosted-glass window. A large antenna protruded from the top. The sturdier man tried the door. It appeared to be locked. He heaved his shoulder against it. Surprisingly the door swung open with a loud creak. It was dark inside but they could see specs of coloured lights. As their eyes became accustomed, it was apparent that these lights were coming from arrays of machinery resting on a metal bench. It looked fairly primitive, probably some old pumping gear, so the birdwatchers ignored the technology and looked for a viewing position. Even with their binoculars pressed up against the window it was still too opaque for their purpose. They pushed the door open as far as it would go and lay on the floor. Their backpacks made good cover and a resting place for their binoculars. They set their sights and waited.

Ralph returned holding the handles of two steaming mugs of coffee in one hand. Carl was still bent over peering at the monitor.

'Where do you want this?' asked Ralph.

Carl didn't reply.

'Hey, take one of these, my hand is burning.'

Carl turned to look over his shoulder. 'Not the only thing that's going to be burned if someone doesn't move their satellite out of the way of this baby.'

Ralph put the coffee mugs down on a pile of papers and leaned over to see what Carl was talking about.

'Not there,' spat Carl. 'They're the printouts of the orbits. If you really want to know what's going on why don't you check those out?'

Ralph looked around for somewhere else to put the coffee. Not finding anywhere, he placed one on the floor and picked up the printouts. It didn't take him long to work out what was going on.

'They've not got much time. Have you contacted the satellite operator?'

Carl gave him a sarcastic glare. 'Oh yeah, worked out the trajectory, printed out all the data, and I've had plenty of time to look up "White Pages" whilst you've been making two cups of coffee.' He bent down and picked his off the floor. 'Without even going to the fridge for the milk by the look of it.'

Ralph sat down in front of his own terminal. 'Fair enough, I'll check through the database. *PhreeSat*, what sort of name is that?'

'Old school, launched in the early nineties I think. Let's hope they're still around to move the bloody thing, otherwise we're going to have another thousand bits of junk to follow.'

Ralph was used to Carl's exaggerations but, if this bit of debris hit the *PhreeSat* satellite, it would certainly make a mess and the trouble with this mess was there would be no one to clear it up.

'I reckon they've got about half an hour. Strange we didn't notice this object before.'

'You accusing?'

'No, of course not, you're the best tracker at the Ops Centre. Just saying they don't have much time, that's all.'

'Backhanded compliment accepted. Now why don't you stop nattering and message the guys who own that thing.'

The Whiskered Tern swooped into the view of the binoculars. Southern Kazakhstan was an ideal place to follow their migration. Despite the fact that the bird was more than a hundred yards away, the birdwatchers held their breath.

'Camera?' whispered one after a while.

The other birdwatcher shuffled backwards slowly and reached into his bag. The Zenit camera bore a long lens and either the movement or the reflection of sunlight disturbed the bird. His partner swore as it flew into the distance. They settled down with their binoculars once more, scouring the horizon. Not a bird in sight but in the distance a cloud of dust coming, at speed, directly towards them. In unison they refocused their binoculars. A dark object was tearing along the dirt track, apparently ignoring the ruts and rocks. As it came closer some markings became visible. They were military. The two men dropped their glasses, looked first at each other and then behind them into the interior of the room. The machines were still blinking. Evidently not a pumping station. A military installation perhaps. The armoured car was now nearly upon them. The flat brushlands stretched for miles, pointless to run. The man with the camera pushed it back into his bag and clumsily pulled out his papers and his bird handbook. He waved them at the soldiers who were running towards the building, shouting and brandishing their PKM machine guns.

The next few moments were a blur as the soldiers kicked away their bags and threw the birdwatchers onto the ground. Heavy boots were placed on their backs and questions were shouted in Russian. One of the men began to answer in his native Kazakh, but a gun butt in the head forced him to plead clemency in Russian. Their bags were searched, their papers scrutinised, and the camera confiscated. They were made to lie face down whilst a soldier inspected the interior of the building. He seemed satisfied and nodded towards his superior. The birdwatchers were dragged unceremoniously towards the armoured car. Plastic strips were placed around their wrists as they were heaved into the back. Looking out of the small slit windows of the vehicle they could see one of the men placing a large padlock on the metal door. He pulled at it violently to see if it would hold before jumping back into the driving seat and turning the ignition. They lurched forward recoiling up and down to every movement as they sped along the dirt track back to the main highway.

The offices of MalaySat Corp fill most of the seventy-fifth floor in Tower 2 of the Petronas Twin Towers in Kuala Lumpur. Today was a particularly fine day and shards of light glinted from Symphony Lake in the park way below them. Jenny Kang never tired of the view. She had graduated in astrophysics at Berkeley some months earlier. This job as a satellite operator was in a building as close to the sky as she would ever get. Her work to date had been fairly routine, monitoring communication satellites; not exactly the space travel excitement that she had yearned for. But the views from the Towers were spectacular and, like now when she had little to do, she would stare out of the windows and dream. There was a 'ding' from the desk behind her. No one else was in the office this evening. It must be her mobile. Perhaps the guy she met last night asking for a date. She strolled over to her desk, trying not to be too eager to see his number on her screen. It was a message but not from him. It was one of the contacts that MalaySat had asked her to store in her phone. JSpOC, she couldn't remember what the initials stood for. The company had mentioned something about a tracking station but she had been so keen to impress that she hadn't asked too many questions. She clicked open the message.

Your satellite PhreeSat in the path of space debris approx. 10cm diam. Collision estimated 30 minutes. Please advise of any action taken.

It took a while for Jenny to take in this information. It seemed so casual for such a catastrophic event. She scrolled down further to note the exact coordinates of the orbits and the potential collision point. *PhreeSat,* not a name she was familiar with. The main satellites she was monitoring covered major broadcast and telecommunications from Eastern Africa to Australia. They were modern and well maintained and to date she had had little to do. She looked at her watch: thirty minutes, not a lot of time if it was one of theirs. On the other hand, she didn't want to call her employers and appear in a panic; that would do little for her chances for promotion. She tapped at the consul, searched for the name. Not in the main file of operational broadcast satellites. Perhaps it had been a mistake, or even a scam. Twenty-five minutes to go. Worth another attempt. She stumbled across some back files; satellites procured from other companies in past takeovers. Most had been decommissioned but she found one that, although on the decommissioning list, was still in service. Her Malay was rusty so she took a while to find the source. Someone had filed it phonetically, *FreeSat*. Twenty minutes to go. The name had to be too coincidental. Jenny typed in the orbital path that was described in the text message and aligned it with the satellite in the file. It was an exact match. She scrolled through the list of numbers on her phone to a number she had been given. The text alongside was written in capitals. *ONLY TO BE USED IN EXTREME EMERGENCY.* She hesitated. She had been employed to monitor and control the company's broadcast satellites. Wasn't it this that she was supposed to do? The room was getting warm, or was it that she was flushed with anxiety? She pointed her smart phone at the aircon, turned it down a few notches, and went back to her station. She had done the satellite manoeuvre many times in simulation. This should be no different. Now that she had the codenames it shouldn't be too difficult to link with the control station; where was it, somewhere in Kazakhstan? A computer signal to the station would automatically instruct them to direct the radio waves on a frequency that would open the small rocket boosters. Just a little nudge, enough to move it a few degrees and out of the way of the 18000 miles-an-hour missile coming towards it.

She opened the channel. Fifteen minutes to go.

In its geostationary orbit at 22000 miles above the Earth's surface, despite its age, the satellite *PhreeSat* was operating perfectly. The videotape recording of *Challenge the Leader*, although suffering from the occasional dropout from the scratches on the old magnetic tape, suffered no lack in quality by being bounced from the satellite to the dishes in the small footprint on the Malaysian Peninsula. Nor was the transmission interrupted as small jets of propulsion came from the vehicle that carried it. Smoothly the old Boeing satellite bus moved a few degrees off its normal trajectory into the empty space around it. Seven thousand miles away the piece of metal space debris hurtling towards it had no intelligence on board to know that its path of destruction had been avoided.

Jenny Kang was cooling down. The monitors were showing the right data. She recalculated the plot of the new course a number of times before reaching for her phone and texting back to the tracking agency. She tried to make it as cool as the one she had received. *PhreeSat moved. Collision averted.* Followed by the coordinates of the adjusted orbital path. No need to ring the emergency number or her employers. When they discovered how professional she had been she would modestly say that she was only doing her job. Just to be sure, she checked the orbits of her mainstream satellites. There they were, normal flight paths, transmitting on their usual frequency. She breathed a sigh of relief and strolled back into the corridor to look out of the window once more. Downtown Kuala Lumpur was as busy as usual, the traffic running along the freeways like ants scurrying towards their nests. It was a real privilege to get this aerial view of the city. Tourists often had to queue for hours and pay nearly a hundred ringgits to have this experience. Jenny could take a look any time she liked. She glanced at her watch. Without her calm actions, in two minutes' time, one of MalaySat's vehicles would have been dust. She decided to take the pleasure in watching the near miss on her screens. Admittedly it would be in numbers but satisfying, nevertheless. The office was quietly humming with the sound of the aircon. The temperature was fine so she left the setting alone. The monitor was still locked onto her priority satellite. *Birdsong* they called it. It was strange to think that this object in space was providing most of Australia with its main news channel. Now where was *PhreeSat*? The access codes were still scribbled on a pad next to her screen. She typed in the numbers but the pathway didn't look right. She typed them in again. Still the same orbit, the original one that she had moved it from only a few minutes ago. Something was wrong. Very wrong.

Challenge the Leader was coming to a climax. The last standing contestant had only one question to answer to win the $10000 prize. The throbbing music built the tension.

'What is the capital of Australia?'

The Leongs shouted at the screen. 'Sydney, it's got to be Sydney.'

The contestant smiled. 'I know this one,' she said.

But the Leongs never did get to know if she did or not. The screen on the television silently cut to black.

Twenty-two thousand miles above their heads the reaction was a little more dramatic. The piece of space junk travelling at thousands of miles an hour hit *PhreeSat* with extraordinary force. The satellite broke into hundreds of pieces, the wreckage spreading far into space, joining the half a million or so other fragments of debris circulating planet Earth.

Two

The Soho offices of Bagatelle Films were unusually quiet. Their last investigative television programme was aired on the BBC the night before, to great acclaim but, for the first time in five years, there was no other active project in the production line. Geoff Sykes, the proprietor, flicked through his old back files. A number of great programme proposals and highly creative treatments but, as most were on topical investigations, they were now out of date. The problem with being an established film company, Geoff thought, was that established commissioning editors eventually moved on. Broadcast slots were becoming more and more difficult to win. Younger avant-garde companies were putting in ideas at half the cost, many videoed on iPhones and edited in back bedrooms. The halcyon days of 16mm film with a five-man crew were over, replaced by reality TV that was shot by the yard. Perhaps it was time to stick his film awards into a loft cupboard and pack it all in.

The intercom on his desk made a loud buzz. He pressed the button and spoke into the microphone.

'Film producers' retirement home, can I help you?'

The mellifluous voice of Stefanie, his PA, came down the line. 'Not me, Geoff. Nathalie's just dropped in; wants to know if there's any work going.'

'I wish,' said Geoff. 'Best bloody film director in London looking for a job and we haven't got a vacancy. There was a time when I could have done with three Nathalies.'

'What shall I tell her?'

'Tell her that, unless she's got an imminent shoot this afternoon, to come on in and cheer up an old man.'

After a few moments Nathalie bounced through the door. 'The

old man feeling sorry for himself is he? Why not enjoy it, you could do with the rest.'

Geoff removed himself from his swivel seat and gestured towards the easy chairs in the corner of his office. 'You know me, Nathalie, if I haven't got eight programmes on the go I can't sleep. How are you anyway? Saw your doc on knife crime; very good, although, I'm sure it would have been better if we had produced it.'

Nathalie laughed, 'Same old Geoff, can't stand complimenting another production company. Well you'll be glad to know they haven't got any more commissions either.'

Geoff put his feet on the coffee table. 'Bad times, Nathalie. So, besides knocking on my door, what else are you up to?'

'Oh this and that; been putting a few of my own ideas together.'

'Anything that would interest us?'

'Not sure. Although I did have one strange phone call the other day. Some sort of scientist. Saw that programme we made on Ebola and terrorism. Said he liked the hard-core investigative approach. Don't know how he got my number; must have seen the credits and found me in one of the production guides.'

Geoff took his feet off the table and put his arms behind his head, a gesture he normally made when becoming interested in a topic of conversation. 'A scientist you say.'

Nathalie could see where this was leading. 'Yeah, but not a medic, doesn't want a follow up.'

'So, what's his field?'

'Cosmology.'

Geoff looked surprised. 'Cosmology?'

'Yes, astrophysics sort of guy, looking at the universe.'

'I know what a cosmologist is. What's he doing asking you about the Ebola programme?'

'It wasn't the Ebola that interested him. It was the way we did the investigation. He said he had an idea, wanted to know if I could help him.'

'I get hundreds of people ringing up saying they've got an idea. What's so special about this guy?'

'I'm not sure, he just sounded interesting. Works on something called Cold Dark Matter. Says a lot of his job involves tracking a telescope they've put up recently.'

'Put up?'

'Yes, into space, like the Hubble. Looking for remnants of the Big Bang apparently.'

'Don't think that one will fly; dozens of programmes about that sort of stuff recently.'

Nathalie got up to stretch her legs. 'Not sure he was thinking of a programme on cosmology. It's the methods we used he was interested in. Says he believes there's something fishy going on.'

Geoff was becoming attentive again. 'Space telescopes. Fishy? Has he contacted the authorities?'

Nathalie looked up at the row of international clocks on the wall. The UK one was reading one forty-five. 'Christ is that the time? I said I would be at Vibrant Productions at two. Authorities, yes, no. He thinks they might ridicule him. Hasn't got enough evidence. That's why he rang me.'

Geoff rose to show her out. 'Okay, on your way. Sounds fascinating though. If you hear from him again let me know.'

Harry Stones felt the sun on his back as he strolled down the flower-bordered walkway to the Cosmat building. The three-storied glass-fronted structure had won an architectural award only a few months before the incumbents had gone bankrupt, and the administrators had put it up for auction. At the time a benefactor had funded a collaboration between MIT and London University to research Cold Dark Matter. The building was not far from the Surrey Satellite engineers in Guildford and, as there was expected to be some communication between the two, it made the ideal location. The project had been running for five years and, although no ground-breaking discoveries had been made, the data was promising. But today Harry had other things on his mind. He swept through the rotating doors, waved his security badge towards the reception desk and took the familiar route to the lift. Some seconds later, as the mechanical voice announced 'first floor', he stepped out of the lift and slid the glass door sideways to enter his office. He could smell the coffee from the percolator but made straight for his desk. The hum of his computer told him it was still on, as always.

'Centauri, search News for satellite malfunctions.'

The blue light flashed on the electronic personal assistant device. Within moments it provided the answer.

'*The Straits Times* Singapore reports a problem with a broadcast satellite in Malaysia.'

Harry was used to multitasking, and he tapped at his keyboard whilst asking another question.

'Centauri, what is the name of the satellite with the malfunction?'

The black box flashed again, and this time it took a few seconds longer to reply.

'No data on that question.'

But Harry had beaten Centauri to it. The change in tone of the computer indicated that the program that he had left running overnight was churning out the calculations. He pressed a button on the laptop and it read the numbers to him.

'Shit,' he said to himself. 'Another one, and this time a direct hit.'

'Harry.'

He turned towards the voice at his door.

'Sorry to disturb. Video-conference link meeting next door. MIT want to discuss the latest gravitational wave data from the telescope.'

'Video-conference,' Harry laughed. 'Okay, Bernard, I'll be with you in a minute. Just need to print out this stuff first.'

The irony wasn't lost on Bernard. Harry was practically blind. He was also, by far, the best astrophysicist on their team. He had joined the team at its inception, a no-brainer for the interview panel. A genius they said, an obsessive but a genius. Perhaps it was this obsession that led him to ignore his diabetes which resulted in the retinopathy that slowly degraded his sight. Typically, Harry focused on his work yet ignored the signs of deteriorating vision until it was too late. He refused to resign and simply carried on in an attempt to resolve his calculations.

'We are trying to find Cold Dark Matter,' he had said. 'The point is, *no one* can see it; not having sight shouldn't make an atom of difference.'

And he had proved them right. He had geared his office with voice-activated software and continued with his work as if nothing had happened. This had been fine for the last two or three years but, recently, he had been asked to monitor their new space telescope. This device was revolutionary. It had the capability of searching out low gravitational waves as well as mapping structures in the infrared. Both useful functions in determining the existence of Cold Dark Matter and how galaxies were formed in the early universe. Unfortunately, the telescope satellite had come with a warning, 'Beware of Space Junk'. It was this warning that had led Harry's obsession to take a different turn.

Bernard left the office door open. 'That stuff's not to do with your…?'

'None of your business,' snapped Harry. 'I said I would be with you in a minute.'

Bernard shrugged. 'Fine, we'll wait for you.'

The MIT team could sense that Harry's mind was elsewhere. He had developed a technique of placing his eyeline in the view of the monitor and was normally sharp with the relevance of his data.

Today, however, his eyes wandered towards the ceiling and his answers were vague.

'Did you get that, Harry?' asked Bernard, tapping him on the shoulder. 'The Nevada lot are questioning our basic principles; say we should be looking into our satellite's atomic clock.'

Harry shrugged him off. He hated the patronising touch of his colleagues. 'Just because I can't see, doesn't mean I can't hear them,' he snapped. 'They think the satellite passes through a topological defect; the defect should cause the satellite's atomic clock to skip a beat. All crap. One jump in one atomic clock isn't enough proof for their topological defects. Nothing wrong with our methods. The stuff coming in from the satellite is giving us a good foundation for predicting Cold Dark Matter. Now defects, that is a problem. I keep telling you that there is shit going on up there. Something's not right with satellite trajectories. We need more resources, keep an eye on it. If something hits our bird it will set us back years.'

The group heaved a communal sigh of despair. Harry had been going on about some sort of trajectory anomalies for weeks. It had been since his deterioration in sight had hit a low, so they had made allowances. Now it had developed into an irritation. His real work was suffering and all he seemed to think about was the movement of satellites and space junk.

Bernard rose from the table. The Zoom conference was becoming an embarrassment. 'Hey, you guys,' he said into the camera lens. 'Think we'll call it a day. Send us that paper on topological dark matter and we'll come back to you. Let's say this time next week.'

The faces on the monitor nodded sympathetically and the link was terminated.

'Next week!' exploded Harry. 'Next week we might not have a satellite to link up with them.'

'Harry,' said Bernard, once more touching him on the arm.

'Get the fuck off, and don't you "Harry" me,' he barked. 'And the rest of you can stop staring,' he added, casting his non-seeing eyes around the room.

The group shuffled uncomfortably in their chairs and, one by one, quietly exited the room following the sideways indication of Bernard's head.

'So, now you've got rid of that lot tell me that you are going to fire me.'

'Don't be stupid, Harry, fire you? You're the best brains on this project. You need to refocus though; get your mind back onto what matters. This sight thing, it's hit you harder than you think. We shouldn't have put you on this satellite tracking business. Thought it would ease you back into work but you've become obsessive about it. Anyway, it's beneath your intellect. Look, take a week off, you're due some leave. When you get back, we will set up a proper academic tour for you. You've been in this office too long. Get out, visit some colleagues, get some telescope time, put yourself in the front line where it really matters. If anyone's going to find Cold Dark Matter, you should be leading the field.'

Harry took a deep breath and sat back down in his chair. He intertwined his hands and tapped his thumbs. Head bent down, he seemed to think for a moment. 'All right, I'll take the leave, as long as you put Trevor on satellite tracking and he reports directly to me if there're any anomalies.'

'Done. And the field trip?'

'All-expenses-paid, and the institutions and locations I want to visit?'

'Absolutely, just flag them up and we'll make the arrangements.'

'Shake on it?' Harry stood again and held out his hand.

Bernard took it firmly in his. 'One condition.'

'Which is?'

'No bothering the authorities with your space junk ideas.'

Harry made a firm handshake in acquiescence. 'Now, if I'm off to my sun lounger I better get back to my office and make some end-of-term notes for Trevor.'

Bernard watched him make his way out of the meeting room. He only hoped he had made the right decision. Harry was indeed the best brains of the outfit. It was worth the arrangements and disruption to keep him. If after a month he was still in the same place, perhaps then he would have to let him go.

Harry found his chair by touch and felt for the keyboard. He started to type, first with two hands and then with one as he reached for his phone. 'Nathalie Thompson, Bagatelle Films,' he whispered into the microphone.

Bloodcurdling cries could be heard from the cell next door. The two birdwatchers cowered in the corner. They had been waiting in this damp stone-floored room for hours. On arrival they had given their names and addresses and had been rudely locked up in what they could only describe as a dungeon. No one had visited them since. From the small barred window high above them they could see that it was now getting dark. They were cold, hungry and frightened.

The door was flung open. The silhouette of a Russian army officer in full regalia filled the frame.

'Get up!' he shouted.

The two men didn't move. They were scared and at first did not quite understand the Russian phrase.

'Get up!' this time in Kazakh.

The two scrambled to their feet.

'Why are you keeping us here, Sir?' asked one in stumbling Russian, trying to appease the man.

'Ah so you do understand Russian,' said the soldier. 'Come with me.'

They followed him down the passageway, past a number of metal doors towards a shaft of light. They had only seen this stuff in movies. What next? A lichen-draped room with bizarre instruments of torture. The man at the rear began to shake at the knees. The officer turned and chided him.

'Hurry up, they've come some distance. I wouldn't like to be in your position when you meet.'

The birdwatchers groaned.

The light at the end of the corridor led to a simple anteroom. The two men looked around in dread of their fate but, instead of the iron manacles and coils of electrodes, they found two familiar figures sitting on chairs next to a samovar of tea.

They were met, first by abuse, then by hugs of tears as their wives wrapped themselves around their shaking bodies. The soldier laughed.

'They're letting you off lightly. Not an easy journey from your Homestead to the army barracks, but it's the only way we could verify your story.'

The birdwatchers were nonplussed. 'But why were we held in the first place? We were only using an old building as a bird hide.'

'We know that now, but I think it's best for you not to ask any more questions. And definitely not to go anywhere near that building again.'

After a warming cup of black Russian tea, the two men were given their backpacks and binoculars. Papers were signed and stamped and they were escorted into the barrack's car park.

The four-door Hyundai Accent pulled out of the compound lighting up the road ahead. The soldier was right, it would be a long way back to their Homestead. They probably wouldn't get there before the early hours. The wives took the front seats and the men slouched glumly in the back. After half an hour of silence one of the rear seat passengers plucked up the courage to start a conversation in their native Kazakh.

'What did they ask you?'

His wife, who was driving, kept her eyes on the road. 'Who you were, what time you went out, what you were doing and, believe it or not, whether you had anything to do with the Cosmodrome.'

'Cosmodrome?'

'Yes, you know, that enormous space station place.'

'What did you say?'

'Say? I laughed.'

'What did he say?'

'Think he got the idea. A man who can't even count his chickens' eggs working for a space station. I don't think so.'

The woman in the front passenger seat turned around. 'Strange though, thinking you were both something to do with the space station. That building you were hiding in must be something to do with it; overheard one of the soldiers saying that they'd received a warning but that nothing in the "control station", I think he called it, had been touched. Perhaps that's why they let you go so easily.'

'That and us driving hundreds of miles to confirm who you were,' interrupted the driver. 'That's the last time you two go out looking for birds. Stupid thing to be doing anyway. Two grown men tramping around the countryside searching for creatures they can find in their own farmyard.'

'Make a good story on Facebook though,' said her husband reaching for his phone.

Three

Nathalie peered into the window of Patisserie Valerie in Old Compton Street. It was mid-morning, the early birds had long left and the lunch crowd had yet to arrive so there were few people inside. It shouldn't be difficult to pick him out. The sunlight glinted off the polished plate-glass obscuring some of the colourful cakes on display. Not quite her thing at this time in the morning but, when he had called, it was the first place that came into her head. She opened the door and walked past the counter. A couple of women in one corner were bent over their cappuccinos and, opposite, a young hipster-looking guy was reading a media magazine. Perhaps she was too early. Then she spotted him at the rear of the café cradling an espresso. In his mid-fifties, hair greying at the sides, intellectual sort of face. Had to be him.

'Doctor Stones?'

The man rose from his chair and held out his hand. 'Nathalie Thompson?'

She took it and smiled. 'That's me. Pleased to meet you.'

They sat and he held his arm in the air to catch the waitress's attention. 'Coffee, cake?'

'Oh, a cappuccino for me,' said Nathalie turning to the waitress who had turned up. 'And another espresso for you?'

'No thank you, Ms Thompson, got here early, I'm on my third. I just want to thank you for agreeing to meet.'

Nathalie felt slightly uneasy. There was something different about this man but she couldn't quite put her finger on it. 'Nathalie, please call me Nathalie. No problem, Doctor Stones. Your story sounded interesting, and my job is interesting stories so I couldn't resist it.'

Stones played with the handle of the diminutive cup, spinning it around in the saucer. 'Harry, if we are on first name terms, it's Harry. You must be a busy young woman so I won't waste your time. I'll get to the point. As I told you, I'm a cosmologist studying Cold Dark Matter, but that's by the by. A few months back I was asked to monitor a satellite we're using to aid our research; make sure it doesn't bump into something.'

Nathalie's coffee arrived. She thanked the waitress which seemed to distract Harry Stones so she asked him a question.

'What do you mean bump into something?'

'Another satellite, a piece of space junk, you know.'

Nathalie stirred her coffee, still trying to get to grips with this man. 'No I don't know. Space junk?'

'Oh yes, sorry.' Harry reached into his bag on the table beside him and pulled out a small laptop. He opened the lid, typed a few keys, and spun it around. 'There, space junk.'

She looked at the screen. It held a picture of the Earth with what looked like thousands of insects buzzing around its surface.

'Extraordinary, isn't it, when you see it for the first time. Each one of those dots is a piece of junk or a satellite, all travelling at thousands of miles an hour. From time to time they bump into each other, causing more space junk. It's a bloody nightmare for someone launching a new satellite into all that stuff, or making sure that the ones you've got up there don't hit anything.'

'Wow!' exclaimed Nathalie. 'Is it that bad?'

'Bad, I should say so. Imagine there's an accident on the M1. Nobody clears it up. A bit later an accident on the M25. Nobody clears it up. Now imagine you are in space, get the idea?'

Nathalie nodded. 'Interesting topic for a television programme but I'm more into the investigative documentary stuff. You know, crime, terrorism, ill-gotten gains by large corporations.'

Harry placed his hand under his chin. 'Yes, I know, that's why I contacted you. I've been tracking satellite orbits for over a month. And there's something not quite right up there. A few of these things are moving out of their normal trajectories. A couple have actually hit something. I don't think these are natural events. I'm convinced that human hands are controlling these operations. And that person or those persons are up to no good. Things could get really dangerous.'

'Have you reported this?'

'Who to?'

'Well, the people in charge of space cyber security.'

Harry laughed. 'Cyber security. There is none. It's the Wild West up there. No laws, no space-police, no security.'

'Well, there must be some sort of international convention. The UN?'

'Oh, there are plenty of conventions. Mostly gentlemen's agreements, but actual hard-nosed legislation with real consequences? Nope. And before you ask, yes I have made overtures to all the treaty bodies I know of. None are interested. Not enough evidence. Apparently I'm a bit of a nuisance, imagining things, after...'

'After you lost your sight,' said Nathalie gently.

'Oh, you noticed.'

'Not at first, you're very good. How do you use that laptop?'

'Practice. I can touch type, know what keys will open files. You're thinking "How can someone, who is practically blind, make a programme on space sabotage?"'

'Make a programme?'

'Yes. No one seems to believe me so, if I could research and direct a programme that gives some answers like your investigative documentaries, they'll have to.'

Nathalie sat back. 'Well that's a first. I've had many people wanting to help research a project, but direct it!'

'Not a first actually, I've heard of several so-called blind film directors. And those are my conditions. If you want my expertise and my story, you will have to have me as a director.'

Nathalie stared at the man. He certainly sounded confident

and she was intrigued by his story. 'Well, it wouldn't be up to me, I'm only a freelance minion. The company that would put up the cash and get the commission is Bagatelle Films. The guy that runs it is called Geoff Sykes. And, if I'm not mistaken, knowing Geoff, he's going to take some persuading.'

'A blind film director!' Geoff's derisory voice came down the phone. 'Now I've heard it all, political correctness gone mad. Not only can the guy not see but he's not even made a film before. You've got to be crazy, Nathalie. Just because neither of us have got any work, there's no need to be clutching at straws.'

Nathalie waited for the rant to subside. 'I know it sounds odd, Geoff, and I must admit at first I thought it was crazy too but the more I talked to the guy the more interesting it got. If he's right it would make an amazing programme.'

'So who is this bloke? A cosmologist you said?'

'One of the leaders in his field. Checked him out on the internet. Incredible CV. In line for a Nobel Prize, they say. Anyway this television programme. He says he can do the research in the three-week trip he has planned. Apparently he can go where he wants all-expenses-paid by his project grant. Can't you donate a small bit of seed money so that I can go with him?'

'Yes, of course, that's not the problem. It's the fact that he's using his knowledge to make us hire him as the director of the programme. A director that can't see!'

'I've been thinking about that. I've always said that my cameraman is my eyes. If we hire a good one, they could be his.'

'But you say he's never even made a film before. Not even a wedding video. How on earth…'

'Okay, it's not going to be easy, but he's a really intelligent guy,' she laughed. 'Brain the size of a planet, you know. And I could keep a close eye on him. Produce the project; hands-on.'

'You're not going to let this one go are you?'

'At least meet with him.'

'Oh, all right, I've nothing better to do at the moment but I'm not promising anything.'

'Thanks, Geoff, you're a real star. You won't regret this.'

'Famous last words,' said Geoff after he had put down the phone.

It was seven in the evening in Kuala Lumpur. A glittering burst of light, the last before the burning sunset, flashed across the windows of the Petronas Towers. For once Jenny Kang didn't appreciate the view. She had been sitting in the boardroom of MalaySat Corps for the last three hours being interrogated by the chief technical officer and a number of other suits who had not provided their titles. Papers were thrown across the table in front of them – printouts of timesheets and satellite data taken from the days before, during, and after the *PhreeSat* crash. They had been over the event nearly a hundred times. When was she first alerted to the danger of the impact time? Who had made the first contact? What action did she take? Why didn't it work? And most importantly: Why had she not reported the first warning?

Jenny sat there with her eyes closed, head in hands, trying not to cry. She was exhausted. She had explained that she had taken evasive action but these men would not let up. There was a knock at the door. Another suit entered, whispered in the ear of the man to the right of the technical officer, handed him a piece of paper, and slipped out of the room. The man, a brutish sort of character, stood up and banged on the table.

'Miss Kang, I'll ask you for the last time, why did you not telephone your superiors when you were contacted by JSpOC?'

JSpOC. Jenny now knew what these letters stood for. The Joint Space Operations Centre in the United States. A focal point for worldwide joint space forces, and an organisation that alerted satellite operators regarding collision possibilities. She knew why she had not contacted her boss. She was keen to show she could handle what should have been a straightforward manoeuvre. The problem was she couldn't or, at least, it looked that way. She was sure she had carried out the correct procedures. For goodness' sake the satellite had actually moved. But they didn't, wouldn't, believe her.

She looked up at the man who was glowering at her. 'I thought I could handle it, I did handle it,' she pleaded for the umpteenth time.

'Well, one thousand pieces of orbiting shrapnel would seem to contradict that statement, Miss Kang.'

Jenny could hold her tears back no longer. 'But I moved it, I really did, there must be a record of it somewhere.'

'Well, fortunately for you, Miss Kang...' he held up the piece of paper that had been given to him, 'there is. At 18:00 hours on the day of the collision the records of the tracking station in the United States have noted a slight deviation of *PhreeSat* at the time you say you made your operational decision.'

Jenny started to breathe heavily. 'There, I told you, I told you. I moved it. It shouldn't have collided.'

'I was about to continue, Miss Kang, before I was interrupted, that they noted a deviation but after...' he looked down at the paper he was holding, 'after two hundred seconds, the satellite was repositioned to its previous course. Why did you re-plot its course?'

The tears began to flow again. 'I've told you; you really must believe me, I didn't touch it.'

'So you're telling me that it moved back onto its collision orbit all by itself?'

The chief technical officer, noting the distraught and exasperated expression on Jenny Kang's face intervened. 'Or there's someone else out there who moved it,' he said quietly.

The meeting had been set up for eleven o'clock in the morning at Bagatelle's offices in Soho Square. Geoff had nothing else in his diary and Harry Stones had said sarcastically that he was on a week's gardening leave so they agreed to Nathalie's suggestion that, after their chat, they could take an early alfresco lunch in London's warm summer sunshine. Nathalie found Harry tapping his way along Greek Street after his journey in on the tube.

'Hi, Doctor Stones, can I help you?'

'Harry, it's Harry,' he replied cheerfully waving his white stick in the air like a conductor's baton. 'Yes, of course, what a wonderful day.'

She looped her arm through his, and they walked slowly northwards taking in the smells of the local coffee shops.

'Come far?' asked Nathalie.

'Guildford, easy train to Waterloo and then a couple of stops on the Northern line.'

'Amazing, on your own, no dog?'

'Ah the last thing I want is to be dragged around by a dog. No, people are generally very helpful; let me know when my stop has arrived, help me across the road if there's a lot of traffic. But today is okay, I know this route well, used to go to scientific meetings just around the corner. And you?'

'Me?'

'Yes, you. Where have you come from?'

Nathalie suddenly realised that she might have been a bit patronising; asking him where he'd come from and how he had made the journey. He was only replying in turn as any other person would. 'Fulham, I take the District line. Like you it's a familiar journey. Bagatelle Films is practically my second home.'

'And this Geoff Sykes?'

'Bark worse than his bite. Nice guy really, but doesn't suffer fools, you know the sort. If he starts to become dogmatic and argumentative don't worry about it.'

'Oh, I think I can hold my own.'

Nathalie looked at the man walking beside her. 'Yes,' she thought, 'I bet you can.'

To Nathalie's surprise Geoff and Harry hit it off immediately. Neither was good at what she would call diplomacy, but their blunt, no-nonsense approaches seemed to conspire rather than create any antagonism.

'Okay, let me get this straight,' said Geoff. 'The data you've been collecting over the last few months has shown a number of satellites veering off course and then some of them returning to their normal orbits. Two of these have resulted in collisions. One, an experimental astronomical satellite just wandered into a piece of "space junk" as you call it, and recently, an active media satellite that was taking evasive action was moved back into a collision course.'

'Got it in one,' said Harry. 'These movements are not normal or accountable by any natural processes. They have to be manipulated by someone on the ground. My worry is that this is just the beginning. If this person or organisation can remotely control other people's satellites, then we really could have Armageddon. One slip and something could even hit a piece of military space hardware.'

'And no one seems to be interested in taking any action?' murmured Geoff, almost to himself.

'Except if you guys can broadcast a programme showing the dangers, or even the culprits if we can find them.'

Geoff got up from his chair and walked over to the window. Common habit of his when he was trying to think. It was a blazing late-spring day, not a cloud in the sky.

'And you think this is still going on up there, right now?'

'Can't be sure of it but that's why I'd like to use my mini-sabbatical to find out.'

'And this stuff is all paid for, you can go where you want?'

'Absolutely.'

'Then why can't you do that, and then report back to us? If there's anything in it, Nathalie could make the programme.'

Harry Stones picked up the laptop he had been using to show his presentation. 'I told Nathalie, that's not the deal. If I find anything, I'd like to film it on the hoof. I'm not prepared to trust anyone else with the data I discover. Either I direct it, or we part ways. Amicably of course,' he added.

Geoff glanced at Nathalie and raised his eyebrows, but this sort of story was right up Bagatelle's street. He didn't want to let it go without a fight.

'Believe me,' he said genuinely, 'my reticence isn't because of your lack of sight, although I can predict there might be problems there too, but we could get over those. I can see from your manipulation of the computer that you're highly skilled in communication and getting around. No, my problem is with your lack of film experience. It sounds easy, but it takes years to become a good documentary film director.'

'I'm not naive, Mr Sykes, I realise that there are skills and techniques that I've not even thought of, but any film director won't have *my* skills. Tens of years of physics, cosmology and extra-terrestrial data. Personally, I think it would be easier to teach me how to direct a film than a director how to manipulate the science.' He pushed his laptop into his bag and began to rise. 'However, I can understand your concerns. Thank you for your time.'

Nathalie glowered at Geoff. She shook her head indicating that he should intervene. Geoff moved back behind his desk. 'Please don't go yet, Harry. We promised to take you to lunch.' He looked at his watch. 'It's a great day for a stroll and there's a table booked at the Orrery for 12:30. It's got a wonderful outside terrace.'

'That means,' chipped in Nathalie, 'as it's midday, he's got half an hour more for you and me to persuade him.'

That half-hour was intense. Nathalie's premise was that, for a very small budget, she could accompany Harry as a producer on the project. If there was anything that needed filming she would get the crew and, if necessary, help him as an assistant director. She argued that it would be only for three weeks and that they wouldn't be paying Harry a penny as he had all expenses provided. In fact it was a no-brainer, a win-win. Harry noted the way the tide was turning and explained how he would go about the project. He had carte blanche with locations and knew a number of his colleagues around the world would be able to help out with tracking down unusual movements of extra-terrestrial objects and how they were being manipulated. Because of his reputation and autonomy, he could easily do this under the guise of his current project brief of searching for Cold Dark Matter.

The phone rang rudely interrupting the onslaught. Geoff took the call. He grunted one or two affirmatives into the mouthpiece and hung up.

'Sorry about that. The good news is that the commissioning editor wants to see me about a proposal I put in some time ago. The bad news is that I won't be able to come to lunch with you as he would like to see me now. I'm in no position to turn down any opportunities at the moment.'

Nathalie jumped up. 'So does that mean you're not going to turn down Harry's opportunity either?'

Geoff looked at her out of the corner of his eye. 'Well, Nathalie Thompson, you can be very persuasive sometimes; I suppose I'll have to consider it.'

'So that's a yes then,' she said, taking Harry lightly by the arm. 'You'll love the Orrery Harry, great food, and just the place for us to start planning our trip.'

Four

Many restaurants in central London are full of the hustle and bustle of metropolitan life. Today the exterior terrace of the Orrery was no different: difficult to have a quiet and possibly sensitive conversation about potential terror plots. Nathalie guided Harry out of the lift into the quiet dining room where one side was lined with white-clothed tables nestling in secluded booths. She gave her name to the receptionist and asked for a change of table in order that they could sit in the quiet interior. She did this with a little trepidation; not that she was worried about changing Geoff's booking but, the last time she had come here, she was doing her research incognito and had used a different name. She only hoped that the guy wouldn't notice. If he did, she needn't have worried, he merely ushered them to a side table in the corner. Harry felt for the seating and settled on the banquette on the inside. Nathalie asked for the menus.

'This one's on Geoff,' she laughed. 'He says there's a great value lunchtime set menu. That means that's the one we have to choose from.'

Harry discreetly felt for his place setting: knife, fork, glasses. 'My lunch yesterday was a chicken sandwich so a Michelin star set-meal is fine by me. Would you like me to fund the wine?'

'Certainly not. The old man gave us such a hard time back there that I'm sure Bagatelle can squeeze in a full bottle.'

The waiter arrived with two menus, handed one to Nathalie and was slightly perplexed when Harry didn't take the other.

'The gentleman can't see,' said Nathalie gently. 'Just leave it there and I'll tell him the choices.'

As the waiter backed off with slight embarrassment Nathalie read out the choice of starters and main courses.

'I think I'll start with the ravioli and try the sardines,' said Harry. 'Fish is easier to eat than meat in establishments such as this and, fortunately, I'm quite partial to sardines.'

For the first time Nathalie considered how Harry would eat his meal. How would he know where things were on his plate, what to cut up, what to combine with what?

'Fish easier?' she asked. 'Why fish?'

'It's soft, I can prod around and slice it with my fork. You get used to it. Steak is more difficult, unless I ask someone to cut it up for me. No, in posh places such as this, I usually plump for the fish. If some drops off my fork I don't mind embarrassing myself by picking it off the table and popping it into my mouth. If that's okay by you of course?'

Nathalie smiled and reached over to touch his hand. 'Harry, you are a marvel. The way you walked in here no one would think you have a problem with your sight. The waiter even waved the menu under your nose. But, as you are heading a project on cosmological research, I shouldn't be surprised. You know, I had my doubts but now I'm beginning to think that we can make this directing thing work.'

Harry tapped her hand back. 'Well I was going to say, Ms Thompson, that it's not rocket science, but in some ways this is what this project may turn out to be.'

They decided on a bottle of Provence rosé. Nathalie refused to tell Harry the price. If Geoff thought that his meeting was more important than theirs he would have to put up with it. The waiter poured a sample for Harry to taste. Nathalie reached over, took the glass, swilled the wine around the rim, and gave it a sniff.

'It's fine,' she said to the waiter. 'And it's best not to assume,' she added.

The waiter flushed a little, it was obviously not his day. 'Of course madam, and shall I pour out some for the gentleman?'

'Yes please,' said Nathalie swapping the glasses. 'Oh, and I'm sorry, that was a bit rude of me.'

Harry was listening intently. 'No you're quite right, why should a bloke take the responsibility for a corked wine.'

Nathalie couldn't quite decide if he was joking and covered her embarrassment by telling Harry where the water and wine glasses were placed on the table.

The starter arrived and they began with small talk – where they had grown up, their universities and their career paths. Nathalie then moved the conversation onto the filming project.

'Harry, I expect that in the documentary we're going to be interviewing people. I was concerned that you might have a problem in doing that but your eyeline is incredible, how do you do it?'

'Experience,' said Harry, reaching for his glass and taking a mouthful. 'Very nice wine, are you sure...' Harry must have anticipated Nathalie's shake of the head. 'Well, you must thank Mr Sykes from me.' He found a space on the table with one hand and lightly put down the glass.

'I've had this condition for a few years now. At first people started patronising me, stopped listening to my scientific ideas. Then I realised that I wasn't holding their attention because I wasn't looking at them, engaging them. So I've learned to find the eyeline by ear, if that makes any sense.'

'Absolutely. I must admit I'd never even thought about it before.'

Harry laughed. 'There is one problem though. I can't be absolutely sure that you're looking at me. For instance, if you were bored with my chatter you might be eyeing up some young man at the next table.'

'Harry! As if.'

'Oh don't worry, I'd get my own back. If I became bored with your conversation I'd just tune you out and earwig on someone else's. But enough of this impaired sight thing. I understand that we still have to get the final approval from your boss. What else do you think he needs?'

Nathalie paused while the waiter served up their main courses.

Harry had a good point. Geoff was nearly there but she really wanted his full commitment. She noticed Harry reaching for his cutlery.

'Your sardines look good,' she remarked trying to be as unpatronising as she could. 'They are layered on the right of your plate with some sort of squiggly vegetable on the left; ornamental courgette I would describe it.'

Harry felt the sardines with his fork and, finding the vegetables, scooped some up and placed them in his mouth.

'Excellent observation, Ms Thompson; fancy courgettes it is, and very good too.'

They spent a few minutes savouring their meal and, by the time a suitable pause had arrived, Nathalie had hatched her plan.

'You asked what would clinch the deal with Geoff. He's a great one for lists – locations, plans of action. If we could come up with some places that you want to visit, why you want to go there, and some ideas of who might be moving these satellites, I think he'll buy it. Doesn't have to be concrete facts, just some plausible explanations.'

Harry was deftly piercing the last sardine on his plate. He waved it lightly in the air. 'That's a good start, like writing a scientific research proposal and, although I say it myself, I'm quite good at that. Okay, put your iPhone on record and here goes.'

Nathalie reached into her bag and pressed her voice memo app. She missed the first few words as Harry had already started.

'…months ago I was tasked with monitoring our new satellite. There's a lot of junk out there and one small piece could hit something sensitive and blow our whole project. I must admit I was a bit pissed off about the remit; a junior research associate could have done the job. Oh, you had better scratch that last bit.' Harry took a sip of water, composed himself and began again. 'During routine monitoring of our satellite I noticed a number of aberrations in the paths of certain bodies within a few kilometres of our orbit. Not close enough for any collision but things out of place interest me, I'm inquisitive, you know.'

Nathalie smiled. 'I can see that, go on.'

'Well, to cut a long story short, I have evidence of at least five satellites being moved without official authorisation in the last four months. One or two could have been data error or someone correcting an orbit without reporting it but five, I don't think so. And the most recent one is very interesting. As I was telling Mr Sykes, a small satellite was on a collision course with some junk when it was moved.'

Nathalie interrupted. 'Isn't that normal? Surely other operators monitor their satellites like you do?'

'Oh yes, very normal. There's even a station set up to contact anyone in such an eventuality. But this one was different. A couple of minutes later the satellite was moved back onto the collision course. And bang, it's now in pieces floating with the rest of the junk around our planet.'

Nathalie paused her audio. 'Mm, and you think that could have been done on purpose?'

'Absolutely. You still recording?'

Nathalie clicked on her iPhone and nodded.

Harry leaned forward. 'Is that a yes or a no?'

'Oh sorry, yes.'

'The next thing Mr Sykes is going to want to know is how we are intending to discover who is actually moving these things and why.'

Nathalie temporarily paused the audio. 'And what sort of pictures will provide the proof?'

'And what sort of pictures will provide the proof?' repeated Harry, popping the last sardine into his mouth.

Nathalie waited as he chewed thoughtfully.

Harry brought his eyes in line with hers. 'Okay here's what we do. I still have some days of this gardening week remaining. Bernard, that's my boss at Cosmat, is expecting me to draw up a field research plan. He thinks the distraction will take my mind off rogue satellites. Don't get me wrong, there's some useful stuff

I could be doing for my gravitational wave project, but there are some interesting people out there with some very sophisticated kit. People with the ability to move satellites and instruments that can detect any strange goings-on. The observatory at Las Palmas for example. What I need to do is to draw up one of your boss's lists that marries the two. Places where I can genuinely benefit from what you would call my day job, and places where we can do some digging around. How does that sound?'

'Sounds good to me,' said Nathalie. 'And after I've typed this up with a few subtle embellishments, I'm sure it will sound good to Geoff Sykes too.'

The view from the Petronas Tower had not recovered its charm. Jenny Kang fiddled with the paperclips at her new desk. She could still see Symphony Lake but from a slightly different angle. What she couldn't see were the rows and rows of satellite monitors that were normally ranged out before her. Since her little encounter with *PhreeSat* she had been given a different office, and a different job. What the new job was, she was not exactly sure of yet. All she had been asked to do to date was a bit of archive filing. At least they hadn't sacked her. At the end of her grilling, for that's what she was calling it, the chief technical officer and his henchmen had gone into a huddle. It was apparent that the henchman, Zikri Amin, as she now knew him to be called, or rather *Mr* Zikri as he insisted, was all for throwing her out of the building there and then. Yet for some reason the chief had other ideas. Perhaps it was the thought of a large redundancy payment but, after he had whispered a few choice words into Mr Zikri's ears, the guy seemed to acquiesce and agree that she should have a second chance; if that second chance was cleaning out old filing cabinets, in a borrowed office, that is. She was pulled out of her reverie by the blinking of the intercom button on her telephone.

'Jenny here.'

The tinny rasping voice of the female operator came through the speaker.

'Miss Kang?'

The question was officious and unnecessary, but Jenny answered politely.

'Jenny Kang here, yes?'

'You are expected at Mr Zikri's office in five minutes. Please do not be late.'

Jenny looked at her watch. The twin Petronas Towers were vast; being late would depend upon where Mr Zikri's office was. Jenny took a deep breath, she was determined not to lose her temper.

'Of course not, but please could you tell me where his office is?'

The voice barked back. 'I assume you have an office directory, Miss Kang?'

The receptionist didn't wait for an answer and the intercom button went blank.

'Bitch!' snapped Jenny, looking around her small office. No sign of a directory. She scrabbled around in the drawers of her desk. A few bits of paper left by the last incumbent, but no directory. Four minutes to go. No way was she going to ring back that receptionist. She took her jacket from the back of the chair, slipped it on and stepped into the corridor. Rows of identical doors, and not a soul in sight. There was a ding in the distance, the elevator was arriving. She slipped off her high-heeled shoes and, carrying them in one hand, ran towards it.

The stainless-steel doors were closing but the person inside must have heard her footsteps for, as she arrived, they slid apart again. The young man, in a crisp white shirt and tie, looked her up and down with amusement.

'Not good if you are in a hurry,' panted Jenny waving her shoes at him.

The man smiled, 'I would think so, not that I have many opportunities to wear them. Floor?'

His reply made Jenny a little nonplussed. 'Floor?'

'Yes, which floor do you want?'

'Oh yes, floor,' said Jenny entering the elevator car. 'Ah, not sure. You don't happen to know where Mr Amin's office is? MalaySat Corp,' she added in partial explanation.

'I don't think he would like you calling him that. Amin – disrespectful to his family name. Zikri isn't it, Mr Zikri?'

'Yes, that's right,' said Jenny, hopping on one leg and putting a shoe on the other.

'Ah, now I see why you're in such a hurry, bit of a taskmaster, doesn't like people being late.'

'Absolutely,' said Jenny, squeezing on her other shoe.

'Well, I've got good news and I've got bad news,' teased the young man.

Jenny looked at him with pleading eyes.

'The good news is that we are on the sixty-ninth and he is on the forty-third floor and we are going down.'

'And the bad news?' sighed Jenny

'We are in Tower 1 and he is in Tower 2.'

Jenny groaned.

'How long have you got?'

'Two or three minutes,' replied Jenny closing her eyes in despair.

'Well, if you take those shoes off again, you might make it.' He grinned. 'The skybridge is on the 42nd. I'll stop the elevator there and you can run across.'

Jenny could have kissed the young man. 'Thank you,' she sighed, reaching down to remove her shoes once more.

She arrived at Amin's office with twenty seconds to spare. Not that it mattered. His receptionist told her to sit in an anteroom and she had been waiting there for nearly half an hour. Not even a cup of coffee offered. There was plenty of time to study the room. No view but a high-tech feel to it – glass shelves, calf leather chairs, expensive looking avant-garde paintings. She wondered why the office wasn't annexed to the other MalaySat offices on the other floors. There was no sign of their logo, just a small silver plaque with the words Satellite Security Systems engraved into its surface. An offshoot company thought Jenny. She was running her finger along the typeface when she was brought up with a start by the receptionist who had quietly opened the door behind her.

'We would be grateful if you didn't touch that, Miss Kang,' the receptionist uttered melodically. The reprimand was worse than if she had shouted it. 'Mr Zikri will see you now.'

Jenny followed her down a short corridor and into a large vestibule. The decor was opulent. A large Henry Moore-like statue dressed the centre of the room and Magritte-like paintings adorned the walls. She was invited to sit in the sling-back chair, another item looking as if it had been taken from a gallery. The receptionist pointed towards the vast panelled doors. 'When they open, please enter and sit at the desk opposite Mr Zikri and do not speak until you are spoken to.'

Jenny nodded. Was all this meant to intimidate her? If it was, it was working. She watched the receptionist turn on her heel and leave the vestibule. A moment later and the large doors opened. They must have been electronic for no person seemed to be near them. Jenny was about to follow her instructions but the office took her breath away. Two of the walls were towering plate-glass; one with a view of the other tower across the bridge and the other looking towards the city.

'Impressive, yes, Miss Kang?' Mr Zikri's voice came from the other side of the room. 'I chose this office from the plans before the building had been constructed. Turned out very well don't you think?'

This was not the sort of tone that Jenny was expecting. She had been girding herself for a tirade. Instead, here was the man making polite conversation.

'It's stunning, Mr Zikri, beautiful design and amazing views.'

'Please sit down, Miss Kang. Would you like some tea?'

'No thank you, Sir,' said Jenny, placing herself in the comfortable armchair that faced his desk.

'To business then,' said Amin, throwing down a small file in front of her. 'This is the report on your little *PhreeSat* adventure. Data from the computers on the day that you moved the satellite. Data which also shows that the satellite was returned to its original position. The monitoring and care of the satellite was contractually the responsibility of MalaySat, and the reparations could be substantial. As the duty officer that evening, would you not agree that the company and the leasers of *PhreeSat* could lay the charge of the satellite's demise at your door?'

Jenny kept silent. It seemed that her initial optimism was premature. In fact, things could be worse than she had even imagined.

'No answer. Maybe a good thing. You will also note in the report that you have in front of you, your disclaimer. The fact that you were alerted to the satellite's path and corrected it to avoid collision. Also the fact that you swear that you did not attempt to move the satellite again.'

Jenny thumbed through the first pages of the report and nodded.

'Well, if we are to believe you and, after some preliminary investigations, we think we do, then some other source must have taken control of the satellite.'

Jenny's eyes widened. Perhaps she was going to be let off after all.

'Now, not all people may believe us including, I'm afraid, the broadcasters who used *PhreeSat*. As a result we are making a proposition. MalaySat will smooth over the waters, so to speak, and you will be retained as an employee with a very specific remit.'

This was beginning to sound interesting and Jenny sat up in her chair.

'Remit?'

'Yes, a specific task.' Mr Zikri was sensing Jenny's excitement and relief. 'But this employment is conditional.' He handed her a sheet of single-spaced typed paper. 'Conditional on the fact that you sign this document which states that you are sworn to confidentiality and that any lawsuit, unfavourable publicity, or adverse consequences will be solely your responsibility, and that any action that you take will be deniable by MalaySat.'

Jenny started to read the tightly printed contract. 'And if I don't wish to participate in this task whatever it may be?'

'Then I'm afraid you will not only have no job but, I would imagine, months or maybe even years of litigation for bringing down a very expensive piece of equipment.'

Mr Zikri steepled his hands together and placed them under his nose. 'But, as I said, the choice is entirely yours.'

Five

There was no one within miles to hear the screams. The red pickup truck sat idly beside the desolate farmhouse. Everything in the yard was peaceful, a few chickens pecking at corn and a lone cat basking under the clear blue sky. It would have made a great photograph, and it would have hidden everything, including those terrible screams. Inside the house it was a different matter entirely. Furniture strewn all over the place, a broken rear window and a man crudely tied up in a kitchen chair. His wrists were bound to the wooden arms by electrical wire. His thumb and forefinger were missing and, if one looked down, there they were lying on the rough floorboards. Surprisingly, there was little blood, just a few brown splashes next to the severed digits. There were two other men in the room. One was in the corner ferreting through an old desk. Crumpled bills and farmers' magazines were scattered amongst the pens and notebooks. The other man was perched against a sturdy pine table facing the man in the chair. He held a pair of pincers in his hand. He spoke quietly in heavily accented Russian.

'Let's begin again. Where is your partner?'

The man in the chair began sobbing and muttered something through his dribbling mouth.

The man by the table sighed, eased himself from its edge and, placing the pincers under the other man's chin, lifted his head so that he could stare into his eyes.

'Now we've been through all this before, Alen, none of your bucolic Kazakh. Russian, if you please, and a little more clearly. I'll repeat the question in case you didn't get the message, where is your partner?'

Alen stumbled for his Russian, he wasn't fluent at the best of times but in this situation he couldn't think. The two men seemed to have come out of nowhere. Visitors were rare in this part of the woods and he had thought them to be either lost or some sort of salesmen bartering agricultural foodstuffs. He had invited them in but had become suspicious when he had heard their accents. Obviously foreigners; neither Kazakhstanis nor Russians. How he had been bound into the chair he couldn't exactly remember. It now seemed hours ago. All he wanted was to sleep, forget any of this was happening. Where was his partner? He had repeatedly told them, and was praying for him to return at any moment. He finally found the Russian words from somewhere in his scrambled head.

'I told you, my partner, his wife and my wife have gone into Zalagash. They are buying provisions. It's a monthly thing. We take it in turns. It's my turn to look after the farm.' He began to sob again.

'And remind me once more, when will they return?'

The tears were now pouring down his cheeks. 'I don't know, I told you I don't know. It depends. If they haven't got all the goods they want they could stay over with Ravil's aunt, or they could be back this evening.' His whole body was shaking. 'Please, please let me go. I don't know who you are, what you want, I don't know anything.'

A mobile phone was pushed under his nose. 'Well your friend Ravil knows something doesn't he? Why else would he be putting pictures of this on his Facebook page?'

The finger flicked through the screens. Blurred images of the area where they had set their stall for birdwatching, only a week ago now.

'I don't know why he did it, when he took the pictures. We were only looking for terns, they love those marshy habitats. We didn't know what the hut was, or is, for. The Russian soldiers believed us, why don't you?'

The mobile phone was taken from his view and he was stroked gently on the head. A sinister sort of stroke.

'Ah yes, the Russian soldiers.' The man snicked the pincers by his side. 'Take me through the interview again.'

Nathalie strode purposefully along Greek Street. This was the day, she thought. Geoff would either buy the project and she would be off around the world, or he would be his miserly old self and she would have to spend the rest of the day toting around CVs. Harry had called her the night before and declared he had come up with a plan. He had seemed excited, not a characteristic she had noted him for. More than a list of locations, he had said, and already a sniff of a plotline. What he had meant by plotline she had never discovered as he was whisked away to a teleconference meeting. The word had made her anxious. This wasn't a soap drama to be aired on television. It had the potential to be a hard-hitting investigative documentary. Perhaps Harry didn't know what he was doing after all. She took in the aromas of freshly brewed coffee from the Soho brasseries. It was a great place to work. Even if Geoff did give it the thumbs down, she was in the right place. The streets around here were crammed with production houses and studios. She was sure to bump into someone she knew either rushing between editing suites or taking a break for a quick snack. That was the film industry for you. The right place at the right time. One day you would be out of a job and, on another, a brief encounter with a television producer would set you up for months on the road. She passed Milroy's on the right. Used to be a wine shop but now famous for its range of whiskies. Nathalie couldn't understand why people raved about the stuff. Tasted like petrol to her. Only a few yards to go before she would arrive at Bagatelle's offices in the square. She recalled how many times she had rushed up those steps, first as a rookie researcher and, later, as a fully blown documentary maker. The sun was out, perhaps today it would be a taste of the latter.

Stefanie greeted her with the news that Harry Stones had already arrived. He was in Geoff's office. They had been there for some time and, by the number of espressos they had consumed, were getting on like a house on fire. Nathalie was surprised; she had thought the meeting was for ten, and it was now five to. She tapped on Geoff's office door. No answer. She placed her ear to the panel only to be regaled by barks of laughter. Nothing for it but to burst in.

Geoff looked up. 'Oh there you are,' he glanced at the wall clock. 'Punctual as usual. Harry here had an hour to spare so, hope you don't mind, we started early.'

Harry swivelled his chair around to face her. 'Good morning, Ms Thompson, sorry to jump the gun but there was something I really had to sound out on Mr Sykes. Didn't want to waste your time if it went down like a lead balloon.'

Nathalie shrugged her shoulders. She was about to say that she was only the producer on the project, but thought better of it. After all, it wasn't even a project yet. 'No problem, and did it?'

Harry looked puzzled. 'Did it what?'

'Go down like a lead balloon?'

Geoff got up and pulled over a chair for her. 'Absolutely not. Harry and I have had a good chat and I think that Bagatelle are prepared to put some funds into the thing. Initially anyway.' He waved a piece of paper at Nathalie. 'A list of locations that Harry is funded to visit. If you're happy with them, I'll fund you – a daily rate, travel and accommodation – to go with him. If after two weeks we've got a real story I'll budget the full thing. How does that sound?'

Nathalie sat down slightly taken aback. She was expecting a full discussion, pros and cons, and a possible halfway outcome. However in the last hour it looked like these two had stitched the whole thing up. She didn't know whether to be pleased or irritated.

'Okay you two, it seems that you both have an idea on where this thing is going. Now, if I'm to be producer on this project, even if it's only on the two-week pilot, don't you think I should take some part in its planning?'

Geoff turned to Harry. 'I told you that she might react like this,' then sensing Nathalie bristling, 'and rightly so. She is really good at this stuff. I suggest I back out and the two of you go into the boardroom and come up with a schedule.'

Nathalie glared at him. Harry, sensing some sort of atmosphere, rose from his chair and held out his hand. 'I'd be grateful if you would show me the way, Ms Thompson.' Nathalie could do no more than take him by the arm and lead him towards the door.

'Oh, Harry,' said Geoff, 'might be good to start with your Academic Star Wars idea.'

Nathalie turned to him and narrowed her eyes.

Geoff put up his hands. 'Just saying.'

The boardroom was chilly. 'Not been used for a while,' explained Nathalie. 'I'll turn up the heating.'

'A bit frosty in there too,' said Harry feeling for a chair and sitting down. 'I hope I didn't upset things by coming in a bit early.'

Nathalie sat in a chair on the opposite side of the table. 'Misogynistic old bastard. Two guys sort it all out and bring me in at the last minute.'

'Oh I don't think so, Nathalie,' said Harry looking towards her voice. 'He thinks a lot of you, it's obvious. We got carried away. It's my fault, we should have waited.'

Nathalie played with the list of locations in front of her. 'No, you're right, Harry. I'm only lashing out. Misogyny is the wrong word, in fact he treats all his staff the same, male or female. He's a bit old-fashioned, that's all. And I didn't mean to lump you in with my gripes. He acts like some kind of uncle sometimes. Assumes that I'll just fit in with his plans. This was my idea in the first place and I did introduce you to him. The least he could have done would be to wait for me to make the final decision.'

'I think you're being a bit hard on him. If he acts like an uncle he's a very caring one. You would have been embarrassed in there to hear him sing your praises: professional, laser insight, nose for a story. I could go on. Anyway, I thought you'd be pleased that he'd stump up the money.'

'It's the principle, Harry. I don't want him to assume that I'll fall in with what he wants. If things go wrong it's me who gets the blame.'

'Fair enough, but I'm sticking my reputation on the line too. Now, are you going to help me with this thing or not because, from what he said in there, it's obvious that I can't do it without you.'

Nathalie looked down at the list of locations that she held in her hand. Carefully typed addresses – observatories, universities, research sites – all with notes written alongside. This was followed by a long paragraph entitled '*Academic sabotage – Theory and evidence*'.

Nathalie read the title out loud. 'Is that what Geoff was referring to when he mentioned Academic Star Wars?'

Harry looked up and instinctively found her eyeline. 'Oh is that what the pregnant pause was for, you were taking a look at my proposal?'

'Oh sorry, Harry, I keep forgetting…'

'That's a good thing,' said Harry. 'Being judged on my own merits, no concessions. I'm beginning to like it. And, to answer your question, yes, the Star Wars thing. Not my title I assure you but the idea has always been at the back of my mind. It was our meeting the other day that brought it into focus.'

The boardroom was warming up. Harry took off his jacket and hung it over the back of his chair. 'You asked me to write a proposal based around locations. You're a film director, you think in pictures. I'm a scientist. There's an anomaly in the system and I want to find out what it is.'

Nathalie continued scanning the document. 'So writing the list has crystallised some of your ideas?'

'I suppose you could say that. Initially I just wrote down places where there are experts who could assist in tracking and finding patterns in satellite movements but, as I made the list, it became pretty obvious where we should start. Take a look at paragraph 4.2.'

Harry gave Nathalie a little time to read the notes. 'See the first location, the U.S. National Observatory at Kitt Peak. This houses more telescopes in one place than anywhere else on the planet. Why? It's on a mountain in the middle of the Arizona desert. Great climate, clear unpolluted air. Now look at the second, the Boulby mine in Cleveland. Quite the opposite. A hidden laboratory a mile underground. Not a star in sight. Why's that there? It's looking for Cold Dark Matter in the universe. But I can fill you in on that later. The point of these two locations is that, recently, the hardware has been commissioned by two very competitive groups of scientists, both heavily sponsored by corporations from different countries and both wanting publicity and prestige.'

Nathalie had been listening patiently. 'Yes, all very interesting but what has this all to do with satellites?'

'I'm coming to that, bear with me.' Harry reached into his satchel for his laptop and placed it on the table. He flipped it open and turned it towards Nathalie. 'Click on the icon labelled WCMB Associates.'

Nathalie did so and the screen filled with a glossy website. Stunning images of galaxies, telescopes and satellites. Thumbnail portraits of men and women were aligned down one side.

'Not your normal academic website is it?' remarked Harry. 'The guys you can see on the left are some of the top brains in the business. I was in Cambridge with one of them. They've all been lured away by some Russian billionaire who's set up a think tank. I don't blame them for joining. They have enough funds to buy practically any telescope time they want and even to launch any number of satellites. They're in it for the reputation, the Nobel Prize perhaps. The billionaire? I'm not sure. Publicity for his business? Celebrity status? Prestige for his government perhaps?'

Nathalie clicked through a few more pages. 'Sure, very

interesting but I come back to my first question. What's all this got to do with satellites?'

Harry passed her a printout. Nathalie glanced at it and all she could see was a mass of symbols and numbers.

'Sorry, still none the wiser.'

Harry took in a deep breath. 'No, I'm the one to be sorry. I'm making assumptions, been working with cosmologists too long.' He tapped the paper. 'It's a list of events, orbits, trajectories and so on. All the things I've been monitoring in the last few months. And a few before that.'

'Yes but they looked like the scribblings on Tutankhamun's tomb to me,' said Nathalie. 'Where is this taking us?'

Harry shook his head from side to side. 'Not sure but it could be a start. You see, the first item on the list I found from the records before I started monitoring the things myself. It was a satellite that had been taken down about six months ago by some space junk. When researching my proposal I discovered it belonged to WCMB. It was a small thing, by satellite standards inexpensive, the bus carried some sort of experimental telescope, but it must have set their research back months.'

Harry reached forward and tapped on the laptop. 'Now open the file labelled FastTrack.'

This time another website, less glitzy, more austere. The plain text listed a number of research projects, published papers and astrophysics associates. Nathalie read a few lines and it began to dawn on her what Harry was getting at. 'This lot, the FastTrack group, also sponsored by some rich guys, yes?'

Harry retrieved the laptop and snapped it shut. 'FastTrack were set up only a few months after WCMB appeared. Difficult to discover where the funds came from. I'm still working on that but I think it's from somewhere in the States. The thing is, there's a lot of money washing around in these outfits and it's really unusual for them to be private and not run by university departments.'

Nathalie drummed her fingers on the table. 'So your theory is that these are two wealthy rivals, both seeking some sort of esteem and reputation, and one has taken the other's satellite down.'

'It's a distinct possibility,' said Harry.

'But what about the others? You said there were five; they can't have all been astronomical satellites'

'Yes you're right there. A bit of a fly-in-the-ointment for my theory but not enough to knock it down. There are a number of possibilities. Perhaps it's someone experimenting with the technology or, conceivably, there could be different people taking down different satellites. Another option: there's an individual out there who knows how to do it and is hired by different groups.'

'A bit tenuous,' said Nathalie. 'How did you get onto these two organisations in the first place?'

'While I was researching the list of locations that had the ability to track and control satellites, I checked out the outfit that was buying time on Kitt Peak. That led me to WCMB and then their rivals FastTrack. Thought the story would sway your boss.'

'Well it certainly seems to have done that. Let's hope we don't disappoint him.'

Harry began packing his computer into his bag. 'I can sense your scepticism, Nathalie. Like you I'm a bit puzzled why a media satellite should have been taken down if it's a war between these two academic groups. But someone or some people are manoeuvring these things, and it's the best bet we've got at the moment.'

He stood up and made his way to the door. 'And the only way we can find out is to go out there and visit them.'

Nathalie rose and opened the door for him. 'Couldn't have put it better myself. Before you go I'll introduce you to Stefanie; she's a real rock when it comes to schedules and arranging film crew. We'll need someone on standby out there if you can sniff a story.'

'Sounds like a good idea, Nathalie. Next stop, Arizona.'

Six

The officials at the Cosmodrome could not have been more helpful.

'Of course, Miss Kang; your documents and licence are all in order, and it's a pleasure to have one of MalaySat's operatives to visit us in person. We do hope you will allow us to take you out to dinner this evening. Perhaps we could discuss a little business.'

Jenny was relieved by the reception. Mr Zikri had bundled her off with a visa and accommodation vouchers to Baikonur in Kazakhstan. She had been taken through the desert to her hotel in a bus full of excited tourists. A trip to see the latest rocket launch apparently. As they disgorged from the coach she had been dismayed by the institutional facade of the Sputnik Hotel. Now, some hours later at the Cosmodrome, her spirits were rising. Her hosts were gracious and charming and their offices state-of-the-art. It was evident that their concern over the loss of *PhreeSat* and its impact on future business was putting her at a distinct advantage.

'I'd love to,' she said, playing along. 'The restaurant at the hotel?'

The man in an ill-fitting suit – imitation Armani, from the Russian chain store Lillies, by the sight of the label – pulled out his mobile phone from an inside pocket. 'I think we can do better than that, Miss Kang. The roasted goose at Nebo's is a delicacy in these parts and I know the owner so we are sure of a private table.'

He switched seamlessly from the fluent English they were using to Russian as he made the booking. He must have seen a flicker of interest in Jenny's face.

'Kazakh restaurant, Russian speakers, but you will be pleased to know they provide a menu in English. No doubt you wish to return to your hotel to change. Our limousine will take you there and collect you again at, say 7.30, if that's all right with you, of course.'

Jenny nodded with a smile. 'Of course, that's very kind of you. And once we've established the technical fault that brought down *PhreeSat*, I'm sure my company will be only too willing to embark on the launch of another more state-of-the-art satellite. Will there be someone this evening who may be happy to help in these matters?'

The man in the Armani-copy suit looked towards his colleague. 'Anatole here is our head of security and will be joining us. I, as you know, control all the commissioning and maintenance contracts for our satellites so, between the three of us, I'm sure we will be able to smooth a path for the current investigation and a future relationship between our companies.'

He certainly was a cool customer she would give him that. She had arrived feeling frightened and nervous, not knowing what to expect. Her remit was to discover who or what had crashed MalaySat's satellite. Fingers at her company were already pointing to her but the people at the Cosmodrome hadn't seemed to have heard of that. They were all too keen to smooth over the waters and to get more business. So she had become a little braver, mentioning the possibility that helping her with their investigation would open up avenues to further contracts was her first step, and it seemed to be working.

'That's wonderful,' she said glancing at Anatole. 'I know MalaySat would be extremely pleased with your cooperation.' She stuck her neck out a little further; even if she was making it up, a dangling carrot was sure to help. 'And I have the authority to open up initial contract negotiations with our satellite program over the next few years. The three of us should make a good team.'

The journey from the Cosmodrome to Baikonur took about forty minutes. The tarmac road was surrounded by featureless flat rust-coloured desert. As they entered the town the landscape was hardly more cheerful – geometric Eastern European office blocks and apartments were interspersed with the odd stoic statue and, bizarrely, an old steam train on a plinth. A far cry from bustling Kuala Lumpur. Jenny Kang took a deep breath. Her first meeting had gone well, hopefully she wouldn't be here long. She retrieved her key from reception and went to her room. A small double bed covered in a gross floral counterpane was placed against a green plastic headboard. Either side were two small polished wooden side tables with bedside lamps. A small uncomfortable looking chair sat in one corner so she perched on the bed and keyed in her office number. The phone call was short, Mr Zikri was in a meeting and his secretary was her acrimonious self. She took down the details of Jenny's arrival and logged that she was meeting with the satellite people over dinner. She ended by saying that Mr Zikri expected a full report by the end of the week. Jenny entered into the tone of the conversation and ended the call without a goodbye. She tried to check out the restaurant on the internet but the WiFi wasn't working, so she opened her case and mulled on what to wear based on her conversation with the two Russians. 'A private table' suggested somewhere upmarket but, from the little she had seen of Baikonur, not that upmarket. She selected a simple woollen calf-length cheongsam dress, put it on a hanger and went for a shower. The needle-hot water relaxed her whole body and it was only then that she realised what stress she had been under. She towelled down and flopped onto the bed. Sleep must have been instant because the next thing she remembered was a loud knocking on her door.

Jenny reached for her phone on the bedside table. It was only seven o'clock, they were half an hour early.

'Wait a minute, I'll just put a dressing gown on,' she said putting her feet over the end of the bed, wrapping the towel closely around her.

The loud knocking continued. 'Open the door now please, Miss Kang,' the voice was aggressive and heavily accented.

Jenny was confused. Her Baikonur hosts had been so gentle

and polite. Their chauffeur however seemed anything but. She threw off her towel and grabbed the cheap hotel towelling gown from behind the bathroom door. She understood that she was a guest in a foreign country but she wasn't going to put up with rudeness. She slipped on the gown, pulled the cord tightly around her waist, marched towards the door and threw it open.

'How dare you...' she began. Her face turned from anger to horror as she was confronted by two heavily armed soldiers.

'Miss Kang of MalaySat?'

Jenny nodded involuntarily.

'You are to get dressed and come with us at once.'

Jenny was speechless. One of the soldiers stood by the door and the other entered the room, stood with his legs apart and placed his hands behind his back waiting.

'You just can't... I'm a guest of the Cosmodrome...' stumbled Jenny, trying to regain her voice.

The soldier stared impassively towards the wall. 'We are quite aware of that, Miss Kang, they have been informed. You are required to come with us. There has been a murder.'

It was six o'clock in the morning, Tucson Arizona time. Despite an eighteen-hour flight and a tedious change at Los Angeles Airport Nathalie found she couldn't sleep. The Hilton Garden Inn was comfortable enough but she couldn't help worrying that she was on a wild-goose chase. Had she been taken in by the charm of Harry Stones? Perhaps Geoff's original reaction was right. Maybe it was crazy to have a blind film director guide the project. And what project? A tenuous lead of a few rogue satellites, and the suspicion that two academic astrophysics groups were at loggerheads with each other? At six o'clock in the morning it was starting to become a bad idea. A very bad idea.

The Garden Grill looked more like a corporate canteen than

a hotel restaurant but at least it was open at this unearthly time of the morning. Nathalie dragged her laptop to one of the stark, brown Formica tables, grabbed an upturned mug from one of the place settings and poured herself a cup of weak coffee. Weak coffee because it was the only sort available from the self-serve dispenser.

'Hi, another early bird I hear,' came a voice from behind her.

She turned to see Harry Stones at the doorway. 'Oh good morning, Harry, coffee?'

'Good idea,' said Harry. 'Dark and strong, please.'

Nathalie met him at the door and guided him to a seat. 'I'm afraid you will be disappointed there. Piece of toast?'

Harry sat back and yawned. 'Well, espresso and a croissant are usually my thing but, hey, if that's all they've got; when in Tucson.'

'Oh you prefer grits…' laughed Nathalie. 'What are you doing up at this time of the morning?'

'Could say the same thing to you. I've always been an early riser and nowadays it doesn't matter whether it's light or dark. Thought it a good idea to work out a strategy to get what we want without arousing suspicion.'

Nathalie put two pieces of toast on a plate and grabbed the handles of the coffee cups. She sat alongside Harry and indicated where his coffee was by making a loud noise as she smacked it onto the table. He reached for it and grimaced as he took his first gulp.

'I think they wave the bean at the water from a hundred metres away; at least it's hot and wet.'

'I think Geoff's got a solution to that.'

'Improving American coffee?'

'No, even Geoff hasn't got that sort of influence. Solution to the suspicious investigation thing.'

'Okay…?'

Nathalie took a bite from her cold toast. 'Two birds with one stone,' she mumbled.

Harry turned towards her. 'Now my hearing is going as well as my sight; what on earth did you say?'

Nathalie took a swig of coffee and swallowed. 'Two birds with one stone,' she repeated.

'None the wiser.'

'Got a reason why we are here rooting around asking strange questions and a cameraman for you all in one fell-swoop,' said Nathalie. 'And you're right about the coffee.'

'Cameraman?'

'Yes, you told Geoff that one of the reasons you wouldn't be just a researcher was that you wanted to film on the hoof. A bit difficult without a cameraman. I persuaded Geoff to provide one.'

'Impressive.'

'More than that, a stroke of genius. I reminded him that he made a film on the planets for the BBC's *Horizon* strand many moons ago, pun intended. They filmed on Kitt Peak in the Mayall telescope. Something to do with Pluto I think.'

'Yes the telescope predicted that there was frozen methane on the thing,' interrupted Harry. 'You people get around don't you?'

'We do but that was before my time. Anyway, the astronomer he filmed is now a professor at the Department of Astronomy in Tucson. Geoff gave her a ring and said we were interested in getting some archive footage for a possible revised version of the old programme. Said he was a personal friend of yours and that he understood you were having meetings at Kitt Peak. Asked whether they minded if I tagged along.'

'Clever. I was wondering how I could explain who you were.'

'A bit young for you?' said Nathalie with a smile in her voice.

'Not at all, no I didn't mean it in that way.' Nathalie hadn't seen Harry embarrassed before. He gathered his composure. 'Let me start again. I was wondering how I could get around your lack of knowledge on cosmology.' He sighed. 'There I've done it again haven't I?'

'You could say that,' said Nathalie enjoying the situation. It was the first time since they had met that she felt she was getting the upper hand. 'You're right though. I'm not usually slow on the uptake on scientific matters but I don't think I could pass off as one of your Cold Dark Matter team.'

'So, who's this professor?' asked Harry, trying to change the subject.

'Alison Perez. She knows your WCMB group. In fact, she's the person responsible for allocating telescope time. Couldn't be more convenient.'

'Alison Perez.' Harry closed his eyes to remove the little light that he could still see. 'Alison Perez. Yes, the name rings a bell. Never met her but must have seen the name in a directory somewhere. She's not working directly on our project, which could be a good thing. The Mayall telescope work on Pluto was confirmed by a satellite flyby a few years back. Might be a good place to start when asking about any suspicious events.'

'So,' said Nathalie leaning back in her chair, 'you're the director. What do you want to do with this cameraman?'

'Ah, Ms Thompson, afraid you've got me there, hadn't quite worked that one out. I suppose I thought we might find something out of place and film it as we went along.'

'Doesn't quite work like that, Harry. You have to set things up. Geoff taught me that. Used to say, "Point a camera at a cat, not much will happen. Tie two cats' tails together and throw them over a washing line, serious action."'

'That sounds terrible,' protested Harry.

'No, of course he didn't really mean it. Knowing Geoff, he's left all his money to a cats home. He just meant that when making a documentary things aren't always going to occur when you want them to. You have to create the right conditions for action to happen when the camera's there.'

Harry thought for a moment. 'So if we ask to film Professor Perez in the Mayall, drop a few questions about satellite malfunctions in the interview, and have some of the WCMB group along at the same time, we might get some reaction.'

'Got it in one, Harry. Now finish that coffee and we'll take a stroll in downtown Tucson before it gets too hot.'

Their meeting was scheduled for nine in the Steward Observatory, they had plenty of time. Nathalie waited in the lobby whilst Harry gathered his things and used the time to phone for a cab. The offices of the Steward Observatory were part of the University of Arizona and were situated downtown. A short stroll should get the cobwebs out of Nathalie's head and she scrolled through the map on her phone.

'Maynards,' came the voice from behind her.

Nathalie turned around puzzled.

'Receptionist told me you had asked the number for a cab to take us downtown,' continued Harry. 'I was telling him that we weren't too impressed by their breakfast. He told me not to tell the management but he agreed with me. Got a recommendation. Maynards Market and Kitchen, only a couple of miles from Steward. They even serve croissants apparently.'

Nathalie stared out of the cab window as they headed downtown. Tucson appeared as a saucer of buildings set in a ring of mountains. Beyond, to the south-west, was the San Xavier Indian Reservation with its famous saguaro cacti. As the streets rolled by Harry ignored the complaints of the taxi driver and wound down the window.

'Aircon may be a great smell to you,' foiled back Harry, 'but I prefer to get a sense of the city. And at the moment I'm getting some weird aromas from fast food restaurants. Now I would say that's a Mexican outfit that we passed back there.'

The cab driver checked out Harry in his rear-view mirror. 'You wanna stop for a Mexican?' he drawled.

Harry sat back in his seat. 'Nope, just taking in the sights,' he replied putting his arms behind his head.

Despite the early hour the journey took them forty minutes. 'Traffic gets worse every day,' grumbled the driver taking the dollar bills from Nathalie's hand. 'You wanna book a return trip?'

'Thank you no,' said Nathalie. 'I prefer to go the direct way back,' she added under her breath.

'Well that was a pleasant drive,' said Harry, a little sarcastically. 'Can you see Maynards or have we another block or two to walk?'

'It's right across the street,' said Nathalie, grabbing his arm. 'I paid the cab, it's your turn to cough up for the croissants.'

Maynards' croissants were unlike any Nathalie had seen before. They were cut into two like a hamburger bun and were crammed with ham, eggs, cheese and rocket. Harry picked up the sandwich with both hands and took a large bite. He chewed for a while and reached for his cup to swill it down with his double espresso.

'Now that's more like it, real food and real coffee. I even feel the neurones feeding back into my brain. If you're ready, I'll outline the agenda for this morning's meeting and my proposal for a site visit. Then perhaps you can tell me more about this cameraman character and how we can fit him into the schedule.'

Harry opened his laptop and tilted it towards Nathalie. One by one he went through the table of events: introductions to the WCMB team, the Dark Energy project they were working on and how it could be compatible with Cosmat's work, and, finally, an agreement on what work could be shared.

'Now here's the crunch,' said Harry. 'I know they're pretty keen to get hold of some of our stuff. They may have the money but, putting modesty aside, we have the brains. I think they will move heaven and earth, to use a cosmological metaphor, to get me on board. However I could make it a little uncomfortable for them. Perhaps I might be a little concerned about their security, losing one of their satellites for instance.'

'You really think that it was taken down on purpose?' asked Nathalie, wiping the final crumbs of the giant croissant from her lips.

'Can't see how it fell out of the sky by itself.'

'And you think one of their rivals, like FastTrack, could have done it?'

'Possibly. But I'm pretty sure, if it was my satellite, I would have done everything I could to find out why it bumped into something. They've got the money and, according to some people I know, highly sophisticated satellite technology. Even if it's not FastTrack I'm sure they'll have some idea of how and why it was done.'

Nathalie looked at her watch. 'Well if we are going to have that two-mile stroll to the university we had better get a move on. Do you plan to confront them at the meeting?'

'No. I thought it would be better to save that until our site meeting on Kitt Peak. It's a spectacular location. Your cameraman will love it.'

Seven

Grit and dust were thrown into the scrub by the Russian military Humvee as it tore through the dimming Kazakhstan light. The acrid smoke from the driver's cigarette seared through Jenny Kang's nostrils as she recoiled from the movement of the vehicle. She had been bundled out of her hotel room still trying to pull a sweater over her head. They had taken her passport and pushed her into the back of this ominous looking mode of transport. Neither of the soldiers had responded to her questions so she sat silently staring out of the window. Her watch and phone had been left on the bedside table, and she had no idea of the time that had passed when they eventually drew up into the yard of a small holding. The driver jumped out of the cab and slammed the door behind him. Jenny watched him walk over to a pair of black Mercedes which were sinisterly lurking by the farmhouse door. It was now dusk and the cigarette being stubbed out by the soldier's heel threw sparks onto the straw-laden cobbles. Her escort in the front passenger seat remained motionless and stared into the distance.

'Can you *now* tell me what's going on?' protested Jenny. 'I have a right to know. I shall report this to my government,' she added, trembling but trying to sound authoritative.

No gesture, no answer.

Jenny tried the handle of the door. Her guard didn't even turn around, it was locked. She peered out of the darkened windows. The driver was talking to another uniformed man who was pulling something out of his pocket. He spoke into it and pointed to a large barn on the other side of the yard. There was a bright flash and Jenny threw herself to the floor of the Humvee. No sound followed.

She reached the sill with her fingers and pulled herself up to stare nervously into the yard.

Initially she was blinded by the glare but, after squinting her eyes, she realised that the whole scene had been lit by giant floodlights. Now she could make out more buildings, all with striped plastic tape surrounding their perimeters. A murder they had said, this must be the crime scene. But what on earth had it got to do with her?

Two ghost-like figures appeared from the barn. They were dressed head to toe in white canvas clothing. One was carrying a large clear plastic bag, a pinkish inside. They held it up to the soldier and the other uniformed man who scrutinised the contents and pointed to a large truck that Jenny now noticed in the far corner of the yard. As the men walked towards it the soldier indicated to the Humvee; the other man nodded and they both headed in Jenny's direction.

The rear door clicked and was roughly pulled open.

'This is the inspector of police. He does not speak English. You will address all your answers to me. I will translate. You are to come with us.' The two men stood either side of the Humvee door waiting for her to step down.

Jenny realised it was pointless trying to protest or ask more questions. She meekly climbed down out of the vehicle and stood between them. The police officer led the way and Jenny and the soldier followed. As they reached the farmhouse door it was opened by another officer who saluted and stood aside for them to enter. The interior had a warm glow from the electric light but contained a large bare wooden table and an unlit fire hearth. Looking around Jenny could see that it would have been a cosy farmhouse scene; would have been, except for three distraught figures bent over in their armchairs, one of them weeping and wailing.

The policeman pointed to a position in front of the three chairs. Jenny was so nonplussed by the situation that she stood rooted to the spot.

'Stand where the inspector has asked you,' snapped the soldier.

She was guided by her arm around the room to stand bewildered in front of the three seated people. Now she could see that, although their heads were bowed, they were coarsely dressed bucolic farmers. A man and a woman, both with gnarled hands gripping onto the armrests, the other a woman, face in hands, still howling. The policeman strode up to the silent seated couple. One at a time he lifted their heads for Jenny to see. He spoke to her brusquely in Russian.

'Have you met either of these people before?' translated the soldier.

Jenny stared, too distraught to speak.

The inspector lifted the man's head again and once again barked out some Russian.

'This man, have you seen him before?' the soldier reiterated.

Jenny stared at the man whose vacant black pupils stared back at her. She shook her head.

The policeman lifted the other person's head. More Russian.

Jenny didn't wait for the translation. The woman of indistinct age, possibly in her forties, looked straight through Jenny. Her eyes were red and swollen, her face puffed and burning. This face was more than weather-beaten, it held hours of agonising distress.

'I have never seen either of these people before in my life. What have you done to them?'

The soldier interpreted her remarks.

The inspector ignored him and moved to the other woman, now exhausted, sobbing silently. He pulled her hands away to expose a distorted face. There was no need for him to ask the question. Jenny shook her head and breathing heavily shouted at him. 'I have never seen any of these people before, any of them!'

She turned to her interpreter. 'Ask him what has he done to them and why am I here?'

The soldier talked quietly to the police officer who seemed to ignore the comments. Instead of addressing Jenny he spoke to the three seated people. This time she noted a different language. They appeared to understand for they shook their heads vigorously, even the crying woman. He spoke again, this time at length and more gently. Again they shook their heads and for the first time the man spoke, his hands held together in prayer. Jenny couldn't understand a word but it was obvious that he was pleading with the officer to believe him.

Jenny was ushered away from the scene into a small kitchen. Unwashed crockery sat in the sink, and an empty chipped Formica table held the centre of the room. The policeman pointed to one of the tubular metal chairs and left the room. She walked over to the small window. It was dark outside, as the window faced out from the rear of the house, away from the glaring spotlights. She didn't know why but she closed the tiny checked plastic curtain and, as there was little else to do, she moved over to the kitchen table, drew up a chair and waited.

The Steward Observatory offices were unimpressive. A four-storey concrete structure with narrow oblong windows set in panels of orange brickwork. Nothing like the high-tech sci-fi architecture that Nathalie was expecting. She said none of this to Harry as she led him up the concrete steps to the reception. They were expected apparently, badges already printed. If they took the elevator to the second floor they would be met by Professor Perez. Nathalie was surprised to see Harry press the correct button until she noticed the raised dots and dashes in the metalwork.

'You can read Braille?'

Harry grinned. 'Observant woman. No, I've not time for that, just learned a few useful signs on the hoof. Things like "male toilet" and "poison", you know.'

A diminutive dark-haired woman wearing owl-like spectacles came into view as the doors slid open.

'Welcome, Doctor Stones. We are privileged to have you as our guest and, good morning, Ms Thompson.'

Before Nathalie could guide Harry towards the professor he had already stepped out of the lift and proffered his hand which was taken in a warm handshake. Harry returned the palliative compliment and asked her to lead them to the meeting room.

Apart from Perez all of the members were men. Nathalie sensed that the formal introductions were slightly frosty and was rather annoyed at being introduced as an assistant film researcher. She also took an instant dislike to the leader of the WCMB consortium, Sechenov. His ill-fitting suit and black slicked-over hair didn't exactly help his disdainful demeanour either. The astronomer to the left of him was more genial and his name, Rodin, would be easier to remember. The other three members were referred to as 'affiliates of the team' and passed over quickly. Despite being the apparent guest to the party Harry took charge. He thanked the group for the invitation and hoped that this encounter would be the beginning of a long and fruitful collaboration. As they knew, Cosmat had an established reputation in the Cold Dark Matter field and was eager to put heads together with any new burgeoning enterprises. Although Harry couldn't see the expression on Sechenov's face, at the mention of the word 'burgeoning' Nathalie realised that this was the nature of the response he was seeking. Antagonise your partners, make them come back with boasts, and indulge you with more information than they might want you to know. Harry concluded his speech by asking the consortium about the use of the Mayall telescope's new Dark Energy Spectroscopic Instrument, adding spikily that he was surprised to hear about the amount of time they had been allocated for the DESI project. There was obvious discomfort around the room. Harry and Nathalie had already established that the one-month period, a normally unheard-of amount of time, had been allotted after a large donation had been bequeathed from an unknown source.

Sechenov ignored Harry's last remark and launched into a

convoluted lecture on the scientific goals of their project. Nathalie couldn't grasp all of this but she had made films on science before and pieced some of the jargon and technical language together to make sense of it. Essentially, these scientists were trying to establish the fate of the universe. They believed it was expanding; whether it would expand forever or implode back on itself would depend on how much matter there was. Current calculations said there was nearly enough to stop the expansion. If they could find a small proportion of extra mass then it would stop the universe expanding altogether. Freeze it in a stable state, a neat idea. The problem was, they couldn't see this mass or detect its heat. So as often happens in science they described a complex problem with a simple label – Cold Dark Matter.

'Excellent, gentlemen,' interrupted Harry, detecting that the speech was becoming repetitive. 'Any clearing up of expansion history theory and large-scale structures would be welcome. As for actually how you're measuring it, I think it would be better to talk about this in situ.' He turned to the chair next to him where the professor was sitting. 'I'm sure that Alison – if I may call you that – might arrange it for us, this evening perhaps?'

'Of course, Doctor Stones. In fact...' Alison Perez paused while she flicked through the notes on the table in front of her. 'In fact,' she continued, 'Ms Thompson's boss, Mr Sykes, has already negotiated a visit with the university. He's asked for a cameraman to take some pictures of the interior of the telescope. I was going to mention it. This evening would be a suitable time as the DESI project is not scheduled to start until tomorrow. However, perhaps someone from Mr Sechenov's team could accompany us and talk you through some of the technical methods of his project at the same time.'

'I would be delighted,' said Doctor Rodin, speaking for the first time. 'Spectroscopy is my speciality, and if Yuri doesn't mind...'

It was obvious he was referring to Sechenov who nodded his head in agreement.

'That's decided then,' said Rodin. 'And I'd like to bring along Terry, our intern. Get him out of the computer room and into a real telescope for once.'

The young man with long golden hair blushed. He opened his mouth to speak but, glancing at Yuri Sechenov, thought better of it.

'Right, it's three of us from here and we could pick up yourself and Ms Thompson from your hotel,' broke in Alison Perez. 'It's about a forty-minute drive to Kitt Peak and I'd like you to see the telescope as the sun is setting. It's an amazing sight. Would six o'clock suit you?'

'Perfect,' began Harry, but Nathalie interrupted. 'What about the film crew? They will have quite a bit of equipment and will require some time to set up.'

'Our people carrier can take the...' she counted on her fingers, 'three, four, five of us, and the crew will no doubt have their own trucks. If they meet us at the hotel we could go in tandem.'

'Great,' said Nathalie. 'Would five-thirty be too early? If the sunset is as good as you say it is, it would be great to get a shot of it as the telescope opens.'

'That's right,' said Harry, realising that as the covert film director he should have suggested it first. 'That would be very useful – for Mr Sykes's company I mean.'

Alison Perez looked at Doctor Rodin who nodded. 'Consider it arranged,' she said. 'We will pick you up at your hotel at five-thirty.'

Boyd Anderson was an imposing character. Broad shoulders, over six feet tall, with a mane of white hair. He greeted Nathalie with a wide grin.

'Good to make your acquaintance,' he drawled. 'Heard a lot about you. Got the brief from my old buddy Geoff, but I expect you'd like to fill me in on the detail.'

Nathalie put her tiny hand into his enormous palm. 'Pleased to meet you too Boyd. I'm not sure how much Geoff has told you but I'm the producer on the project. Harry here is the named director.'

Boyd turned to Harry, put his hand on his shoulder and shook his hand. 'Yep I've been briefed on that too. Harry, I believe that I've to be your eyes on this one.'

Nathalie breathed a sigh of relief, at least she wouldn't have to go through that explanation. 'Take a seat, Boyd, I'll let Harry go through what he's trying to do.'

Boyd seemed very relaxed with Harry's approach. He'd shot in the Mayall before and knew the location well. Pictures of the telescope and the spectroscope should not be difficult. The challenge was getting an interview out of one of the WCMB people when they were meant to be there picking up archive shots for a rehashed film.

'Shouldn't be too problematic,' said Harry when Boyd raised the issue. 'Cosmologists are notorious for wanting to talk about their pet project. I'm sure that if I put Comrade Rodin on the spot and ask him if he would talk about the spectroscope on camera, he wouldn't be able to help himself.'

It was dawning on Nathalie why Geoff had allowed Harry to nominally direct the project. He was highly respected in the field and these guys would probably do anything for him.

'So we have a plan,' she interjected. 'I'll busy myself pretending to tick off the list of archive shots we need and Harry can loosen up Rodin. I'll ask the sound recordist to take some atmos of the telescope doors opening, and that can be the cue for Harry suggesting that we get a bit of Rodin's wisdom on tape.'

'Worth a go,' said Harry. 'Once he's well into his spectrographic stuff, I can slip in the odd question about satellite malfunctions.'

'Spoken like a true director,' laughed Boyd. 'I'm looking forward to it.' He looked at his watch. 'We had better get going, it's nearly half past five, the two guys in their truck outside will be getting restless.'

Alison Perez was right about the spectacular view. As the small convoy passed through the Indian reservation framed by the saguaro cacti, Kitt Peak rose in front of them. A desert mountain landscape littered with the white domes of alien-looking telescopes. It looked like someone had juxtaposed the set of a sci-fi movie alongside a John Wayne western.

'Quite a sight,' said the professor, almost to herself. 'I never tire of it. One of the largest gatherings of telescopes in the northern hemisphere, and here is the largest,' she added as they drew up outside the massive dome of the Mayall telescope.

The crew were all local, had spent most of their working lives filming these telescopes, and so Nathalie's job was an easy one. She passed Boyd the list Geoff had e-mailed her and let him and the lighting guy get on with setting up. Whilst they did so, she walked over to the base of the telescope where Harry and Perez were standing. The telescope was enormous, stretching many metres into the interior of the dome. At its base was a cradle-like chair for the operative to sit and guide the massive instrument to point at its target. As she approached, the professor was sidling her small frame into the seat. Nathalie caught the end of her conversation with Harry.

'At three o'clock in the morning – I'm sometimes here all on my own staring at the universe – I say to myself, "This is all mine."' They both laughed.

'I remember the scale of it well,' said Harry. 'Quite a telescope, but there was no spectroscope last time I was here. Perhaps you could describe it to me.'

'Of course, I had almost forgotten that you can't see it now,' said Alison. 'It's like a massive donut-shaped device wrapped around the outer cage of the telescope. It's open at the top and connected to an array of spectrographs aligned here, to the right of us. I'm not an expert on the instrument, I'm afraid, but our colleague Doctor Rodin is. You may wish to ask him about it.'

'I certainly intend to do that,' said Harry. 'I even wondered whether it might be worth recording some of his words for posterity as we have film crew here.'

'What a good idea. Why don't I go over and ask him?'

As the huge dome rotated, and the massive doors slid open with a growl, the sunset-shot was every film-maker's dream. The burnt-orange light streamed into the telescope's interior, creating an illuminated panel of the sky. At the top of the mountain the air was clear and cloudless, the reason for this location in the first place. As the firmament darkened, the glow would turn into a black night studded with the millions of bright objects that this instrument had studied for decades.

'Breathtaking,' said Boyd, finishing the shot and taking the camera off its tripod. 'What's next up?'

'I think Harry has wangled the interview with Rodin,' whispered Nathalie. 'Looks like your lights are in the right position to record it with him sitting in the telescope's control chair. Wait here, I'll go over and ask them.'

It made a great shot, Rodin seated at the base of this enormous instrument with the spectroscope array around it. Harry's eyeline was perfect and he deftly asked how this new instrument would probe the expansion history of the universe and the mysterious physics of Dark Energy. Rodin became more and more excited as he raced through the answers – how the DESI would be transformative in grasping the expansion rate of the universe at early times, one of the greatest mysteries in the understanding of the laws of physics. Harry realised that this was the time to strike. With Rodin in full flow about how the panel at his side could control the pitch and yaw of the instrument towering above him, he changed tack.

'Doctor Rodin, your project is very ambitious. How much has the communications link to the project been impaired now that your satellite has been brought down?'

Rodin was taken off-guard and looked stunned. He turned nervously to his intern Terry who was standing alongside and, in doing so, flicked one of the controls. The telescope cage responded and veered violently towards where Harry was perched on a side rail. Harry heard the noise but didn't see it coming. Alison Perez screamed as metal met with bone.

Eight

The Kazakhstan sun crept through the small brick window. Inch by inch it illuminated the sparsely furnished police cell. As it reached Jenny Kang's face she woke with a start. Anxiety flooded through her body. It wasn't a bad dream. This event at a farmyard in the middle of nowhere had actually happened to her. She sat up from the narrow single bed and swung her legs around so her feet touched the stone floor. She had a sudden urge to urinate. In the corner of the room was a simple wooden table and chair. Underneath, a bucket. Too urgent to be proud now. She dragged the bucket across the floor, pulled down her jeans and relieved herself. Humiliating and disgusting but what else was she to do. She pushed the bucket back under the table, sat on the crude chair and laid her head in her arms on the table. Her chest was cramping with panic and she tried to take deep breaths to slow down her heart rate. This was all a big mistake. A possible case of mistaken identity. Why else was she driven to some farmhouse in the middle of nowhere? She had been questioned again and again about those three pitiful creatures and yet the police seemed not to believe her when she protested that she had never seen them before. At the start they had mentioned a murder, but whose murder? Was she being accused of this? If not, why had they taken her from the farmhouse and driven for hours through the night until they had locked her into this cell in this strange building? They hadn't been rough but had been firm, and she was told that they were waiting for someone else. She would have to stay the night.

The door opened behind her. She turned to find a suited character standing in the doorway. He spoke with calm authority in perfect English.

'Good morning, Miss Kang. I'm so sorry that the accommodation could not be more comfortable. It was all the officers had to offer in the circumstances.' He sniffed the air and glanced towards the bucket under the table.

'And I must also apologise for the sanitary arrangements. I will have a word with the station chief. Please follow me and I will show you to the officers' toilets. You can tidy up before we have a chat over breakfast.'

Jenny was lost for words so she followed the man, taking in his elegantly cut suit as she did so. He showed her to a bathroom, far from luxurious but adequately equipped. She washed her face and hands and combed her hair. On the exterior she now looked more presentable; on the interior she still felt a mess.

'Please could you tell me who you are and what all this is about?' she asked as she walked into the corridor.

'Of course, Miss Kang. My name is Nikolai and we can discuss "what all this is about" over breakfast. I have asked the inspector here to provide some coffee and Butterbrots in his office.'

Jenny had no idea what Butterbrots were but, after her torrid night, coffee sounded a good idea. Once more she followed the sharp suit down the corridor and into a wooden-panelled office. It had a large window and light was streaming in, warming the polished desk and surroundings. She was offered a chair and sat looking at a tray with coffee cups and slices of bread covered with ham. She suddenly realised how hungry she was; not a bite to eat since yesterday lunchtime.

Nikolai took a pot and poured out two cups of strong black coffee. He pushed one towards Jenny and waved his hand towards the open sandwiches.

'Please take one.'

Jenny bit into the sandwich; it was a bit dry but she would have eaten practically anything. She swilled it down with a deep gulp of the bitter dark coffee and sat back in the chair feeling a little more assertive.

'When I asked who you were, I wasn't being friendly asking for first names. I was asking what your position is in all of this. I am a guest in this country, have been taken from my room without any explanation, and refused access to my Consulate or even to my hosts at the Baikonur Cosmodrome.'

'Ah, my position. That for the moment need not concern you. Suffice it to say that you were accommodated overnight so that an English-speaking person of authority could talk to you. I am that person. Now, your connection to the Baikonur Cosmodrome – that does interest me.'

Jenny sighed exasperated. 'Interest you, it interests you. I'm being held here captive against my will, and you say that my visit to the Cosmodrome interests you. What is that meant to mean?'

Nikolai leaned on the desk and steepled his hands. 'All right, let me start at the beginning.' He took his hands apart and reached into his pocket. 'I would like you to take a look at this.' A clear thick plastic bag was placed into Jenny's palm.

She looked inside the bag, and dropped it on the table in shock. Vomit filled her throat and she did all she could to swallow it back.

'What is that!' she screamed.

Nikolai picked up the bag and dangled it between his fingers. 'What does it look like, Miss Kang? Something a friend of yours might own. Or, something a friend of yours might have taken.'

'It's a human ear, you know that don't you. Why are you trying to frighten me? It's repulsive.' She turned around looking towards the door. 'You have to let me go, or call my Consulate. I shall report you. This is an international outrage.'

Her interviewer placed the plastic bag gently on the table. 'You may be right about that, Miss Kang, an international outrage. I would like you to know that we have found many more parts belonging to this gentleman. Many of them unrecognisable but fortunately or, for some, unfortunately, a few quite identifiable. I used to think tattoos were unnecessary adornments but, in my line of business, I've now come to find them quite useful.'

'You're sick,' spluttered Jenny. 'I demand to see the authorities.'

'Well, I will grant you that one,' said Nikolai. 'You see, I am probably the highest authority that you could ask for. Quite a privilege I would say. But we should stop playing games.' He poked the plastic bag. 'Would you like to know where this came from?'

Jenny shook her head vehemently.

'Well, you may know the parts belong to an adversary of yours. A person with the knowledge of your substation and the ability to take down one of your satellites.'

Jenny shook her head in disbelief. 'Knowledge of our substation?'

'Knowledge which unfortunately he no longer possesses as the majority of him has been consumed by a litter of pigs.' Nikolai gave a sinister smile. 'Litter, I'm rather proud of that word. I looked it up. Initially I thought "herd" but it seems the dictionary prefers "litter".'

Jenny felt sick. The ear on the table, and the repellent thought of someone being eaten by animals. She remembered the pink object the soldiers handled at the farmhouse. That must have been them rescuing bits of the body.

'This has nothing to do with me,' she protested, her stomach still turning. 'I have no idea who those people at the farm were, I've never seen them before. I've never even visited Kazakhstan before. Yes, I have some knowledge of a satellite substation. I've not seen it yet. I'm here to take a look at it, find out what went wrong. But I've no idea what these people have got to do with it. You have to believe me.'

Jenny sat up with a start as Nikolai smashed his hand onto the desk. The inane smile that he had been wearing instantly disappeared. 'Believe you? That is what I'm finding extremely difficult to do, Miss Kang. Look at the facts from my point of view. One: you enter the country enquiring about a satellite. Two: that satellite is controlled from the Cosmodrome Substation 241. Three: a man who was found to illegally enter that substation has been found murdered, and,' Nikolai wrinkled his nose in revulsion, 'his body fed to his own pigs. All a bit coincidental don't you think?'

Jenny closed her eyes trying to take all of this in. A thought came to her. 'All right, I have entered the country enquiring about a rogue satellite. As for the substation I have no idea where it is and haven't even visited it yet. You can ask my hosts at Baikonur, they had arranged to take me tomorrow.' She glanced at the clock on the wall, 'No, make that today. And Mr Policeman or whoever you are, how do you think I would know that anyone had illegally entered the substation? I've only just arrived in the country.'

Nikolai reached into his pocket and pulled out a large mobile phone. He turned the screen towards Jenny. 'Have you never heard of Facebook, Miss Kang?'

The tall saguaro cacti stood like sentinels in front of the Tucson Medical Center. The paramedics had been alerted beforehand, and they moved with efficiency as they gently manoeuvred the patient onto a trolley under the illuminated hospital sign and into the emergency unit. Harry Stones paced up and down under the Tucson night sky.

'How bad is it?' he asked for the umpteenth time.

Alison Perez touched his arm trying to arrest his walk. 'She's in the best of hands, the medical centre has all the facilities.'

'That's no answer,' Harry barked back irritably. 'How bad was it? All you have told me is that she pushed me out of the way. Tell me the truth.'

Alison tried to keep him still. 'It's like I said, the telescope swung out of control and was about to hit you when Nathalie jumped in its path. I'm afraid she took the full force of it. Knocked the poor girl to the floor and she went out like a light.'

'I heard that much, sounded awful. Foolish thing to do trying to protect me. I'm far bigger than her. Stupid bloody eyesight. I couldn't bear it if, if...' Harry tailed off and once more started pacing up and down.

Alison Perez turned to Doctor Rodin and his young intern. 'I think it best if you take a cab back to your hotel. The film crew won't leave until they find out more and I'm sure the hospital don't want too many of us hanging around. I'll let you know what's happening in the morning.'

Rodin nodded and gestured to his assistant to follow him to the taxi rank. As they walked past the film-crew truck, Boyd Anderson jumped out and confronted the astronomer.

'You had the controls of that thing. For your sake I hope she's all right. I think you should make a statement to the police right now.'

Rodin looked up at the intimidating frame of the cameraman in front of him. 'You saw, it was an accident, I slipped.'

'Slipped because you were looking at young Terry here,' snapped back Boyd pointing at the intern. 'You know how sensitive those controls are. You should have been more careful.'

'It was an accident,' protested Rodin moving around Boyd and hurrying with Terry towards the row of cabs.

'If you don't report it I will,' Boyd shouted after them.

Alison Perez tried to calm the situation. 'You're right, Mr Anderson, it should be reported and we will do so, but first we must find out how she is.' She glanced towards the pacing body of Harry and lowered her voice, 'I haven't told Doctor Stones but I think it's quite bad. She took a terrible blow to the head and it looked like she had broken her legs. If you must wait, stay in the truck while I take Harry into the medical centre to see if we can find out anything more.'

Boyd could see that he would only make things worse if he made a fuss so he acquiesced and joined his colleagues in the vehicle.

'As soon as you know anything, right?'

'Of course, I'll take Doctor Stones in right now.'

The waiting area was nearly empty. A neon bulb flickered above them as Alison Perez and Harry Stones sipped their lukewarm coffee out of the hospital cardboard cups. They were told that Nathalie had gone in for x-rays and scans. She was still unconscious but no more information was available. Harry decided that ranting and raving wouldn't improve the situation and so he sat meekly in a plastic chair, rocking gently.

An hour passed, but it felt more like ten to Harry. The hospital was still going about its nightly business: a few drunks with cuts and bruises, a very pregnant woman breathing hard, and an old man with dementia haranguing the patient desk staff. Each time footsteps came from the corridor Harry stood and raised a question, but each time he was answered with a shake of the head. And each time Alison interpreted the reply.

'I'm sure they'll tell us as soon as they know anything,' she said to Harry. 'It's nearly three in the morning. The film crew might have to work today. I'll give them my number and tell them to go home. They can't sit in that truck all night and there's nothing more they can do here.'

'Good idea,' said Harry. 'Why don't you go outside and persuade them?'

Harry waited until Alison's footsteps had disappeared and then called out to the desk.

'Excuse me, would someone show me the way to the male toilets? I have a small sight problem here,' he added pointing to his dark glasses and extending the telescopic white stick he held in his pocket.

'Of course, Sir,' said a nurse from the desk walking over to guide him. 'Take my arm and I'll direct you.'

She took Harry down the corridor and, as he heard the noise from the reception behind them fade, he stopped in his tracks.

'Is there anyone else around?' he asked.

'No,' answered the nurse, thinking it strange that a grown-up man should be shy of going to the toilet.

'Well,' he whispered. 'I'm afraid that I've brought you here under false pretences.'

The nurse stood back a little apprehensive.

Harry noticed her movement. 'Oh nothing like that I can assure you. You see, I merely want to ask you a small favour.'

'Favour?'

'The young lady, Nathalie Thompson, the one who was admitted after an accident at the observatory...'

'Yes, she was taken in about an hour ago.'

'That's her. You see I'm not exactly her next of kin, more sort of in loco parentis.'

It was evident that the nurse had no idea what he was talking about. He continued. 'An uncle, you know, been told to keep a close eye on her by her parents. I feel responsible. Is there any way you can get me in to see her?' He pointed to his sunglasses. 'Or, as you have gathered, not exactly see her but find out how she is.'

The tone was rather compelling, a poor blind man taking the responsibility of someone else's daughter. The nurse glanced up and down the corridor. It could do no harm. The patient's room was the second on the right. The doctors were awaiting the results of an MRI scan. There would be plenty of time to slip him into the ward.

'It's against the rules but I don't see how it can hurt. Let me take you to the room but we can only be a few minutes.'

Harry took her arm and tapped his way down the corridor. The nurse opened the door and shut it quietly behind her. Harry could hear the respirator and tried to assess the bleeping of the heart-rate monitor.

'Her breathing sounds okay. Can you tell me if she's awake and what her medical reports say?'

The nurse picked up the chart at the end of the bed. 'She's not conscious I'm afraid: been like that since admission and sedated while they wait for the MRI report. The good news is, the x-rays show no broken bones. It's the head injury that they're worried about.'

'Head injury?' Harry tapped his stick to try and find the edge of the bed. 'How bad is it? What does she look like?'

The nurse looked at Nathalie's swollen purple face, scarred with a gaping wound. For a non-medical person it would appear pretty frightening, but she knew these things often calmed down after twenty-four hours. 'She's a bit bruised, but we won't know how she is until the scans come back.'

'Worst-case scenario?'

'A haematoma on the brain,' she rested her hand on Harry's. 'But that's the worst-case scenario. She's a fairly light creature and apparently was swept to the floor easily. With luck, it should be only concussion. I can assure you she's in the right place and they are doing all they can.'

'Can I hold her hand?'

The nurse looked at her watch. There was at least five minutes before the next ward round. 'Of course, I'll take you over.'

She lightly guided Harry's hand onto Nathalie's. He felt the warmth of her tiny fingers. They both remained there motionless in their own darkness.

Nine

Reflections of the sun skidded across the grey swathes of lakes nestled in the Kazakhstan interior. Despite the almost transparent blue sky the flat plains surrounding them were a monotonous beige. The windows of the Mercedes were left wide open and the cool May turbulent air assaulted Jenny Kang's hair. She attempted to tie it back; better that than ask for the windows to be closed and suffer the acrid smoke of the Russian cigarettes emanating from her front-seated guardians. They had been travelling at high speed for an hour, initially on smooth metalled roads, but now they had turned off onto a wide dusty side track. Jenny continued to stare out of the window, miles and miles of flat featureless plains. She was alone on the back seat feeling naked without her handbag and mobile phone. She was almost too tired to feel frightened and sat there in a hypnotic trance. The passenger in the front seat turned around to face her.

'Not far now, Miss Kang.'

Her interrogator, the sharp-suited Nikolai, had changed into less formal attire – combat trousers and a military-looking sweater. He pulled out a mobile phone from one of his many pockets and scrolled through some texts.

'You will be pleased to know that we will be having a small reception committee. Your friends from Baikonur.'

This was the first time her 'friends from Baikonur' had been mentioned since the acrimonious ending of her interview. Not Jenny's words, but those of Mr Nikolai here. She would have called it more of a grilling or an intimidating examination.

'So you're letting me go?' she asked hopefully.

'I didn't realise we were actually keeping you, Miss Kang. As

I said, you are helping us with our investigations. This is merely another part of our enquiry.'

'Well it would help if you told me where we were going,' protested Jenny.

'Ah, I thought that was obvious. You informed me that you had come to Kazakhstan to inspect a satellite control substation. Your friends at Baikonur have confirmed this intention. I'm merely facilitating the purpose of your visit. And I'm pleased to tell you that, with a little persuasion, your friends have agreed to join us.'

Jenny didn't like the way he ominously accented 'a little persuasion' but she was pleased to know that she would be reunited with her hosts and, with a bit of luck, a return to some sort of normality. She decided to keep silent, for every time she opened her mouth she felt she was getting deeper and deeper into trouble. She would try to act as normal as possible. If they really were visiting the substation she would have to remember her training and have all her wits about her. Her task had been to determine how the satellite had been moved. If it had been from the substation there would be tell-tale signs. The problem was that Mr Zikri had told her to keep the signs from her hosts and retain them for MalaySat's own potential use. This left her in a real quandary. She didn't know who to be more frightened of – Mr Zikri or the smooth-talking Nikolai. The Russian was the more imminent threat. He had her passport and was sitting right in front of her. But if she got out of this without information on *PhreeSat*, Zikri would be waiting for her. Neither prospect was attractive. She would have to keep a cool head and try to talk her way out of this one.

'There you are, in the distance…' Nikolai pointed to a small aberration on the horizon. He turned to the driver, indicated to a rutted side track, and snapped something in Russian.

The driver swung the wheel around to the left and the limousine exited the main thoroughfare. The furrows along the stony trail had been made by wider vehicles and didn't match those of the Mercedes. In response it bucked to and fro, in and out of the ridges.

Jenny was thrown across the back seat and into the footwell. The two men in front continued to sit upright, the driver clenching onto the wheel and Nikolai holding onto the shelf in front of him.

'I must apologise for the discomfort, Miss Kang. The station did offer me their Humvee but I have to return to my office this evening and preferred to take my car and driver.'

Jenny's heart leaped. Returning this evening he had said. Hopefully that meant he would leave her with the hosts from the Baikonur Cosmodrome. She crawled out of the footwell, grabbed onto the sill and thrust her head out of the window. Her heart beat a little faster. There in the distance, next to a wire-surrounded hut, was a mud-spattered pickup truck and she could just make out a rocket-shaped logo on the side.

They were greeted by three men emerging from the pickup truck. Two of them, introducing themselves as Doctor Valery Bykov and Anatole Molchalin, Jenny had met before at the Cosmodrome. The third was dressed in police uniform and stood to attention as Nikolai approached. Nikolai ignored him and with a sweeping gesture invited the group to enter the substation. Molchalin, who Jenny remembered as the head of security, took a large bunch of keys from the policeman and tried them one by one until the new padlock swung open.

'Apparently we had a couple of intruders recently,' he explained to Jenny. 'The police here kindly threw them out and padlocked the external wire gate. I've got the key to the substation door here.'

The aluminium pole and chicken-wire gate was pulled outwards cutting a curved groove into the gravel and Molchalin walked the few yards to the green-painted metal door. He began to insert the key but found that the lock had rusted and the door had been left slightly open.

He spoke in Russian to the policeman who replied curtly.

'Ah, no need for concern,' he said to Jenny. 'They didn't touch anything. Seemingly, they were apprehended using the station as a bird hide, would you believe.'

Recalling the severed ear she had handled recently, Jenny thought there was not much she could believe but she said nothing and, taking the cue from Nikolai, entered the substation. Molchalin and Bykov waited nervously outside accompanied by the policeman.

The interior was murky, lit only by a small panel of light from a dirty window set high up in one of the concrete walls. Red and green pinpoints of light flashed from the desk set along one side. Cream and grey polished-metal instruments slowly morphed out of the darkness as Jenny's eyes became accustomed to the gloom. She stepped back in alarm as there was a sudden flash of cold light.

'I thought you might wish to see a little better,' said Nikolai, taking his hand from a wall switch that led through a plastic conduit to a flickering single fluorescent tube on the ceiling.

'Of course, thank you,' said Jenny taking a deep breath and trying to maintain her cool. Now was the time to use all of her scientific expertise and yet think on her feet. She took a stride to the instrument bench and swept her finger across the dust to form a smear.

'Will Doctor Bykov be joining us?'

'I understand he has come in more of an administrative capacity. In other words, I don't think he has any understanding of how this thing works. I believe you are the expert, and the one who requested the inspection, so here you are.' Nikolai pulled up a metal crate that was standing by the door and sat on it with his arms folded, waiting.

Jenny tried to shut out from her mind all that had happened to her and attempted to focus on the instrumentation. It was an antiquated device, built several years ago to control satellites directly by radio waves. As such the technology was simple. She looked for recent activity on the controls. The dust itself would have been moved by any interference. Nothing. A thin untouched film covered the whole instrument panel. Yes there was disturbance on the floor by the entrance but, if that was made by the birdwatchers, they had nothing to do with *PhreeSat*. It had been taken down some time before they had arrived. She checked the power that would send messages to the satellite thrusters, thrusters that were no longer there. The power was on and, if there had been a satellite, the controls would still work; she could determine that at least. She slowly surveyed the room. To one corner behind the main consul was a small innocuous box. It didn't tally with the layout that she was expecting. She traced her finger under the bench and found a set of small cables clamped to the underside. She had no phone or torch so she felt their passage by touch to a junction box set in the floor. She prised it open, breaking her fingernail in the process, and knelt on the floor to take a closer look. Seeing the feet of Nikolai beside her she tried not to look surprised. A USB connection, something she would not have expected in this relatively primitive substation. She closed the box gently and nodding got to her feet.

'All that's fine,' she said hoping that it didn't sound too false. 'I just need to check the transmission base. If I'm right it should be on the left-hand side of the bench.'

Nikolai didn't move as she turned her back to him and threw some switches to make him believe that she was checking the apparatus. She now knew how someone could have taken down *PhreeSat*. They would have had to have been extremely clever but, in theory, it could be possible. A lot more work would need to be done and she would have to persuade Zikri that it would take time. For now, her challenge was to pacify her interrogators. She looked around by the switches and found a compact lever connector. It was slightly rusty but it would do. Using a fingernail to avoid disturbing the dust she raised the lever and carefully pulled out the wire.

'Ah, this could be the problem,' she cried excitedly. 'Probably due to heat expansion or a frost at night.' She turned to face Nikolai. 'Look here, see, the connector has lifted. It's possible that the wire could have oscillated and caused some sort of signal. These stations are old and becoming obsolete; nobody's fault but I'll report this to my company and ensure that future satellites are controlled by more up-to-date technology.'

Nikolai slowly rose from the metal casing and peered at the connector.

'Is it not more likely that someone could have done this on purpose?'

'Look for yourself. It's covered in dust, hasn't been touched for ages. And besides, if you're thinking of those poor farmers…the satellite controlled by this instrument crashed many days ago. Why would someone revisit the station after the event? It doesn't make sense.'

'You're right there, Miss Kang, it doesn't make sense. But I have an unsolved murder to investigate, and I find it strange that on one day these farmers are being apprehended for trespass on a sensitive satellite station and, on another, one of them is being picked out in pieces from a pig pen.'

He turned to walk into the sunshine. Jenny shaded her eyes and followed him.

'And can you see me capable of such a terrible thing?' asked Jenny.

'No, Miss Kang, I don't think I can,' replied Nikolai. 'Maybe some of your associates…' He added glancing at Molchalin and Bykov who were nervously pacing up and down by their pickup.

'But I hardly know them,' said Jenny. 'I only met them the day I arrived. You can check that out can't you?'

'Oh I intend to, Miss Kang,' said Nikolai walking towards his Mercedes. 'I understand that you are to fly out on Wednesday. If our enquiries are satisfied by then, we will return your passport to your hotel.'

'Is that it?' exclaimed Jenny.

She received no reply and stood there watching the black Mercedes kick up dust as it rocked its way down the gravel track.

'So you found the problem?' Anatole Molchalin moved alongside her looking a lot less agitated than he had a few moments before. 'I'm sorry you've been put through all of that.' He looked around to ensure that the policeman was out of earshot. 'The authorities have been quite intrusive with us, too. I hope that they are now satisfied.'

'Me too,' said Jenny.

'Well, it's getting late and you must be hungry. I hope you will be free to take up our invitation to that restaurant we were talking about.'

'As long as they don't serve Butterbrots,' laughed Jenny, feeling an almost hysterical relief flow through her body.

The security officer looked puzzled. 'I don't think so, Miss Kang. They serve delicious kebab dishes though.'

Jenny didn't bother to explain. 'I'll need to clean up at my hotel if that's okay, and change of course,' she added looking down at her soiled jeans.

'The police officer insisted on accompanying us to the site but, once we've dropped him off, we can take you to your hotel.'

The two Cosmodrome officials accompanied her to the truck. Jenny sat in the back with the policeman, who hadn't spoken a word. As the vehicle pulled out of the clearing she looked at the horizon. The sun was now dipping behind the low hill that surrounded the plain. The sky was turning to purple and orange making long shadows out of the shrublands. She wasn't sure whether it was her imagination as a sudden flash of light entered the scene. It was from the skyline, and Jenny had the unnerving thought that it was the glinting reflection of watching binoculars.

Jenny had a feeling of déjà vu as the taxi picked her up from the Sputnik Hotel. She was half expecting to be kidnapped by Russian soldiers but, instead, a courteous local taxi driver beckoned her to his well-labelled cab. Baikonur Taxis was written in English, Kazakh and Russian in gaudy letters across the side. He didn't speak English so they sat in silence for the short journey to Nebo's Restaurant. As she pulled out her purse the driver waved the money away. By his symbols and utterances she guessed that he was saying it was all paid for. She tried to give him a tip but even this he refused. He pointed to the restaurant and made eating gestures with his hands and mouth. Jenny decided not to push it any further and thanked him using the only Russian word she knew.

The restaurant was plain but intimate, a row of modern sofas facing low tables adjacent to plate-glass windows. Deeper into the interior were black-pointed white-brick walls, some adorned with decorative plates bearing the images of cosmonauts and space rockets. The smells emanating from the open-fire grill pervaded the restaurant reminding Jenny that she was famished.

'Ah, Miss Kang, you beat us to it.' The accented voice of Doctor Bykov came from behind her as he entered the restaurant.

'Anatole will be joining us shortly; I have reserved a table for the three of us. Please follow me.'

The waiters fussed over them and brought gaudy unordered cocktails. Jenny sipped the sickly liquid and smiled politely. As soon as the security officer had joined them Doctor Bykov clicked his fingers and was immediately brought a long wooden sharing platter containing some sort of deep-fried meats, noodles, salad and fries.

'I hope you don't mind, I have taken the liberty to order. Much easier than trying to translate the menu.' He bore a rare smile. 'I believe the English is more difficult to understand than the Kazakh version.'

Jenny smiled back and tucked in. She would have eaten practically anything but in fact the food was quite nice. Her two companions seemed less assured than they had been on the previous day. The intervention by the police or whoever they were had obviously shaken them. Initially they skirted around the subject but, after a few vodkas, Anatole decided to broach the issue.

'Terrible thing this murder. We understand from the police that you volunteered to help with their enquiries.'

Jenny raised an eyebrow.

'Because your company was renting the substation where the victim had been seen,' he added.

'Volunteered' wasn't exactly the word that Jenny would have used but she decided to hold her rant for another time. In the circumstances, she thought, the less she said the better.

'And did they involve you in their enquiries?' she asked deflecting the conversation away from herself.

'Only natural,' replied Molchalin. 'I'm head of security for all the substations around Baikonur and apparently one of them was broken into. No damage I was assured, only a couple of birdwatchers using it as a hide.'

Jenny took another sip from her violently coloured cocktail and leaned forward to look at Molchalin across the table. 'Did you report the break-in to MalaySat?'

Molchalin shuffled uncomfortably in his chair. 'We didn't think it necessary. After the accident the substation was inactive. I don't think any more would have been said about it until it became part of a murder enquiry. I doubt it had anything to do with the substation but, you know, they like to cover all angles.'

Valery Bykov could see that this conversation was becoming detrimental to his cause and so he intervened. 'Miss Kang, you mentioned at our first meeting that, after your investigation, you deemed it possible your company might procure further satellites, more high-tech, less chance of any problems should we say.'

Jenny noticed the change of tack and decided to go along with it although, after what she had seen at the substation, 'high-tech with less chance of problems' seemed far from the right sort of equation.

'Well, as you know, *PhreeSat* was at the end of its natural life anyway, and I understand that my company has moved its transmissions to a land-based service in Malaya. Of course I shall report back your proposals and, I'm sure that if MalaySat receives a special discount for a new launch, they would be willing to overlook any possible negligence or security issues with the old substation.'

The two Cosmodrome officials looked at each other in slight dismay. 'Of course, Miss Kang,' said Doctor Bykov. As we said we absolutely deny any negligence on our behalf but I'm sure, because of our long-standing relationships, we could provide a very reasonable quotation. I'll send our proposals to your superiors by the end of the week.'

Jenny kicked off her shoes and sat on her bed in the Sputnik Hotel. She pondered over the evening's events. It had been superficially polite but with an undercurrent of discomfort. No mention was made of the inspection of the substation, or of her findings, overtly disclosed or otherwise. She now had a clue as to how *PhreeSat* could have been moved. How, but not why. She still had a suspicion that Bykov may have had something to do with it. Both men were rather sleazy, and both men would reap the benefits from an old satellite coming down and for a new one to be commissioned in its place. And then there was that terrible murder and the bizarre belief that she had something to do with it. She froze as there was a loud knock at her door. Not again. She opened it and her fears returned as she was confronted by a large uniformed officer. Her heart began to palpitate, panic surged through her body.

'Miss Kang?' asked the officer.

Jenny nodded gasping heavily in short breaths.

'This is for you and for your eyes only,' said the officer, thrusting a large manila envelope into her hand. 'Good night,' he added, turning on his heels and closing the door behind him.

Jenny stood there shaking. Blood had rushed to her head and she could feel it throbbing as if it would burst. She sat cross-legged on the floor where she had been standing and tore open the envelope. Inside was a passport, two pieces of paper and a letter.

Dear Miss Kang,

I here return your passport and wish you a safe return journey. I also enclose two copies of a log that I have obtained from the Baikonur Cosmodrome. The first, as you will see, is highly redacted and was requested through formal channels. The second, an identical page from the log, was obtained sometime later from, let us say, informal channels. You may be interested in the redacted sections which, if I'm not mistaken, may coincide with your findings at the substation. We are still pursuing the homicide case but corporate espionage is beyond my remit. I therefore trust that you may make your own enquiries in this regard.

Sincerely, Nikolai Turgenev. MUR

Ten

'You'll wear the carpet out,' said Stefanie.

Geoff paused, stared at the polished mahogany floor beneath his feet, and turned to his PA who was standing in the doorway.

'I haven't got a bloody carpet,' he snapped.

'You know what I mean. I keep telling you, I have rung every hour, on the hour. There's still no change.'

Geoff slumped in the swivel chair behind his desk and swung it towards the wall. The international clocks were set in a line. The one labelled Pacific time was the nearest to Arizona. He mentally deducted an hour.

'Nine o'clock in the morning there. According to Boyd she's been out for about fifteen hours. What in the hell are they doing!'

'Everything they can, Geoff. It's a top hospital and, from what I understand, they've done every test on the planet. She's taken a hit to the head and I expect they will bring her round slowly.'

Geoff Sykes rose from his chair and started to pace up and down once more.

'I knew I shouldn't have sent her on a wild-goose chase with that guy. He may be bright but he can't see a thing. And we've no idea whether it was an accident or done on purpose.'

'Well according to Boyd it could have been a lot worse. The telescope was coming straight for Doctor Stones; might have killed him if it wasn't for Nathalie pushing him out of the way.'

'Yes, and she gets a blow for her efforts.'

'A glancing blow, according to Boyd.'

'Glancing enough to put her out for fifteen hours,' barked Geoff.

'Well the hospital say the scans are all normal. They sedated her and she's asleep. It's now just wait and see.'

Geoff looked at his watch. 'It's four o'clock, where's Nick?'

'He is on his way, don't be too cross with him. I called him as soon as you heard from Boyd. He said he would drop everything and get here as soon as he could.'

'It takes over two hours to get to Cambridge. They'll shut up shop soon, those academic places often knock off early.'

'They're an Astrophysics Department, Geoff, they're used to working in the evenings. Anyway, you needn't worry, I've made an appointment for 7.30. The professor was very accommodating, especially after I told him we were working with Alison Perez on Kitt Peak.'

'You didn't mention the accident.'

'No, of course not. I merely said that we understood Doctor Rodin had been a visiting astronomer there and would like to know more about their spectroscopic research in case it could be of use for one of our television programmes.'

'Right, perhaps we're sending the wrong guy then. Nick's more known for his special forces than this special-oscopy or whatever it's called.'

Stefanie opened her mouth in disbelief. She had protested to Geoff that Nick was not the best person to send but he had insisted. 'Nick knows Nathalie, he'll get to the bottom of this accident thing,' were his actual words.

Geoff ignored her, walked over to the window, pulled open the Venetian blind, and stared into the Soho streets. It was pouring with rain and people were rushing between one another, umbrellas held high. All except one. A large broad-shouldered man was marching towards his office, shirtsleeves and head uncovered.

Nick Coburn, ex-Special Forces and general dogsbody as he described himself, strode into the office and pushed his fingers through his wet hair.

'Like you said, I dropped everything including the bloody jacket they lent me and came straight over. What's the latest?'

Geoff pushed a chair towards him. 'Still no news on the Nathalie front. Stefanie's getting hourly bulletins and keeps telling me that there's nothing to worry about but...'

'But you're worried shitless,' said Nick, finishing his sentence.

'Trying to piece the bits of the jigsaw together,' said Geoff. 'The observatory lot are swearing it was an accident. Trying to protect their own arses and convince everyone not to call the police.'

Nick sat down in the chair. 'But you think different.'

'All I have is Boyd's observations. He's a really good cameraman, notices the smallest of things. He said the interview was going fine until Harry mentioned something about the satellite. He was on a close-up of Rodin's face. The guy looked dazed for a moment and glanced to one side. That's when he pressed the wrong button on the telescope control panel.'

'Rodin, what sort of name's that? Sounds more like a statue.'

'He's a Russian astronomer, one of the guys that Stones and Nathalie are trying to suss out for a project we're doing.' Geoff threw a small file onto Nick's lap. 'You can read it, all in there, on your train journey. You did say you could make yourself free.'

'Only too pleased, merely an ex-forces reunion at the RAC Club. Not my sort of place. Wouldn't let me in without a jacket. Would you believe it, they have rails of them to lend to people like me? Which reminds me, if you're sending me across the country, I'll need your anorak. Bloody freezing out there for this time of year.'

'You're welcome to it but I thought you Scots were hardy types.'

'So where am I going, the North Pole?'

'Cambridge, the university. I want you to check out the background on this Rodin guy. See if there's anything sinister there. Stefanie discovered that he was a recent guest lecturer at the Cavendish Laboratory.' Geoff looked down at his notepad. 'She's made a 7.30 meeting with their head of department. Someone called Professor Watts. The guy's a bigwig in astronomy, in charge of Cambridge's new centre of astrophysics. Knows everybody in the field.'

'It's Nathalie, so I'm willing and able, but are you sure I'm the right guy for the job? Sounds like you need more brain than muscle.'

'That's what Stefanie said, but I have a feeling that your persona might get more out of him. We have no time to pussyfoot around. If we have any evidence, or even suspicion, that Rodin was the type of guy to do this on purpose we need to get someone to report it to the police. And we've got to do it soon.'

The Battock Centre for Experimental Astrophysics was just off the Madingley Road. Nick nearly walked past it. He was expecting a geodesic sci-fi construction of steel and glass. Instead he was confronted by an orange-brick, horseshoe-shaped building, windows tilting outwards, similar to those of a 1960s secondary school. He felt like a schoolboy himself in Geoff's undersized anorak but at least it had kept some of the rain off. He pulled back the hood and walked up to the reception. The woman behind the desk was on the telephone facing the other way. Despite being a few minutes late, Nick didn't interrupt and used the time to flick through last year's alumni magazine. After a short time she finished the call and turned to face him.

'Nick Coburn, Bagatelle Films,' he announced, handing one of Geoff's cards to the receptionist.

'Ah just in time,' she said. 'I was about to close up. Professor Watts is expecting you. I'll give him a buzz.'

'No need, Jilly,' said a white-bearded man, appearing down the staircase. 'Good evening, Mr Coburn. If you don't mind, I think it would be more comfortable if we had our chat in the local pub. Wouldn't like to keep Jilly longer than necessary.'

'Pub sounds good,' said Nick holding out his hand for a firm handshake.

The Punter pub was a white-washed brick, old coaching house on Pound Hill. Despite its name, not a river to be seen. Bare wooden tables were surrounded by odd chairs and random prints hung from the tacky wallpapered walls. Just Nick's sort of drinking place. Professor Watts seemed to be known by everyone.

'A pint of heavy?' asked the professor making a reference to Nick's gravelly Scottish accent.

'Not the same as it used to be,' smiled Nick. 'A pint of the local bitter would be great though, thanks.'

Watts placed the two brim-full glasses onto the table. 'Now, Mr Coburn, your company's project sounds intriguing, what can I do for you?'

Nick took a large gulp from his glass and licked his lips. 'Nearly as good as Scottish ale,' he commented. He sat back on the chair, leaning on two of its legs. 'I'm not going to beat around the bush, Professor. I'm no scientist and haven't got a clue what Geoff's programme's about. I'm more what you would call a fixer, checking out participants and locations.'

The professor smiled. 'Somehow I didn't see you as an academic type, and the name's Jim by the way.'

Nick soon established that Jim Watts had not become Cambridge University's head of astrophysics by chance. He had been suspicious since the very first mention of Rodin's name and had made enquiries about Bagatelle Films. He noted that, alongside some of their scientific productions, their main claim to fame was for major investigative documentary journalism – corporate crime, government scandals and espionage. Marat Rodin had a fine reputation for spectroscopy but there was also another side to his CV. He came with the association to some serious Russian oligarchs and, shortly after his spell at Cambridge, had joined a mysterious privately sponsored astrophysics group. Jim Watts had yet to establish how this group was funded and why they were so uncompromising in the field of Cold Dark Matter. The Battock Centre had been formed to merge some of the greatest minds in cosmology, and yet this WCMB group seemed reluctant to share any of their results. He hadn't even been able to determine what the letters WCMB stood for.

'So there you have it, Mr Coburn. I'm afraid I can't supply you with any endorsement of Doctor Rodin other than he is one of the world's top experts in astronomical spectroscopy. But I'm not sure whether that's exactly what you're looking for, is it?'

Nick drained his glass. 'Another one, Jim? And, as we're on first name terms, it's Nick, by the way.' He sauntered to the bar and, using the time, tried to calculate exactly how much of Geoff's 'Star Wars dossier' he should share.

The phone vibrated in his pocket. It was Geoff.

'She's come around, she's fine apparently. Too fine for my liking. Phoned me herself. Insists that we don't make any complaint about Rodin. Says it will ruin her investigation. Tried to discharge herself but the hospital insists she stays in for observation. Apparently we're not to worry. If I hear that one more time from anyone I'll…'

Nick whispered into the phone. 'I get it, I'm glad she's okay. Things are getting interesting here though. I'll keep you in the loop.' He pressed the disconnect button and slipped the telephone into his back pocket.

'Good news?' asked Jim Watts, noting the smile on Nick's face.

'Yes, a sick friend feels a bit better. Let's drink to it.' Nick raised his glass and Watts clinked it in return.

'Okay. Geoff's programme covers a little more than this Cold Dark Matter thing. We are interested in this WCMB outfit – how they got their money, and why they're putting it into academic research when this sort of stuff is usually done by you guys. From what I understand it's usually either about knowledge or prestige, Nobel Prizes and all that sort of thing.'

Jim Watts wiped the froth from his moustache. 'The Nobel Prize, yes there are a great many of us who would do a lot for that. Some would even try to fake academic papers but, millions of dollars of private money, I'm not so sure.' He stroked his chin in an afterthought. 'Mind you, the Russians spent billions on space research for prestige so why not be the first to uncover and publish the secrets of the origins of the universe?'

'Doesn't sound as sexy as a race to put a man on the moon,' said Nick.

'You'd be surprised, it's the holy grail of physics. Why are we here? How are we here? How did it all begin? How will it all end? Cold Dark Matter as a theory could explain our fate. I don't know whether you call it sexy but I would think it's one of the most fundamental concepts for human thought.'

Nick drained his second pint in one. 'All a bit too deep for me. I'm a simple journeyman trying to get through life without being bored.'

'If I may say, you don't seem the bored or boring type and, while you're trying to work out how much you should tell me, it's my turn I think.' He pinched the two glasses between his fingers and headed for the bar.

Nick stared after him. He was right, how much should he tell him. Geoff's dossier was pretty thin but it was obvious Nathalie and this guy Stones were tracking down some nefarious characters involved in satellite sabotage. Professor Astronomer here hadn't mentioned anything about satellites. Maybe it was best that Nick kept that bit to himself. Rival cosmology groups however seemed fair game. There had already been mention about WCMB Associates. Perhaps it wouldn't hurt to bring up the other group that Geoff had mentioned in his report.

'There, two more pints of the good stuff,' said Watts spilling some of the contents on the table.

'Thanks,' said Nick, scooping the spattered beer away from the table edge with a beer mat. 'FastTrack, does that mean anything to you?'

'So you have been doing your homework. Yes it's another privately funded research group. Came out of Stanford. I think the Yanks had their noses put out of joint by cosmology financed by Russians and subsidised a small group of academics themselves. Nothing like the scale but several million dollars of government money matched by private enterprise. Wish we could get the same deal over here.'

'What do you know about them?'

'Quite a bit actually. One of our brightest stars, to coin an astronomical phrase, has joined them.'

'A Cambridge lecturer?'

'She was offered a post but, no, one of our PhD graduates, Sarah Nowak, extremely talented. We were sad to lose her, but the salary was no contest.'

Watts took a large gulp from his beer glass, wiped his mouth with the back of his hand, and smiled to himself.

Nick noticed that he was about to say something more but had stopped himself.

'So was it just the money?'

Watts interleaved his fingers and put his hands on his lap. 'Probably, but she was getting a bit of a reputation.'

'Reputation?'

Watts looked around the pub and, seeing no one within earshot, leaned forward and lowered his voice.

'Shouldn't be saying this sort of thing in this day and age but she was a very good-looking young woman. Gobbled men up for breakfast.'

'And that made her want to move on?'

Watts sighed. 'Well there were a few members in the department getting jealous.'

Nick changed the subject.

'And this FastTrack, they are in competition with the Russians?'

'I'm not sure I would say competition, but both groups are working in a similar field. As we all are, in fact. Probing the diverse aspects of cosmology – from Dark Energy to alternatives to general relativity, and from neutrino masses to the early universe.'

Nick put up his hand. 'Now you are losing me. You say they're working on similar things. Is there a race to see who will get there first? For instance, would it be advantageous for one group to scupper the other?'

Jim Watts put down his beer glass and looked straight into Nick's eyes. 'Ah, I can now see where you're going. Bagatelle Films would like to portray a sort of cosmological battle, one where dirty tricks are played on both sides. Deep investigative journalism, is that what they call it?'

Nick winked back. 'Not my call, I'm just the monkey dancing on the organ.' He picked up Geoff's folder and waved it in the air. 'I've no idea where these media-types get their ideas from, or how they put them on television, but they're pretty good at it and, if I can help out, all well and good.'

The professor pulled out a business card and placed it on the table. 'Well, Nick, I can't pretend I'm not interested in all of this. I'd love to know how and where WCMB get their money. So, if I can contribute in any way, you know where to find me.'

The trains to London were every fifteen minutes. Nick caught the 21.20, grabbed a coffee and scribbled a few notes on the envelope containing Geoff's proposal. The phone vibrated in his pocket. It was Bagatelle's number.

'Still at work?'

'Got some catching up to do.'

'Nathalie – any more news?'

'I keep phoning her but she's now getting cross. Says if I wanted her to get on with the project I should let her get some rest.'

'She's got a point.'

'I told her I don't give a damn about the project as long as she's all right.'

'And?'

'You know what she's like, says she is fine, a small bump to the head. A small bump to the head my arse, she was out for fifteen hours.'

'Have you talked to the doctors?'

'Have I talked to the doctors? I could have been awarded a medical degree for the time I've spent on the phone.'

'And?'

'They say she'll be fine. Cuts and bruises but no internal damage. They just want to keep her in for a few days. Protocol apparently.'

'Well, that's okay then.'

'You think so? Can you imagine Nathalie, on a job, staying in a hospital bed for two days?'

Nick didn't reply.

'Nick, you still there?'

'Just smiling. Want to hear about Rodin?'

'Yes of course, that's why I've rung.'

'Well it's interesting,' he glanced at his scrawls on the envelope. 'I'm just writing up a few notes. Professor Watts is as interested in the WCMB group as we are. Apparently Marat Rodin has some connection with a billionaire oligarch. Says it's unprecedented that so much money has been donated to a private group for cosmological research. I think he also has similar thoughts to your idea.'

'My idea? What idea?'

'The Star Wars thing. Two companies at loggerheads.'

'It wasn't my idea, it was Harry Stones's.'

'Whoever's idea it was, he'd heard of FastTrack. Even lost one of his best PhD graduates to them. Thinks you could be onto something concerning a rivalry.'

'Bloody hell, Nick, how much did you tell him? We haven't got proof on anything yet.'

'No worries, didn't mention anything about satellites. But I have got an "in" to FastTrack...' he hesitated, 'if you've got the budget.'

'There is no budget, but what's this "in"?'

'Jim Watts can get me an introduction to his prodigy, Sarah Nowak. She's working for FastTrack at Fermilab in Chicago. I think he's as interested as we are to know more about the outfit. Said if I wanted to meet them he could contact Sarah and say a friend of his was going to Chicago and would she show him around?'

There was a moment's pause while Geoff made some quick calculations. Nick waited knowingly. Eventually Geoff came back onto the phone. 'Are you free this week?'

'First-class flight and the Peninsula Hotel?'

'Economy and Holiday Inn or nothing.'

'Same daily rate?'

'Same daily rate.'

'Done, nice doing business with you. I'll pick up my tickets from the airport.'

'What about my anorak?'

'Sleeve's a bit ripped but otherwise it's okay. Oh, and there's one other thing. I noticed a name in one of Nathalie's recent e-mails in your dossier. Some sort of sidekick to Rodin. I saw it again in the Cambridge alumni magazine. Funny thing is, Watts didn't mention him.'

Eleven

Nathalie looked at herself in the mirror. It was a good thing that Harry couldn't see, she thought. One side of her face looked almost twice its size and the blackened bruises were now turning to purple. The bandages had been removed that morning exposing the large stitched wound. She was more shaken than she had let on but, if she was to convince Harry that she was fine to be let out of the hospital, she would have to hide that fact. The nursing staff had been reluctant to return her clothes but had agreed that, if Doctor Stones would look after her quietly in her hotel room, she could be discharged. Being discharged was her number one objective. The other, to meet with Rodin and his sidekick to find out more about the telescope malfunction. She had spoken to Boyd on the telephone and had heard his account of the incident. It had taken all her means of persuasion to stop him contacting the police but eventually he had yielded to her arguments. She heard footsteps from the corridor and quickly slipped back into the bed. She plumped the pillow, took a sip of water from the bedside table and sat up waiting for Harry Stones.

'And how is my favourite film producer today?' asked Harry, feeling for the side of the hospital bed.

'All the better for seeing you, Harry,' said Nathalie trying to talk as normally as she could through her swollen lips.

Harry sat on the edge of the bed and Nathalie grasped his held-out hand.

'They said they'll discharge me if you agree to escort me back to the hotel,' she said, squeezing his hand a little.

'A little more than escorting I think,' said Harry removing his hand. 'They want me to ensure you have a quiet few days in your room.'

Nathalie looked around to make sure the nurse was out of earshot. 'Well we can talk about that at the hotel,' she whispered. 'Have you made any more contact with Rodin?'

'I have. He's agreed to see me this afternoon. I think he's worried we'll report the incident to the police; was very accommodating when I said I'd like to talk to him.'

'You mean, *we* would like to talk to him.'

'No, just me, you are meant to be resting in your room, remember.'

'Must be the knock on my head but I don't remember anyone saying that. I'm sure that the plan was for both of us to see him.'

'But…'

'No buts, Harry. If I turn up with you I'm sure I can get more out of Rodin by insinuating that I may not pursue the investigation of the accident if he answers some of our questions.'

'The hospital recommended that you stay another night.'

'The operative word there being "recommended", Harry. They can't keep me here. Geoff's insurance premium is going up by the day and I am within my rights to walk out of that door right now. Saying that you will look after me for a while will just make them feel better.'

Harry shook his head. He could hear by the tone of her voice he was not going to win this one.

'All right, Ms Thompson, I'll play along. But any symptoms – dizziness or headache – you will let me know.'

'Promise,' said Nathalie, crossing her fingers behind her back.

The full force of the sun hit Nathalie as she stepped out of the taxi onto Cherry Avenue. The high-rise buildings seemed to spin as the contrast of the aircon and the thirty-four degrees in the shade took their toll. Nathalie grabbed the door handle to steady herself with one hand and put a finger to her lips with the other just as the cab driver was going to make a comment. She glanced at the other side of the taxi where Harry was getting out, obviously oblivious of the scene. She palmed the driver a more than generous tip and connected with Harry's arm, ostensibly to guide him to the sidewalk but, in reality, to stabilise herself. They made their way slowly towards the entrance of the Tucson University Astronomy Department. The reception was refreshingly cool and Nathalie sat in a chair whilst Harry made his enquiries.

'We have an appointment with Doctor Rodin,' he said feeling his way along the front of the desk. 'We'd appreciate it if he would send someone down to guide us to the meeting room.'

From the reaction of the receptionist Nathalie assessed that she had no idea of Harry's eyesight condition.

'Right away, Sir, if you would like to take a seat.'

'I'll stand thank you,' said Harry, swivelling around and leaning casually with his elbows on the desk.

They didn't have to wait long. The lobby elevator doors opened to reveal a surprised-looking Terry Jacobs.

'Oh my,' he started to say, staring at Nathalie's face.

Before he could blurt out any further expletive Nathalie leaped up, shook him by the hand, and covered the young man's embarrassment by asking him to guide Harry to the elevator.

Doctor Rodin's expression showed he was shocked by Nathalie's appearance as they reached the first floor. This was one time when Harry's sight didn't complicate the issue and, after initial pleasantries, they walked in silence towards the meeting room.

'I thought it apt for Terry to join us today,' began Rodin nervously. 'He was a witness at the accident and we both wish to say how sorry we are that...'

'That you spun a nine-ton telescope into my head,' completed Nathalie.

'I assure you that...'

Nathalie put up a hand to silence him. 'We're not here to argue with you, Doctor Rodin. It's possible that it was completely accidental. On the other hand…' she paused, '…on the other hand the police may think differently, if they get involved that is.'

She waited for this veiled threat to sink in.

'What I think Ms Thompson is getting at,' intervened Harry, 'is that, if we get full answers to our questions, the police may not even know about the unfortunate event.'

Rodin stared at Terry Jacobs who was about to open his mouth.

'I have made a full apology to yourselves and the department here who are also concerned not to take the matter further,' said Rodin. 'Considering the health and safety restrictions on the research projects they think it would be better for everyone all round.'

'I dare say,' said Harry, 'but Ms Thompson here has taken a rather nasty blow, and we would like to know how and why that happened.'

'Not to beat around the bush,' said Nathalie, 'if you understand that phrase. It was pretty obvious to our cameraman that the mention of the words "satellite malfunction" caused Doctor Rodin to lose his concentration. A quick glance to Terry and a slip of the finger and the next thing he sees is a whopping telescope veering its way towards Doctor Stones.'

'And if it wasn't for this lady here, as I couldn't see the thing coming, this so-called accident could have been a lot worse,' added Harry.

Rodin and Jacobs looked at each other. Nathalie could see that Rodin was in a dilemma as to how to respond. But it was Terry who spoke first.

'You're right, it might have been to do with the mention of the satellite.'

Rodin, looking horrified, put his hand out to stop him but Terry waved him away and continued.

'It's all right, Doctor, I'm sure it was just a distraction and a complete accident but I think they ought to know.'

'Go on,' said Harry leaning forward.

Nathalie could see that Rodin's face was turning almost as purple as hers but Terry was determined to have his say.

'You asked about our satellite malfunction. It's true that we had our satellite go down. I'd been looking into it and that's probably why Doctor Rodin glanced at me.'

'It doesn't seem a major issue for such a reaction,' said Nathalie. 'Boyd said he looked extremely agitated.'

'Yes that's because of the covert work we are doing,' explained Terry, looking at Doctor Rodin. 'I'm sorry, Doctor, but I think I ought to clarify the situation.'

Nathalie thought that Rodin was about to explode. He began spluttering and protesting but Terry calmly continued.

'That research satellite cost several million dollars. One day it suddenly crashed out of the sky. Although I'm only an intern I have a fair bit of IT knowledge so the company asked me to look into it.'

'And?' asked Harry.

'And I'm still looking into it. But what I think Doctor Rodin is worried about is that we might divulge some of our suspicions. That's why he was anxious about what we should tell you.'

Nathalie pointed at her own face. 'Well if you want all this to go away then I would suggest you tell us everything you know.'

The tips of the Petronas Towers were shrouded in haze. It was nearing the end of the monsoon season but Jenny Kang sensed that it was going to rain. The humidity was still high so she had left her raincoat in her apartment but fortunately she had taken her umbrella because here it came. When it rains in Kuala Lumpur, it rains; needles of piercing water that score your skin. Jenny flicked open the umbrella just in time and ran towards the pillars embellishing the entrance of Petronas Tower 2. Under the vast swirling ceiling of the lobby tourists were shaking off the water from their coats and standing uncomfortably in the ticket queues.

Jenny bypassed them and used her MalaySat authorisation to take the elevator. She felt herself shaking. The last time she had entered Mr Zikri's office she had been furnished with cryptic warnings. Come back with some answers or else. Well, she had some answers but not the complete story. She doubted whether there would be enough to satisfy Mr Zikri though. The elevator was remarkably quiet and swift. It was not long before it hissed to a gentle halt, the indicator light showing she had arrived at Floor 43. Jenny took a deep breath and made her way out of the sliding doors. She had spent most of yesterday planning her strategy: keep it cool, present her findings as if they were the keystone to Zikri's demands, depict the next step as a logical move that would provide all the answers whilst, in reality, she had no idea where it would take them.

The sullen secretary scowled at Jenny as she entered Satellite Security System's outer office, and silently pointed towards a tall painted jar standing in the corner. Jenny was at first puzzled and then realised that her umbrella was dripping all over the immaculate marble floor. She produced a forced smile and with an exaggerated movement placed the umbrella into the jar. Jenny waited to be lambasted but this was interrupted by the buzzer from the reception desk. Mr Zikri's voice came over the speaker.

'If Miss Kang has arrived please send her in immediately,' he snapped.

The secretary walked over to her desk, pressed the intercom and replied that Miss Kang had just arrived. The large panelled automatic doors slid open silently and Jenny walked sheepishly into his office.

Mr Zikri was behind his massive desk poring over some documents.

'Sit,' he said without looking up.

Jenny did as she was told, placed her thin leather briefcase on her lap, and began to take out her files. She sat there in silence waiting. After what must have been at least five minutes Zikri looked up and put his palms on the desk, his thumbs resting outwards along the lower ledge. He drummed his fingers.

'So what have you got for me, Miss Kang?'

Jenny pushed one of the files across the desk and orientated it towards her superior.

'A very profitable trip, Mr Zikri, I hope you agree.'

Zikri flipped open the file. 'That depends, Miss Kang.' He perused the top sheet of paper. 'Looks like a lot of black lines to me.'

'Yes that's the point, or one of them. It's a redacted document from the Baikonur Satellite Company.'

'Well what's the use of that, if we can't read it?' asked Zikri, irritation rising in his voice.

Jenny leaned over and revealed the second sheet of paper underneath.

'The fact that it's redacted makes it interesting. This is the version that Baikonur gave us on an official request. However...' Jenny paused for dramatic effect, 'if you look at the other sheet you will find the original unredacted document.'

Zikri held the two pieces of paper in both hands and looked from one to the other for comparison.

'Mm, so what do you deduce from this?'

'What's interesting are the parts which Baikonur have redacted. They obviously wanted to hide those actions. You'll see in the original that those sections refer to the recent installation of an internet connection to the substation. We were not told about this. Our channel for communicating with the satellite was fairly primitive through a secure line to the substation that could control the bus and its payload by basic radio waves. I believe that MalaySat assumed that the substation was either at Baikonur central or hardwired, and that our commands were implemented manually by local operatives. As it happens the substation is miles away. I expect, that in the unlikely event that they would have to make any adjustments, they covertly connected the instruments to the internet. I found a fairly new USB connection in the hut.'

Zikri thumbed his way through Jenny's file.

'So what does that tell us? Are you any closer to finding out how someone took down the satellite?'

This is what Jenny had been toiling over. How to convince Zikri that she was making progress and stopping him from either firing or suing her.

'I think it tells us that someone can use the internet to lock into the satellite. And, if so, we're closer to finding out how to do that.'

'You mean *you're* closer to finding out how to do that.'

'Yes of course. The USB in the substation was connected to a simple domestic router, just like the one that was in my hotel room. I would assume that, either Doctor Bykov was lazy and didn't want someone tramping out to the substation or, it was put in so they could take the satellite down themselves.'

Zikri looked up from the papers and seemed to be paying attention for the first time.

'You're running a bit ahead of me there, Miss Kang. Bykov?'

'He heads up the corporate satellite section at Baikonur.'

'Lazy you say?'

'It's a possibility. The substation was old and *PhreeSat* only a means of getting someone out of a complicated contract. Not their priority. The satellite could have been controlled manually either by someone driving out to the substation, or through a landline which may have been rusted or cut. Either way, it would have been a pain to keep to their maintenance contract, so a quick plug into the domestic internet…'

'Also the possibility of taking it down themselves you said? Why would they want to do that?'

'It's an option. Why would they want to redact the fact that they put an internet connection in? Okay, we could claim that it was insecure but without physically inspecting the connection we wouldn't know that…' Jenny paused for her coup de grace. 'They're very keen to get new business. A state-of-the-art satellite to replace *PhreeSat*. With the old one out of the way what better time to sell a new one?'

'And you think that is reason enough for them to crash the thing?'

'Using their new concealed router, yes. I was getting the really hard sell at the dinner they took me to. Business must be slack as they were falling over themselves to give discounts and proposals.'

Zikri pulled open the drawer at the side of his desk and pulled out a printed e-mail. 'A proposal like this you mean,' he said throwing it across the desk to Jenny.

While she read it he stood and walked over to the enormous windows looking over the city of Kuala Lumpur and the shadowed backdrop of the mountains behind. It had stopped raining and the mist from the drying highways could be seen rising from the streets below.

'I said they sounded keen,' said Jenny.

Zikri continued staring out of the window. 'All right, there's a vague possibility that they could have moved the satellite themselves but, as you say, with an unsecure internet connection anyone could have done it.'

'Perhaps not anyone but someone with high IT skills,' said Jenny addressing Zikri's back and being slightly unnerved by not seeing his facial reactions.

'Well, Jenny, I'm not so interested in who took the satellite down but in how they did it. So what do you intend your next step to be?'

Jenny took a while to answer. She was shocked by him using her first name – he hadn't done that before – and if this was some overture of detente she would have to play her cards carefully.

Zikri spun around from the window and, to her surprise, smiled at her.

'Well?'

'Since returning I've been doing a little research and I feel that with the IT resources of MalaySat we could trace the ISP of the router and, from there, the source and means of the satellite movement.'

111

'The IT resources? You couldn't manage this yourself?'

'My degree is in astrophysics not computing science. I know more than most but not sophisticated enough to trace ISP sources. It's possible for people to bounce signals around the world to avoid being detected. MalaySat have a cutting-edge technical department. There must be someone there who could help us.'

'Help *you*, Miss Kang,' retorted Zikri returning to her family name. 'This operation must be kept confidential, the fewer people involved the better.'

'It's the best chance we, I mean *I*, have,' said Jenny noting the new softness in his voice. '*PhreeSat* was one of ours. It won't seem unnatural for the technical department to lend you one of their bright sparks to investigate its demise.'

'And you feel that this router – internet lead – will reveal how someone can remotely take down a satellite?' asked Zikri, returning to his desk.

'Absolutely,' said Jenny.

Twelve

The lobby at the Tucson Garden Inn Hotel was quiet. Harry and Nathalie had chosen it as a meeting venue instead of their sparse bedrooms and sat in front of the faux fireplace. It had obviously been designed for decoration rather than function as the hotel staff were surprised to see them there. Nathalie assured them that they were happy to sit there and ordered two cups of coffee. She had led Harry to the more comfortable armchair and perched herself on one of the foam-filled bench-like sofas.

'Sounds quiet,' said Harry. 'You think it's all right to talk here?'

'Apart from the odd staff member there's not a soul to be seen,' replied Nathalie. 'The hotel is mainly used by airport passengers changing flights or for a short meeting downtown. I don't think we will be disturbed.'

'How are you feeling?'

Nathalie didn't want to concern him with her dizziness and headache so she shrugged it off. 'Fine, Harry, don't worry about me. Like a cat with nine lives, as my mother used to say. You're worse than Geoff but, at least, my little confrontation with the Mayall has got him funding some more research for us.'

'Yes, interesting that. Fermilab you say. We should liaise with your other researcher so that we can coordinate our plan.'

'I'm not sure I would call Nick Coburn a researcher,' laughed Nathalie. 'Geoff only pulled him in on the project because he wanted to see if it was worth prosecuting Rodin. Got more than he bargained for though, as Nick came up with another lead.'

'I don't think I've quite grasped how Bagatelle works,' said Harry. 'Is that coffee I can smell?' he added.

Nathalie took the two mugs from the young man who had just

entered the room. She thanked him and waited until he was out of earshot before peering into them and reporting the contents to Harry.

'I'm afraid the smell is deceiving, Harry. They call it coffee but it looks like thin brown water.' She placed the handle of one of the mugs into his hand. 'At least it's hot, careful how you hold it.'

Harry took a sip and grimaced. 'Shouldn't complain, it's better than the stuff that came out of the machine. Now, down to business. What did you think of Terry's explanation?'

'Curious,' said Nathalie. 'It was obvious that Rodin wasn't pleased with him saying anything at all. It sounds like they have the same suspicions as us.'

'You mean, they think someone at FastTrack has taken down their satellite to slow them down.'

'Well he didn't actually mention the name FastTrack but the description of a US-sponsored cosmology group doesn't fit many other candidates. No, what I found fascinating was that Rodin didn't want us to know that he was asking Terry to use their computer resources to trace the source. Why not? Seems a natural thing to do.'

Harry took another sip of the coffee. 'Doesn't get better,' he grimaced. 'I don't think that's so unusual. For all they know it could be a random collision. Pointing fingers without any actual proof could be damaging to their reputation.'

'Yes, but you said the data shows that it was deliberate, the satellite had been manipulated by someone on the ground.'

'I know that, but the general public don't. I think in this instance WCMB wanted to keep any publicity away from themselves. They seem quite a secretive outfit, as was proven by their reluctance to give us the address of their main offices.'

Harry heard footsteps and sat back in his chair waiting to see if another guest was joining them. Nathalie turned to see a business woman with a trolley case, obviously checking out.

'Have a safe flight,' she said, mainly for Harry's benefit.

They waited until the woman had left the lobby before continuing their conversation.

'It's all right, she's gone,' said Nathalie. 'The offices, yes, funny that. I was struck with admiration in the way you charmingly flushed the address out of them. I've never heard such alluring threats. What was it? Assault on a journalist, public outrage, scientific malpractice?'

Harry laughed, 'I'm sure it wasn't that devious but I could see they were keen to brush the whole episode under the carpet. A simple address wasn't much to give.'

'Yes but what intrigued me was the reluctance of them to give it. You and I actually have business cards we give out showing where we work. Suspicious or what?'

'The fact is we know where they are based now. And fortunately the location is on our list.'

'Looking forward to it,' said Nathalie. 'I've never been to the Canaries.'

'Mountains with a vista,' said Harry putting on a bad Spanish accent. 'My favourite hotel is very close to the Herschel telescope, and if I've got my diary right...'

Nathalie interrupted him as she saw, through the window, a coachload of tourists draw up outside.

'I think we're about to be invaded,' she said. 'A thousand new guests about to check-in. I think we should continue this conversation elsewhere.'

Harry felt for a side table and put down his coffee mug. 'My stomach was telling me it was lunchtime anyway. Let me treat you to a healthy veggie meal. I know of this farmers-market-come-restaurant, only a ten-minute cab ride away.'

5 Points Market Restaurant was a charming place. Bare wooden tables set against exposed brickwork walls covered in artwork. The

clientele were mainly young arty types chatting over their vegan fare. Harry ordered two wheatberry salads and, for the hell of it, freshly squeezed prickly pear juice. Nathalie studied her salad. She liked her meat, but this didn't look too bad: roasted vegetables and farmhouse pickles. She was less sure about the rather pink prickly pear juice.

'The juice, a favourite of yours?'

Harry felt for his glass. 'Why, is it yours? I've never tried it before.'

Nathalie laughed, 'So I'm the guinea pig.'

'Drink it up, it's supposed to be healthy. You've just come out of hospital, it'll be good for you.'

'All right, Dad,' she said sarcastically taking a sip.

'The verdict?'

'I'm wrinkling my nose, it's an acquired taste.'

'Like Doctor Rodin,' said Harry. 'What do you think's going on there?'

Nathalie scooped a few vegetables into her mouth to clear the taste of the juice. She chewed slowly for a while.

Harry waited.

'Definitely something going on,' she said at last. 'The friction between Rodin and Terry was palpable. Despite the fact that Rodin is Terry's boss he seemed frightened of him.'

'Yes I felt that too. He wasn't keen on us knowing that WCMB were checking to see if FastTrack had manoeuvred their satellite. I even wondered whether he had something to do with it.'

'Can't see why he would want to damage his own research. Another funny thing, no mention of the demise of that media satellite from either of them. You would think if Terry is the IT whiz-kid that we suppose he is, he would have noticed the similarity between the two collisions. Both satellites being manoeuvred into space junk within weeks of one another.'

Harry took a swig from his prickly pear juice, and suddenly remembered what it was. He pointed at his nose. 'Wrinkling in sympathy,' he chuckled. 'But back to business. It seems that your colleague may be able to look at the other side of the coin. Who is this astrophysicist working for FastTrack? I don't think I've heard of her.'

'Don't know much about it, just that Geoff e-mailed me with details of Nick's chat with Professor Watts of Cambridge.'

'Now Watts, of course, I've heard of him. So what did this Nick guy come up with?'

Nathalie dug out her phone and read the e-mail to Harry. He listened carefully.

'Ah yes, Sarah Nowak, now it rings a bell, a co-author on some obscure stuff from the Cavendish. So she's joined FastTrack and is working at Fermilab. Must be quite a high flyer. Difficult to get time on that thing nowadays, so many different projects going on.'

'Such as?' asked Nathalie.

'Oh, a deep underground neutrino experiment, their proton project, and a number of dark matter experiments. I would imagine she's on one of those unless…'

Harry threw his unseeing eyes upwards.

'Unless what?' asked Nathalie.

'Unless she's working on the Dark Energy Spectroscope. Fermilab built the barrel that contains the instrument's lenses.'

'Is that the spectroscope that's in the Mayall that nearly wiped me out?' asked Nathalie.

'Got it in one,' said Harry. 'Perhaps you could ask Nick to check that out.'

'Not sure if that's his forte,' said Nathalie smiling, imagining Nick trying to pronounce the word. 'But if you want to find out if she's up to no good, he's your man.'

Nathalie's perception of Nick Coburn's attributes was based on some of her past documentaries. As a fledgling researcher, she had been introduced to him by Geoff Sykes. Geoff would often call upon Nick when he needed some muscle or a cool head in a dangerous situation, which is why she was slightly puzzled that he had become involved now. Things did not seem that bad, and it appeared to her that Geoff was overreacting to the telescope incident. But it was Geoff's money and, if he wanted to give it to Nick, that was up to him. She couldn't help feeling though that it might have been better to put a scientific researcher onto the job.

In Chicago's O'Hare International Arrivals lounge Nick Coburn was thinking exactly the same thing. For once, his flight had landed early and the cab that Stefanie had kindly pre-booked had not yet arrived. He sat on his case and pulled out his call-sheet and notes. He was still trying to get his head around this Fermilab thing; America's particle physics' laboratory apparently, with an accelerator investigating the smallest things human beings have ever observed. He flipped through the brochure again; most of the stuff seemed to be underground. From what he could make out they fired tiny particles in opposite directions around massive great circular tubes. When they collided they made smaller particles, what for, he wasn't sure but that was okay. He was just a tourist, a casual drinking friend of Jim Watts. When Jim discovered he was going to Chicago he recommended a tour of Fermilab. And not just a regular public tour, he had a contact who could get him special access. Sarah Nowak was all too pleased to help out, especially after she had seen Nick's photograph that her old professor had sent her for identification. Nick looked at his watch, the cab should be due any moment. He would just have time to shower and change before his initial rendezvous at Sarah's hotel this evening. He pushed the brochure into his inside pocket. Only a tourist. He hoped he wouldn't make too much of a fool of himself.

On Geoff's instructions Stefanie had booked the cheapest room in the downtown Holiday Inn. Nick threw his suitcase onto the bed and looked around. Clean and adequate and, being Chicago, a bed long enough that his feet wouldn't stick out of the sheets at night.

The shower was blissfully hot and shook off the aircraft's fumes and cushioned the jetlag. Nick was not normally a shirt-and-tie person but he needed to make an impression. He held the collar under his chin and looked in the mirror. The shirt was creased to pieces. He threw it in a corner and picked out a thin round-neck sweater. Under a jacket it would look just as good. The bedside phone rang and the concierge told him that his taxi had arrived. He pushed back his hair and made his way to the lobby.

Rooms at The Langham cost more per night than at Nick's hotel for a week. The entrance was impressive. The cab pulled up in its dedicated side road and a porter appeared from under the vast spangled lobby canopy to open the door. Nick stepped out and looked up at the skyline. Lights were already appearing like opening eyes in the glass skyscrapers. He thanked the porter and made his way to the lobby desk on the second floor.

'I've an appointment with Ms Nowak. I'm not sure of her room number but I was told to check-in here.'

The receptionist smiled and consulted his computer. 'You have a first name?'

'Yes, Sarah, Sarah Nowak. She said to meet here around seven.'

A few taps on the keyboard later and the young man seemed to find something. He lifted the receiver of the telephone.

'Ms Nowak? I have a visitor for you,' he looked at Nick and asked for his name.

'Nick Coburn,' said Nick proffering his passport for ID.

The receptionist repeated the name and, after listening to the handset, passed Nick a small brochure.

'She says she's on her way and will meet you in the Langham Club lounge. The map in there will help you get around the hotel. Is there anything else I can do for you?'

Nick flicked open the brochure – a hotel big enough to need a map, that was a good one.

'No, and thanks,' he waved the brochure in the air. 'Very useful.'

He didn't need the map. The elevator indicated that the Langham

Club was on the top floor. Nick walked into a large cream-coloured lounge decorated with geometric furniture. Floor-to-ceiling plate-glass windows rewarded the club members with spectacular views across Chicago. The sky had darkened, heavy grey strips of cloud were tinged with red and the city was now alight.

'Your Clubcard, Sir?' asked a waiter.

'He's with me,' came an English voice from behind him.

'Of course, Madam,' said the waiter deprecatingly. 'Your usual seat?'

Nick turned to face his invitee. Jim Watts's description didn't do her justice. More a Hollywood film star than a 'quite attractive young lady'.

Nick was not normally stage-struck but it took him a few seconds to realise that she was holding out her hand.

'Mr Coburn? Of course it is. I'm Sarah, Sarah Nowak, welcome to Chicago.'

Nick gathered himself and took her hand, hoping that she hadn't noticed the hiatus. 'Thank you, Sarah, it's really good of you to spare the time. I hope Jim didn't foist me on you.'

Sarah gestured towards a pair of armchairs facing the city. 'Of course not. After you, best view in the house here. Would you like a drink?'

She gestured to the waiter. 'Bourbon on the rocks for me and…?'

'A single malt, please. Glenlivet if you have one.'

The waiter nodded, took the small card that Sarah was waving, and made for the bar.

'Of course, a Scotsman. You must think I'm a philistine,' said Sarah with an alluring beam.

'Maybe just a little, but who am I to judge when you're going to so much trouble.'

'Oh no trouble at all. In fact, I love showing people around. It's quite a privilege for me to share such an amazing place. As soon as Jim mentioned that a friend of his was coming over I jumped at the opportunity. How did you get to know him?'

Nick was prepared for this one. He and Jim had decided that it was best to say that they had met in The Punter pub, which in a way was true, but he was to make it seem as if they were regular drinking partners.

Sarah listened with interest. 'Are you also from the university?'

Nick laughed, 'No, haven't even got a GCSE. Just came out of the army and thought I'd spend some time travelling, for pleasure this time, before looking for a job. The two things that Jim and I have in common are beer and the great outdoors.'

'So why Fermilab?'

'Oh that was Jim's idea, always trying to broaden my mind. Told him I was touring the States, mentioned Chicago as my starting point, and he said I had to visit Fermilab. I'd never heard of it but, when he said he had a contact there, how could I refuse.'

'Yes, Jim can be very persuasive, especially when trying to involve people in astronomy. Ah, here are our drinks.'

They clinked a toast and Sarah explained that she had arranged for them to visit the site tomorrow afternoon. She had an engagement this evening and some work to do in the morning but she could pick him up from his hotel at noon. It was an hour's drive to Fermilab which was on the eastern outskirts of Chicago. They would get there around one o'clock, grab a sandwich in the canteen, and start the tour at two.

'Sounds great,' said Nick. 'I noticed in the brochure that a lot of experiments are done there. Which one are you working on?'

Sarah looked around the room. 'Well it's a little hush-hush at the moment. I've just joined this new consortium and they're coordinating a number of projects. But what I can tell you is that they're looking at why we live in a matter-dominated universe.'

She noticed that Nick was looking a little puzzled.

'To find out why we're here I suppose. We are all made of stuff, which we call matter: billions of particles. Some of the stuff, like in us, we can see and some we can't. I have some expertise in computing science and will be helping analyse the results from our neutrino experiment. Neutrinos are all around us but we know very little about them.'

It was Nick's turn to look around. 'Well they must be bloody small. Will I see any of these things at the lab?'

Sarah laughed, 'Don't worry, the particles might be small but the accelerator is huge, nearly four miles long. You won't be able to miss it.'

'Bloody mystery to me why you need something that big to look at something so small.'

'We smash these tiny things into each other at high speed. You need that sort of distance to get the acceleration.'

'A good run-up, like a fast bowler,' quipped Nick.

Sarah couldn't contain herself, she shook with hilarity. Nick thought it made her look quite captivating.

'I'm going to use that one on the next tour,' she managed to say at last. 'If you have any other ideas like that please write them down; we are always trying to think up ways of explaining things to the public.'

Nick wondered whether now was the time to bring up the subject of satellites. Geoff's dossier had said they were looking for possible evidence of someone hacking into a guidance system. She had already mentioned her expertise at computing but he couldn't yet see an elegant way in without her becoming suspicious. He would bide his time, get to know her a little better, and make a few innocent enquiries when she was off-guard. He looked across at his companion and thought of some of his recent assignments. In comparison, this could be quite a pleasurable one.

Thirteen

Nick took a late breakfast in the Holiday Inn coffee shop. There was a six-hour difference between Chicago and London so he decided to give Geoff a call.

'Hi, how's Nathalie?'

'Is that you, Nick? You sound muffled.'

Nick wiped his mouth and swilled the last piece of the waffle down with a slurp of coffee.

'Sorry, eating breakfast.'

There was a short pause whilst Geoff did a quick calculation.

'At ten in the morning? What am I paying you for?'

'Information,' drawled Nick in a mock American accent. 'My visit to Fermilab isn't until this afternoon. And, if you want me to be more efficient, you could have booked me in at The Langham rather than this place.'

'The Langham? Thought you preferred the Peninsula,' said Geoff sarcastically.

'Yeah I do but it's where Sarah Nowak is staying, club membership and all. Anyway, you haven't answered my question about Nathalie.'

'Apparently she's fine. Apparently. She wouldn't tell me if she wasn't. Got an obdurate streak that girl.'

'I wonder where she got that from. And I don't think she'd like you calling her a girl.'

'What else do I call her; getting so you can't say anything nowadays. Mind you, it's all right if writers use it. *Girl on a Train, Gone Girl, The Girl with the Dragon Tattoo.* I read somewhere that most books with girl in the title are written by women. And you know what?'

Nick was getting tired with one of Geoff's hobbyhorses. 'No, but you are going to tell me anyway,' he sighed.

'Nearly a fifth of the so-called "girls" in the title of books written by men end up dead.'

Nick shook his head. 'You've got too much time on your hands, Sykes. What happened to that guy who snapped instructions down the phone – fix this, sort that, and by yesterday?'

'Sorry, not enough work, I'm twiddling my thumbs here. Not used to it. Had a long chat with Nathalie though. They're no further forward on who's hacking the satellites but have their suspicions – Sarah Nowak being one of them. What have you found out?'

'Well first, that she is an absolute stunner but, more than that, not a lot. I'm hoping to find out something this afternoon.'

'Who's being sexist now?'

'Not sexist, just an observation. And in a way it's relevant. She flirts; gives you the eye. Watts said she had a reputation with men. *FastTrack* is about it with that girl. Now you see, you've got me using the word.'

Geoff snorted. 'So what's your plan?'

Nick shuffled a few of the papers that were scattered around his breakfast table. 'I've been doing some reading about Fermilab, trying to find a link between their experiments and either computers or satellites. Most of it's gobbledygook to me but there're a few mentions of internet communications and satellite function. I thought I'd try and get the conversation around to that and see her reaction. It is evident that she has the skills to get into computers, the access and, if what Jim Watts says about the rivalry between WCMB and FastTrack, a motive.'

'Yes but what's worrying me is this media satellite thing. Doesn't seem to fit Harry Stones's theory.'

'I've thought about that one. Nowak seems an ambitious type, living a bit beyond her means. I mean, what's an academic scientist doing swanning it up in The Langham? Could be that someone noticed her ability and paid for her to shoot another one down.'

'Bit far-fetched.'

'We've only had a casual drink together but I wouldn't put it past her. Confident woman, easy in her own skin. I've met these types before in the army. Ruthless if they want to be.'

'Well, the best of luck. If we don't get a better story soon I think I'll drop the project. A couple of minor satellites falling out of the sky won't exactly compete with *Game of Thrones*.'

Unbeknown to Geoff his 'better story' was being announced on CNN at that very moment. Nathalie and Harry were waiting in the American Airlines' departure hall. They had decided there was not much more to be gleaned from meeting again with Rodin and had booked a flight to Las Palmas via Madrid. Harry had an excuse to go there. His company, Cosmat, had booked some time on the telescope and they were intrigued to know about WCMB's offices on the island. It was 9.30 Standard Mountain Time and, as their flight was late, they grabbed a coffee and sat in the lounge. Whilst Harry put his headphones on and sat back listening to music, Nathalie surveyed the passengers around her. From time to time she glanced involuntarily at the mesmeric flickering of the large television screen on the wall.

'Christ!' she suddenly shouted, and realising that Harry couldn't see the images, shook him on the shoulder.

With one hand Harry yanked his headphones off. 'Time to go?'

'No, not yet anyway. It's the pictures on the news. It's horrendous.'

'What's horrendous? They have sound on that thing?'

'No, just subtitles. There's been a horrific accident in the Mediterranean. Fire and bodies everywhere.'

'What sort of accident? An auto-route pileup?'

'No, an accident actually *in* the Mediterranean. Two massive ships have collided. Wait a minute, I'm reading the text. "Super-tanker *Zircon Master* collides with the cruise ship *Wind of the*

Seas. Nearly a million barrels of oil spilled, a lot of it on fire." Jesus Christ, it's terrible. A chopper must be filming it live. The cruise ship is almost at right angles, half of it is submerged in the water. Those poor people.'

Harry reached out for her hand. 'Nothing you can do. What else do they say?'

Nathalie tried to compose herself. The camera had cut to a studio presenter. The scrolling text printed out his speech. She read it out loud.

'The four-hundred-metre-long super-tanker was travelling in misty conditions and apparently ploughed right into the midships of the cruise vessel. Twelve hundred people are reported to have been on board, travelling from Ancona to the Greek Islands. Most of the passengers are reported to be Italian nationals.' Nathalie paused. 'They've put up an emergency number to call.'

'Couldn't be much worse,' commented Harry. 'Those tankers are enormous and can take miles to stop but, with today's…' He broke off. 'Oh shit, it couldn't be could it?'

'Be what?' asked Nathalie impatiently.

Harry was reaching for his phone in his jacket pocket. 'What time is it in the UK?'

'Between five and six in the afternoon I think. I rang Geoff first thing, remember?'

'He should still be there then. I might be paranoid but…'

Nathalie was mystified. She looked back at the screen but the news channel had moved on. A mass shooting in Illinois. What a terrible world.

Harry was dexterously tapping out a number. It was amazing how he could do it without seeing the keys. The dial-tone turned to a ring.

The reply sounded as if it was next door. 'Cosmat Research Group, how may I help you?'

'It's Harry, is Trevor there?'

'Oh, Harry, how are you? Enjoying your trip in the States?'

'Trevor, I need to speak to him. Now.'

Harry's tone of voice did its trick.

'Trevor, of course, putting you through now.'

It was starting to dawn on Nathalie what Harry was doing. She waited patiently by his side, eavesdropping into the portable telephone.

It took Trevor a few minutes to answer. 'Oh, hi Harry, they said it was you. How's things?'

'Things would be a lot better if you could get to the phone quicker,' barked Harry. 'That satellite surveillance Bernard asked you to do. Are you still on it?'

There was a hiatus whilst Trevor considered his answer.

'Are you still on it or not?' insisted Harry.

'Sort of,' said Trevor. 'Things are busy around here you know.'

'No I don't know. What does "sort of" mean, are you monitoring those things or not?'

'Well yes, and no. I take a look now and again. Nothing to report.'

'Trevor,' Harry said his next words slowly and deliberately. 'I want you to take a look now – any aberrations in satellite movement in the last six hours? Did you get that?'

The Tannoy announced the flight departure to Madrid. Harry felt Nathalie tap him on the leg.

He turned to her. 'Yes I heard it. I'll get Terry to e-mail his results so we can look at them when we land.' He pressed the digital watch on his wrist for the audio time. 'That gives him until ten tomorrow morning. For Christ's sake I hope that there's nothing to report.'

Nick was unaware of the tanker crash, he was too busy studying his Fermilab printouts and, if he had checked out the Holiday Inn's TV screens as was the way in the US, they were now concentrating on the Illinois shootings. The literature was hurting his brain. It appeared as if the lab was doing hundreds of experiments for different groups around the world. Most of it was underground stuff, slinging particles around at horrendous speeds. The phrase 'unravelling the mysteries of matter, energy and space' seemed to crop up all over the place but what they meant by that and how they were solving it was, to Nick, another mystery. He fished out the file on the satellite again. It seemed like it was looking for the same material, Cold Dark Matter and Dark Energy. They really were keen to find this stuff, the answer to all their problems apparently. So if it was a race for these groups to solve the mysteries of the universe, like any race, it might be good to spike the opposition. Could he imagine someone like Sarah Nowak doing such a thing? Yes, perhaps he could. He looked at his watch. Five to twelve, he should make his way down to the lobby.

The race-red coloured Mustang pulled up at the forecourt, exactly on the stroke of twelve. Nick was about to open the car door when he realised the car was left-hand drive.

'You can drive if you like,' said Sarah, giving him that alluring smile again.

Nick skipped around the back of the car and slipped into the passenger seat.

'Sorry, wrong country. Thanks for the lift.'

Sarah put the car into gear and Nick could almost feel the G-force as she accelerated into the traffic.

'Are we late or something?' he chuckled.

'Oh sorry,' said Sarah initially, slowing down. 'I did tell you though, acceleration is my business.' The car picked up speed again.

They took the 290 west towards Hillside and then Route 88 towards Batavia. Nick kept looking behind them to see if there were any speed cops. He thought it lucky that there were tolls to slow them down. Enquiries from the police about the reasons for his visit were the last thing he needed. After about forty-five minutes on the road Fermilab came into sight. He recognised the main building from the brochure – a tall concrete building looking like someone had bent two thick cards and leaned them against each other.

'There she is,' said Sarah pulling into a side road and flashing her pass at the entrance barrier.

'You must be hungry, let's take a bite in the cafeteria and I'll tell you what I've lined up for you.'

Wilson Hall cafeteria was an enormous room lit by slanting side windows and panels of artificial light on the blue and orange panelled ceiling. They both chose a club sandwich and some fresh fruit from the restaurant bar and sat at one of the Formica tables. Sarah threw down a wad of pamphlets in front of Nick. He could see by the titles that they were similar to the ones he had been studying at the hotel. He didn't mention this to Sarah.

'Okay,' said Sarah munching on her sandwich. 'I realise that you just want to look at the spectacle of this thing but it brings it more to life if you know some of the background. Stop me if you think I'm being a bit patronising.'

Nick shuffled through the pamphlets. 'Oh don't worry about me, patronise away. I thought astronomy was all to do with telescopes and satellites.' He watched her face carefully on the mention of the word. Not a flicker so he continued. 'This underground stuff, when did it start?'

'Well it was in the early eighties mainly. The scientists here were amongst the first to bring the worlds of astrophysics and particle physics together. They recognised the importance of studying matter on a very tiny scale and comparing it to the information they were getting from large-scale structures in the universe.'

Sarah picked up Nick's apple. 'You must have studied gravity at school.'

Nick laughed. 'Didn't listen much at school, but I did do ballistics in the army.'

'Ah well, compared to that, this will be simple. She dropped the apple onto the table. You see, the gravity of the Earth pulls the

129

apple towards it. Now imagine that the apple is a star. It moves towards something but there's no Earth there, or at least we can't see one. What's pulling it?'

Nick picked up the apple and took a bite out of it. 'You tell me.'

'Well if there is no visible matter moving these stars there must be some unseen mass exerting the gravitational pull.'

'Ah,' said Nick. 'Got it, Dark Matter. Sounds like something out of a Pullman book.'

'Pullman?'

'Haven't read it, they're doing it on the telly, but don't let me stop you. You said you were doing some experiments to find this stuff.'

'Well FastTrack are. We've got a number of projects going, as I said. Mine is analysing the data from neutrino particles, but others in our group are coordinating ventures with other establishments elsewhere.'

Nick suddenly remembered something that Watts had told him. 'The spectroscope in Arizona. Jim told me they made bits of it here. Is that one of yours?'

Once again, not a flicker. 'No, that's a Mayall project. Similar objectives but operated by a competitor.'

'A competitor? I thought you scientists shared all your work.'

'I wish,' said Sarah. 'Some of us do but there are some of us who don't.'

'You sound a bit bitter about that.'

'I think we've got a right to be bitter. For instance, the group on that spectroscope project are funded by billions of dollars.'

Nick had eaten his apple to the core and placed it in his saucer.

'The Eagle has landed,' he said. 'So where does this money come from?'

'That's it. Nobody seems to know.' Sarah pointed at his apple core. 'Take your Eagle. NASA-funded, transparent government money from the federal budget. Now take FastTrack. Stanford University-funding, admittedly subsidised by a huge federal grant, but still transparent.'

'And this other lot?'

'They are called WCMB Associates. No idea what the letters mean. Vast sums of money. They seem to be able to buy any amount of telescope time they want. They've already set up a privately funded Cold Dark Matter project in the Canary Islands. '

'And the money? Not openly from government sources I assume.'

'Absolutely, it's all private. Rumours are that a Russian oligarch is involved. Could be prestige or access to some of the most sensitive astronomical equipment in the world. Who knows?'

'You sound jealous.'

Sarah Nowak rocked back in her chair and put out her arms full length onto the table.

'Sorry, do I? Shouldn't be. They were inaugurated before us. In fact, it's most likely that FastTrack was set up as American competition. It's only now, I think, that people have realised how much money WCMB have got pouring into them. We just can't keep up.'

'I hear they lost a satellite,' said Nick, seizing his opportunity. 'I expect that set them back.'

For the first time Sarah Nowak seemed a little disconcerted.

'Where did you hear that?'

'Can't remember, must have been from Jim Watts I think.'

Sarah made a conscious move of looking at her watch and standing up.

'It's nearly two o'clock. I promised the accelerator guys that we wouldn't be late. I think we ought to go down there now. We could continue this chat later.'

Nick followed her to the elevator. She showed her pass and they accessed some of the lower floors. When the doors opened they were met by a young man in a safety helmet. Sarah went to shake him by the hand but realised that he was carrying another two helmets, one in each hand.

'Hi Frank, thanks for arranging this. This is Nick, the friend of

Jim Watts I was telling you about. Would you like us to put those on?'

'If you don't mind,' said Frank, handing over the helmets. 'Nothing's ever fallen on my head but it's health and safety, you know.'

Nick took one from him. 'No worries, I'm used to wearing helmets but in my case I've found them very useful.'

Frank looked a little nonplussed so Nick avoided any further explanation by reinforcing Sarah's thanks. The three of them walked down a long corridor fitted with enormous aluminium pipes.

'The Booster Accelerator is just around the corner,' said Frank. 'That and the new Neutrino Detector are probably the most impressive bits of hardware I can show you.'

Nick looked up at the enormous structures. No effort was made to place the equipment into neat shiny containers. Everything looked inside-out with wires projecting chaotically like an enormous telephone exchange. In one area, a group of engineers were working on a colossal hexagonal structure. It was so large that one of the men was sitting inside it, on one of the enormous sides.

'Wasn't expecting this,' said Nick. 'If the aim was to impress, you've succeeded. What's this piece of kit for?'

'The new neutrino experiment,' replied Frank proudly. 'The one that Sarah here will be working on. This is only a small part of it.'

'Remember I told you that neutrinos were the most ubiquitous particles in the universe, Nick,' broke in Sarah. 'Well this is where we make and capture them.'

'Make them?'

'Yes, this thing smashes protons into a target where they decay into neutrinos so we can study them. The next stage is to accelerate the protons even faster. To do that we're going to fire them from here to South Dakota, nearly eight hundred miles away.'

'Bloody hell,' said Nick. 'I hope you are telling everyone to get out of the way.'

'You wouldn't even notice,' grinned Sarah. 'They would go right through you.'

'All the same,' said Nick, 'let me know when you're switching the thing on and I'll make sure I'm way clear of South Dakota.'

He sensed his banter was relaxing Sarah. She had seemed a little tense since his mention of the crashed satellite and, if he was going to get more information, he would have to gain her trust. Perhaps a few late-night drinks in the Langham Club bar would loosen her tongue.

Fourteen

The journey back to the hotel was less hazardous than the one to Fermilab, as the late afternoon traffic had slowed them down. Nick went straight to his room and opened his laptop. He googled 'astronomy satellites' to see if FastTrack were involved in any of them, perhaps a new launch to compete with their rivals. There was no mention of FastTrack but, to his surprise, there were hundreds of satellite telescopes of different kinds. He had only heard of one of them, the Hubble. He read the rubric: '*The size of a school bus, travelling 340 miles above the Earth, completing an orbit in ninety-five minutes*'. Shit, that was some missile up there. He scrolled through the others and realised that they weren't all optical telescopes. Some looked at gamma rays, others, things like x-rays and radio waves. It was no wonder that one of them had crashed. He was surprised that it didn't happen more often. Another article caught his eye. '*New internet satellites could make astronomy impossible and create a space junk nightmare*'. There was a plan, apparently, to launch at least sixty new satellites to cover blanket broadband of the Earth. Great, if you found it difficult to get a signal, but a real problem for scientists who were studying the stars. Perhaps Geoff's proposal for satellite sabotage was pie in the sky. He grinned at his own pun. There was so much stuff up there that these things could have bumped into each other all by themselves. He snapped the laptop shut and made for the shower. Still, it was not his job to write the brief. He had been employed to suss out Sarah Nowak and FastTrack to see if they had any involvement with nefarious goings-on in the satellite business. He hadn't found anything yet. He would have to work hard this evening to earn his money.

✳

Shaw's Crab House described itself as a jazzy carefree seafood restaurant. Nick had chosen the location as it was within walking distance of the Langham hotel. It was the least he could do, he had said, after the Fermilab tour. The dinner would be on him. When Sarah dropped him off at the Holiday Inn they had agreed to meet at eight. It was now half past and there was no sign of her. Nick had picked a small intimate table in the corner of the bustling oyster bar. He wanted to keep a cool head so he ordered sparkling water and some Florida stone crab claws, to nibble on, whilst he waited. A lone musician had plugged his guitar into a small amplifier and had started to tune up. The restaurant was nearly full now, its warm lights glowing on the customers' faces. Nick pulled open one of the slatted blinds and peered into the street. No sign of her. He wondered whether he should give the Langham a call.

'Hi, I'm so terribly sorry I'm late, what must you think of me?'

Nick turned to see Sarah rushing towards his table. She looked quite striking in a knee-length figure-hugging dress. Nick put his head to one side.

'In that outfit, quite a lot,' he replied. 'No need to apologise. I'm on holiday, all the time in the world. Take a seat.'

Sarah pulled up a chair and gathered her breath. 'Couldn't wear my work jeans when I'm being invited out to dinner.' She looked around. 'Cosy little place, I've not been here before. How did you find it?'

Nick waved the mobile phone that he was about to make the call on. 'Internet – best seafood in Chicago apparently. And it's within walking distance of your hotel.'

'Yes, I'm terribly sorry. It's only a few minutes away. I meant to be here earlier but got caught up in some work and then…' she gestured down at her dress, 'I had to make myself look respectable.'

Nick handed her the menu. 'Well I've given you one compliment, would sound too smooth to give you another. How do you like oysters?'

Sarah gave him a coy look. 'Oysters? I love them.'

Nick put his phone away. 'Great, me too, and for mains?'

She studied the menu. 'Ooh hard to choose. The spice-crusted yellow-fin tuna looks good.'

Nick waved for the waiter and ordered two dozen oysters followed by the tuna with Shaw's fish and chips.

'Very impressive today,' he said as the waiter moved away. 'Jim told me that it would be worth a visit.'

'I'm glad you found it interesting,' said Sarah. 'Some people find the science all a bit too obscure.' She looked around. 'I don't mean to be rude but could we order some wine?'

Nick signalled for the waiter again. 'Of course, a dry white?'

Sarah nodded enthusiastically.

'And as for obscure…' Nick added, 'I don't think trying to find out why we are here is obscure at all.' He laughed. 'It's just how you're going to do that by firing stuff through eight hundred miles of rock that gets me.'

The oysters arrived on tiers of plates laden with ice and seaweed. Nick had taken many women out for oyster suppers but none that ate oysters as sensuously as Sarah Nowak. It seemed that she was teasing him as she tipped the shellfish slowly into her red-lipped mouth. He didn't mind, the more she flirted the easier it would be for him to catch her off-guard.

'FastTrack?…' he broached, 'how long have you worked for them?'

Sarah slipped down her last oyster and licked her lips. 'About six months. The first part of that in Stanford, getting to know the ropes, and the rest here in Chicago.'

Nick poured her another glass of wine. 'Do you live at the hotel?'

'Thank you. Yes, all-expenses-paid. They're a very generous company.'

'Is that why you joined them? Jim says that they offered you a university lectureship.'

Sarah took a sip of wine and, seeing Nick's glass nearly empty, topped him up.

'Can't see you lagging behind,' she grinned. 'Yes, that's right,' she added. 'A Cambridge lectureship was tempting but FastTrack's offer was difficult to refuse. It's not just the money, they've given me access to some of the best apparatus in the world. Does that make me sound mercenary?'

Nick played with his glass. He was hoping that she wouldn't notice that he wasn't keeping pace with her. 'Not for me to judge, I've no idea how these scientific jobs work. But you must be pretty good if they head-hunted you.'

'Just had the right skill-set I think – particle physics and computing science. Most of the time I'll be analysing data from the accelerator and they want someone to develop new software to cope with that.'

They paused the conversation whilst a waiter came to clear their oyster shells. Nick had managed to manoeuvre the topic to computers. Now all he had to do was to link this with satellite communications. The moment their main courses arrived he decided to dive in.

'Your competitor, WCMB I think you said. When I mentioned their satellite malfunction earlier you seemed a bit distracted.'

Sarah took her time to answer whilst she chewed on her tuna. 'This is very good, how're your fish and chips?'

'Better than those from McTavish's Kitchen,' said Nick. 'The satellite, you don't seem to want to talk about it.'

'Not much to say. It wasn't our satellite. If Jim mentioned it, you probably know more about it than I do. All I know is that it crashed into some space junk. There's a lot of that stuff up there you know.'

'But surely they must have ways of avoiding it. There are thousands of satellites up there, don't hear about them crashing. Must have cost them millions.'

'You're right there, but they have the money. I hear they're launching a second one. We can't even afford one.'

'With your computing skills, could you find out how it crashed?'

Nick noticed that Sarah was tiring of the subject. Her flirtatious demeanour was subsiding and she was becoming irritable.

'If someone paid me to investigate it probably, but it's not my problem. The bottle is empty, shall I order another?'

Without waiting for Nick's reply she turned to get a waiter's attention and waved the empty bottle at him. They finished their meal in silence, listening to the jazz guitarist who was now delivering his set. He was very good and the music seemed to improve Sarah's mood. Nick waved for the bill, ignored her protests and slapped his credit card on the table.

'I said it was my treat. I really enjoyed today; so much better having individual attention than going around in a big public tour.'

Sarah smiled and put her hand across the table to touch his. 'Sorry I was a bit snappy back there. I'm simply a bit tired talking about work all the time.'

'Quite understand,' said Nick leaving his hand under hers. 'I'm just the inquisitive type.'

'I can see that. I feel like I'm getting a second wind. How about joining me in a nightcap at the hotel?'

'Suits me,' said Nick, 'after all I am on holiday.'

The late May evening was balmy, an overture of the summer to come. They strolled down East Hubbard Street and as they turned into the busy freeway of North Wabash Avenue Sarah slipped her hand into Nick's. The romantic gesture was tempered by the sweet smell of doughnuts wafting from a nearby 24-hour coffee shop. Nick gestured with his head to suggest that they could go in, but Sarah laughed and shook her head. The Langham doorman greeted them like a dragoon guard and opened one of the lobby doors with a sweeping gesture. Sarah asked for her key card and turned to Nick.

'The club bar is often busy at this time. Shall we go to my suite? The view is just as good.'

By the way she said it Nick could see where this was going. He smiled and shrugged approvingly.

'A bottle of Glenlivet and two glasses to my room, please,' she asked of the receptionist.

'Of course, Madam, right away,' said the young man, noting her key card.

They started to make their way to the elevator when Sarah turned and added, 'Oh and a large bucket of ice.'

That slightly puzzled Nick but he didn't say anything; perhaps she liked a lot of ice with her whisky.

Sarah wasn't wrong about the view. The plate-glass window in her suite practically filled one of the walls. It felt like standing on the edge of a cliff; the high-rise buildings lit up like Christmas trees, feeling as if they were in touching distance. Below was the river crossed by bridges of late evening traffic but, within the room, a calm restfulness, furnished with a cream king-size bed and a sofa facing a glass-topped table. There was a knock at the door and a porter wheeled in a rather pretentious trolley containing a whisky bottle, two crystal-glass tumblers and a large ice bucket. Sarah tipped him with a ten-dollar bill and, after he had left, walked up to the minibar to remove the tops from two soda bottles. She emptied the contents into some spare glasses.

'I prefer my whisky neat,' said Nick, 'but if you want to ruin yours it's up to you.'

'Oh, it's not for the whisky, I just need some candlesticks,' grinned Sarah, taking two half-candles from her handbag and placing them into the empty bottles.

'Did you steal those from the restaurant?'

'Maybe.'

'You'll set off the sprinkler system.'

Sarah looked around for the smoke alarms. 'Not if I put them over here,' she said, lighting the candles and dimming the room lights. 'Now, doesn't that look better?'

Nick had to admit it did. The candlelight flickered around the room lighting up the contours of Sarah's face. She unscrewed the cap of the Glenlivet and poured it seductively into the crystal tumblers. She handed him one.

He took it and swilled the amber liquid around the glass. 'No ice?'

'Perhaps later,' she smiled.

They moved towards the sofa but didn't sit. Standing side-by-side they sipped their whisky and stared at the view. Chicago by night can take your breath away. It was obviously not the time for conversation. The meal, the white wine and now the warmth of the whisky was having its mellow effect. Sarah refilled their glasses and they must have remained there for at least ten minutes before she made her move. She deftly took Nick's glass from his hands and placed it with hers on the side-table. Turning to face him she gently placed her palms against his cheeks and stared into his eyes. Nick waited for the kiss but it didn't come.

'Unzip my dress.'

She was still holding his face in her hands. He reached behind her neck, found the zip and slowly drew it downwards. She wriggled out of the dress and stood there in her underwear and high heels. He reached for the clip of her bra, but she shook her head.

'Now it's my turn.'

She had clearly done this before; first his shirt, next his trousers and then his shoes. She indicated for him to sit on the bed and peeled off his socks and finally his underpants. He sat there naked and aroused and made to move towards her. She stood up and wagged her finger at him.

'Stay there and lie on the bed,' she said rather strictly.

He did as he was told and she walked towards the wardrobe. When she turned around she was holding three long silk scarves. She wrapped one around her neck and held the others in one hand as she moved towards the headboard. She knelt, as if in prayer, and did something under the corner of the bed.

'Stretch out your arms and legs,' she commanded.

Nick complied and lay there naked, looking like Leonardo's Vitruvian Man.

He watched her as she tied one of the scarfs tightly around his wrist. The other, no doubt, was secured around the bed-leg under the divan. If this was the game she wanted to play, he wasn't

140

worried. He was strong enough. If he needed to, he could probably rip it apart. Why not just join in. Not hurrying, she strolled around the other side of the bed and repeated the action tying the second scarf to his other wrist.

'Stay!' she snapped, as she walked away from him. He heard a rattle from the corner. Ah, that was what the ice bucket was for. His nipples tingled with the shock. The last scarf was being removed from around her neck. It was placed about his head, over his eyes and tied tightly around the back. Now it was her mouth, he could hardly contain himself. She stopped abruptly and he heard her heels click across the floor once more.

'So much better by candlelight, don't you think?'

Nick was blind-folded; he didn't understand the question until a searing pain tore through his body. She was slowly dripping candle wax onto his most sensitive parts.

'Now, Mr Nicholas Coburn, if that's your real name. Why are you really here, and who are you working for?'

Nick was about to protest, that only his mother was allowed to call him Nicholas, when another cascade of hot wax hit his skin.

Fifteen

Jenny Kang sat nervously channel-hopping in her apartment. Her feet drummed rhythmically on the parquet wood floor. She still couldn't concentrate. It had been three days since she had met with Mr Zikri. He would think about it, he had said. If he came up with a solution she would be contacted. Until then she was to take gardening leave, a bizarre choice of words Jenny thought, as her apartment was on the third floor above a pet salon. Kuchai Entrepreneurs Park was a bustling area of Kuchai Lama, a suburb of Kuala Lumpur off the Old Klang Road. She had chosen the accommodation for its reasonable rent and location. It was only eleven kilometres from the Twin Towers but, as Jenny had found from bitter experience, it took a couple of train changes and more than an hour to complete the journey. At least she hadn't had to do that in the last few days. She had spent the time shopping in the local market, cooking and watching television. However, domestic chores were not her thing. She was a first-class astrophysicist after all. But she was stuck. There was no way she could apply for a new job in Kuala Lumpur and, even if she absconded and left the country, any new employee was bound to seek MalaySat for a reference, one that she wouldn't get. No, she would just have to keep drumming her feet and waiting.

She was concentrating so hard on the rhythm sounding from the floor that she hardly noticed her phone vibrate on the side-table. At first she thought it was the echo of her feet but then she noticed the small glow of light. She snapped off the television and nearly slipped on the polished floor rushing to pick it up.

'Jenny Kang,' she gasped.

A cold brusque voice came down the handset. Jenny recognised it to be that of Vikri's secretary.

'Oh, you *are* there. I was about to hang up.'

'No, it's fine. I've been waiting for Mr Zikri to call.'

'Have you now, quite presumptive.'

'Oh, not really, he did tell me that he might make contact.'

'Well he's not, making contact that is. I've been told to tell you that someone will be delivering a message. You are not to write it down or place it on any electronic device. You are to read it and then destroy it.'

Jenny waited silently for further instructions.

'Is that clear?'

'Yes, absolutely clear. Read it and then destroy it.'

The telephone went dead.

Jenny looked for the caller number but there was none. Zikri obviously wanted no electronic trace of any communication with her. And the message, what on earth could that be?

It was not long before she found out. The next morning she woke to find a thin postcard had been slipped under her front door. It was blank on one side and had an address on the other. That was it. No instructions, no directions and no further message. She took the postcard and was about to type the address on her computer when she suddenly remembered her orders; not to put it on any electronic device. This was going to be difficult. She had not lived here long and, although she knew the main landmarks, she was not that familiar with the city. Perhaps she could print out a large-scale map and look at the address on there. But her instructions were very specific – no electronic device. It was still early and she hadn't yet had breakfast. She could grab a coffee at the corner shop. There was a stationer's next door, they were sure to have a city map.

The Secret Loc Café was one of her favourite haunts and she was greeted warmly by the serving staff. She ordered her usual, kaya toast with soft-boiled eggs and a dark hot cup of Malaysian Kopi O coffee, a far cry from her treacle waffles and pancakes in the Berkeley cafeteria. She had even learned the way the locals made the toast. Remove the crusts from two pieces of bread, toast them lightly, add a slice of cold hard butter to one side, and the layer of coconut jam on another. By placing them together the butter merged into the jam – nothing quite like it.

For someone as computer literate as Jenny, it felt strange to unfold the paper map. She used her left hand to munch her toast and a right finger to scour the map. At last she found it. A small street tucked away in Chinatown. She dipped her finger in the cooling coffee and made a smudge around the area. The postcard, she tore into lots of tiny pieces. She would flush them away in the toilet before she left.

Jenny spent the rest of the day in her flat. One moment she was going and the next she wasn't. There was an address, but no time, telephone or person's name. To put it on paper rather than e-mail or text seemed to her a bit extreme but perhaps Zikri needed the confidentiality to be extreme. In this day and age, paper trails were more difficult to trace than electronic devices which left their footprint everywhere. He obviously wanted his hands nowhere near the thing, whatever that thing was. It must be dangerous or illegal that's for sure. She opened the fridge: two cold dumplings and a carton of milk. She would have to go out sometime. She paced up and down her small kitchen. She really couldn't make up her mind. Perhaps she should stroll around the area and take a look at the address. On the other hand perhaps she should confront Zikri and ask what in the hell he was up to. He didn't want to know *who* took down the satellite, she remembered, he wanted to know *how* it was done. Why would he want to know that? Put in place some defence mechanisms? That wasn't it. If that was the case there would be no need for all this clandestine activity. No, the reason he wanted to understand *how* was so that he could do a similar thing himself. Shit! What had she got herself into?

In the end, curiosity got the better of her, and what else could she do? If she didn't go it was certain that Zikri would make life extremely difficult for her, prosecutions, threats and the sack. On the other hand, walking up and knocking on the door of this address could be quite benign. Perhaps someone would give her an envelope to take to MalaySat. It could be as simple as that. Her window was open, it was warm outside, a dry evening by the look of it. Jenny put on a pair of jeans and a light sweatshirt and skipped down the stairs. She checked her paper map again, although she had been staring at it all day and knew the address off by heart – 14 Jalan Balai Polis. It wasn't too far from the famous Petaling Market. She knew that part of town at least – one of the first places that sweet boy had taken her to. Seemed a long time ago, a young man chatting her up at the inauguration party. He had left for a start-up satellite outfit in China. She wondered how he was doing now.

Jenny got out at Pasar Seri station. The street on the map was somewhere to the south but she headed north along the main road towards one of the main entrances to Chinatown. She would grab some of the delicious street food before she plucked up courage to try the address. The Chinese gateway was typical of most cities – enormous red pagoda-pillars topped with golden dragons. A large blue sign advertising *JALAN PETALING* hung beneath the green tiled roof. Beyond, a riot of colour, smells and sounds. She walked into the thoroughfare. It was getting dark but the ubiquitous lanterns lit up the market-fare: everything from fruit, flowers and mobile phones. The odour of noodles and sesame fried fish permeated the air and she suddenly realised how hungry she was. She had not eaten since the kaya toast that morning. She avoided a street seller pushing coloured sneakers into her face. Another time she may have stopped to barter but tonight she had other things on her mind. Too agitated to sit in one of the side cafés, she found a stall selling noodles and skewers of chicken in disposable cardboard bowls. She handed over the money, tucked the map under her arm and used the wooden chopsticks he had given her to pick up the food. There was nothing else for it, she couldn't delay it any longer. Perhaps they wouldn't be at home. If not, at least she had tried.

Jalan Balai was a small side street to the south of the market.

Jenny made her way through the back streets, across a small concrete arched bridge towards her destination. Things were quieter here. A few ragged lanterns hung from wires across the narrow streets and the windows were closed up with peeling pale-blue shutters. Turning the corner she faced a stained wall with rows and rows of air-cons, purring away in the still-night air. She should be nearly there but could make no sense of the street signs. Finally she found a landmark. Under a shabby arcade was a café – *KAFE OLD CHINA Restaurant and Antique Gallery* was enigmatically painted in thick cream letters above the door. But what was more interesting to Jenny was the address written in English below the menu stuck on the wall – *11 Jalan Balai Polis*. If the café was number eleven, fourteen should be close by. She peered into the café doorway. The warmly lit interior looked inviting; ancient Chinese prints on the wall and odd wooden tables and chairs scattered around the room. One solitary man sat with his back to her reading a newspaper. Not wanting to approach him Jenny returned to the street. It was a poor area with a number of buildings closed up with iron shutters. There didn't seem to be many houses on the other side and so she hoped the street was in simple numeric order, not odd numbers on one side and even on the other. She walked first one way and then the other away from the café, counting the buildings as she did so. The numbers didn't seem to make sense. Next she turned the corner to find a small brown door set under a paint-peeled archway; scratched on the side was the number fourteen. There was no bell so she knocked. No one came so she knocked again and put her ear to the door. Not a sound. Feeling almost relieved she was about to turn away and go home when suddenly an electronic buzz came from above the door.

'Good evening, please identify yourself by standing back and looking upwards.' The voice was tinny, in a Chinese accent, but quite distinct.

Jenny stepped back and looked above the door. For the first time she noticed a small box, a grill to one side and a small circle to the other. Speaker and camera she thought.

'Come in, down the stairs and the passage on the right.' The door made a mechanical click.

She pushed at the door and it opened easily. In front of her were, dimly lit, steep concrete steps leading to a basement. She gingerly made her way downwards and, following the instructions, turned into a narrow side passage. At the end was another door, already open, with a man about her age standing in the entrance.

'So you found it. Good. For all intents and purposes you can call me Kenneth. I know who you are from photographs. Please come in.'

No hand was offered so Jenny merely followed the man into the room behind the door. What confronted her made her freeze momentarily.

'It's all right, you are quite secure here,' said Kenneth. 'Please take one of the chairs and I'll get you a cup of tea.'

It all sounded so normal, a cup of tea. But the room was far from normal – rows and rows of computer screens lit up like a NASA control room. In front of them, two chrome and leather swivel chairs. Kenneth pointed at one and disappeared into a side room. Jenny was speechless. She sat down and swivelled the seat towards the monitors, some carrying images of satellites and spacecraft, the others streaming torrents of symbols and numbers.

A few moments later Kenneth appeared carrying two small ornamental cups of Chinese tea. He placed one in front of Jenny and took a sip from the other.

'A bit hot, you might want to wait a little.'

Although she had guessed, Jenny still asked the question. 'What's all this?'

'What it looks like, computers. A little more powerful than your average Dell, but computers all the same.'

'And their purpose?'

'I think you know that. I'm here to help you.'

'To find out who took down our satellite,' stuttered Jenny.

'And how,' added Kenneth.

'And how,' repeated Jenny.

Kenneth sat down in the other chair and tapped at a keyboard.

'Shall we get started? Can you tell me the exact date and time that the satellite was repositioned? Oh and, to save me a bit of time, your personal MalaySat password.'

Jenny wondered how much she should trust this wiry Chinese man. All she had been given was an address. No instructions or contact name. She had sworn her passwords to secrecy: part of her contract. 'Save me a bit of time' he had said. By the look of the equipment he probably could do without it. She had come this far, how much else could she lose?

'It's quite long and complicated,' she said. 'Have you a pen and paper?'

A flash of yellow teeth. The first time he had smiled. He pushed one of the keyboards towards her.

'No paper here,' he responded.

She typed in the fourteen-character password from memory. No phonetic phrases, just a jumble of letters, numbers and special characters.

Kenneth watched her. 'Ah good, that would have taken me at least half an hour. Now the date and time, please.'

Jenny sat back and sipped her tea. She found it quite calming.

'The date is easy, but the exact time, I'm not quite sure. I know when I moved it and I know when the incident happened but the actual time, to the second, that it was moved back on a collision course I couldn't exactly tell you. I wasn't actually watching the screen for someone to move it. Why would I?'

Kenneth's hands tripped across the keyboard like a concert pianist.

'Okay, I've put in the time of the collision, and assume you changed the orbit within five minutes before that. Did you do anything else in that time? Put on the kettle, open the fridge?'

Jenny tried to make sense of all of this. How did he know the collision time? And what did kettles and fridges have to do with it?

Kenneth could see her thought process. 'I have the collision time from MalaySat,' he waved at his computers, 'but it's in the public domain anyway. Kettle, fridge any other domestic appliance that you may have used during that time?'

'During that time'. Now Jenny started to understand what he was getting at. Many modern appliances were so-called 'smart-devices', possible to be switched on remotely through the internet.

'No, I don't think so. We don't have a fridge and I normally get my coffee or tea from the cafeteria.'

'Think please, Miss Kang. Anything electronic, anything at all?'

Jenny sat back, closed her eyes and tried to replay that fateful day. It was quite hot, she remembered. Ah that was it, the aircon.

'It was quite a nice day but stuffy in the office. I used a remote to control the room temperature. Does that help?'

'Maybe,' said Kenneth turning to his keyboard. Jenny watched and listened as the soft keys clicked at an alarming rate. One by one the screens began to respond – spooling characters, flashes of code, and equations that would have given her a headache at Berkeley.

Kenneth peered from one screen to another seeming to understand the displayed hieroglyphics.

'Aircon, yes, a portal opened at the same time. That's how they got in. Now,' he muttered, 'where did that come from?'

More concertos on the keyboard. More flashing images.

'Clever, quite a run-around.'

'Run-around?' asked Jenny.

Kenneth replied without looking at her. 'It's normal to bounce your ISP off different locations – send the signal around the world a few times – but this guy or girl knows their stuff. Quite a few red herrings.'

Jenny smiled at the maxim. It sounded strange coming from Kenneth's mouth.

'They have sent me down a few blind alleys, but I think I know how to get back on track.' Jenny could see that Kenneth was enjoying the challenge.

'Got them!'

Jenny nearly jumped out of her chair at the exclamation from the quiet Chinaman.

'So who are they?' she asked.

Kenneth ignored her for a while still clipping away at the keyboard. He suddenly stopped and turned towards her.

'We won't know that physically for a while but what we do know is where they are in the ether, and roughly how they are doing it.'

He sat back with admiration. 'Got to hand it to them, extremely dexterous, very, very clever. I believe you wish to know how to replicate their actions. I'm not sure without meeting them I could do that but we're halfway there. I don't think it'd take long to know where they are geographically as well as virtually.' He seemed to be saying the last few sentences to himself.

'So how long will that take?' queried Jenny.

But Kenneth had been distracted. He was staring at one of his screens and manipulating some of the numbers with the mouse.

'How long?' repeated Jenny, this time more impatiently.

Kenneth tilted his head. 'Oh by tomorrow I should think, but look at this, really extraordinary.'

Jenny peered at the monitor he was pointing to but couldn't make head or tail of it.

'In the last twenty-four hours, look.'

'What?' She was becoming exasperated. 'I don't know what you're talking about.'

'They've done it again. Risky by the look of it.'

'Done what?' she nearly shouted.

Kenneth flicked up an image on one of the monitors that Jenny could actually recognise. It was a satellite telescope, one she had read about in the *Astrophysical Journal*.

'It's *Diophantus ll*. It was launched six months ago by a European consortium.' She pointed at the screen. 'What's it doing there?'

Kenneth sat back and started to twiddle his thumbs. 'Well, it's not doing anything anymore. Our clever friend here has moved it into some other object. It has been completely annihilated.'

Sixteen

They both felt exhausted. Nearly eighteen hours in the air and two changes of aeroplane had taken their toll. Nathalie hadn't told Harry but she had nearly fainted in the Madrid transit lounge. The headaches seemed to be getting worse rather than better. Harry hadn't detected this because he was too obsessed with trying to contact Trevor. He had tried to access the public WiFi but with no luck. As they struggled with their luggage from the Las Palmas arrivals hall, they were met with a pleasant twenty-six degrees, not that Harry noticed as he was still battling with his mobile phone. Nathalie steadied herself and hailed a cab.

'Leave it, Harry, it won't change anything; contact him from the hotel.'

Harry knew she was right and, stuffing the phone into his pocket with one hand, was led by the other into the back seat of the waiting taxi. Nathalie closed her eyes throughout the winding journey and sighed with relief when the taxi driver announced their arrival at the parador.

Harry had booked the hotel and had waxed lyrical to Nathalie about its heritage. Tourism Paradors in Spain are state-run, usually historic buildings which were initiated in the 1920s by the King of Spain to promote tourism. The fact that there are now more than ninety of them is testament to their success. Nathalie opened her eyes to survey this one. The Parador de Cruz Tejeda was certainly impressive. Perched on a volcanic tip it surveyed the undulating island. In the distance, silhouetted on the top of the craggy rock, perched a telescope dome.

'I think I can see the telescope, Harry, right at the top of the highest peak.'

'Ah, it must be a clear day then,' said Harry climbing out of the cab. 'Ironic. The last time I was here a few years ago, I couldn't see it because of the clouds. Now...'

Nathalie sensed the tremor in his voice. It was the only time she had heard any regrets about his lack of sight. She tried to deflect the mood.

'What happens if it's cloudy, do they have to postpone the viewings?'

'Postpone? No, usually cancel. If you miss your window you're out. Fortunately most of the year, even if there is cloud, the blanket sits in a layer below the telescope. It's like flying in an aeroplane; clear skies sitting on a field of clouds. At dusk it's magnificent.'

Nathalie wondered what it felt like to have been deprived of the planet's visual wonders. Selfishly she thought of her own sight; she had had phases of blurred vision ever since that bang on the head. Until now she had been trying to ignore it but the conversation with Harry brought back the anxiety. She took a deep breath and retrieved her suitcase from the driver.

'Okay, Harry, let's check in and go to our rooms. I could do with a shower and I expect you'll want to contact Trevor. Shall we meet in the bar in an hour?'

The iced cold beer was delicious. The shower and a ten-minute nap had revived her and Nathalie felt ready to tackle the world again.

'Over here,' she shouted, seeing Harry in the doorway. 'One frosted cerveza is sitting on the bar waiting for you.'

Harry tapped his way to the bar and felt for the stool. Nathalie placed the beer glass into his hand. He drank deeply from it and put the remainder on the counter.

'I needed that,' he wiped his mouth on the back of his sleeve, 'especially after what I've just heard from Trevor.'

'Go on.'

'As I feared. He or she has done it again.'

'Done what again?'

'Crashed a satellite. *No*, crashed *two* satellites!'

'And this information was from Trevor?'

Harry nodded his head sadly. 'When I heard about that terrible shipping accident – but no, again, it was no accident – when that awful collision occurred, those burning and drowning people, I feared the worst.'

'You wouldn't talk about it on the plane, so what's the actual story?'

'I didn't want to talk about it because I hoped that it wasn't true. I wished that it was just some sort of awful error.'

'The satellites? How could they have anything to do with it?'

Harry reached out for his beer and drained the glass. 'A year ago a new European satellite launched with a payload of technology that is used for electronic navigation and other bridge systems around the Mediterranean. It links with an existing geo-stationery satellite which is part of the European navigation overlay system. It revolutionised maritime navigation in the area, so much so that the captains of vessels have almost become dependent on the device. It would seem that the captain of that super-tanker did so anyway.'

'So the satellite crashed and blanked the *Zircon Master*'s guidance system?' gasped Nathalie.

'That's about it,' said Harry. 'I asked Trevor to track any satellite aberrations and in retrospect he found that a space telescope veered off its course and into the navigation satellite. Made a hell of a mess apparently, thousands of pieces of space junk.'

Nathalie sat up on the barstool. 'A space telescope!' she exclaimed.

'So you're now thinking what I'm thinking. An astronomical satellite – possibly of use to one of our suspects – is taken down in a flash, literally.'

'Do you know anything about this telescope? I mean could it be of use to WCMB?'

'Or, could it be of use to FastTrack? A possible revenge motive?'

Nathalie rooted in her bag for her phone. Hearing the keys being pressed Harry protested, 'You needn't look it up, I know all about *Diophantus*. It's an *ESA* medium class astrophysics...'

But Nathalie wasn't listening. She tapped Harry on the arm and continued scrolling through her screen.

'Fuck the space telescope. I want to see what those bastards have done to those wretched passengers on the cruise ship. From these reports it looks an absolute disaster.'

The final Cosmat Observatory session had been booked for the hours of darkness on the day of their arrival in Gran Canaria. After her outburst of rage in the bar Harry had told Nathalie to get some rest for the night's work. She hadn't protested; her body still ached all over with the bruising and she knew she had to unwind. The perfect solution presented itself with the hotel's curious spa facilities. The blue-tiled indoor swimming complex extended under an arched wooden bridge onto the exterior terrace. This three-metre-square mini infinity pool was surrounded by a Perspex fence allowing the bather the most spectacular view of the volcanic island. Nathalie borrowed a costume from the spa receptionist and slipped into the warm water. Resting her elbows on the side she slowly paddled her legs whilst taking in the panorama. Her anger now was turning to remorse. Why hadn't she been quicker with her investigation? It had started with a casual enquiry about an old media satellite. Now nearly a thousand people were dead: drowned or burned alive by a super-tanker inferno sinking their luxury cruise ship. She was meant to be a television journalist for God's sake, one with a nose for international crime. Why hadn't she seen the warning signs earlier? She was brought back to the present by a voice from the terrace.

'I heard that you were out here. Exotic little spa pool from what I remember. Good idea, it should ease your muscles. I expect you've still got some painful bruising.'

Nathalie looked up to see Harry walking over the little wooden bridge.

'Oh they are not too bad,' she said wincing as she tried to turn her body around. 'There's a lounger on the terrace right in front of you. You said we were going to be up all night, why don't you take a rest there.'

'Will do,' said Harry feeling for the steamer chair. 'Now you've calmed down a little perhaps I could tell you more about that telescope satellite.'

It wasn't exactly the conversation that Nathalie wanted right now but Harry had appeared less affected than her by the Mediterranean incident. He seemed more interested in the satellite crash than the demise of the ships.

'Well if you think you can…' she hesitated. She was going to say, 'close your eyes and relax' but stopped herself in time – '…relax while giving me the lowdown, I'll paddle away here and listen.'

Harry sat back and indeed did close his eyes. 'Well I've been thinking. *Diophantus* is the name of the space telescope that, according to Trevor, was manoeuvred into the orbit of the navigation satellite. From his calculations it would seem that the choice of navigation satellite was purely incidental. It was the nearest orbiting object to the telescope's trajectory. I doubt whether the perpetrator even considered the collateral damage. *Diophantus* is fairly new, launched from Baikonur only a few months ago.'

Nathalie turned away from the view and floated on her back. She paddled gently to keep her ears above the water.

'So what did it do? Anything that would be of interest to our main protagonists?'

Harry put his hands behind his head and took in the early evening air.

'Very much so.'

'Well aren't you going to tell me then?'

'It's fairly complicated.'

'I think I can handle it,' said Nathalie, raising her eyebrows and almost submerging her head in the water. 'Try me,' she spluttered.

Harry turned towards the pool, 'You okay?'

'I'm fine, go ahead, it will be dark soon.'

Harry put on his lecturing voice and began. 'The *Diophantus* mission is primarily to understand why the expansion of the universe is accelerating. Currently we think the source for this acceleration is something we call Dark Energy. This Dark Energy represents about three quarters of the energy of the whole universe. Together with Dark Matter it dominates the universe's matter-energy content. Both of these things are mysterious and unknown but they control the past, present and future evolution of our universe...' Harry paused. 'With me so far?'

Nathalie was looking up at the twilight sky in awe.

'The universe expanding, getting faster, being pulled by dark forces. Scary.'

'But that's the point,' said Harry. 'Fear often comes through lack of knowledge. *Diophantus* was exploring how the universe evolved over the past ten billion years and trying to track the imprints left by Dark Energy and gravity.'

Nathalie turned back onto her front and slowly let her feet drift to the bottom of the pool.

'Sounds important. So this bastard has not only killed thousands of people, they have lost the answer to the universe. Great.'

'It's damaging of course but there are other satellites and terrestrial-based telescopes like the one we are visiting tonight. Cosmat's work here is equally as important. We are creating a map of the universe, also looking into the past. I think you'll find it impressive. I've taken years in calculating where the galaxies should be. The team have been aiming the telescope at these coordinates and recording the images. Tonight is our last night. With luck we should end up with an enormous sky map containing the structures of the whole universe.'

Nathalie pulled herself out of the pool and reached for her towel. She found Harry's last comments unsettling. They were those of a competitive scientist. Instead of lamenting the consequences of the crash, Harry's voice had turned to the excitement of his own project. But perhaps she shouldn't be too harsh in her disapproval. She remembered her first meeting – an obsessive cosmologist excited about the stars in the universe and the satellites orbiting the Earth. It's what drove him to overcome his lack of sight.

'I'm going to change,' she said. 'The taxi's due in an hour. See you in the lobby.'

The sinuous road to the top of the mountain offered astonishing views of the island. Rocky crags protruding from dry ochre soils, tipped here and there with the red tinged clouds. Nathalie could see why they chose to build a telescope here – clean air, high altitude and very little rain. Harry sat beside her tapping into his phone and listening to some audio on his headphones. Since the beginning of their journey he had become a man possessed, focused completely on the night's observation.

'Thank God the weather is fine,' he had said, rubbing his finger and thumb to feel the atmosphere, as they had entered the cab. 'Cosmat's last allocation was a disaster. Storms for two weeks.'

Nathalie was realising the importance that this project had to Harry. Time on the 4.2-metre Herschel telescope on the island was at a premium. Cosmological rivals around the world had to tender for a slot. Normally they would only get two or three days; however, this time Harry's proposal had persuaded them to give a couple of weeks.

'Even that hasn't been enough time to do what the team want,' he had complained.

Nathalie was concerned that Harry's attention had started to drift away from the satellite enigma to his quest for mapping galaxies in the universe. As interesting as this was she was struggling to see how this project would help find the perpetrators of the satellite crashes. When they had first met in London she was sure he had mentioned that the Cosmat team at Las Palmas would have the instruments to help. She turned her thoughts to the offices of WCMB – and they were in the main town, not up here on the top of a mountain. Still, Harry's work had got them this far. Tomorrow she would persuade him to visit the address they had been given in the suburbs of Las Palmas.

As they rounded the last corner, the sight nearly took Nathalie's breath away. The telescope was enormous. A vast white gleaming ball sat on a huge cubic building. Harry sensed the taxi slowing and was almost out of the door before it had actually stopped. He was greeted by one of the Cosmat team who had come to meet them. Nathalie felt somewhat neglected as the men shook hands and immediately started up a conversation about red-shift measurement. She had to cough loudly to interrupt and made Harry introduce her.

'Sorry,' he said, without really meaning it. 'Jake, this is Nathalie, Nathalie this is Jake, the most important guy here tonight.'

Jake smiled at her knowingly. 'Heard a lot about you,' he looked up at the sky. 'Got your smart phone? It's nearly time. We're just about to open the doors.'

He noted the puzzled look on Nathalie's face.

'I hear you're a film director. If you want the shot of a lifetime, stand over there and we'll give you a show.'

As they walked over the scrub to a small knoll overlooking the telescope and valley, Jake unclipped a walkie-talkie from his belt and barked some instructions.

Nathalie was unused to taking photographs or film for anything other than recces, but she was quickly getting the message. She put her mobile phone onto video mode and pointed it at the observatory. Jake was right, it was the shot of a lifetime. The white telescope dome was in partial shadow set against a cloud-filled valley below them. The sun was dipping and the cloud layer appeared like an orange tinted field of snow. She was startled by a rumbling noise. The whole dome was rotating whilst at the same time its gigantic doors growled open creating a window of artificial light.

'Wow!' exclaimed Nathalie. 'What I would have done for an Arri cameraman and a Nagra operator – 16mm film and sound,' she added in explanation.

'Glad you liked it,' said Jake. 'I saw the clouds gathering below the mountain peak and when they do that there aren't many scenes that beat it.' He looked up at the sky. 'Fortunately for us we are above them and tonight should be a good night. Follow me and I'll show you the laboratory.'

It was only when she was inside that Nathalie realised the scale of the telescope. She was led to one of the surrounding platforms containing rows of instruments and computer screens. Through the glass she saw the monster of a thing; criss-crossed tubular girders surrounded the four-metre telescope. As she took her place on the gantry the man next to her was tapping a keyboard like some sort of organist. The cage swung around and enormous shiny metal tooth-like plates retracted to expose the lens. It looked almost organic and reminded Nathalie of the giant squid's beak in *Twenty Thousand Leagues Under the Sea*. And then in an instant it was gone, pivoted towards the open dome window and the now star-studded sky.

'Quite something, isn't it,' remarked Harry, plugging some earphones into a computer. 'Nearly ready to go.'

'So what are we exactly doing here?' asked Nathalie. 'Is there someone that can help us with the satellite issue?'

Harry continued fiddling with the equipment. 'Not tonight, these guys won't have a clue. No, tonight we are measuring red-shifts.'

'Red-shifts?'

'Yes, Cosmat are in a race against the Stanford group to

produce a 3-D map of the universe. We've got a 2-D section of the sky imaged by satellite telescopes. What we don't have is how deep these galaxies go.' He tapped the computer in front of him. 'In here I've got the 2-D coordinates of more than ten thousand galaxies. Tonight we are going to point the telescope at about a hundred of them and measure their red-shift. That means some going.'

Nathalie could see that Harry was now in a world of his own. The satellite quest was obviously off the agenda for the time being. She would just have to be patient and pick up the leads tomorrow. But time was running out and, noting the emotional energy he was already expending, she wondered what shape he would be in by the morning. Harry hadn't noticed that Nathalie's attention had wandered and was still nattering away like an express train. She tuned back in.

'...and as you know red-shift gives us distance. Some of these large-scale structures are five hundred million light years away. If we can make this map, before anyone else, we will be able to show a fossilised imprint of the Big Bang; show how the universe began.'

It wasn't the first time that evening that Harry's words disturbed Nathalie, and it wasn't concerning the scale of the universe, it was the phrase 'before anyone else' that troubled her. These guys were really driven. In the next few moments she would see how driven they actually were. The Cosmat team suddenly came to attention like Pointers on a hunt. A brief moment of silence and then Harry started shouting out orders.

'Q fifteen: twelve!'

The clatter of keys and the immense instrument veered skyward.

'Exposure ten seconds.'

She watched as Jake recorded the image.

'Next object, J fourteen: six!'

The telescope deviated once more.

They were going to do a hundred of these things? So much for astronomy being a leisurely gaze at the stars.

Nathalie realised it was going to be a long night. She wondered how Nick was doing. Reaching for her mobile phone she slipped into the back of the observatory.

Seventeen

Nick felt the phone vibrate in his back pocket. Thank God he had put it on silent; not the time he wanted to draw attention to himself. Without looking at the screen he switched it off and continued down the alleyway. The sun had dipped below the high-rises on the shores of Lake Michigan but it would be an hour or two before it got dark. Why they couldn't have waited he didn't know but she had been adamant. The offices closed at six-thirty and the cleaners came in at eight. It would be the right time. He was expecting a different environment to the one they had found themselves in. South Shore sounded rather exotic but the characterless red-brick buildings belied any atmosphere of a glamorous beach resort. Sarah had parked her car at the back of the buildings in Southlake Park Avenue. They had walked past rows of green dumpsters to arrive at a featureless brown door with a small square tinted-glass window. She tapped a six-digit code into the aluminium lock and pushed the door open. Turning to put her finger to her lips she held up her other hand to indicate that he should stay put. She disappeared into the dark interior and, after what seemed an age, reappeared.

'All clear, usually the last one out clears the shredder. It's empty and I can't hear anyone so it's probably okay.'

Nick followed her into the building. A lot of strange things had happened in the last forty-eight hours. Raiding someone's offices, albeit their temporary ones, didn't seem exceptional.

'His office is in the front of the building, overlooking the lake. With a bit of luck he won't have locked his door.'

Nick wasn't happy with this but after he had come clean with Sarah – well partially clean anyway – about his business, she had convinced him that this was the only way of finding the truth. On that first night, tied on the bed, he had given a lot of thought to what he should tell her. It would have been easy to rip away the silk scarves and turn the tables, but it was obvious that she wasn't stupid and knew he couldn't be an age-old buddy of Professor Watts. He wasn't getting anywhere with the satellite thing anyway so he decided to change tack. He wasn't a tourist, he was a hired gun from a small-time Malay newspaper. Nothing to shout about but he'd been given the brief to find out why some of their TV stations had been shut down. He had tracked it back to a satellite malfunction, and then to companies that might control them – media organisations, meteorologists, astronomers and so on. The media organisations were hard to crack but scientists like the ones in FastTrack were easier to approach. He still wasn't sure how much she bought the story, and he hoped she wouldn't be ringing Professor Watts any time soon, but the rest of the night went well. He still had the wax burns to prove it.

Sarah had reached the front office and tried the door. A shaft of light from the lakeside window pierced the dark corridor as it effortlessly swung open.

'Great, empty. Now all we need to do is to find those papers. Have you got your gloves on?'

Nick slipped on the pair of surgical gloves that they had purchased from the local pharmacy. That really made him feel like a criminal. What in the hell was he doing here? After that first challenging night they had spent the whole day in Sarah's hotel room skirting around the subject. Eventually she came straight out with it.

'You think FastTrack has something to do with bringing down that satellite!' she blurted out suddenly after they had consumed nearly a whole bottle of Glenlivet.

This woman had a PhD in astrophysics, there was little point in denying it. Nick conceded that it had crossed his mind.

'So you're going to interrogate *me* now?' she had slurred seductively.

It didn't take long for Nick to take up the offer. It also didn't take him long to get the information he wanted from a naked astrophysicist bound and splayed over a drinks' trolley.

That morning they had woken feeling like their heads and bodies had been put through a centrifuge. After several espressos from the hotel machine they had sat down to consider their options. Sarah had claimed that she had nothing to do with it but could see Nick's reasoning. Cosmology could be a cut-throat business. Who was going to publish what first? 'It's all about Nobel dreams,' she had said. Quite possible that rival groups could try and spike each other's progress. Bringing down an old media satellite could have been just a rehearsal for crashing a space telescope. Whether it was her company FastTrack, that was another matter. Normally she had a sense for these things but there hadn't even been a rumour. Three or four groups were in the race for the holy grail of Cold Dark Matter: WCMB, Stanford and Cosmat among them. The name Cosmat struck Nick like an anvil. He tried not to seem too eager as he probed her about the company. She reeled off some names. One of them was a real obsessive she had claimed, would do anything to be there first. Before he could challenge her on this she had made a surprising proposal. One way of checking out her own company would be to take a look in the files of FastTrack's temporary office in Chicago. She had access so it would be easy. Nick was reluctant to break in, even if he was with someone who had the keys, but what had really persuaded him were her aspersions on Harry Stones. If they were true Nathalie was in real trouble, and he would do anything to stop that.

The office was compact, neat and tidy, upset only by a few half-drunk coffee cups. Cheap imitation-wood laminated furniture, a whiteboard looking like Einstein had attacked it, and various computer technology furnished the room. A large plate-glass window gave a view over the lake which was turning grey in the shadow of the building. Sarah made her way quietly towards the filing cabinet in the corner.

'I'll check this, you look in his desk drawers.'

'I thought you said we weren't going to break into anything,' said Nick, sliding one of the drawers open.

'Well, this filing cabinet's not locked and neither is his desk by the look of it,' said Sarah. 'Looking for a report that I've mislaid in my boss's office isn't exactly burglary.'

'What report?' drawled Nick.

Sarah smiled, 'Oh, you must know the one, I think he filed it next to the satellite data file by mistake.'

Nick shook his head, this woman was really something. One minute she was a dominatrix, the next a cat burglar. He thought he heard a noise.

'Shh, is that the cleaner?'

Sarah glanced at the clock on the wall, 'No chance, she's not due for another half-hour. Must be the wind or something.'

Nick sidled back to the door and peered down the corridor. 'No one there, but she could be early. Why didn't we come later when it was dark?'

Sarah stood up and put her hands on her hips. 'Yes that would be great wouldn't it? The two of us found wandering about at midnight. Nothing suspicious in that. Look, stupid, if someone finds us now, no problem. I work here. Just showing a friend around and taking in a spectacular view of the lake.'

Nick saw her reasoning. But then he looked at his gloves. He held them up.

'Oh yeah, but what about these?'

Sarah sighed with exasperation. 'If you hear something stick them in your pocket and stare out of the window. No wonder you ended up working for a crummy Far Eastern newspaper.'

Nick was about to protest when he suddenly remembered his story.

'After this scoop, next year the *Washington Post*,' he said with a grin and started to rummage through the drawer.

It took them fifteen minutes to find that her boss wasn't the best in keeping records on paper. The desk contained humdrum things like expenses claims and theatre tickets. The filing cabinet, nothing more than published research papers.

Sarah switched on the computer.

'Whoa!' exclaimed Nick. 'You are really going to hack into that?'

Sarah ignored him, sat down and tapped at the keys.

'Looking for your lost report is one thing,' whispered Nick. 'Breaking into the guy's computer...'

Sarah stopped typing and stared at him. 'Look you silly boy, why don't you stand by the door and see if anyone is coming. If there is, wave at me and I'll shut this down. I thought you wanted to find out who crashed a satellite?'

Nick nodded compliantly and walked towards the door. Geoff was going to kill him when he found out what they were doing. At least on active duty it was straightforward. You were given orders and you carried them out. A simple chain of command. Geoff had asked him to discreetly look into a scientist's background to see if she had anything to do with satellites. Here he was aiding and abetting hacking into her boss's computer, not exactly discreet. The natural light was beginning to fade and he watched as Sarah's face was lit up by the computer screen. From her expression she had obviously got in. Now she was leaning over, staring, moving the mouse and pressing the odd key.

'Eureka!' she suddenly exclaimed. She sat back and grinned at Nick.

'Get it?' Then seeing Nick's face, shook her head and muttered something about philistines.

'I assume you found something,' said Nick laconically, becoming a little irritated by Sarah's patronage.

'Yes it's all to do with maths. You won't believe this guy. He's a professor of particle physics and hasn't got a clue about cyber security.' She turned back to the computer.

'So what have you found?'

'E-mails, and only after the twelfth attempt.'

Nick peered down the corridor nervously. 'Twelfth attempt?'

'Mathematicians. You wouldn't credit it, the guy's got a brain the size of a planet and he uses mathematicians as passwords. I should have got it earlier: Gromov. He didn't even use his full name, Mikail Leonidovich Gromov.'

'And that let you into his e-mails?'

'Yes,' she said waving her arms theatrically at the screen. 'Come and look.'

Nick glanced at the clock on the wall. Ten to eight. The cleaner was due at any moment. They would have to be quick. For a large man Nick could be agile. He skipped around to the side of the desk so that he could see the screen. Sarah was already scrolling through the names. One caught her attention and she expanded the correspondence.

Cancellation of Diophantus project. Owing to the collision of the Diophantus satellite telescope it is with great regret that the consortium have had to suspend activities hence rendering your application for data acquisition unviable.

'Shit,' hissed Sarah in a loud whisper. 'Collision, when did that happen?'

Nick was beginning to put two and two together. 'Satellite collision. Remember that news on CNN, terrible shipping accident in the Mediterranean. They thought it was something to do with a navigation satellite. Maybe it hit this *Diathonese* thing. No one told you anything about it?'

'*Diophantus*,' corrected Sarah. 'No they bloody didn't. Fucking FastTrack and their need-to-know policy. I'm on their main neutrino project for God's sake. We are all working towards the same aim. I didn't even know they had applied for time on the damn thing. Just you wait until...'

'I don't think that's wise do you?' interrupted Nick. 'Not

sure whether your boss would like to know you've been playing mathematical mastermind with his passwords.' He looked up at the wall clock again, five to eight. 'We are running out of time, and you need to close this thing down so he doesn't know we've been here.' He was thinking of Nathalie. 'Any closer to knowing if Cosmat had anything to do with this?'

Sarah typed the word into the search box. A couple of hits came up but, before she could expand the e-mails, they heard a door open from the end of the corridor.

'Quick, nip into that side office on the right. I'll shut this down and fend her off. Say I've had to work late. If I can hold her talking with her back to the door you will be able to slip down the corridor and out the way we came in.'

Nick was about to ask if she had glanced anything about Cosmat but she was already switching off the computer.

'No time,' she snapped, guessing his purpose and waving him away. 'See you at the car.'

The cleaner was more concerned about the dirty coffee cups than with Sarah and it had been easy for Nick to creep down the corridor unobserved. He waited by the car. Why did she have to have such an obtrusive red one? Sarah took her time.

'Didn't want to appear to be in a rush to get out. She wasn't interested in talking so I flicked through a few journals to avoid any suspicion.'

'Did you get any more out of the computer?' asked Nick sliding his large frame into the low passenger seat as she remotely opened the car door.

Sarah sat behind the wheel and looked at him askance. 'What do you think? Reading a printed journal is one thing but sitting at your boss's desk studying his computer? Come on Nick.'

'I know I know, but we were that close.'

Sarah put the car into gear and pulled away, so quickly that Nick was thrown back in his seat.

'Close to what? We know that a space telescope has been destroyed. We would have found that out by the news anyway. Okay, we found out that FastTrack were trying to get time on the thing. Bit weird that they would be in the frame to bring it down then. Cosmat? Who knows? They've got their own satellite. I know they're competitive but would they really kill thousands of people to spike the opposition?'

Nick held onto the dashboard as Sarah swung the car around the corner. 'Say they didn't know the consequences. Say they just wanted to move the thing out of its normal orbit; mess up the figures sort of thing.'

'Mm. You've got a point there, but I don't know how we can find that out. Being found in the boss's office once is fine. But twice, I can't take the risk. I really don't think FastTrack have anything to do with your satellite story. I've done what I can but I'm not prepared to put my job on the line for your news scoop.'

Nick was about to tell her that breaking into the office was all her idea but thought better of it. Her argument about FastTrack's interest in keeping the *Diophantus* satellite in the sky didn't apply to the earlier crash. She was right, they weren't much further forward, except perhaps that Cosmat did have a motive, albeit a tenuous one. Tenuous or not, it worried Nick. His mind was racing as fast as Sarah's sports car. What if an obsessive, like Harry Stones, wanted a competitive advantage? What if the *Diophantus* telescope was gathering more data than Cosmat's? Would he be crazy enough to spin a story to a production company that he wanted to make a film about satellites? Looking for perpetrators when he was the actual culprit? Throw people completely off the scent? Nathalie had already been put into danger on this project once. What if her so-called film director was a madman? It didn't bear thinking about. He would have to call Geoff.

Sarah turned into the underground car park with a squeal of

tyres and pulled on the brake. She glanced at Nick who was staring through the windscreen.

'If you've noticed, we've arrived,' she said. 'What's up with you?'

Nick snapped out of his reverie. 'Just thinking. I've got to write a story up soon; my editor will be losing patience. I should give him a call.'

Sarah did a quick mental calculation. 'Well, Malaysia is about thirteen hours ahead of us so it should be mid-morning there now. You can call from my room if you like.' She lowered her head and raised her eyes. 'That's if you want to come up,' she added mischievously.

Nick suddenly remembered the time difference. It would be three in the morning in London. Geoff would not be happy.

'Well if you think we can get past the concierge again,' said Nick trying to think on his feet. 'And, on second thoughts, I wouldn't want to ruin our evening, the old man can wait. I'll send him a text and write something later.' He took out his phone. 'You go on up, I won't be long.'

Sarah shrugged, 'Keep my name out of it won't you.' She turned and walked to the elevator. 'I'll order some drinks,' she shouted over her shoulder.

Nick leaned with his back on the car and typed out a message.

Need to talk. Have you done any background checks on Harry Stones? Concerned he may be playing you. Have information that could put Nathalie in danger. Call me 7am Chicago time. Nick.

Seven in the morning! He took the elevator to the fifth floor. They had better take it easy tonight.

Eighteen

'Interesting!' exploded Jenny. 'Interesting doesn't quite cover it when the thing has killed thousands of people. It's outrageous. And now MalaySat will have to believe me. It wasn't my neglect that caused *PhreeSat* to crash.'

Zikri Amin looked around the ornamental gardens to see who was in earshot.

'Keep your voice down, Miss Kang. The reason we are sitting on this park bench in the sunshine is so that no prying electronic ears can hear us. Pointless if you're going to shout the information to the whole of Kuala Lumpur.'

Jenny leaned back against the hard bench and took a deep breath. In normal circumstances this would be a pleasant location – a shaded pillared pagoda underneath a riot of orange hibiscus, immaculate gardens stretched out before them, the odd person bending over to take a closer look at the different exotic species – but these weren't normal circumstances. After her encounter with Kenneth, Zikri had sent her another note. He had heard from their mutual friend and was interested to hear more from Jenny. Wanted to meet, but not in the Petronas Towers – somewhere quiet, a neutral venue. Thinking this sounded more like a spy novel than a business meeting, Jenny jokingly had said the first thing that came into her head. The Perdana Botanical Garden. He had accepted her suggestion without taking a breath. Now here they were, sitting side-by-side, talking about satellite mayhem as if it was a conversation on horticultural practices.

'I say "interesting" because the data on two satellite manipulations should be able to give us coordinates on the perpetrator,' muttered Zikri into his lap. 'And once we find the person or persons responsible I'm sure we'll be able to find out how they did it.'

Jenny thought this encounter was becoming weirder and weirder. She couldn't understand why they hadn't met in his office. Surely now here was the evidence to prove that it wasn't her who crashed the satellite. All they had to do was check out the data and reinstate her. The new collision hadn't been anything to do with media. They were navigation and astronomical devices. Nothing to do with MalaySat's business. She thought of going over Zikri's head to the CEO but he had covered his tracks. Only she and he knew about Kenneth and the tracking data, he had made sure of that. Even if she had been able to contrive a meeting with the CEO, and that wouldn't have been easy, Zikri could have denied everything. She was only making it up to save her own skin. Where was this high-tech basement? In an impoverished back street of Chinatown? Likely story. And she suspected that Kenneth and his equipment were long gone.

'Miss Kang. Did you hear what I was saying? A chance to track down this person. Seeing the trouble they put you in I'm sure you want to meet them as much as I do.'

Jenny wasn't so sure about that. She was struggling to make sense of all of this. She had the terrible feeling that her earlier instinct that Zikri wanted the information for himself to control other people's satellites was seeming more and more likely. But it was obvious that he was not going to let her go. She had no alternative but to play along until she could see a means of extricating herself. With a bit of luck, if they found this person or persons and blackmailed them into divulging their methods, Zikri might have no more use for her.

'Yes, Mr Zikri, I heard you. I was just upset that you hadn't expressed any concern for the people who suffered as a consequence.'

Zikri put his arm on the rail of the bench as if he was with a consort in the back seat of a cinema. He turned to Jenny. It was surprising how quickly this man could change his demeanour.

'Of course I have concern, wouldn't anyone? But it's happened. What we need to do is to make sure it doesn't happen again. I know you're with me on that, Jenny.' He was using her first name again. 'You're a bright girl, and now we've got Kenneth's data. It shouldn't be too difficult to track them down, but we have to do it without broadcasting the fact in case they go to ground.' He looked around the park. It was nearly closing time and the last stragglers were making their way home. 'That's why I thought it was a good idea to meet here, unofficially so to speak. Now, can I depend on your cooperation?'

Cooperation. What else was she supposed to do? This creepy man could turn at any moment. She had seen his ire in previous meetings. At first she had been worried about losing her job. Now knowing Zikri's access to henchmen, it could even mean losing her life.

'Of course.' She held her knees to stop them shaking. 'We've come this far; with a bit more triangulation of the data I'm sure we can track them down.'

Zikri squeezed her shoulder. 'I'm sure we can Jenny.'

She tried not to flinch. Was this guy really trying to make a pass at her? She tried to make a quick calculation of what she should do if he came any closer. But she needn't have worried. With one swift movement her escort rose from the bench and skipped out of the shade into the blazing sun.

'I have to get back to the office. When you've done some more calculations and have an idea where our target is, phone me.' He pointed to the bench where he had recently been seated.

She looked down, there next to her was a cheap mobile phone.

'Only use it for me; the number is stored in the memory. Keep it with you at all times in case I need to get hold of you.'

Jenny was about to ask why but he had already begun marching briskly along one of the garden's mazy paths.

She picked up the phone and switched it on. Not a smart phone, a simple pay-as-you-go ordinary phone. One number was in the memory. It would no doubt connect to another simple pay-as-you-go phone. She put it in her pocket, looked up and stared at the diminishing figure of her tormentor. He had turned to the south-west. Why was that? The nearest station to the Petronas Towers was Hang Tuah, in the opposite direction. She had taken the route a hundred times. Even if he was hailing a cab, why walk to the opposite side of the park? Her curiosity got the better of her. Grabbing her bag she followed Zikri into the sunshine. He was becoming only a speck in the distance so she started to jog. She was so focused on her prey that she didn't notice an oncoming elderly gentleman. His cane and her bag spiralled onto the grass verge. Fortunately neither of them fell and the old man just stood there looking dazed as Jenny grabbed their possessions and thrust the walking stick back into his hand. She apologised in three different languages and flicked her head around to find Zikri. He was now out of sight, not even a dot in the distance. There was nothing for it but to run in the direction that she had last seen him.

At the edge of the botanical gardens was a large gate leading to the main thoroughfare. She caught sight of the suited figure crossing the street and melting into a small crowd even though there was more space on the side where Jenny was panting, her hands on her knees. Did he know he was being followed? She was no expert at these things. The nearest she had experienced was watching thrillers on TV. She gathered her breath and strolled in a parallel course in the same direction on the opposite side of the street. Now and again she caught sight of him, stopping to tie his shoelaces or to glance into a shop window. It certainly looked suspicious, but she was too far away to be seen in a reflection and he hadn't glanced towards her. As a precaution she took a silk scarf from her bag and wrapped it around her head. The area had a large Muslim population and this would help draw attention away from herself.

Her quarry cut into a side street but was still heading south. She guessed the destination, Bangsar Station. That would be a tricky one. If he was going south the line split into two – one track to Port Klang towards the west, the other to Kajung. She would have to keep up to see which ticket he bought. The trains were on an elevated platform. She pulled her scarf over her face more tightly and ducked in and out behind the following passengers as they mounted the stairs. He had reached the ticket booth window but she was too far behind. She took a guess. Providentially they ended up on the same platform and the train was pulling in. She got into the carriage behind and peered through the window. He had his back towards her. She sat down out of view in case he turned around.

The next stop was Abdullah Hukum. Jenny leaned forward to peer at the doors of the next carriage. She leaped to her feet as she saw his suited trousers step onto the platform. A large woman with a suitcase blocked her way. She watched helplessly as the passengers streamed down the staircase to the street below. By the time she had stumbled around the obstructing luggage the doors were closing. She put out her hand but withdrew it quickly as she noticed out of the side of her eye that Zikri had stepped back onto the train. The fat woman was now haranguing her and people were watching. The train lurched forward throwing Jenny to the floor. She stayed there on hands and knees for a while, at least she couldn't be seen from the other carriage.

She got out at the next station, walked quickly past Zikri's carriage and, seeing that he had stayed on board, slipped into the carriage on the other side. Here it was easier to observe him. The carriage was nearly full and there were a number of people standing in front of her, partially obscuring her presence. At each stop she peered around to see if he stepped off. Stations came and went as they ventured into the suburbs. At Petaling he made his move. The platform was nearly deserted, a few people waiting under the shaded covers. Jenny left it until the last moment. She was the only other person to alight. Remembering the phone, she took it out of her pocket and leaned behind a pillar pretending to make a call. By the time she had turned around, he had passed through the ticket barrier and had disappeared.

'Great,' she thought. 'All this way to the middle of nowhere and I've lost him.'

She slipped her ticket into the slot and the barriers parted. Beyond some tiled steps was a grassy bank. This was commuter belt, greenery interspersed with low rise suburban buildings. She skipped down the steps and scanned to the left and to the right. Not a soul to be seen. There seemed to be more buildings to the right so she took that path. After a hundred yards or so she came across a small private estate; terraced, neat white houses lined the street. She turned the corner to a more salubrious area. A two-storey detached house stood on its own surrounded by palms and banana plants. She stopped in her tracks as she saw the black BMW in the drive. She recognised the plates; she had seen it at the airport when she had first arrived to be greeted by MalaySat's chief technical officer. It couldn't be a coincidence. She felt deflated. Had she come all this way to find that Zikri Amin was merely visiting the home of a work colleague? She had become almost excited by the spy-like tradecraft. Fantasised too much about a mundane social visit. She was about to turn forlornly for the station when she had a second thought. He had said he was going to the office, and what was he doing looking into windows and stepping on and off trains? That wasn't normal behaviour. It was as if he was making sure that no one was following him. What was the motive that had to be kept so secret? She heard voices from the back garden. A low rattan fence boarded the side of the property. Jenny took off her shoes and crept down the adjacent path. There was only one way she was going to find out.

The afternoon was muggy, the scent of orchids and ixora filled the air. She prised open two pieces of cane to view the garden. A riot of colour from the lush grounds filled the foreground; beyond, seated around a round white fretted table, were three men engaged in lively conversation. She recognised Zikri and the technical officer but the third man had his back towards her. He was slight, and less animated than the others. She strained to hear their voices. One had a definite Chinese accent: she couldn't hear the words because he was softly spoken but she was sure it was Kenneth. Zikri's piercing voice on the other hand came across loud and clear.

'We are nearly there, only a few more pieces and we should complete the jigsaw.'

She could just make out the technical officer's reply.

'So the girl is still playing along?'

'So far, Adi. She's scared out of her wits and if we keep it that way we should get results.'

The man, who she assumed was Kenneth, gesticulated with his arms and mumbled something softly. She caught the words 'data' and 'location' but no more.

The other two nodded in agreement.

'It would make sense if we sent someone there,' said the technical officer who Zikri had referred to as Adi.

Kenneth mumbled a reply.

Adi was shaking his head. 'No, we can't risk you, has to be someone who won't draw attention and knows the lie of the land.'

'Well we all know the obvious choice,' said Zikri. 'She's been before; all we need is another excuse to send her there.'

'Can you trust her? And didn't she get arrested for something the last time?'

'Nothing to do with us. She just happened to be near a crime scene – in the wrong place at the wrong time – was all cleared up, that's what I understood anyway.'

Jenny who was on her toes leaning forwards nearly fell into the fence. Kenneth, hearing a noise turned to face her. She froze, still keeping the split between the canes slightly open. The aperture was so small that she was sure, from that distance, he couldn't see her, but she was unnerved by the way he glared at the boundary. The other two seemed not to notice and after a while Kenneth turned back to the table. Jenny breathed a sigh of relief and found a more stable spot to eavesdrop. Adi was walking around the table refilling the men's glasses with a sickly-looking bright pink juice. It looked like air bandung – she had tried it in her local coffee shop – a mixture of condensed milk and rose syrup, disgusting. Still, in the late afternoon sunshine the men seemed to be enjoying it. They broke off the conversation for a while and Adi appeared to be showing them around his garden. She held her breath as they passed the fence and admired the hibiscus on the borders. Fortunately for her they gathered in a small group, standing near her but looking away from the fence. Now she could hear every word.

'I've got it,' said Zikri suddenly, changing the subject from the vibrant flora. 'There's a new launch coming up.' She could only see his back, but it appeared as if he was checking something on his phone.

'Yes, within the next week. A company called WCMB are launching a new satellite from Baikonur. Perfect.'

Kenneth spoke softly, but this time she could hear him. 'How can that help us? It's not a MalaySat project.'

'No, but that doesn't matter. Baikonur are really keen for us to launch another satellite to replace *PhreeSat*; bending over backwards to get us to sign. All we have to do is to say we would like to observe their operation, see how smoothly it goes.'

'And that would get us an invitation?' asked Adi.

'Absolutely and, of course, we will send our brightest star to attend.'

The technical officer started to make his way back to the table and his words became less distinct but she caught enough of them – '…the skills to track our target when she gets there…'

What was all that about? What skills? And why would she have to go back to Baikonur to try them out? She didn't like the sound of this at all.

Kenneth's soft voice answered her questions.

'I think so, she was pretty good in the temporary ops room. I

178

thought I could triangulate from there but the dominant signals go through Baikonur. A simple hacker could trace them if they're actually in Baikonur using a domestic router.'

'That's decided then,' said Adi. 'Amin here gets the invitation and you, Kenneth, can prep the hacking codes.' He turned to Zikri, 'This better be worth it, we're taking a big risk here. Are you sure you weren't followed?'

'Absolutely,' protested Zikri. 'I didn't start out from the office anyway, I was in the botanical gardens. The chance of someone from MalaySat being there at this time of day would be slim. Besides, I covered my tracks just in case.' Jenny could almost hear the smile in his voice. 'Just like in the spy movies,' he added, before draining his sickly-sweet drink.

Nineteen

The alarm from the telephone was so loud that the vibration nearly ejected it from the bedside table. Nick snapped out his left arm and, without opening his eyes, grabbed the handset. He lay there for a second, the phone still ringing in his hand, before he started to prize his lids open. He looked to his left and saw Sarah's bare feet sticking out from under the duvet and resting against the pillow. There was a groan from the foot of the bed.

'Aren't you going to answer that thing?'

Nick looked at the phone. Six o'clock in the morning. Bloody Geoff Sykes!

'Yeah, sorry.' Nick swung his legs off the bed and patted where he thought Sarah's bottom might be. 'I'll take it in the bathroom.'

He staggered across the floor and into the hotel suite's enormous wet-room. Two of the walls were covered in mirrored tiles. He glanced at his rear. Black and blue stripes. What in the hell had she done to him this time? The phone was still ringing angrily. He sat heavily on the lid of the WC and nearly jumped up again with the stinging.

'Sykes, I thought I said seven o'clock Chicago time. Can't you bloody add up?'

'Can't you bloody answer the phone? And yes, I can add up. It's midday here and six there. If it's as important as it sounded I thought that wouldn't be too early for an ex-army officer. Besides, it's lunchtime here and I've got a restaurant booked for one.'

'I'm not in the army anymore. I wanted to be awake enough to gather my thoughts. And, while we're on that subject, hang on a minute while I clear my throat with a glass of water.'

He stood up and reached for the wall cupboard, took out a

180

couple of tablets and dropped them into one of the tumblers standing on the marble sink. He ran the tap, holding his finger under to make sure it was cold, and filled the glass. Returning to the WC he sat down, but this time gingerly.

'Okay I'm ready. Wanted to pass something by you.'

Geoff had been sitting patiently in his office swivelling in his chair, feet on the desk, handset pressed closely to his ear.

'Headache?'

'What do you mean headache?'

'I'm sure that was Alka-Seltzer I heard there.'

'What of it? Can't a guy have a few drinks now and then?'

'No wonder you're balking at six o'clock in the morning; there have been times when you've called me at three.'

'I'm not sure if it's that urgent, could be nothing, and I've no proof, but if it does turn out to be true I wouldn't forgive myself.'

'Nick, you're talking in riddles. Blurt it out man.'

'Okay. In a word, or two words actually, it's Harry Stones.'

The midday sun had burned off the mist and Nathalie could see clearly across the peaks and valleys of Gran Canaria. Red soils and rocks were interspersed with patches of green forests and the metalled roads appeared as sinuous rivers winding their way down to the coast. She rested her outstretched arms on the handrail. The hotel terrace had been built for such viewing. In the distance, atop one of the peaky crags, the white dome of the telescope glinted. They had spent all of the night and the early hours of the morning there and she was exhausted. The lack of sleep hadn't done much for her headaches and the dizzy spells still came and went. But she was desperate to pursue their research, especially after the Mediterranean fiasco, and had called Harry's room as soon as she had woken from her two-hour nap. The response she had got was brutal, most unlike Harry. Why had she woken him? Did she not realise how hard he had worked in the night? He would get up when he was ready. She had tried to cajole him, gently reminding him that the reason they were there was to visit WCMB in Las Palmas. Without him she had no entrée. He had sworn at her and put the phone down. That was over an hour ago. She had grabbed a late breakfast in the coffee shop and, with nothing else to do, had strolled onto the veranda. Time was ticking away; if they were going to visit WCMB they would have to start off soon. She sat in a lounger and flipped open Google Maps. The very least she could do was to explore the lie of the land. The route was winding and the forty-odd kilometres would take them at least an hour. The offices were situated on the north-east of the island adjacent to the Avenue de Canarias in amongst other business complexes. She expanded the map and studied the street views. White and cream rectangular tower blocks surrounded by shaded car parks. Not the exceptional surroundings she was expecting for a Russian billionaire's enterprise. Nothing to sell but publicity, no need for show she supposed. She thought about hailing a cab and taking the journey alone. But what would be the point? There was no way without Harry she would get past the front door. He on the other hand had a very good reason for visiting them. The results from last night's IR survey for one.

'If I scratch their back, they might scratch mine,' he had said. But that was a few days ago. After this morning's tirade she doubted whether he would be sharing his precious numbers with them at all. The whole point of doing this trip was to track down possible satellite saboteurs. Originally when Geoff had suggested Harry do the research on his own and report back, the man had insisted on being the director on the project; wanted to film things as they went along he had said. To date, all they had got was some meagre footage from the Mayall in Arizona, some telescope shots that would be useful for voice-over, and a partial inconclusive interview. He hadn't mentioned a camera since. Not the way she would have gone about things. Maybe she should take more control. The story was certainly simmering anyway. Yet without him she wouldn't have the contacts or the access and, if there was one thing that you needed to make a documentary, it was access. She looked at her watch, nearly one o'clock in the afternoon. She would give it one more chance. She would wake Harry again at two o'clock. If he didn't play ball she would quit, even if it meant paying for her own fare home.

Geoff had cancelled his lunch meeting. He had spent the last half-hour listening to Nick's theory about Stones. Initially he had told Nick he was crazy. Why would an avuncular blind guy want to smash up other people's satellites? It didn't make sense. He was an academic, okay an obsessive one, but it was too far-fetched to believe that his investigation was to put people off the fact that he was doing it himself. But the more Nick told him the more worried he became. Stranger things had happened. Even if there was a slither of possibility, they should tell Nathalie. She was on the ground. They should leave it up to her to make the call. Geoff paced up and down his office. Work was coming in again, he didn't really need this project. Maybe he should cut his losses, abandon it and tell Nathalie to come back to the UK. He hadn't realised it but he was saying his thoughts aloud down the telephone to Nick.

'Doesn't sound like you,' said Nick. 'From what Sarah and I found at FastTrack I think you've got a great story.'

'Oh it's Sarah now is it,' said Geoff, sensing something in Nick's tone of voice.

'That's her name,' snapped Nick defensively. 'She's been very helpful as it happens. She's no more idea than we have if her company is involved but there's something really funny going on up there. Space machines bumping into each other causing havoc. We are sure someone is doing it. It's right up your street – espionage, corporate crime. You can't back out now.'

Geoff went over to the corner of his office and slouched on one of the easy chairs. If Nick Coburn was becoming interested, there might be something in this thing. Nick had a poor attention threshold at the best of times.

'This Sarah thing,' he asked perceptively, 'have you got something going on there?'

Nick shuffled on the toilet seat. His rear was really becoming sore. 'Well you did say get close to her and find out what I could.'

'Yeah but how close, Nick? I mean is she taking you for a ride?'

'A ride?' Nick laughed. 'Maybe, but not in the way you think. I don't think someone who is trying to con me would hack into her boss's computer.'

Geoff sat up in the chair. Nick now had his full attention.

'I thought I told you to be subtle; suss out the ground. When did all this happen?'

'Subtle is my middle name, Geoff.' Nick moved over to the bathroom door and opened it to see if Sarah was still sleeping. 'Wasn't my idea, backed into a corner so I challenged her. She claimed no knowledge of it but was interested as I was to see if there was any funny business going on. Ended up breaking into her boss's office.'

Nick could visualise Geoff's eyebrows hitting the ceiling. There was a silence and Nick continued.

'Discovered FastTrack were going to buy data from a satellite that crashed. Would be strange for them to have done it. That's what made us think of who else was in the frame. Sarah mentioned Cosmat as a rival in the race. Said that people like Stones would do almost anything to publish first.' Seeing that Sarah was fast asleep he gently closed the bathroom door again.

'But don't worry, I haven't mentioned anything about Nathalie and Stones. Sarah thinks I'm working for a two-bit Malaysian newspaper trying to find out who blanked out one of the local TV stations.'

This part of the conversation had Geoff's head spinning.

'I thought you were meant to be a tourist, introduced by Professor Watts.'

'Oh yeah, things have moved on since then. I was going to update you in my next report.'

'Next report? You never make reports.'

The two men were on the phone without vision but both of them could imagine each other's expressions.

Geoff was the first to speak. 'Right, if things are as interesting as you say they are, we'll carry on. I'll get Stefanie to do some background checks on Harry Stones. See if he has any misdemeanours in his past. Meanwhile I think we'll not say anything to Nathalie. You should wrap up there, before this lady gets an idea that you're not working as a Far Eastern journalist, and I'll look up Nathalie's next port of call. I'll get you to join her there so you can keep an eye on things.'

'Won't Nathalie be suspicious? Me turning up unannounced.'

'No, I'll think of something. Are you okay to stay in Chicago until I find out where and when?'

Nick went to the basin and took his toothbrush from the glass. 'Oh I'll occupy my time somehow,' he said. 'Might be a bit of a bind though.'

There was no need for Harry to be given a second wake-up call. He appeared on the terrace nursing a cup of espresso. Nathalie waited for the invective.

'Is that you there?' he asked hearing the creak of the steamer chair.

'Good morning, Doctor Stones, I was about to call you again.'

'Yes, I'm sorry about that. I was shattered, please accept my profound apology.'

'If you're up for taking a trip downtown in the next half-hour, apology accepted.' Nathalie rose from the lounger. 'After all, that is why we are here,' she added tartly.

'I know, I know, got carried away. When you've spent an academic lifetime trying to map the universe, it's hard not to get excited. Not often you get the opportunity to operate a one-billion-euro telescope.' Harry drained the last of his coffee.

'So if my apology really is accepted, I'm back on duty. The good news is that WCMB replied to my e-mail this morning. They are really keen to know some of our results from last night's vigil. I gave them a call and we have an appointment with them at four o'clock this afternoon.'

Nathalie was right about her estimate of an hour for the journey. The taxi skidded its way around the dusty narrow roads without fear. Of course, Harry couldn't see the precarious drop to one side and the millimetre gap that the driver spared, but he could feel the tight grip of Nathalie's hand as they swung around each corner.

'They're pretty good these drivers you know,' he said, after a particularly hard squeeze. 'They must travel this road a thousand times.'

This was of no comfort to Nathalie. She had heard an almost identical phrase told to her by a Machu Picchu guide. The sight of a burned-out bus in the ravine hadn't comforted her then either.

'It wouldn't hurt for him to slow down,' she said. 'These dizzy spells are bad enough as it is.'

Harry turned towards her with a surprised expression on his face. 'You still having those? I thought that all of that had cleared up.'

Nathalie realised what she had said and wished she had bitten her tongue.

'Mainly, yes, but I get the odd spin. It's just that this taxi slalom isn't helping.'

Harry leaned forward and tapped the driver on the shoulder which he instantly regretted for the driver spun round and they nearly slewed off the road.

'Could you slow down a little please, we're getting thrown around a bit back here.'

'Por supuesto,' said the driver, putting his foot on the accelerator.

Eventually, as they neared the coast, the road levelled out and they joined the main avenue. Nathalie looked out of the window at the glinting ocean and began to relax but not for long as their taxi driver, believing that Harry had asked him to hurry, started behaving like Fernando Alonso and weaved perilously through the traffic. The hotel manager had given the driver WCMB's address, and he had been prepaid with a large tip, so it was with great aplomb that he screeched to a halt outside a corner office block, jumped out of his cab and swung open the back door with a large grin on his face.

'Hemos llegado, muchas gracias.'

'Muchas gracias,' said Nathalie in return, helping Harry out of the cab.

The blue double-entrance doors were set into the corner of the deco-looking building. There was a small brass plaque in one corner of the covered portico inscribed with the name 'Western Cosmological Mission Bureau' with the words 'Oficinas Registradas' in smaller script underneath.

'Strange title for a Russian-based company,' said Nathalie as she watched Harry trace out the letters with his fingers.

'Yes, we don't really know who the main benefactors are or exactly where they're from. When they started up the board at Cosmat they did a search but all they could come up with was that the money and some of their top scientists came from Russia.'

'Why the "West" bit do you think?' asked Nathalie.

'Give it some sort of kudos here in Spain I suppose. They've spent a lot of money getting time on the Herschel.'

'And you don't think they will be suspicious with you dragging me around?'

'I kept to our original story. Sechenov was told that you were a film researcher checking out observatories. He was obviously the leader on the Arizona project so the information must have got back, especially as you were whacked with the telescope. I simply e-mailed them to say you were shadowing me to recce…' Harry said the word awkwardly, '…to recce the Herschel as part of your astronomy film.'

'Well, I'll keep mum like last time, let you do the talking. Remember, if you get the chance, distract them so I can see if I can sniff out any paperwork.'

'Okay, but be careful young lady.'

Nathalie balked at the "young lady" bit. 'You do your bit and I'll do mine,' she retorted. 'I've done this sort of thing before; just leave it to me.'

'I'm sure you have,' said Harry remembering why he had contacted Bagatelle in the first place. 'I think we should go in. Can you see a doorbell?'

Nathalie looked around the entrance and saw a small camera high up on a ledge. She moved to one side and it followed her.

'I don't think we need a doorbell,' she said. 'They know we are here. I hope they haven't got sound on that thing.'

A sharp buzz emanated from the doors and they swung open. Nathalie led Harry inside towards a small hallway with black and white floor tiles. A carpeted staircase led upwards but, to one side, was a single stainless-steel elevator. As they entered the lobby, it arrived with a loud ding and a green light above the door which slid open.

'I believe this is for us,' she said still holding onto Harry's arm. 'There are no floor buttons to press so I assume we just step in.'

The elevator door slid quietly closed behind them and they felt a rush as they were propelled upwards. A gentle cushioned stop and the door opened as quietly as it had closed. They were met by a large moustachioed man in a pale cream suit. He held out his hand.

'I am so pleased that you have come to see us, Doctor Stones. I have read all of your papers. It's a privilege to meet you in person.'

Harry, sensing the man in front of him, proffered his hand and clumsily grasped his host's.

'It's a privilege to meet you too, Professor Petrov.'

Twenty

The nutty aroma of freshly brewed coffee cut through the cold metallic smell of the air conditioning. Petrov led Harry and Nathalie through a tiled antechamber to a modern but cosy open-plan office. Carpeted floor – unusual for this part of Spain – and tastefully upholstered easy chairs surrounded a smoked-glass coffee table. His enormous desk, carrying at least six computer screens, was ranged in the corner overlooking a large plate-glass window. The sea, reaching as far as the Western Sahara, could be seen sparkling in the distance. Petrov gestured for them to sit down.

'Please, take a seat. I've taken the liberty of preparing some espresso. I always take it black but I know the English…'

'No milk for us,' interrupted Harry finding an easy chair and lowering himself into it.

'Very kind of you. Just what we need,' added Nathalie. 'We've been up most of the night.'

'Of course, the terrestrial IR survey. I can't wait to hear about it,' said Petrov, making his way to a side door. 'Give me a minute, I'll fetch the coffee from the kitchen, and be with you.'

Nathalie waited until he passed through the door and listened for the wheezing and hissing of the espresso machine before she shuffled closer to Harry and whispered into his ear.

'Twelve-metre-square office, we are in one informal corner. There is a large desk against one wall containing computers and a dividing screen that I can only assume is an admin area with filing cabinets and smaller desks scattered with papers. When I get the chance I'll nosey around. There must be other rooms leading from the kitchen – the loo and so on. Later, you might want to take a bathroom break, ask him to guide you there.' She raised her voice to indicate that Petrov was returning. 'And so, I really think there's a great opportunity to film the observatory. We would need you to get permission of course.'

Petrov laid the tray on the table and passed around the espressos. Unlike a lot of people, he didn't seem awkward about placing one into Harry's outstretched hands.

'Sugar?' He noted the shake of heads. 'Oh, that's where we do differ. I like my coffee dark and sweet.' He stirred several heaped spoonfuls into the small cup. 'I couldn't help overhearing but, if you're trying to gain access to the Herschel for filming purposes, I have to tell you that WCMB have commissioned it for the next four weeks. Time's too precious for us to entertain a film crew I'm afraid.'

Not wanting to get off on the wrong foot Nathalie smiled. 'We haven't even had our programme proposal accepted yet. It could be months before we think of filming.'

Petrov took a sip of the bitter coffee. 'That's all right then. I would hate to upset a friend of Doctor Stones.'

'Not exactly friends, more acquaintances,' said Harry. 'The company Nathalie works for called me to see if I was interested in helping them make a scientific documentary; would they mind me showing a researcher around. I said fine as long as they didn't get in the way of *my* research. I have to say Ms Thompson here, as an observer, has been good as gold. I do hope you don't mind her coming with me today. I must admit there's a bit of quid pro quo as she's been very useful in helping me get around.'

Petrov placed his coffee cup back into its saucer. 'Of course not, I'm delighted to see you both. Now, I do hope you had a profitable evening last night. I believe the skies were clear.'

'On the top of the mountain, yes,' said Harry. 'An excellent session, broke a record on IR measurements. It will take some time to analyse the data obviously,' he added evasively.

Petrov was nodding, 'Of course, we look forward to reading

the paper. However I doubt if the terrestrial measurements will compare with our IR telescope survey. We hope to be producing the largest 3-D cosmological map by the end of the year. A major breakthrough for our science, don't you think?'

'I thought I heard that your satellite malfunctioned,' said Harry provocatively.

Petrov's reply was spoken in less friendly tones. 'A minor hiccup. We will be back on track soon, don't you worry about that.'

'Oh I assure you we're not, and, talking about on track, have you heard any progress from that new United States consortium? FastTrack I think they call themselves.'

'We focus on our own work, Doctor Stones; we have enough to do without analysing the data of others. I think the community will be very surprised at our latest theories. Our terrestrial work and large-scale structure surveys are tying in quite nicely.'

Harry drained his espresso and placed the cup deftly into the saucer. 'No chance of any early spoilers I suppose?'

Petrov started to clear the cups onto the tray. 'I think you know us better than that but, be assured, you will be one of the first to have the published paper across your desk.'

Nathalie was listening to this apparently mild banter with sinister undertones with amusement. Like a couple of boys squabbling about their football teams she thought. But the conversation didn't seem to be going anywhere so she nudged Harry with her knee. Harry could hear Petrov clearing the cups and took Nathalie's hint.

'Ah Professor Petrov, if you're taking those back to the kitchen, I wondered if you would guide me to the gents. Coffee seems to go straight through me these days.'

'Of course, I can manage the tray with one hand so, if you would like to take my other arm, I'll lead the way. It's a bit of a complicated route as we have to have a lobby between the kitchen and the toilets; health and safety I believe.' He turned to Nathalie.

Nathalie put up both her hands to demonstrate that she was

fine. 'Don't worry about me. I need to send a short text to my office anyway.'

She took out her phone as the two men made their way out of the office. She waited until their voices had faded before she got out of the chair and strode towards the computer desk. All of the screens were blank and so she tiptoed to the space behind the screen that she had described to Harry as the admin area. Papers were strewn everywhere. She ignored the printed journals with titles such as *Astrophysics and Space Science* and *Classical and Quantum Gravity* and focused on documents that looked like correspondence or e-mail printouts, but there was nothing of interest there. She heard Harry's voice booming in the distance. He was obviously talking loudly to alert her that they were returning. She was about to return to her seat when she noticed a thin blue file with an important looking Russian title. She opened it and spread out the contents. Shit, everything was typed in Cyrillic. Her heart began to beat faster as she heard footsteps. Taking a gamble she began photographing the documents with her phone. A loud crash came from the kitchen. She heard Harry's expletive.

'Bugger! Sorry, I made a wrong turn, hope I haven't broken your best china.'

The reply was indistinct but Petrov was obviously telling Harry not to worry. Nathalie used the diversion to slip the papers back into their folder and skipped back into her chair. As the two men returned to the office they found her engrossed, still tapping away at her phone.

The return taxi ride was more sedate than their journey to Las Palmas. The driver took the main road along the coast before cutting inland towards the mountain peak. Nathalie sat in the back seat alongside Harry nurturing her phone.

'I thought you said you didn't know who ran WCMB,' she said scrolling through her pictures.

'I didn't, at least I didn't before I telephoned to make the appointment.'

'What's that meant to mean?'

'Just what I said. I didn't know that Petrov ran the European HQ of WCMB.'

'You seem to know each other.'

'Never met before. We've heard of each other through cosmological journals. He was a bigwig at Moscow University, the doyen of gravitational waves. I only realised he was fronting WCMB when I called the secretary of the CEO. At first she tried to put me off but when she mentioned my name to her boss the path became clear. He must have been inquisitive to find out how this blind physicist operated.'

'Yeah, thought that was strange; he wasn't fazed at all by the fact you couldn't see.'

'That's me nowadays I'm afraid. More famous because of my so-called disability than my work on CDM.'

Nathalie sensed the bitterness in his voice. 'I think he was more angling for your observation results than to see how you were coping,' she said. 'He didn't seem a bit bothered by showing you to the loo.'

'I stayed in there as long as I could, and I had to fake a stumble to delay things further. Did you find something?'

'Well that's what I'm looking at now,' said Nathalie. 'Took some photographs.'

'Anything interesting?'

Nathalie held the pictures up to Harry, momentarily forgetting that he couldn't see them. She put the phone down again not telling him. 'I've no idea,' she said perfunctorily.

It was getting hot inside the cab; the aircon was obviously not working properly. Harry could feel that they were now snaking upwards towards the mountaintop where the air was cooler. He wound down the window.

'That's better. So have we wasted our time?'

The air from the open window swept across Nathalie's face blowing her hair into her eyes. She brushed it to one side and peered again at the photographs.

'Well it looks important, but I don't understand it.'

'Read it to me; I'll translate the science.'

'Oh it's not the science,' said Nathalie. 'It's written in Cyrillic. Even if you understand Russian I can't read it to you, I've no idea how to pronounce the letters.'

'What made you pick that one out?'

'There was a lot of random stuff in the office. Most of it in English but boring travel itineraries and telescope schedules. I'd almost given up when I saw this smart shiny blue folder on the corner of the desk. Looked like someone had forgotten to file it. It had a sticker on the front with red writing, you know, like you see in James Bond films, "Top Secret" and all that. Trouble was the writing was in Russian, or I assume it was in Russian. So I opened it up and took some pictures. Great move of yours that, the bull in a china shop scenario. He could have caught me red-handed. I was struggling to think of an excuse.'

'I knew you would stick your neck out. I thought I'd buy you as much time as I could.' Harry sensed that the car was slowing and wound up the window. 'So how do we find out what all this stuff says without getting arrested for espionage?'

'We're here,' said Nathalie opening the door of the cab. 'Oh I wouldn't worry about that. I've texted the photos to Stefanie at Bagatelle. She's very resourceful. We should expect a translation by tomorrow morning.'

The arrivals exit at Heathrow Airport had yet to recognise it was nearly June. The cold wind lashed the rain into Nick's Coburn's face as he pulled his Mac around him and tried to hail a cab at the same time. It was eight-thirty in the morning. He had taken off from O'Hare around six in the evening the previous day. Bloody Geoff Sykes had called him to say he wouldn't pay for another night at the Holiday Inn. He hadn't even been staying there for God's sake but there was no way he was going to explain that to Geoff. He told Sarah that he had to go to London for his paper and she had taken him to the airport to see him off; nearly killed him in that red car of hers on the way. She asked him to keep in touch and promised that she would look out for any satellite stories. The glint in her eye and the half smile on her face told Nick that she hadn't believed a thing about his cover story. Sarah was one-of-a-kind, he would miss her. The black-cab driver was a typical London cabbie so Nick wound him up with the latest political scandal, sat back in his seat, and closed his eyes for a nap while he let him drone on. He was woken with a jolt by the guy tapping on the dividing glass.

'Soho Square, mate. That'll be fifty quid.'

Nick rubbed his eyes, sat for a while listening to the throb of the ticking diesel engine and then reached for his wallet.

'Receipt please,' he said handing over the cash. He could hear Geoff's words in his head as he did it. 'Next time take the fucking train.'

Bagatelle Films had occupied this corner of Soho Square for more than thirty years. The brass nameplate had ceased to be polished and the engraved letters were filled with London dirt, but the entrance had had a facelift in the last few months and the glass doors opened silently as Nick pressed the doorbell. He looked up at the camera in the corner.

'Can't quite get used to all this Big Brother stuff,' he said into the microphone. 'Does it make me a cup of coffee? If so mine is strong and black.'

He was met by Stefanie on the first floor.

'Welcome back, Mr Coburn. If you want to go straight in his Lordship is waiting for you. Oh, and no doubt, Big Brother will bring you your coffee in due course,' she added with a smile.

Nick thrust a box of cheap duty-free perfume into her hand. 'Don't say I never think of you,' he said giving her a peck on the cheek. 'And no Scotsman's jokes, if you don't mind.'

Geoff was engrossed in some images playing on his large television screen and waved at Nick to sit in a chair opposite. Nick did so, picked up a ballpoint pen from the desk and started to click it in an irritating manner.

Geoff turned to face him. 'Do you have to do that?'

Nick persisted and tapped the pen even louder. 'If it gets your attention, yes. I've just come off a seven-hour flight at your beck and call, so one would expect a more pleasant greeting – nice to see you, Nick, or, hi, Nick, thanks for dragging your butt all the way back here. How are you?'

Geoff pointed the remote at the screen and shut it down.

'Oh a bit sensitive are we, being dragged away from your girlfriend?'

Nick threw the ballpoint at him. 'Strictly business, well strictly anyway. Told you, had to get close to dig out the information.'

'And did you? Dig out the information?'

'We found out about the crashed satellite didn't we? And, if you had let me stay longer, I'm sure we could have found out who did it.'

Geoff pulled out a file from his in-tray and flipped open the cover. 'The crashed satellite is now international news and I'm not sure you're impartial on the Sarah Nowak involvement in all of this.'

'She's got nothing to do with satellites – studies tiny particle things – and she is quite open to the possibility that another department of her company, FastTrack, could be involved somewhere. She's promised that she will keep an eye on that side of things.'

'Okay, let's start again. I called you back because you're worried about Nathalie. Correction, we're both worried about Nathalie. If what you suspect about Harry Stones is even half true, I'd like you to keep an eye on her. She knows you and trusts you. We don't even have to tell her about our doubts on Stones because, if we find out he's not involved, well I'll leave it to you to think about how she would react.'

Nick nodded, 'Wise man.'

Geoff picked up his file again and ran his finger over one of the pages. 'Right, let's see what we've got so far. Late February a Russian telescope satellite, owned by a company called WCMB, crashes into some space junk. Now, from Harry Stones's early notes, we find that between March and April a number of satellites were moved out of their orbit. However, in early May a media satellite veers into more space junk and is put out of action.'

Nick leaned forward and tried to peer at Geoff's notes. 'The media satellite? What's that got to do with us? I thought we were looking at astronomy type stuff.'

Geoff spun the paper round so Nick could see it more clearly. 'True, but at this stage we don't know who's doing this stuff or why. It could even be more than one person or outfit. What would make the programme interesting is the threat – Satellite Wars, Lawless Space, who controls the sky, and so on.'

Nick scanned the document briefly and gave it back to Geoff. 'If you put it like that. You've always had a way with spinning a story. Go on.'

'This is where Stones came in; said he had some information – mooted the idea about two cosmological companies in competition with each other – enough ambition to spike each other's operations.'

'Bet he didn't mention his own company's interest though,' interrupted Nick.

'No but, putting that to one side, let's see how things progressed.' Geoff turned to another page in the file. 'While Nathalie and he were checking out WCMB to see who would have an interest in taking down one of their satellites, we determined that their main competitor was an American sponsored company called FastTrack.'

'Of Sarah Nowak fame,' said Nick. 'Yeah I know that, move on.'

'Well, according to your report,' Geoff sighed, 'or rather your informal telephone call, one of the satellites that FastTrack are going to invest in was taken out by a navigation satellite, resulting in a thousand people dying in the Mediterranean Sea.'

Nick started drumming his fingers on the desk. 'Looks like someone is upping the game. Much more of this and it's going to be raining chunks of metal.'

'Which is why you're going to join Nathalie in her next location. Say Bagatelle are really keen to get this documentary out there, putting more staff onto the project. We've already got a researcher checking out some material that she found in the Spanish headquarters of WCMB. I'm sure Nathalie will be grateful for any further assistance she can get.'

'So where is this next location?'

Geoff looked down at his notes. 'Cleveland.'

Nick nearly exploded. 'Cleveland! You bastard, I've just spent nearly eight hours cooped up in an aeroplane that departed from Ohio.'

Geoff sat back, grinned, and lingered to enjoy the moment.

'No, Nick, not Cleveland, Ohio. You're going to Cleveland in Yorkshire. Hope you've got your hardhat. It's meant to have the deepest mineshaft in Europe.'

Twenty-one

The aircraft was full. It had an end of term atmosphere. Holidaymakers making their way back from the Canaries, package tours most likely. Nathalie and Harry were squeezed into the tiny seats in the back of the plane. It was all that was left, either that or travel first-class to Heathrow. Even Harry's academic tour budget didn't reach to that. Nathalie scrolled through the e-mail from Stefanie. It was full of apologies. First, the documents that she had received were not in Russian. They were in Kazakh. She thought she could find someone to translate but that would take a little longer. Second, the travel and accommodation arrangements were proving complicated. Harry had insisted that they visit the Rutherford Appleton Laboratory near Didcot before moving onto the Boulby mine in Cleveland. The Cambridge international airport had closed a year or two back and the train connections weren't great, so she had done the best she could with an economy trip to Stansted and a hire car. The hissing of the air ducts was nearly as loud as the passengers and Nathalie had to cup her hands to shout the itinerary into Harry's ear.

'A hire car? Well if it's better than changing trains a hundred times. I assume you've got a licence. I don't think they'd like me driving.'

Nathalie nudged him in the ribs. 'Yes, of course, but why can't we go direct to the mine? What's so special about the Rutherford?'

'I've a good friend there, Adam Brookes. He oversees the Harwell campus. You moaned about my going off-piste in Gran Canaria. Well, here I'm making up for it. We're going to kill three birds with one Harry Stones.' He chuckled at his own joke.

'Three birds?'

'Yes, the first is that Adam has access to one of the best departments of computing science in the country and, second, he's in charge of the underground laboratory in Cleveland.'

'And the third bird?'

'The people who are currently using part of that underground laboratory for their Cold Dark Matter experiment are called FastTrack.'

'You've been keeping that one up your sleeve.'

'Thought you'd be pleased. And I've even more good news. Our Trevor at Cosmat is feeling guilty about not tracking my satellites. Also, after the Mediterranean chaos, even Bernard is conceding that I'm not as crazy as he first thought. They've both pulled together and come up with some great data – orbits, trajectories, possible communication issues. What we need now is some equipment and the brains to digest it.'

A ding alerted Nathalie to the seatbelt sign.

'We are about to land. The Rutherford you say.'

'If their computing outfit can't crack it, nothing will,' said Harry buckling himself in.

The M11 wasn't busy and the hire car comfortable, so the journey to Cambridge was quite pleasant. Nathalie could sense from the smell in the air and the glittering chrome from the oncoming traffic that summer was coming to England. Less than an hour after they had touched down they could spot the doughnut-shaped Rutherford Appleton Laboratory set in the fields beyond. Harry showed his ID at the gate and they were greeted like royalty. One man in uniform took their hire car to a car park whilst the other drove them into the main site in an elegant golf buggy.

'Harry!' He was greeted like a long-lost friend.

'Adam,' said Harry wrapping his arms around the man in front of him.

Nathalie stood to one side, slightly uncomfortable, waiting for the two men to finish their hugging and backslapping. Harry was the first to break away.

'Adam, this is Nathalie, the young woman I was telling you about. Nathalie this is Professor Brookes,' he gestured with widened arms. 'The master of all you survey.'

Brookes laughed and shook Nathalie's hand. 'Pleased to meet you, Nathalie. Ignore this flatterer, it's simply Adam. Now come, from what I've heard, the two of you don't have much time.'

Brookes led them into the main building, up a short staircase and invited them into his office. It reminded Nathalie a little bit of Geoff's at Bagatelle – an efficient looking area with screens and a desk, a window with a view and an easy-chair comfortable corner.

'Please sit,' Brookes indicated to the easy chairs. 'Coffee is on its way. Where would you like to begin?'

'Did you get the data I asked Cosmat to send you?' asked Harry.

'Absolutely, my people are working on it as we speak. They didn't take much persuading after they heard it was to do with the *Diophantus* crash. The head of scientific computing said that with the two collisions they should have enough triangulation points to track down the source, if it's one person that is.'

Until the recent conversations on their flight this was all new to Nathalie. Now it seemed to be progressing faster than she had realised. If they could prevent a further collision it would be wonderful. If they could actually find the perpetrator it would be a coup for their documentary.

'How long do you think it will take?' she asked.

'Can't exactly say,' said Brookes, 'but they're the best in the business. Should have some solid results by the time you get back from Boulby.'

Harry intervened. 'Ah yes, Boulby. Adam, I encrypted the message because I didn't want to mention the real reason I was visiting. Are you okay with that?'

Adam tapped the table twice to reinforce his reply. 'Absolutely.

I can see where you're going with this Harry and why it needs to be confidential. If the people who are using the underground lab are involved, you don't want to alert them. On the other hand, if they're not, you could be open to a libel suit.'

Harry sensed Nathalie was shifting in her chair. 'Don't worry, Adam is an old friend. If he's to help us, there are things he needs to know. He's also asked us to limit the information we give him; not tell him anything he doesn't need to know. Happy?'

Nathalie turned to Adam Brookes, 'It's not that we're doing anything illegal here; in my business we like to protect our sources that's all.'

'Quite understand and, from what Harry here tells me, if you get to the bottom of this it should be intriguing.' He gave a broad grin. 'That's if I'm invited to the premiere.'

'We are a long way off that,' said Nathalie, 'hardly shot a foot of film yet.'

Brookes suddenly opened his mouth and pointed his finger in the air. 'Oh, that reminds me,' he began to search his inside jacket pockets and, after a bit of minor wrestling, pulled out an envelope.

'I was contacted by your office yesterday – very polite man called Geoff something – asked me if we would mind a film crew at the mine.'

'Geoff Sykes,' said Nathalie, wondering where the 'polite man' bit had come from. 'Yes, he's my boss. What did you say?'

'I said of course, any friend of Harry Stones… He's sending a crew to Boulby tomorrow. Says they'll be accompanied by one of your staff. A chap called…' he opened the envelope to read the name, '…Nick Coburn.'

Nathalie was trying to take all of this in when the coffee arrived. It was a useful break. Whilst Harry and Adam reminisced over old times, she gathered her thoughts to plan what she could best do with the film crew. If FastTrack staff were there at least they would have shots of both of their suspects. What on earth Nick Coburn was doing with the film crew God only knew. Scratch that, replace the word God with Geoff. She would have to have a word with him at the end of this meeting.

'Right,' said Adam as soon as they had finished their coffee. 'If you're going to film Boulby I better fill you in with the details. But before I go into the politics, if Harry doesn't mind, I'll tell Nathalie about the science.'

Harry shook his head in compliance, so Adam walked up to his whiteboard.

'As Harry may have told you, many of us are looking for the elusive Cold Dark Matter. Now I know you've been looking at telescopes and satellites, and I guess that makes sense. People are looking for the material that helps form the galaxies we can see out there. So why has the Rutherford got an underground laboratory looking for the stuff? The Boulby mine is one of the deepest in Europe. Over a kilometre down. Its main function was to mine potash but it's a fantastic place to do experiments. We have about twenty going on at the moment. Gamma spectroscopy and microbiology merely two of them. The CDM work has just been taken over by FastTrack. We have a contract with them for a minimum of two years. In that time they have access to the mine, can bring in new equipment, and so on.'

'Is there any connection with the satellite work?' asked Nathalie.

'Ah, not directly but satellite projects and small particle experiments are all needed to answer the same question.'

'The origins of the universe, the meaning of life, why we are here,' laughed Nathalie.

'It sounds funny when you put it like that but, yes, that is exactly the question.'

'So how do you find this stuff down a mine?'

'You really want to know?'

Harry stepped in. 'Yes, she will want to know.'

Brookes took out a felt pen and drew on the whiteboard.

'We are looking for something so dark, so cold and so small it's almost impossible to find. If we take a particle detector and point it around us, we get nothing but noise, too much noise from everything – radiation from the sun, particles flying through the air, emissions from the Earth. We estimate that the particle we're looking for would hit the detector about once a day. Impossible to distinguish it from the billions of other particles on the surface of the Earth.'

Brookes drew a primitive diagram on the board. The Earth's surface represented by the horizontal line, a narrow shaft and chamber at the bottom.

'If we go a kilometre underground most of the particles up here are absorbed by the rock. Dangle a detector here,' he pointed to the underground chamber, 'and you might find the one-a-day particle of Cold Dark Matter.'

'Sounds simple,' said Nathalie. 'A hole in the ground and a particle detector.'

'Would it *be* so,' sighed Adam. 'The problem is that the rock itself radiates particles. To get rid of these we have to build a large lead tank and fill it with pure water, put the detector inside, *then* we might find the one we are looking for.'

'And FastTrack are doing all of this?'

'They've been working there for about a month now. They were intending to link the results with the *Diophantus* project, but now who knows? After the crash there was a rumour that they might pull out, but their investment has been so large that I think they may look for time on another satellite.'

'Fits in with our tit-for-tat theory, Nathalie,' said Harry. 'If we can get close to them, maybe we can persuade some malcontent to talk.'

'Down that mine you are certainly going to be close to them. It's pretty claustrophobic down there, believe you me. Pitch-black without the light of the generators too.'

'Well that's where I have an advantage,' beamed Harry.

Nick recognised the film crew by their attire – three of them, blue denim jeans and white trainers. One was arguing with the station guard whilst the others were making their way to the baggage compartment.

'We have to pull out, Sir. Please would you mind stepping down from the train.'

The young man stood there, one foot on the platform the other on the carriage step. 'Not until we get our camera-kit off. It's not our fault the train is late.'

'You're obstructing the rail network...' started the guard officiously. He stopped suddenly as Nick put his large frame between the two adversaries.

'And you're obstructing a film crew going about their everyday business,' said Nick threateningly. 'I suggest you hold the train for two minutes whilst I help these guys with their gear.'

The guard looked Nick up and down and then at the green flag he was holding in his hand. He made a snap decision and put the flag behind his back.

'Good man,' said Nick. 'Now, if you could help us with a trolley.'

Within minutes the guys had manoeuvred the dimpled aluminium boxes from the train onto the platform.

The man on the train put out his hand. 'John McCord, I believe we've met before.'

'I do think we have,' said Nick. 'I've a people carrier in the car park, hope it's big enough to get us all in.'

John turned round and watched as the train moved out of Whitby Station.

'Thanks to you, at least we've got some kit to try and fit in. Don't think Nathalie would be too pleased, me turning up without a camera.'

It was a squeeze but the four of them, the six metal boxes and the two plastic cylinders just about fitted into the Volvo XC 90.

'Know by bitter experience the kind of stuff you guys carry,' said Nick pulling out of the car park. 'Was told this thing had the biggest boot space. Hell of a job to find a hire company that had one.'

'Appreciated,' said John. 'We've often had to hire two or even three cars when travelling by train. How far is it by the way?'

'About twenty miles.' Nick looked at the massive watch on his wrist. 'Should be there in approximately half an hour, just in time to meet up with Nathalie and this guy Stones.'

'Yeah, Geoff told us about him. Bit odd isn't it, first-class director like Nathalie handing over to a novice?'

'That's only the half of it,' said Nick pulling onto the main road. 'I'm here to keep my eye on that bloke, but you're to keep mum on that. Just do the job you're paid to do, you know, point that thing where they ask you to.'

John McCord laughed. 'I'll have a go, Nick. Trying for my fourth "best pointer" Academy Award this year.'

Nick joined in the laughter and put his foot down on the accelerator.

The tall slender tower with vapour falling from its top could be seen miles from the site. The mine buildings were surrounded by green fields, and a passing tourist would be surprised to know of the hundreds of metres of tunnels nearly a mile below them. It was a fine early June day and a warm breeze blew the few skimpy clouds across the clear blue sky, but Nick had been down a mine before and he pulled on his thick puffer jacket as he got out of the vehicle. Nathalie had already arrived and was waving at him from the other side of the Boulby car park.

'Hi Nick, good to see you,' she shouted. 'Over here, and ask the guys to bring their gear with them.'

Nathalie had worked with John McCord many times before and they greeted each other with a smile and a nod. John introduced the others.

'Nathan on sound and Jack the sparks,' he indicated.

John knew Nathalie's habit of always speaking to the soundman first and he busied himself unpacking the camera.

'I'm technically the producer on this one,' said Nathalie to Nathan, 'but the director is chatting to the laboratory staff so I'll fill you in. It's a kilometre deep down there. I don't know what to expect in terms of atmos but there will be the odd truck and machine I suppose. We are going to try and grab an interview; standard Sennheiser mic on a boom should do. Usual thing, we won't need the questions on mic, just enough to cue us in for the edit.'

She noticed that Jack had unpacked the lights and was walking up to her.

'Not sure what to expect,' he said. 'Normally mines are dangerous places for film lights. One small spark and we could have an explosion.'

Nathalie smiled, at least she had been given a pro.

'No need to worry, Jack, it's not a coalmine, it's potash; shouldn't be a problem, but thanks for the heads-up. I'll put you in touch with their engineer as soon as we reach the bottom. Okay with you?'

Jack nodded and moved over to help Nick who was loading the lights onto a flatbed trolley.

Nathalie looked around; all of the guys looked set. She raised her hand and pointed it towards the lift shaft like commanding a wagon train.

'Okay guys, let's go.'

A small changing room was adjacent to the shaft. Harry was already wearing his helmet and boots. Nathalie introduced him to the crew whilst they put their shoes in lockers and togged up.

'The director of the mine says that he will introduce me to the FastTrack team when we get to the bottom,' explained Harry. 'There are three of them at the moment – a technician and two scientists. One of them, a Doctor Webber, has agreed to do an interview. It would be good to get him standing next to the water tank. It's huge, apparently, and that would give some scale of the thing.'

The entrance to the shaft was daunting. A simple rectangular cage with a sliding open metal lattice gate, the diamond concertina type that one often saw in old movies. There were seven of them including the director and it was a tight squeeze to get them all in. The camera, lights and the sound recorder didn't help. A burly man drew the gate shut and pulled down a roll of tarpaulin across the door.

'Off you go,' he barked as he pulled the lever.

The lift dropped noisily, the tarpaulin rattling in the downdraught.

'Takes about ten minutes,' said the director. 'Works on a counterbalance system. The lift cage is held by a hook with a 4 cm spliced-metal rope.' He looked at their anxious faces. 'Don't worry it's very strong. When we want to get some trucks down there, we take out the lift and hang their bumpers on the hook.'

This did little to alleviate his passengers' disquiet.

'Oh and I ought to tell you,' he continued, 'you'll know when you're halfway down because you'll hear the counterbalanced cage coming up next to us.'

Five minutes later Nathalie was convinced that this explanation had saved her from suffering a heart attack. The amplified reverberation of the ascending adjacent cage was terrifying. It came with a distant rumble and ended with a climatic roar as it hurtled past them.

'Not quite like the elevator at the Empire State,' said John McCord wiping his brow.

Twenty-two

The cage landed with a jolt on the floor of the mine. The descent seemed to have taken hours rather than minutes and, apart from the director, the passengers breathed a sigh of relief. The tarpaulin was rolled up to expose a broad-shouldered miner – dirt smeared face and classic yellow hard hat. He roughly pulled open the latticed gate. In front of them was a long rectangular grey-walled tunnel disappearing into black. It was lit by a chain of circular lamps linked by looped electric cables. As the group moved out of the cage they looked up anxiously as they heard a reverberating growl echoing down the dusty corridor.

'Ah, your transport I believe,' said the director comfortingly. 'With the driver, should be large enough for five people and the camera equipment.' He glanced at the large man standing next to him. 'May I suggest for your comfort that Mr Coburn and I follow on in my small personal buggy.'

Two pinprick lights appeared out of the darkness, became larger, and morphed slowly into the headlights of a dumpster truck.

'All aboard,' said the driver. 'The lab is several kilometres away. If you want to record your interview and get out before the teatime rush I'd hurry. The guys there are waiting for you.'

The crew kicked into action. They were used to moving their gear around. John McCord sat with the camera on his lap next to Harry in the front bench seat, and the others squatted on the flatbed rear holding onto the rest of the kit. The dumpster did an acute U-turn and rumbled into the mine.

'Several kilometres you say,' said Nathalie. 'How long is this tunnel?'

The driver wrestled the wheel with one hand, manoeuvring the truck along the rough terrain.

'Not one tunnel, hundreds of them, some reaching many kilometres under the North Sea.' He pointed ahead of them. 'There, you see that fork in front of us, we're going right. If you took the wrong turn you could be a long time finding your way out.'

'Unbelievable,' said Nathalie, 'working in conditions like this. Dark, dusty and rough rock walls.'

'That's for us miners,' laughed the driver. 'You wait till you see the laboratory, all fancy in there. Surprised they haven't put up wallpaper.'

The mine was a maze and the driver weaved his way through the different tunnels. Some going off from their course were barely large enough to allow a man through, others large enough for a double-decker bus. Much of the route was lit by the cabled wall lights but, in other places, it was completely dark and the dusty grey road was only lit to a limited distance by the weak dumpster headlights. It was almost as if they were travelling through a monochrome film. Finally the driver began to slow down.

'Just round this corner. If you want to get a good shot of the tunnel entering the test site this will be the place – bare rock meets pristine space age laboratory sort of thing; always impresses.'

The crew leaped off the truck and John slid the long tripod out of the plastic cylindrical tube. While he was mounting the camera, noticing that the laboratory director had pulled up alongside, Nathalie took the opportunity to ask about electrical supply for their lights. It was apparent that other film crews had used this location before and Jack was soon plugging his Mizars and Redheads into convenient sockets lined against the wall. The driver was right about the contrast. The dark, crude rock tunnel opened out into a spotless white-walled area lit up by square panelled fluorescent lighting in the low ceiling. Men and women wearing white overalls and yellow helmets were wandering between brushed-steel cylinders and scientific instruments.

'Don't say it,' remarked the director, 'looks like a scene from a James Bond movie.'

Harry who had been standing close to John McCord coughed. 'John was just describing to me what the setup looks like. I won't tell them John if you don't.'

The director looked at his watch. 'Fascinating stuff but not the experiment that you are interested in. We stopped here because it's very photogenic. When you think you've got enough material we'll move on. The CDM experimental tank is further down the tunnel. It was constructed before the main lab so not such salubrious surroundings I'm afraid.'

Nathalie and John aided Harry by suggesting some generic shots.

'They'll be great for setting a scene,' Nathalie explained. 'We always need good pictures for laying over voice-over. Might be useful in explaining the lengths people will go to for scientific research – from a mile underground to a mile in the sky.'

'Fascinating,' said Harry. 'You're already editing the pictures.'

Nathalie could sense that the mine director was getting agitated. He kept looking at his watch and moving from one foot to the other.

'Are we okay for time?' she asked.

'If we go now, yes, but the mine will close down today at four. These scientists will leave first but there's only one way out and we don't want to get caught up in a queue for the lift.'

'Well we've got all we need here,' said Harry noting the urgency. 'What we really want is to talk to Doctor Webber. You go on with Nick to let him know we're coming and we will follow on.'

Jack was already de-rigging the lamps and so it was within minutes that they were driving into the darkness.

The water tank was a massive container of glittering lead blocks. It was set in its own carved-out cave. The dust from the walls of the rock was held back by large sheets of white nylon yet, in places, one could still see the scoured grey stone peeking through. This was a far cry from the sci-fi lab that they had just left. Nathalie noted that the director and Nick had parked their buggy by the entrance and were talking to three men, one of whom was gesticulating and pointing to the exit. The director turned and walked with the man towards the film crew's truck.

'Very sorry, we have a minor problem here. FastTrack's technician has noticed some fluctuations in the power supply. I'm afraid we'll have to go back to the surface to see if we can sort it out.'

Nathalie closed her eyes in frustration. 'You mean we can't even grab a quick interview while we're here?'

The director looked at his watch for the umpteenth time and sighed. 'I suppose you could, you mustn't be long though. I'll take the technician back to the lift shaft in my buggy and do a swift turnaround. You won't all get in the flatbed truck so I'll be as quick as I can.'

'Right,' said Harry, jumping off the truck. 'Nathalie, show me the way; let's not waste any time.'

The water tank was surrounded by a metal grid walkway which was accessed by an aluminium staircase. Two men were waiting for them at the foot of the steps. One put out his hand.

'I'm Doctor Webber, the project supervisor.' He turned to the young man next to him, 'This is Jerry Fairbanks, my assistant, responsible for maintaining the particle counter.'

Nathalie nudged Harry towards the man's outstretched arm but Harry was already moving towards the voice and holding out his.

'Pleased to meet you, Doctor Webber, Harry Stones. I understand we haven't got much time so I'll cut to the chase and ask you if you'll stand next to the tank for a brief interview. I believe you gave your permission to the director earlier.'

'That I did. Would you like Jerry to climb to the top and pretend he's checking the counter?'

Seeing Harry was looking puzzled he added, 'That's what the other film crew did anyway.'

Nathalie was trying not to interfere but she realised that time was slipping away.

'Great idea don't you think, Harry? If you stand in front of Doctor Webber and give him some idea of the questions you'll be asking, Nick and I will help the crew set up their kit.'

The interview began smoothly. John McCord surreptitiously let Nathalie look into the viewfinder. The shot looked great – Webber in the foreground and Fairbanks in the background inspecting some equipment on top of the water tank. The film lights kicked off the shiny lead structure which was set against the white nylon backdrop. John had angled them so that dramatic shadows were thrown across the background making the whole thing look quite surreal. Webber's answers reflected the story told by Adam Brookes but they were far more technical. The two scientists were becoming involved in their own interests and Nathalie was wondering when Harry would broach the satellite issue. The clock was ticking. She winked at Nathan, the sound-recordist, indicated he should cut by moving her finger across her throat and sidled up to Harry. She whispered into his ear.

'We need to do that again, in close-up. Remember we need it for editing. You also need to get onto our theme pretty quickly or we'll be whisked out of here by the director. He's due back any minute.'

Harry took the hint and explained to his interviewee that, for technical reasons, they needed to do some of the interview again in close-up. Webber seemed an old hand at this game and agreed without any objection.

Once more the interview started smoothly and, when Webber was in full flow about the importance of finding Cold Dark Matter, Harry struck.

'But surely you're falling behind in the race. From my understanding the satellite work is turning up with more answers. You don't seem to be able to compete in this field.'

Webber's face reddened and he was about to make a stern

rebuttal when a loud crackle from his intercom came from his overall pocket.

'I'm sorry I have to take this,' he said unzipping the pouch.

The whole crew heard the message. It was loud and urgent. The mine was being evacuated. There was instability in the power system and they needed to return immediately.

Nick Coburn looked around and did a quick calculation. There were nine of them. The dumpster, with a squeeze, could take six.

'If we leave the camera gear here we might all just get on,' he said, looking at the driver.

The lights in the cavern started to flicker.

'That's not an option,' said Nathalie. 'I'm the producer here. Two of us will have to stay behind and be picked up later.'

Nick was about to argue but he'd seen Nathalie in this mood before. It would waste precious time. His brief was to keep an eye on Harry Stones. He started to suggest that Harry and he should be the ones to wait behind for a second vehicle, but the driver had already spun the vehicle around and was beckoning them on.

'It's a no-brainer,' snapped Nathalie irately. 'Jerry is still at the top of the tank and the crew are my responsibility. The two of us will wait here. You're only wasting time. The quicker you go the quicker someone can return to pick us up.'

John McCord was already packing the gear onto the truck.

'She's right, standing around arguing isn't going to help. Besides there will already be a queue waiting at the lift shaft. We'll keep a place for you. By the time it's our turn to go up you should have caught up with us.'

The driver started to rev the truck. Nathalie stood defiantly at the back of the cavern. With nothing else for it, the others crammed onto the vehicle.

'We'll be fine,' shouted Nathalie, watching the disappearing taillights.

The cavern seemed eerily quiet after the growl of the truck faded down the tunnel. Nathalie looked upwards towards the young man standing on the gantry that spanned across the vast tank. He was bending over slightly, lowering a long wire into the water.

'You okay up there?' asked Nathalie.

The man continued tinkering with the equipment without responding.

'I said, are you okay up there?' she repeated.

He paused for a moment and looked over the side of the tank.

'Securing the collection unit,' he said rather brusquely. 'You can come up and see if you want.'

Nathalie realised it would be a few minutes before the truck returned and so she started to climb the aluminium staircase. The noise of her heavy boots made a metallic sound that echoed around the chamber. The location distorted the perspective of the tank and it was higher than it had seemed from ground level. There was no rail to the staircase or the surrounding gantry and she felt quite insecure.

'Come across to the middle,' said Fairbanks and, seeing that Nathalie was staggering a little, added, 'crawl if you find walking a bit precarious.'

The last thing Nathalie wanted was to seem anxious about the situation but the climb had made her recurring dizziness return.

'Give me a moment I'll just steady myself,' she said, looking straight ahead and trying to regain her balance.

'Up to you,' said Fairbanks in an offhand manner.

Nathalie started to inch her way across the walkway trying not to look down at the crystal-clear twenty-metre-deep volume of water beneath her. She was barely a third of the way across when Fairbanks stood up straight and turned to face her.

'So what are you guys really up to?' he asked quietly.

Nathalie was taken aback. She already felt a little shaky. What was this young man on about?

'Don't pretend you don't know what I'm talking about,' continued Fairbanks. 'You're with that guy Stones. I've heard all about him and his so-called investigation.'

Nathalie tried to clear her head. 'I'm sorry?'

'You will be, if you and Stones keep sabotaging our work.'

'I beg your pardon?'

'Colleague of ours, in Chicago, says she thinks that Cosmat could be up to dirty tricks.'

Nathalie was beginning to wonder if her concussion was making her hallucinate.

'Cosmat? Dirty tricks?'

'You heard me. And now that we are stuck out on this gantry, why don't you tell me all about it?'

'What in the hell are you talking about?' asked Nathalie indignantly, temporarily forgetting her unsteadiness. 'Are you threatening me?'

'If that's how you see it,' said Fairbanks menacingly. 'You've been following the guy around. What's he up to?'

Fairbanks began to slowly move towards her. He had a large hooked pole in his hand that he had been using to lower the particle detector into the water. He held it between his hands like a tight-rope walker. In normal circumstances, Nathalie would have turned and skipped the ten or so metres back to the gantry but she was still tottering from waves of nausea. She started to shift backwards. The enormous boots on her feet didn't help as the crenulated souls kept wedging in the grille. She decided to try to play for time.

'So what do *you* think he's up to?' she said mimicking his words. 'And what's this colleague of yours got on Cosmat?'

'Nothing specific, but it makes sense. Who else would try to scupper both us and WCMB?'

'WCMB? What have they got to do with it?'

'That's what I'm asking you. You two have been sniffing around our research outfits, probably trying to get a heads-up on unpublished stuff. The big guy even tried to check out our Fermilab work.'

'You're losing me,' said Nathalie, realising that every step she took backwards was followed by Jerry Fairbanks taking a step towards her.

'Academic espionage I think they call it.' He stumbled slightly but steadied himself with the pole.

'Absolute rubbish,' said Nathalie. 'It's just like-minded scientists exchanging ideas.'

'Exchanging ideas is one thing, sabotage is another.'

He was now close enough to Nathalie that she could see from his expression that he had almost forgotten where he was standing. She looked down at the water, things were getting dangerous.

'What sabotage?' she protested.

The hook of the pole he was holding wavered alarmingly close to her midriff. 'That's what you can tell me,' he said. 'Two astronomical satellites crash within six months of each other; a bit of a coincidence don't you think?'

It was now dawning on Nathalie what this young American was on about.

'You can't think Harry Stones had anything to do with that can you? He's the one trying to find out who did it.'

Fairbanks was now gesticulating at her.

'Great cover, don't you think? Who has most to gain from the demise of those two satellites? Not one of Cosmat's was it?'

Nathalie tried to steady herself. The pole, balancing in his hands, was looking precarious. She looked around the chamber. The lights were still flickering and her dizzy spells were getting worse. She listened vainly for the returning truck. Not a sound, just the echo of their voices.

'Look, Jerry,' she said trying to address him in more informal terms. 'I've known Harry for several weeks now, he's not the sort of person...' she paused as she remembered the evening in Gran Canaria, a different side to Harry perhaps.

Fairbanks noticed the hesitation. 'Not the sort of person to use everything he's got to publish first? The guy's an obsessive. He's also very clever. How many other people do you know with the ability to track and manoeuvre satellites?'

Nathalie put her hands up, 'Okay why don't we wait to get out of here and confront him with it?' she said.

'Not that easy, he will deny it of course.' He made another step towards her. 'Whereas you, you are in no position not to tell me the truth. Admit it, you and Harry Stones…'

He didn't finish the sentence – with an almost silent 'pop', the whole cavern was plunged into darkness.

Twenty-three

John McCord was right about the queue. It stretched for many metres down the tunnel. Grimy faced miners were shaking their heads as they impatiently waited for the lift to return underground. They hadn't passed the director's buggy in the tunnel and Nick anxiously looked around for someone who could help.

'Any of you guys know where the director is?' he asked, pushing his way through the crowd.

'Gone up top,' said one of the miners. 'You with the film crew?'

'Yes. He said he would go back to pick up our remaining crew,' said Nick.

'Oh right. He was in a bit of a hurry but told me to tell someone to turn the truck around and go back and fetch them. Got a few problems on his hands. The power seems to be shutting down section by section. The whole mine has to be evacuated. No problem for your guys though. Even if the lighting goes in the tunnels, the driver knows his way and the dumpster's got headlights.' He gestured to the long queue in front of them. 'They'll be back long before this lot is cleared. Bloody scientists, last in first out. I've just had an eight-hour shift and need my tea.'

Nick turned, shoved his way through the agitated group of miners, and began searching for the film crew. But he was too late. Harry Stones must have also heard the news for, as Nick broke through the knot of men, he saw Harry, next to the driver of the dumpster, tearing down the tunnel.

'Shit,' exclaimed Nick. Running after them was useless. He shouted angrily to no one in particular. 'Anyone got another vehicle down here?'

*

The driver sensing Harry's urgency put his foot down on the accelerator. The truck veered and bumped violently across the uneven floor.

'Don't you worry, know this route like the back of my hand. We'll be with them in a jiffy,' yelled the driver over the echoing noise in the tunnel.

Harry held onto the side of the truck counting the turns. Even with his impaired sight he could tell when they passed through areas with and without lighting. It concerned him that, in the lit sections, he could gauge that the lights had started to flicker.

'Overheard that sections of the mine were losing power,' he shouted. 'Do you know what sectors are affected first?'

'The ones furthest away from the pit shaft. It's happened once before. Bang, bang, bang – one pocket after another. Took an entire day to get the whole thing back up and running.'

'You mean, the water tank cavern might already be in darkness?'

'Probably, but the young scientist guy in there knows what he's doing. They just need to keep still and sit tight.'

Nathalie and the young scientist were certainly not sitting tight. Once they had recovered from the initial shock of total darkness, Fairbanks started waving the pole frantically about trying to find the edge of the tank. Fortunately, Nathalie heard the swish and had ducked in time, otherwise she would have been pitched headlong into the water.

'Keep still Jerry,' she shouted. 'You'll take both of us in.'

'Keep back then,' his voice was panicking. 'Get out of the way; I need to get to the side.'

'I think it's best if we both sit down and wait,' said Nathalie, trying to keep him calm. 'Do you have a mobile phone on you?

You could switch on the light. I was told to leave mine on the surface.'

'Stupid woman, we all have to leave our phones up there; anything that could interfere with the experiment.'

Nathalie remembered how Brookes had told her that any small radiation from electrical circuits or batteries could interfere with the results. 'Of course, sorry Jerry. I should have known that. Will the change of lighting affect your work in any way?' she asked trying to engage him in a harmless conversation.

'I know what you're doing,' he snapped, 'trying to change the subject. Well it won't work.'

Nathalie felt a sharp point of pain as the pole found her ribs.

'Careful Jerry, keep that pole still. It's pitch-black in here. Wait until the lights come on.'

'Fuck the lights, we were talking about Stones. Admit it, he's the one manipulating the satellites.'

Harry Stones had more to worry about than satellites at that very moment. The truck he was careering in suddenly came to an abrupt spluttering halt.

'Don't believe it,' spat out the driver. 'Last night's shift has only forgotten to refuel the tank.'

'Can you walkie-talkie for help?' asked Harry.

'Haven't got one with me,' said the driver. 'Normally no need.'

'Well this isn't "normally",' hissed Harry in frustration. 'We need to get those guys, and we need to get them quickly.'

The driver was already climbing out of the truck. 'You just sit tight. I'll go back to fetch a can of diesel. Be as quick as I can.'

Harry had no idea if the driver knew he was blind or not and decided not to enlighten him anyway. He waited until the footsteps had almost receded before getting down off the dumpster and delving into his overall pockets. He pulled out his telescopic cane and began tapping his way down the tunnel towards the water tank cavern.

The cavern was in absolute darkness. There was no way that Fairbanks could tell where Nathalie was other than from the sound of her voice. He was merely thrashing out with the pole blindly looking for the edge of the tank. She decided her best course of action was to keep low and stay quiet.

Fairbanks was becoming more frenetic.

'Tell me won't you, tell me all of it. He took down WCMB's satellite didn't he? And if that wasn't enough, he took down the one we were going to invest in.'

It was pointless Nathalie trying to argue with him. He had made up his mind. Any movement or sound she made would put her in the reach of that damn pole. She lay flat on her stomach and peered into the darkness. Normally one's eyes would get used to the dark but, here, there was no light at all – completely pitch-black. She heard the swish of the pole above her head.

'You can't have reached the side yet, I would have heard you.' Fairbanks was breathing hard, pants of breath in between his words. 'It's a conspiracy isn't it? Spike the opposition, take all the glory. Well I've not spent years at university and crawling to the FastTrack hierarchy to lose out now.'

Nathalie heard his heavy mining boots clatter on the caged floor of the narrow bridge spanning the tank. He was inching towards her.

Harry was making good time. It was easier navigating the tunnels than the open spaces above ground. It was evident, from the little he could normally see, that the mine was now in complete darkness. He tapped his stick along the side wall. He had a good sense of direction. Once he had walked a route he could usually do it again. Although he had been seated in the truck on the way in he remembered the turns. Make a mistake now and he could be wandering forever through this underground maze. He passed the area of the first underground laboratory. Not a sound came from it. He shouted out anyway.

'Anyone there?'

He didn't expect a reply. The scientists had been told to evacuate some time ago. The water tank cavern would be now only a few hundred metres away. He started to speed up. It was a mistake. He tripped and fell face down onto the bare rock floor. Getting up he spat the dust from his mouth and continued, this time more slowly, tapping his way down the tunnel.

In a few moments Fairbanks would be upon her. If his large boots stood on her it would be hard to keep her balance. She tried to creep backwards, not turning around but shuffling crablike, one leg at a time.

'Is that you?' snapped Fairbanks hearing the rustling noise. 'Have you reached the edge yet?'

Nathalie heard the pole rattle on the gantry. He was obviously swinging it out in front of him, along the walkway, trying to reach for the side. She tried to move more quickly but her foot caught in one of the stanchions. The pole grazed her face. She heard a piercing metallic noise as he brought it down sharply on the metal grille.

Harry heard a scream. From his calculations he was about fifty metres from the cavern. He attempted to make longer strides.

'Nathalie, are you all right? It's Harry.'

There was no articulate response. Yet a strange noise echoed around the tunnels; a heavy thud, slapping water, and a haunting gurgling sound. Harry repeated his call.

'Nathalie!'

The entrance to the Sputnik Hotel was bathed in thirty degrees of Kazakhstan sunshine. Not that it eased the butterflies in Jenny Kang's chest. She had been dreading this moment ever since that awful pay-as-you-go phone had rung. After her garden encounter with the MalaySat gang she had been expecting it. 'An amazing prospect', Zikri had said. 'Put yourself on the company's map, our brightest representative'. Like hell, she thought. More like a sheep thrown to the wolves. Any slip-up and they would, of course, deny all responsibility. Checking in at reception brought back the memories of her abduction to that awful farmhouse, a sinking feeling in her stomach. But what else could she do? On the surface she had been given the privileged position to represent MalaySat as their senior negotiator. Bykov and Molchalin had nearly fallen over themselves to get her to attend a satellite launch. A wonderful opportunity for you to see how we operate in action they had said. Of course, WCMB wouldn't mind her attending the launch. Their team would be arriving in the next few days. The more publicity they had for their new satellite the better. What the Cosmodrome guys didn't know was that her briefcase contained a brand-new laptop; one whose disc-drives had been specifically partitioned by the man who called himself Kenneth. All she had to do was plug it into her hotel router and feed him back the data. That was for tomorrow. This evening she had to face that terrible room again and try to get some sleep.

The next morning was as bright as the day of her arrival. The sun streamed in the small uniform hotel windows. Jenny pushed her breakfast around the plate. She wasn't hungry and, unlike the weather, felt anything but sunny. The mobile phone vibrated in her pocket. She glanced at the screen with dread and was relieved to see that it was a text rather than a call.

Defer data collection until 18:00 hours.
A few more tweaks needed at this end.
K.

Jenny took in a long deep breath. She didn't know whether this was good or bad news. Good because it put off her dreaded task. Bad because she had to kill time until then. She pushed her plate to the middle of the table, grabbed her coffee cup and returned to her room. She removed the laptop from under the mattress where she'd hidden it and lifted the lid. At least she could check things over and make sure everything worked. It would be terrible if something like the battery failed when she logged on at six o'clock. She pressed a few keys. Battery fully charged. She took out the cable from her case and linked the computer to the hotel router. A perfect fit. Next how to open the partitioned drive. It had been hidden and encrypted and was not easy to access. The codes were written alongside the crossword in the copy of the *Malay Mail* in her suitcase. Why they had to go to that extent she didn't know. She fished out the newspaper and, seeing it was torn, panicked. She frantically turned to the puzzle page and gave a sigh of relief when it was still intact. Everything was now in place; she could relax. She lay back on the bed and closed her eyes and immediately opened them again when she heard a loud knock. Her heart began racing. Not again. She had visions of a uniformed guard standing behind the door.

'Who is it?' she asked timidly, the words hardly coming out of her mouth.

'Reception, Ma'am.'

'What do you want?'

'A message from the Cosmodrome.'

Jenny leaped off the bed, pulled the cables out of the router and snapped the laptop shut.

'One moment.'

She couldn't think or act fast enough. She wasn't expecting anyone. The meeting at the Cosmodrome wasn't until tomorrow morning. What did they want? What could be wrong? She pushed the laptop and newspaper under the mattress.

'Coming.'

The maid was waiting at the door with a note. She looked at Jenny's flushed face with puzzlement.

'Did you wish to reply, Ma'am?'

Jenny tore open the envelope and read the invitation to dinner. She closed her eyes trying to calm down.

'Ma'am?'

Jenny opened her eyes again suddenly. 'Oh yes, sorry, of course. Please tell Mr Bykov I would be delighted to accept.'

The day passed slowly. Felt more like weeks than hours. Jenny hated her room but there was little outside other than a small verge of grass around the hotel with the view of burnt plains blurring into the distance. After she had walked round the block twice she plumped for the hotel bar. The waiter didn't speak English other than the phrases, 'What can I get you?' and 'You're welcome'; so Jenny spent her time nibbling nuts, drinking soda water, and playing a computer game on her smart phone. The digital clock eventually crawled around to 17:30. She nodded to the waiter, drained her fifth soda and took the stairs to her room. She repeated the actions that she had rehearsed earlier: removing the laptop from under the mattress, inserting the cable and switching it on. Kenneth had discreetly implanted the link to the encrypted drive under the word *functions* displayed in the control panel. Jenny clicked on the icon and a new screen appeared – black with luminous green panels. The computer's clock in the corner showed 17:52. Eight minutes to go. It was vital that she entered the code at exactly 18:00 hours. One mistake and the computer would shut down and erase the drive. Her heart skipped a beat as she felt under the mattress for the newspaper. In her panic earlier she had pushed it further in than she had realised. She found it at last and using two fingers pulled it from the bed.

'Shit!' she exclaimed, as the paper started to rip.

'Oh no,' she cried, as she noticed that the tear sliced across the puzzle page.

It was now 17:58. Only two minutes to go. She frantically tried to read the code letters. They had been written in ink alongside the crossword, appearing as if someone was manipulating letters for an anagram. They were all legible apart from one. The gash in the paper had split a letter. It was either a V or a W. The computer's clock was counting down. Kenneth had told her that the code could only be entered once. Her hands were shaking. There were only a few seconds left, she would have to start typing. Fourteen of the fifteen characters flashed back at her in luminous green. One space remained. There was nothing else for it but to guess. She had a fifty-fifty chance. Her finger hovered over the W but on an instinct she drew it down and hit the V. Nothing happened. The computer didn't shut down but neither did the page react. She was about to phone Zikri on her pay-as-you-go mobile, something he had strictly instructed her not to do, when the computer beeped.

Kenneth's voice came through the speaker.

'Good, now reboot your router.'

Typical Kenneth, no greeting, no well done. She walked over to the small cream-plastic router in the corner of the bedroom and switched it off and on again. When the little blue light started to flicker she moved back to her laptop which was sitting on the bed.

She knelt on the floor and watched the screen which was coming alive with scrolls of green digits. Kenneth's voice appeared again.

'Right-hand, top screen. A graph of spikes. When it settles, write down the number the longest spike is pointing at.

Jenny had been briefed to use paper and not electronic devices for recording and already had a pen in her hand. She wrote the number onto her newspaper.

'Now, left-hand bottom screen. Same procedure.'

Jenny watched the animated graph in the small panel, looking like some sort of seismograph. She waited till it froze and took down the number.

'Got it?'

Jenny didn't know what to do, could he hear her at the other end?

'Just nod, I can see you.'

She looked into the little camera iris on the laptop and nodded.

'Good. What you have there is the geographical coordinates of the location where the strongest signal was bounced – should be within a hundred kilometres of you. Check it out, use the same code, and report back tomorrow at the same time.'

Jenny was about to ask what 'check it out' meant when the screen went black. She tapped on the space bar but all that did was return the screen to her original desktop display. Kenneth was no longer in the ether. She looked at the figures she had written down on the newspaper. Now she could see that they were numbers of longitude and latitude. There was no way she was getting a paper map of the local area in this hotel. There was only one thing for it. She opened Google Maps.

Twenty-four

Nebo's restaurant was full. Bykov had reserved a corner table near the window. The waiters fussed around and served them complimentary drinks.

'I'm so glad you could accept my invitation,' he said. 'I'm a regular so they fitted us in.' He gestured around the restaurant, 'Coachloads of tourists, booked-in to see the new launch in two days' time no doubt.'

Jenny played with the coloured paper umbrella that was sticking out of her drink.

'Very kind of you to invite me, Mr Bykov,' she said. 'I'm a bit embarrassed. It should have been my turn; you did the honours last time.'

Bykov raised his hands in protest, 'Not at all, it's my pleasure. After all, we are the hosts, and please call me Valery.'

'Well, thank you, Valery. Will Mr Molchalin be joining us?'

Bykov was looking around the restaurant and raising his hand to attract the waiter's attention. 'I'm afraid not, he has to attend to security issues for the forthcoming launch. I'm sure you'll understand. He'll be disappointed. I've pre-ordered the roast goose, the house speciality. It's a favourite of his. I think I mentioned it when you visited before.'

Jenny didn't want to think too much about her last visit to the restaurant. She had been recovering from the shock of her interrogation. Fortunately, before she had time to say anything, the waiter arrived with two plates of steaming hot food. Bykov smiled and nodded for her to start. They ate in silence for a while. The goose was surprisingly good. After some minutes Bykov began, as most corporate negotiators do, with small talk – the weather, the forecast being perfect for the forthcoming launch, the local wine, and hobbies. He was an ardent golfer apparently. Jenny jumped on the opportunity.

'Do you like horse racing? I hear Kazakhstan is famous for... what do they call them, golden horses?'

Bykov dabbed his lips with his napkin. 'Ah yes, the breed is called Akhal-Teke, they are wonderful beasts. As for actual horse racing, not for me I'm afraid. Why, does it interest you?'

'Love it,' said Jenny trying to sound excited. 'I would really be interested in visiting an authentic Kazakh stud farm. I believe there is one not too far from here.'

Jenny thought that her host appeared a little uncomfortable at the mention of the farm. Her instinct was confirmed by Bykov's reply.

'I would like to give you a tour but I'm afraid it's private, not open to the public. Do you have any other interests?'

It was obvious he was trying to change the subject. Jenny continued to probe.

'Oh what a shame. From the map it looks quite a large set-up. Do you not have any contact there, Valery, you seem a well-connected person?'

She could see him squirming. She was using his first name, being convivial and hinting the favour would ease the negotiations somewhat.

'I really would if I could, Miss Kang...'

She interrupted him, turning the screw. 'Oh please call me Jenny. You must know who runs it.'

Realising he was being backed into a corner Valery Bykov took a sip from his drink to buy himself a little time.

Jenny pressed her advantage. 'It's only about fifty kilometres from the Cosmodrome. At least you must know something about the place.'

Bykov grasped that he had to give some sort of answer. 'Not a lot. As I said, I'm not really interested in horse racing but it's owned by the Usenov family. They come from the Far South.'

'The south?'

'It's where the uranium comes from. The Usenovs own most of the mines down there. That's where they made their money, and other things...' Bykov tailed off.

Jenny leaned forward, sensing a story. 'What other things?'

'I shouldn't have mentioned it, just a rumour.'

'You can't stop now, Valery.'

'Arms dealing. People say that's why they moved up here. The stud farm is located within the borders of the Russian-leased district of Baikonur. Different jurisdiction.'

'I knew the Cosmodrome was controlled by the Russians; didn't realise that the area reached as far as that.'

'Yes, the area leased is a sort of ellipse, reaching nearly a hundred kilometres across. Usenov's stud farm is just inside, surrounded by barbed wire and heavy security. That's why I can't get you in. He doesn't like visitors, keeps himself to himself.'

'So who's this "he"?'

'The head of the family, a guy called Miras Usenov. Recluse billionaire.' Bykov scooped up the last piece of food from his plate. 'I've said more than I should have. Dessert?'

Jenny knew better than to push him further. She had got most of what she wanted anyway. She accepted the invitation of a dessert and moved the conversation onto business. The satellite launch was not until the day after tomorrow but she had been invited to see some of the preparations. By the time the coffee had arrived a meeting had been set up for a rendezvous at the Cosmodrome the next morning. If she played her cards right, she might persuade the driver to take a small detour to pass the stud farm in the afternoon.

As Bykov had predicted the next morning the weather was still holding. Clear blue skies framed the desert steppe of Baikonur. It was the ideal location for launching rockets. In the early days there were stories of debris crashing down on the surrounding farms. Many of these had now been compulsorily purchased and rockets had become more sophisticated. Very little news about mishaps occurred anymore. Jenny's taxi arrived on time. She had insisted on hiring her own driver and Bykov hadn't objected, as the Cosmodrome limousine fleet had been allocated to WCMB who had commissioned the launch. The car overtook a coachload of tourists heading towards the centre, possibly the same crowd who were in the restaurant last night. Cosmodrome tours were becoming increasingly popular and the locals were capitalising on the influx of trade. The visitors would of course be using the public entrance and start by visiting the Space Museum. Jenny, on the other hand, had a private pass – *Access to all areas* it read. Valery Bykov had certainly set out to impress.

Antatole Molchalin met her at the gate.

'Good morning, Miss Kang, I'm so pleased to meet you again. I understand that you had the roast goose at Nebo's. I was quite jealous.'

'It was excellent,' smiled Jenny. 'We missed your company.'

Molchalin widened his arms and gestured around the compound. 'Work I'm afraid. Security here has to be tight in normal times, but just before a launch…'

'Quite understand. Valery said he would show me around the control tower.' Jenny stressed the word Valery. 'Meet some of the people who have commissioned the launch, an astronomical satellite I think he said.'

'An astronomical telescope, yes, but I can assure you that the procedures for media satellites are just the same.' Molchalin stood to one side and indicated towards a glass door at the bottom of, what looked like, an airport traffic control tower. 'Please, after you. Valery is with his other guests now.'

The top of the tower held spectacular views over the Baikonur plains. Glass panels laid out in a hexagonal format allowed a three-hundred-and-sixty-degree panorama. Behind them the ochre-burnt brush of the steppes, to the front the impressive launch pad containing a flame deflector and the framework of the launcher. Inside the framework was a glistening silver and white rocket. Bykov was hunched around the control desk talking to a group of people. He heard Jenny and Molchalin arrive from the lift and turned to greet them.

'Good morning, Miss Kang, Anatole. I would like you to meet Professor Petrov from WCMB.'

Jenny shook his hand, introduced herself as a representative of MalaySat, and thanked him for allowing her to attend.

'Not at all, Miss Kang, all too pleased to share experiences with fellow satellite aficionados.' He waved his hand towards the other members of his team. 'Here are some of my colleagues who have just arrived from the other side of the world. Hope you understand but I won't introduce you individually as they are a little preoccupied at the moment.'

Jenny looked towards the group. They were all men, two with their backs towards her adjusting some of the controls, and another who nodded acknowledgment before turning to peer at the rocket through a set of binoculars. She tried to make a mental snapshot. The small bald-headed man was talking to a guy with long blond hair who had now moved from the desk-controls to his laptop. The man with the binoculars had an Eastern European look – dishevelled suit, pale skin, greasy black hair. The suntanned Petrov was more impressive – large frame, moustache and pressed, cream summer jacket. Zikri had told her to make a note of any of her hosts' contacts. Bykov and Molchalin were still their prime suspects but there was always the possibility of conspirators.

The morning passed quickly. Bykov was keen to involve Jenny at every stage – the preparations for the launch, mounting the satellite onto the bus, checking the fuel load and starting the countdown. After her initial introduction, the WCMB people kept themselves to themselves and became engrossed in checking the calculations. Bykov explained the procedures and the accuracy to which they were working. She had to admit, it was all very impressive. If she really did have the money to commission a satellite launch she would be signing on the dotted line. At the end of the session she accepted the offer of a light lunch and afterwards made her excuses. She had work to do back at the hotel – communicate with her office, draft commissioning proposals, and juggle with a few budgets. She thanked everyone for their hospitality and said she looked forward to watching the forthcoming launch. Molchalin escorted her to the exit where her taxi driver was still patiently waiting.

When booking the cab Jenny had made sure that the driver spoke English. When he had picked her up she found he wasn't as fluent as she had hoped but they had got by. She waited until Molchalin was out of sight and told the driver that she had a change of plan. Instead of returning to the hotel she would like to see some of the district. Could they go to Ayteke? At first the driver didn't understand her pronunciation. She repeated the word and reached over his shoulder to show him the town on her mobile phone map. Fortunately the road was straight for he took the phone from her hand and peered at it closely. The car started veering from side to side.

'Ah, Ayteke,' he said. 'You want to go tomorrow?'

Jenny snatched back her phone praying that the driver would keep his eyes on the road. 'No, not tomorrow, today,' she said.

'Hotel this way,' he said pointing straight ahead. 'Ayteke, that way,' he said pointing to the west.

'I know. I have all afternoon, I want to see the town.'

'See the town,' said the driver.

'Yes,' said Jenny. 'Ayteke,' she repeated trying to correctly pronounce the word. 'How long?'

It was obvious that the driver didn't understand. She leaned over the front seat again and pointed to her watch and then towards the west. 'Ayteke, how long?'

Finally, the driver got the message. 'Hour?'

'Okay, let's go,' she said sitting back in the seat.

She waited apprehensively wondering if he had really

understood her but she relaxed when the car turned west onto the M32. The terrain was flat and the road smooth so they made good headway. She tracked their progress on her phone's GPS. The signal was pretty good, the beacons must have been installed as a result of the Cosmodrome. Her next challenge was to persuade the driver to turn off the motorway towards the stud farm. She waited until they were about a kilometre from the junction before she tapped him on the shoulder.

'Would like to see horses,' she said. 'Farm near here.'

The driver pretended not to hear.

Jenny tapped harder. 'Please stop I would like to see horses.'

The driver pulled over to the side of the road. 'No horses here,' he said. 'We go to Ayteke.'

'No, I've changed my mind, I would like to see the horses.' Jenny pointed towards a green riverbank meandering through the dry scrub. 'The stud farm is over there. Next left.'

The driver looked anxious. 'No horses, we go to Ayteke.'

Jenny pulled out a bundle of American dollars; she knew the currency had kudos here. She waved them in front of the driver's face.

'I see the horses, I give you the dollars.'

'It's private, very private. Bad men there.'

Jenny added to the bundle.

'Horses – dollars.'

She could see that the driver was in a dilemma. The money in her hand was probably worth two months' wages.

Eventually the sight of the green bills got the better of him. 'Okay we go, but not too close.' He ran his fingers across the seat like a little walking man. 'I drive, you...' he struggled for the word.

'Walk the rest,' completed Jenny.

'Yes, money now.'

Jenny divided the wad of dollars into two, one bundle in each hand. She offered him the ones in her right hand. 'Half now, half later,' she said.

He took the bills, thrust them into his top pocket, nodded and put the car into gear.

The turnoff was not signposted. The side road began smoothly enough – metal surface, tidy verges – but it soon deteriorated into a rough trail, grass down the middle, worn gravel tracks. As they neared the river the foliage became greener. Trees and manicured fields appeared on either side. The driver slowed as they approached a bridge. He pointed to the front of him.

'I stop here. Horses there,' he said.

Jenny looked to the other side of the river. Beyond the trees were a group of gated buildings. A long wall surrounded them. On its top a roll of menacing barbed wire. Jenny got out of the car.

'Okay, wait here,' she said.

She strolled over the arched bridge with its neat natural-stone wall on either side. Peering over the edge she saw the long wide meandering river. Lush green foliage boarded its banks. A stark contrast with the yellow Baikonur plains. She sniffed the air; there was the strong smell of horse manure. The stables must be nearby. She walked towards the buildings and saw a set of hefty impressive gates set in the walls to one side. A large sign stood before it – two rows of Cyrillic lettering. One seemed to be headed by a sort of X and the other a C. Both lines were indecipherable for Jenny. She strode up to the gate to look for a bell. Not one to be seen but as she scanned upwards she saw a small video camera veering from side to side as she moved. She waved at it cheekily and jumped as a loud voice came from behind her. It sounded like Russian.

Jenny turned to see a large burly man in a flak jacket holding an intimidating black firearm. She tried to maintain her composure and put on an air of demure innocence.

'Oh, I didn't see you there. Good afternoon, is this the stud farm?'

The man barked at her once more in his own language.'

'Sorry, I don't understand you, I'm on a tour of the Cosmodrome and I am fascinated by horses, especially Akhal-Teke. Saw the stud farm on the map.'

The guard started to wave his gun at her and began to shout again when interrupted by a voice from a loudspeaker next to the camera. He stopped immediately and listened. After a few abrupt sentences the voice from the speaker changed into English.

'Please, give your handbag and mobile phone to the guard and he will let you in. I detect an American accent in your English so perhaps you would prefer coffee to tea.'

The guard slung the automatic weapon over his shoulder and held out his hand. Jenny passed him her bag. He opened it, looked inside, took out the mobile phone and switched it off. She waited for him to return it but he pocketed the phone, put her bag under his arm and pointed towards the large gates that were now opening slowly. Inside was a vast cobbled courtyard surrounded by stables. Here and there the golden head of a thoroughbred horse peered through an upper-gated door. Jenny moved over to stroke one of them.

'Beautiful aren't they.'

A handsome looking man in a white linen shirt and cream jodhpurs ambled towards them. He waved his hand nonchalantly at the guard who turned away in the other direction.

'My bag...' began Jenny.

'Don't worry all will be returned when you leave,' said the man holding out his hand. 'Miras. And you are?'

'Jenny, my name's Jenny. Sorry, I didn't understand your guard, or the sign. I didn't mean to be rude, I just have a passion for horses, especially these beauties,' she added, patting the neck of the one beside her.

'Evidently, young lady. The only reason you were allowed in. The horses are extremely valuable and hence the security.' Miras indicated towards a porticoed door at the end of the stable yard. 'Please, our coffee awaits.'

Jenny followed him into the house and waited whilst a servant removed Usenov's boots in the marbled lobby. The living room

237

was spectacular – frescoed ceiling, expensive looking paintings on the walls and a large plate-glass window overlooking a terrace and swimming pool. In the distance Jenny could see other buildings festooned with satellite dishes alongside what looked like a small observatory. She tried to pretend she had no interest in them and walked up to one of the oil paintings. It was extraordinary, an almost perfect representation of the Eagle Nebula.

'It's a Brown,' he didn't say which one. 'She doesn't normally take realistic commissions, but she made an exception.'

'It's beautiful,' said Jenny inspecting it more closely. 'The accuracy is outstanding.'

'So you are interested in stars?'

Jenny had regretted the moment she had spoken, she was meant to be interested in horses not astronomy. She had to think quickly on her feet.

'Absolutely, a hobby of mine since I was a kid. That's why my family booked me a package tour to the Cosmodrome. I don't understand the science much but the wonder of it all.'

'Well it seems we have two things in common. Horses and stars,' said Usenov. 'Ah, here comes our coffee.'

Jenny used the time to talk about horses. She had done her research the evening before, after discovering Kenneth's coordinates matched the location of the stud farm. Miras Usenov seemed quite relaxed, not even probing Jenny about her background. From the staff and surroundings she guessed that he could find out everything about her if he so wanted. When they had finished coffee, Miras gave Jenny a brief circuit of the paddock before returning her to the main gate.

'I do hope you enjoyed your tour,' he said. 'You should especially like the Space Museum.' The gates opened and Jenny was reintroduced to the guard.

'Oh and by the way,' said Miras with a smile, pointing towards the large sign by the entrance, 'if you see one of these be careful. It says private, keep out, in Kazakh and Russian.'

'I'm terribly sorry,' said Jenny taking her mobile phone and bag back from the guard. 'It won't happen again I promise.'

'I'm sure it won't,' said Usenov. 'My guard will escort you back to your taxi. I'm afraid your driver is in a bit of a state. He's found my men somewhat intimidating. I hope you paid him well.'

Twenty-five

'Drowned? You mean *dead* drowned?'

Geoff Sykes was at his desk, head in hands. Nick Coburn sat on the opposite side, a grim look on his face.

'I'm afraid so, Geoff. Even Harry Stones couldn't stop it in time.'

'Where is he now?'

'On his way. Had to stay behind, answer some more questions from the coroner.'

Geoff Sykes got out of his chair and paced up and down. Nick sat there not knowing what else to say. Geoff kicked the wastepaper basket into the corner.

'I told you to keep an eye on her.'

Nick coughed, 'Not exactly, Geoff, you told me to keep an eye on Harry Stones.'

'Same thing,' spat out Geoff, returning to his desk.

They both sat there for a moment, folded arms confronting each other. Geoff was the first to break the silence.

'Right, take me through it again. Slowly step-by-step.'

Nick unfolded his arms, put both his elbows on the desk, and clenched his hands together.

'I was doing as you said, keeping an eye on Harry Stones. Unfortunately the group was split into two, so I followed Harry.'

'Leaving Nathalie and a nut-case behind,' snapped Geoff.

'Couldn't be in two places at once. Nathalie insisted that she was the boss and should be one of the ones to stay behind.'

'Okay go on. The lights were still on at this stage right?'

'Had started to flicker but, yes, they were still on. When we reached the bottom of the shaft Stones and the driver headed back down the tunnel. It was chaos down there, a bunch of miners all trying to get to the surface. If I could have got on the truck I would have. Probably fortuitous that I didn't. Stones had an advantage over me in the dark.'

'So all the lights went out and Stones reached the cavern on foot.'

'That's about it. He heard a splash and called out. Nathalie was lying on the gantry. The idiot who was with her had fallen in the tank. Harry climbed the steps and helped her down.'

'And you say they found the guy drowned.'

'After the event, yes. Nathalie went berserk, all for jumping in the tank and saving him. Harry restrained her. It was pitch-black, Harry couldn't swim and there was no way he was going to let both of them drown. Wouldn't have made any difference anyway. Apparently the guy knocked his head on the side and was wearing heavy boots. Sank straight to the bottom.'

'Shit,' said Nick. 'Poor guy.'

'Not so poor, he was panicking apparently, could have killed Nathalie. She said to me privately that he was distracted, convinced that she and Harry Stones were sabotaging FastTrack's projects.'

'Did she tell that to the coroner?'

'Don't think so. You know what Nathalie's like; didn't see the need, just said the poor guy had lost his balance and fallen in.'

'So where does that leave us with Harry Stones?'

'Jury still out on that one. True, he probably saved her life but that doesn't mean to say he's not messing about with those satellites.'

'Well, the young kid thought so; wonder where he got the idea from?'

Nick Coburn nodded slowly. 'Yes that was a bit of a revelation, and I think I might know the source,' he looked up at the row of international clocks on Geoff's wall. 'We are six hours ahead. If you let me use the video-link in your boardroom, I'll try and find out.'

✳

'That was some interrogation back there.'

'Been through worse. You ought to be up before the scientific subcommittee,' said Harry settling back into the passenger seat. 'You're sure you're all right to drive?'

'Yes, I'm fine.'

'You weren't fine yesterday. Fainted from your dizzy spells I seem to remember.'

'That was in a cavern, nearly a mile underground, in complete darkness, with a lunatic waving a pole in the air. Hardly the A1 with not a car in sight.'

'That's not what you said to the coroner.'

'I told them the truth, well enough of it anyway. On the gantry above the tank, I felt a bit dizzy, thrown into darkness, passed out.'

'You missed out the bit about the guy nearly tipping you in.'

Nathalie checked her rear-view mirror. 'Poor guy was just trying to get me to talk, waving that bloody pole about trying to keep his balance. I didn't know he had fallen in until you had somehow got me to the bottom of the steps.'

'I heard the splash – no one answered my cries – thought it was you. Felt my way up to the gantry and found your body, breathing, thank God. Gave you a fireman's lift to the cavern floor.'

'That's when I came to. Wondered where in the hell Fairbanks was. You wouldn't let me go back for him.'

'I told you, there was no point. I can't swim, there was no noise, and there was no way you would have found him. Are you sure you're all right to drive?'

Nathalie checked her speed. 'I told you I feel fine, even driving way below the limit.'

They continued in silence. Nathalie watched the green fields flash by and noted the sign to Peterborough as they passed the junction.

Harry was obviously feeling uneasy and he started to drum his fingers on the dashboard.

Nathalie turned to look at him. 'What?'

'The coroner accepted that I did what I could. Accidental death. Could have been two.'

'I know, and I still haven't thanked you properly. It was amazing what you did. I just felt helpless you know.'

'Yes I know,' said Harry. 'It was the one time my lack of sight gave me an advantage; used to finding my way around in the dark.'

'Nick wasn't very sympathetic. Said you should have waited for him at the shaft entrance. Thank goodness you didn't. Your quick thinking probably saved my life. Nearly swept in by that bloody pole.'

'So what was all that about? I understand that you wanted to hush it up in front of the coroner but, now we are on our own, you can talk.' Harry turned his face towards her. 'It was more than a young man panicking in the dark wasn't it.'

Nathalie continued driving for a while. She checked her wing mirrors again and, seeing nothing behind her, slowed down slightly.

'You're not going to like it.'

'Try me.'

'He was accusing you, no *us*, of interfering with the satellites. Said our investigation was a guise to cover up the sabotage. Gave Cosmat a competitive advantage in the race to publish.'

Harry took it calmly. 'So where did he get this idea from?'

'Said he had a source from within FastTrack. Got rather heated. Wanted me to tell him all about it.'

'What source?'

'Wasn't explicit and I was in no position to ask,' Nathalie thought for a while and then nearly swerved off the road. 'Oh shit!'

Harry held onto the door ledge. 'Steady, you having those dizzy spells again? Better pull over."

'No it's not that. I've just remembered what he said. Something about a colleague in Chicago and a big guy checking up on their Fermilab work. It's Nick and that Nowak woman. What in the hell have they been up to?'

243

Harry remained quiet for a while, contemplating what Nathalie had just said. He had a decision to make, give a full account of himself or to keep his own counsel and wait for things to unfold. His phone vibrated in his jacket pocket. He took the call.

'Who was that?' asked Nathalie as he signed off.

'Have we passed the Cambridge turnoff yet?' asked Harry ignoring her question.

Nathalie glanced down at the satnav map.

'Not yet. About another mile or two. Why do you ask?'

'Can we make a detour?'

'To Cambridge?'

'The Rutherford. Adam's got some interesting results. Says we should go and take a look.'

The man at the gatehouse was expecting them and waved them through. Nathalie pulled the car into the director's space by the entrance and helped Harry up the steps. Adam Brookes met them by the door.

'Sorry to sound so urgent,' he said, 'but the guys have been working on it all night.' He waved in protest as Nathalie pointed out where she had parked the car. 'No, leave it there it's fine. Follow me, I think you'll be excited by what they have found.'

Harry and Nathalie followed Adam through a series of corridors and into a rather modest looking laboratory containing a few rows of computers.

'Connected to the mainframe in the building next door,' he explained, noting the disappointment on Nathalie's face. 'Please sit down, the guys have set it all up for us.'

He sat at one of the terminals and pulled up two chairs on either side. After he had typed in a few passwords a large world map appeared on the screen.

'I'll talk you through it, Harry,' he said. 'Here we have a map of all the ISPs and routes that someone has used to try to confuse us. Apparently they are very clever, not the normal run-of-the-mill hacker. Took hours to track them down, could have missed them altogether if it wasn't for one large spike of activity.'

'Spike?' asked Nathalie.

'Yes a huge series of events coming from the perpetrator's computer. Bizarrely, coming from Baikonur in Kazakhstan, at the same time as a rocket launch.'

'Go on,' said Harry calmly. 'Has this computer got a footprint? If so can we trace it like a tracker?'

'I think so, as long as they don't reconfigure their hard drive.' Brookes started tapping on the keyboard. The screen responded by inserting a series of luminous webs across the map. 'But here's the interesting bit. I'm showing Nathalie the pathways of the computer signal. Its final destination to the satellites is very odd. A huge powerful computing centre. Could probably link to any satellite up there.'

'At the rocket launching site?' queried Harry.

'Not quite,' replied Brookes. 'It's in the area but not at the Cosmodrome itself.'

Nathalie peered at the screen and the final flashing dot on the world map before the trace moved into space. 'Have you checked it out on Google Earth?'

Brookes enlarged the map and inserted a window with the Google Earth view.

'There. And, for Harry's information, I'm displaying a blurred picture of a section of the Baikonur area.'

Nathalie leaned forward and peered closely at the screen. 'Can you bring it into focus?'

'No, I'm afraid not, that's the whole point. It's obviously a sensitive area –either the aerial close-up shots have not been taken or someone has pixelated a section.'

'Have you checked on a map?' asked Harry and Nathalie almost in unison.

Adam Brookes tapped on the keyboard again. 'Yes, and that's where the surprise comes in. It's a stud farm.'

It was Nick's turn to pace up and down.

'They're late, what's keeping them?'

Geoff snapped his laptop shut and looked up.

'Stefanie told you. They rang in to say they made a diversion. The Rutherford lab. Important information to look at.'

'Yes, but what important information? We've tried phoning and they've bloody well switched their phones off.'

Geoff looked at his watch.

'Nearly half past five. According to Stefanie they should be here at any moment. And, for God's sake, Nick, sit down.'

'I'm still incandescent with rage because of that Nowak woman.'

'Oh, it's Nowak now. Where's your Sarah gone?'

'Bloody stupid idiot, spreading rumours. It's her fault that kid's dead.'

'You sure about that?'

Nick slumped in one of the office easy chairs throwing his knees over the arm.

'He wouldn't have been distracted, brandishing some sort of grappling hook, if he hadn't got the idea that Stones was bringing the satellites down.'

'*You* thought it possible.'

'Yes, but I didn't broadcast it round the whole astronomical community did I.'

'So what's she going to do?'

'Resign, get some kind of lecture job, as far away from FastTrack as possible I think.'

'Anybody blaming her?'

'No, but she feels as guilty as hell. Not such a hard nut as she tries to appear. Was in tears on the video-link.'

They were interrupted by the intercom and Stefanie telling them that Nathalie and Harry had arrived. Geoff told her to send them up before swivelling his chair towards Nick.

'Okay Nick, keep this to yourself for a while, let's see how it pans out.'

Nick didn't have to wait long.

'Nick bloody Coburn,' screamed Nathalie barging into the office. 'What have you been doing behind my back?'

Geoff Sykes raised his eyebrows, put his hands out, and shook his head.

'Mr Coburn, the floor is yours I think.'

The office became eerily quiet. Nathalie, exhausted by her tirade, was slumped in a chair. Nick, who had been trying to defend himself for the last half-hour, had gone for a walk and Harry was sitting quietly in one corner playing with the earpiece of his phone microphone. It was Geoff who decided to break the impasse.

'Harry, it was my instruction to ask Nick to go to Chicago. What he heard there made him concerned about Nathalie.'

'Yeah right,' exclaimed Nathalie.

Geoff looked at her. 'Nathalie, you've had your turn. We all know your feelings. I'm as much to blame as Nick. We decided not to tell you about Sarah Nowak's suspicions. We were going to see how it played out.'

'So it played out well didn't it. Guy gets killed in a tank full of water.'

Geoff sighed. 'That was terrible, but no one made the guy challenge you.'

'And their suspicions were quite rational,' suddenly intervened Harry. 'Not an unreasonable hypothesis. Obsessive scientist conjures plan to spike opposition. Isn't that what you TV people make movies about?'

'Harry!' protested Nathalie, 'you can't think…'

'Oh yes I can. I felt you twitching when I was making those measurements on Gran Canaria. And you were right. I get really fixated on things. But not enough to play dirty tricks,' he added.

'Ah, did I hear dirty tricks,' said Nick re-entering the office waving a wad of papers in his hand. 'Stefanie has just given me these – the translation of those WCMB documents you photographed. If it's dirty tricks you're after, they're all in here.'

It was seven o'clock by the time they had had the chance to absorb the correspondence. It changed the complete mood of the office. Geoff stood up, grabbed a coloured marker pen and walked towards his whiteboard. Nathalie whispered into Harry's ear.

'We are about to have another of Geoff's famous planning sessions, full of charts and arrows. I'll keep you posted.'

Geoff started by summarising their research to date.

'March – WCMB's experimental satellite is crashed. April – three other astronomical satellites are moved from their orbit. Early May – another satellite crashes, this time a media one. Late May – FastTrack apply for time on the *Diophantus* satellite telescope. Days later the astronomical satellite is crashed into a navigation satellite causing thousands of deaths.'

Nathalie whispered to Harry that Geoff was now drawing three intersecting circles. One for WCMB, one for FastTrack and one for Cosmat. Geoff saw what she was doing and started to explain his diagram out loud.

'Here are our three cosmological giants. All with an interest in satellites and Cold Dark Matter. Harry's Cosmat – based in the UK with their own satellite; FastTrack – United States sponsored, trying to buy time on one; and WCMB – who we now know, courtesy of the translated documents, rather than Russian, are Kazakh-funded with a newly launched satellite.'

Harry spoke up. 'So, Messrs Sykes and Coburn, if you now accept my innocence, I think we probably know where the finger is pointing.'

'But do the Kazakh documents actually confirm that?' asked Geoff.

'With our Rutherford data we're getting pretty close,' said Nathalie.

Geoff handed Nathalie the marker pen. 'You've yet to tell us about that. How did it go?'

Nathalie took the stage. She recapped how the Kazakh correspondence was evidently from WCMB's sponsor, a wealthy arms trader called Miras Usenov. The file included the company objectives of being the first to claim the origins and fate of the universe and the strategies to achieve this. The folder also included letters containing veiled threats of what would happen to staff if this was not accomplished within a certain time scale. One letter to Petrov implied that, if a new arms deal under negotiation went through, there would be funds for a new satellite to be launched from the Baikonur Cosmodrome.

'All in all, sounds like a pretty nasty piece of work,' concluded Nathalie.

'Yes but we've all read this. How does it link with your Rutherford data?' asked Geoff irritably.

'We know the source of the signals that take down the satellites,' said Nathalie triumphantly. 'Now if you believe in coincidences, which I don't in this business, it emanates from Kazakhstan near the Cosmodrome.'

'You've forgotten something,' said Nick. 'The letter in the file that mentions concern over the loss of their first satellite and the security measures at the launch of their next one. Why would they take down their own satellite?'

'Perhaps they didn't,' said Geoff. 'Perhaps someone took theirs down so they retaliated.'

Nathalie drew a crude rocket on the whiteboard. 'I'm sure that will be resolved in due course. For now I'm interested in this rocket. Coincidence number two. The signals that took down the media satellite and the *Diophantus* space telescope came from

Kazakhstan.' She wrote two coordinates on the whiteboard. 'From exactly this location. And surprise, surprise, the reason they found the signal was that there was a peak from the originating source at the precise time of WCMB's rocket launch.' She tapped on the coordinates. 'There is a connection between the source computer at the Cosmodrome and this location.'

Geoff peered at the coordinates and started to tap them into his computer.

'No point,' said Nathalie. 'It's obscured on Google Maps.'

'I can see where this is going,' said Geoff with a groan.

'Yes,' nodded Nathalie with half a smile. 'We have to go there.'

Twenty-six

The rocket launch had been spectacular. Jenny was given prime position on the viewing platform. At first the missile didn't seem to move. A burst of flames and a cloud of smoke at its base. As if in slow motion, it left the ground. It looked as if it would topple but then metre by metre, it was thrust slowly into the sky. Next a roar and an acceleration. The shimmering silver arrow was followed by a plume of white vapour as it climbed into the blue atmosphere. She had seen these launches on television but in the flesh it was awesome. The vibration in the control tower had just started to recede when Jenny had remembered the main reason for her visit. It was to fulfil Kenneth's brief which he had given to her the evening after her visit to the stud farm. It was these events that she was frantically trying to assemble in order as she entered the codes into her laptop.

'Kenneth?'

'No names,' came the curt reply.

Jenny cursed herself and tried to stop her hands from shaking.

'I have the report,' she said breathing heavily.

'I need the exact times.' Kenneth's voice was quiet and calm.

Exact times, what did he mean by that – her access to the Cosmodrome, the launch, the tracking monitoring?

It was as if Kenneth could read her thoughts.

'Ten seconds after the launch, what activity did you see in the control room?'

Jenny looked at her notes. She had been forbidden to write anything down but was too frightened to forget anything.

'14:02,' she read out. 'Bykov and myself sitting and observing. Three members of the WCMB team watching the rocket through binoculars.'

'Any of them touching any equipment?'

'Not at that time. The launch was controlled by Baikonur operatives in a different section of the control tower. We could see them on our monitors.'

'And after that?'

'14:21,' read out Jenny, still with a slight tremor in her voice. 'One of the observing group opened his laptop and pressed some keys.'

'And the other two?'

'Still looking at the rocket through binoculars,' said Jenny.

'That's it!' exclaimed Kenneth in uncharacteristic excitement.

Jenny sat back on the bed and stared at the screen of blinking numbers in front of her. Not knowing what to do or say she waited for another question from Kenneth. A minute passed without any communication apart from the flashing characters on her laptop. She couldn't bear the tension any longer so she tentatively spoke into the microphone.

'Hello, are you still there?'

Kenneth's voice came back instantly. 'Of course, doing some calculations. One more question. Was the laptop that was activated at 14:21 the property of the operator or did it belong to someone else?'

Jenny racked her brains. She had been told to monitor every minutiae of the event.

'I think he put the laptop in his case at the end of the session,' she said after a while.

Kenneth's voice sounded irritated. 'You *think*.'

Jenny started breathing more heavily again. 'No, I'm sure he put it in his case. No one else touched it.'

'Okay, I just need to do one more computation and report back to our friends.'

'Can I come home now?' asked Jenny hopefully.

'As I said, I'm reporting back. No doubt they will contact you. Until then I suggest you sit tight.'

Her screen went black. Jenny flopped back onto the bed, stared at the polystyrene-tiled ceiling and sighed. This nightmare felt like it would never end.

She had a whole day to wait. Within an hour of talking to Kenneth her pay-as-you-go mobile had rung with Zikri Amin telling her that he was on the next flight. First-class no doubt, unlike her cramped economy trip. He had reiterated Kenneth's last instruction for her to sit tight, so that's what she was doing. She spent most of the time playing games on her smart phone and trying to teach the barman some English. He was a poor student but seemed to enjoy the encounter. Towards the evening she was explaining how English didn't have a proper future tense, unlike Kazakh with its suffixes, when she was disturbed by a familiar smell. A large man had sidled up to the bar and was obviously waiting impatiently to order a drink. The barman broke off their tutorial and took his order. They both seemed to understand each other and Jenny assumed they were speaking in Russian. The customer was large-framed with an East-Asian appearance. His Russian, if that's what he was speaking, was tinged with an oriental lilt. But the smell, a cheap eau de cologne mixed with sweat, where had she encountered that before? The barman was pouring out two cold beers. Jenny looked around to see another bulky figure, similar features to that of her neighbour, sitting at the far corner table. Now she remembered. She had seen these two characters on her last visit. They were part of a tourist group visiting the Cosmodrome. Strange that they had returned. The barman wiped the froth from the glasses and put them on the counter. Without looking at her, the man grabbed the drinks in his chubby hands and took them back to the table. Jenny returned to her language lesson.

The next morning Zikri arrived in a chauffeur-driven limousine. Jenny was watching from her hotel window. Holdall in hand, he got out of the rear passenger door and walked straight into the hotel reception without even looking at, let alone tipping the driver. She locked her room and skipped down to the lobby.

'Good morning, Mr Zikri, I trust you had a good journey,' she said as cheerfully as she could.

Zikri finished completing the hotel forms before he turned to her.

'You trust wrong, Miss Kang. Eight hours in the air and a three-hour dusty ride to the hotel,' he looked around the reception area. 'If that's what you can call it. Is there somewhere private we can talk?'

'The bar is very quiet this time of the morning, or we could go to my room.'

'I think the bar; we don't want to start drawing attention to ourselves.'

Zikri unzipped his holdall, took out his laptop and passed the bag back to the porter.

'Take this to my room, I need a drink. Will get the key later.'

The porter was about to tell Mr Zikri that the barman was off duty when Jenny stopped him.

'We'll get some bottled water from the machine. I know the way.'

The porter shrugged his shoulders and sloped off. Zikri followed Jenny down the corridor.

'When I said drink, I meant more than water.'

'Welcome to Kazakhstan, Mr Zikri,' said Jenny bravely.

As Jenny had predicted the bar was empty, the barman nowhere to be seen. She put a few coins into the vending machine and pulled out two plastic bottles of, what was meant to be, cold water. The dispenser was having an off-day and the drinks were lukewarm. Zikri grimaced as he took the first gulp. Jenny gestured towards the corner table where the two East-Asian men had been sitting the previous evening.

'No one will disturb us here,' she said. 'The bar doesn't open till later.'

Zikri sat down and powered up his laptop.

'I don't have much time, have to be back at MalaySat for a vital meeting; a meeting that could put a very different complexion on things if we get this right.'

Jenny was puzzled, both with the 'we' and the 'getting right' but she didn't say a thing.

'Right,' said Zikri, appearing to find what he was looking for. 'This stud farm. Kenneth said you had a look inside.'

'I was shown around the stables,' said Jenny tentatively.

'I didn't mean that,' he pointed at a pixelated section of Google Maps on his computer. 'I meant, when you were inside the compound, what did you see at the back of the house? They've obviously got something to hide.'

'As I explained to Kenneth...'

'I want it explained to *me*,' said Zikri sharply, interrupting her.

Jenny closed her eyes, took a deep breath and started again. 'An enormous complex. Satellite dishes everywhere, and a building that looks something like an observatory. I told Kenneth, this guy is a nut about stars and astronomy.'

'But it's not the astronomy we're interested in, Miss Kang. It's the technology. Did you observe something inside those buildings, anything at all that could resemble a super-computer?'

'I didn't get to see those buildings from the inside. Before I could glean any more information I was escorted out. Pleasantly but firmly.'

'But you did say it looked high-tech.'

'Definitely,' said Jenny seeking approval. 'NASA wouldn't be ashamed of those dishes.'

'Do you think we could take another look?'

Jenny was worried about this bit. 'No chance, huge security. I got away with it the first time talking about horses, and then I'm not sure how much he believed me, but a second time, no. The taxi driver was given a real mauling. If I was found snooping around again I wouldn't give much for my chances.'

Zikri turned his attention to his laptop once more. He pressed a few keys and swivelled it so Jenny could see the trace across a world map.

'Fortunately, due to Kenneth's brilliance, I don't think it will be necessary.' He zoomed in on the map. 'See here – the Baikonur Cosmodrome, and here – the stud farm. There's a definite connection between one of the WCMB computers and the farm. It's the farm that sends a signal into space, but the instruction comes from someone's laptop. Someone who you clocked at the observation tower.'

'Was that why Kenneth was asking me to observe their actions?'

'Absolutely.'

'But no satellite was taken down on the launch day, or was it?'

'No, but that laptop communicated with, what we assume is, a super-computer at the stud farm on every occasion that a satellite was moved off course.'

'Even *PhreeSat*?' asked Jenny excitedly, seeing an opt-out clause.

'Yes, even *PhreeSat*. By activating the aircon with a smart device you allowed the hacker to monitor your adjustments and put the thing back on a collision course with some space junk. All they had to do was to bounce a signal around the world to the substation and from there to…well you know where now.'

Jenny didn't like the way Zikri said '*allowed* the hacker'; she was still not being let off the hook.'

'So our suspicion moves away from our friends Bykov and Molchalin and towards one of the WCMB entourage. I assume you've discovered where they are staying.'

Jenny gulped. That was one thing she hadn't thought of.

'I could give Valery Bykov a ring,' she said trying to indicate that she had a close relationship. 'I'm sure he will tell us where they are staying.'

Zikri slammed his laptop shut and glared at her. 'I'm sure he will, but that's the last thing we want someone alerting them to, the fact we want to see them. No, I'll call Kenneth, ask him to check out local hotels and their occupancy. The WCMB delegation will be none the wiser.'

It was nearly midnight when Jenny was woken by a sharp knock at her room door. Once more she had palpitations and visions of being escorted away by the police or military.

'Miss Kang.' It was Zikri's voice.

Jenny held her breath.

'Miss Kang, get dressed – jeans preferably – and meet me in the lobby.'

Jenny checked her phone for the time. Was the man mad? But the instructions were clear and she wasn't going to annoy him any further. She threw some water over her face and grabbed her jeans from the chair by the bed. What in the hell were they going to do now?

Zikri was waiting for her at the bottom of the staircase, uncharacteristically dressed in a tracksuit.

'There's no one at reception so we can slip out the front door. The car should be round the side.'

'A car? Where did that come from and where are we going?'

Zikri was already on his way out of the hotel.

'You're full of questions, Miss Kang. Yes, a car. Not easy to hire here, but if you pay enough a local taxi driver is all too pleased to let you borrow his cab for the night. And, as to where we're going, I'll explain that on the way.'

The side of the hotel was dimly lit with streetlights, half of which weren't working. An old Toyota was parked against the verge. Zikri felt under the front wheel arch and pulled out a set of keys.

'Get in and don't slam the door,' he said pressing the plip.

They drove south through the deserted streets of Baikonur. The journey only took ten minutes. Their destination was the Central Hotel, where WCMB had made their temporary headquarters. Zikri explained that Kenneth had discovered not only the hotel but the room in which their target was staying.

'So how did he do that? I know he's a whiz at computers but remote video access?' asked Jenny as they drew up by the hotel car park.

Zikri pulled on the handbrake and switched off the engine. 'I wouldn't put it past him, he's one of the best we've got but, no, this time he used the telephone.'

Jenny's face was lit up by one of the sodium streetlights. It bore a bewildered expression.

Zikri appeared amused. 'He checked WCMB's website and looked for someone resembling the description you gave him. There are only two hotels in Baikonur where those sort of people would stay. He wasn't at ours so he called the Central Hotel and asked if he could send a message to our man. They gave him the room number.'

Jenny looked worried. 'And is that where we're going now?'

Zikri began to get out of the car. 'The hotel is big enough, nearly two hundred rooms. No one will recognise us. Walk past reception and head for the elevator as if you are a resident. We'll be heading for the third floor.'

Jenny was in an illicit taxi in the middle of Baikonur at midnight. She had no alternative but to follow her employer into the hotel. It was just as he said, the receptionist ignored them as they walked up to the elevator and pressed the button. Once inside the lift Jenny plucked up courage to ask the question that was nagging her.

'So what do you intend to do? Ask him if he is taking down the satellites?'

'Oh more than that. We're going to ask him if he can do some work for us.'

'What? Why would he do that?'

Zikri gave one of his sickly smiles. 'Because if he doesn't we are going to tell everybody who has been making this mess – the press, his employers, if they don't know already, and the police!'

'That's blackmail.'

'I prefer to call it gentle persuasion,' said Zikri.

The elevator came to a rather jolting halt at the third floor. The doors slid open and Zikri walked out into the passageway waiting for Jenny to follow him.

Jenny was still confounded. 'Work for us? What would he do?'

'Leave that to me,' said Zikri. 'All you have to do is ensure it's the right man. Now be of some use, look for a trolley with some food or drinks on it.'

They scanned the corridor. At one end under a window Jenny spotted a trolley covered in a white napkin. Someone had finished their meal and put out the cart for a porter.

'Perfect,' said Zikri, pulling the cloth away like a magician. 'They've hardly touched it; with a bit of a tidy-up it should look okay.'

He pushed the leftover food around the plate to make it look more presentable and placed the dirty coffee cup onto the floor.

'Room 306. I think it's this way,' he said wheeling the trolley along the corridor.

Jenny followed him into the gloom until they reached an old-fashioned wooden door bearing a plastic room number.

'How's your Russian?' he asked. 'Oh never mind, most of them speak English here anyway.'

He knocked noisily on the door. 'Room service!'

No answer. He knocked once more, shouted loudly and put his ear to the door.

'Ah someone's coming. I'll just put this trolley between me and the door. Follow me as soon as it opens.'

A crack in the door appeared and a bleary face peered into the corridor. 'What the hell? I didn't order room service. You've got the wrong room.'

'Oh I don't think so,' said Zikri ramming the trolley into the door making it swing open.

The man was half asleep, dazed. He had no idea what was happening. A crazy porter pushing some food he hadn't ordered into his room. He sat on the bed protesting until suddenly the porter said something that made him jerk awake.

'Sabotaging satellites. You're very good at it aren't you?'

The man was too dumbfounded to speak.

Jenny crept into the room and closed the door behind her to avoid confrontation with any other hotel residents. The room was even more basic than the ones at the Sputnik Hotel – pale green walls, double-bed with simple wooden headboard and a couple of bedside tables with gaudy lamps. The slightly built man was sitting on the floral counterpane, Zikri looming over him. If it came to a fight she had no doubt who would win.

'We are going to make this very simple for you,' said Zikri, with menace in his voice, throwing a piece of paper in front of the man. 'This is a track and trace map showing that your personal computer was the source and cause of a satellite crash that killed a thousand people.'

The man on the bed picked up the paper and studied it. His expression betrayed the fact that he knew what it was.

'Luckily for you,' continued Zikri, 'we're not interested in reporting this to your employers, or to the authorities for that matter.'

There was a terrible pause.

'Unless…'

Twenty-seven

It was the summer break for some and there were not so many people as usual pouring out of London's Tottenham Court Road tube station. Nathalie stood at the entrance watching people blinking their eyes as they stepped into the sunshine. Despite the sparseness of crowds, the forecourt to the station entrance was surrounded by a cacophony of sound. Enormous cranes and construction machines were tearing up the neighbourhood and replacing old skyscrapers with new. London seemed to be like that nowadays, one eternal building site.

She had only been waiting five minutes when the escalator disgorged Harry Stones. He tapped his way to the side of the entrance and placed his hand against the newly refurbished stainless-steel wall and stood there calmly waiting.

'Harry, right on time,' said Nathalie skipping up to him and taking hold of his arm. 'Beautiful morning, pity we've got to spend most of it indoors.'

'Yes, but at least we can get away from this infernal noise,' said Harry walking alongside her. 'I hear your magician, Stefanie, has been able to get us some flights.'

'Magician is about it. Normally it would have been impossible to get us visas and tickets in time but she's managed to get us on a last-minute Cosmodrome package tour. A couple pulled out at the last moment – thought they were going to see a rocket launch but then realised they'd missed it.'

'Wouldn't have minded being there for that myself,' said Harry. 'The roar, the smell of rocket fuel... Took a bit of convincing to tell my guys at Cosmat that I was going to one of the world's top launch sites to visit a horse stud farm.'

ghed, 'They wouldn't even have listened to you a

hat,' said Harry. 'They are slowly coming round to my
w; watching our bird like a hawk.'
ird?'
sorry, trying to sound young. It's the trendy word for
satellite apparently. They are keeping a close eye on the orbits of
our new space telescope, the one exploring the infrared and low
gravitational waves.'

'That sounds more like my Harry,' chuckled Nathalie.

Bagatelle Films' offices were only a ten-minute stroll from the
tube station. It was still early but couples had taken advantage of
the late-June sun to sunbathe in Soho Square. Nathalie wistfully
half wanted to join them. This film had been a whirlwind tour with
a couple of terrifying moments. She hadn't admitted it to Geoff, but
she was exhausted and the dizzy spells had not completely gone
away. She wasn't going to tell him that now, not with a potential
defining-moment trip to Kazakhstan on the horizon. As they
reached the steps of Bagatelle Nathalie recognised a familiar figure.
It was John McCord. Surely they hadn't wangled another ticket to
give her a cameraman.

'Hi, Nathalie, how's your head?'

Harry turned towards the voice. 'Something she will not talk
about,' he said. 'No point in trying any further.'

John smiled; he knew Nathalie of old.

'Okay no more said. You look great anyway, Nathalie,' he held
up a small cardboard box, 'and I've got you a present.'

The three of them were ushered into Geoff's office. No Nick,
Nathalie noticed. Geoff seemed to be distracted; one minute flicking
on the TV screen, the next typing something into his laptop. After
a few minutes he became aware of their presence hovering around
the doorway.

'Sorry, sorry, new project. Have to have copyright clearance on the
archive by midday.' He glanced up at Nathalie. 'Oh how's your head?'

Harry and John spoke as one voice. 'Don't ask.'

'Where's Nick?' asked Nathalie ignoring them all.

'Only two tickets I'm afraid,' replied Geoff. 'Didn't see the point of him coming.'

'So why is John here? I thought you agreed that it was Harry's project.'

'John isn't going with you, but I thought you might need a tutorial. Don't mean to be rude but I really must get this copyright. The boardroom is yours for the morning. Stefanie will fill you in on the travel details and John will sort you out with the rest. I might join you later.'

Stefanie was waiting for them with coffee and warm croissants. She handed out two files, one for Harry and one for Nathalie.

'I'm sure John won't mind while I talk you through the travel arrangements,' she said in her normal seductive tones. 'Here are your travel packs. You will be going on a group excursion with a travel company under the exotic name of Space Tours.'

Nathalie opened her brochure and described the garish cover to Harry.

Stefanie continued. 'They provide a Kazakh-speaking guide,' she coughed, 'and you are supposed to be chaperoned by them at all times. You will be staying at the Tsentralnaya on Lenin Square.'

'Excellent accent,' commented Harry.

'Thank you, Doctor Stones. As you probably know, this is better known to tourists as the Central Hotel and it is the hotel where the WCMB delegates are staying.'

'What a coincidence,' said Nathalie.

'Not really, there are only two hotels that are suitable for tourists so there was a fifty-fifty chance.'

'What about our tickets?' asked Nathalie looking through her folder.

'I know this is a little unorthodox for a film shoot,' said Stefanie, 'but I have provided you with a voucher that you need to present to the Space Tours' representative at the airport. They will provide you with everything you need – group flight booking, hotel and meals. All you need to do is turn up with your passport.'

'You say film *shoot*,' said Nathalie, 'but I understand John isn't coming with us.'

'Well that's where I will leave you in John's good hands,' said Stefanie. 'I believe he will explain everything you need to know. I'll be in my office if you need me.'

Stefanie smiled at John and left the boardroom closing the door silently behind her.

Nathalie narrowed her eyes and looked straight at John.

'Okay McCord, what's going on?'

John pushed the cardboard box that he was holding towards her.

'Present,' he said.

Nathalie opened the box. Inside was a compact matte black camera with a five-inch screen on the back.

'Well, looks sexy, what is it?'

'It's a Black Magic Pro video camera. Could be taken for a standard stills camera but in reality it's one of the top professional video cameras on the market. Super 35 sensor, wireless Bluetooth remote control, HDR imaging and dual gain ISO for exceptional lowlight performance.'

Harry put his hands out. 'Can I feel it?'

Nathalie nestled it carefully in his palms.

'It's incredibly small,' said Harry, 'and it does all the stuff you said?'

'That and a lot more,' said John, 'but I don't want to overwhelm you both. Geoff says I have to teach Nathalie how to use this thing by lunchtime.'

Nathalie had been a researcher and film director for many years but she had never touched a camera on a shoot. She had been trained under Geoff's old-school rules. 'Your job is to plan the shots, make sure they will tell the story you want. Their job is to take them,' he would say. But needs must and there was no way she was going to get a film crew to Baikonur. John kept it as simple as he could, placing most of the controls on automatic. They practised shooting well-lit shots and pictures taken in almost complete darkness. He wasn't joking about the technology, it was an amazing piece of kit.

'It takes extraordinary pictures for such a small thing,' said Nathalie to Harry.

'What about sound?' asked Harry. 'We might need that.'

'Built-in,' said John. 'Not great – usually would need some sort of external mic – but I don't think they would let you use that where you are going, posing as tourists.'

'Looks a bit flash though,' said Nathalie, turning the object around in her hands. 'Not sure we could pass it off as something to take snaps.'

'Thought of that,' said John pulling a scruffy piece of thick material from his pocket. 'Got it in a charity shop. Tartan camera case, with strap.'

'Used by all the best keen photographer sightseers,' snorted Nathalie, slinging it around her neck. 'How do I look?'

John didn't have time to answer as Geoff burst into the boardroom.

'You won't believe this,' he said grabbing the television remote control. 'On the other hand, perhaps you will.'

He started flicking through the channels. The wall-size flatscreen at the end of the boardroom flickered with the pictures of different programmes. He stopped on one of the channels. A black screen with a small white caption. *No signal.*

'Just had a telephone call from a mate who works for a broadcast magazine,' he said moving around the boardroom table and changing the channels again.

'He spends his life watching TV, sometimes mainstream, sometimes the more obscure channels. Writes reviews and reports on signal strength and so on. He was doing that this morning and suddenly found this.'

Geoff froze the image on another channel. He described it for Harry's benefit.

'No signal, Harry. Completely black. Was working a few moments ago and then it suddenly cut off.'

'How many channels like that?' asked Harry.

'That's it,' said Geoff. 'Dozens.'

'And are they related in any way?' asked Harry, slowly realising where this was going.

'My mate's working on it but, seems so, yes.'

'Another satellite,' said Harry.

Geoff's mobile phone gave a ding. He put his hand up in apology and scrolled through the message.

'Just got a text. I'll read it to you. Channels affected serviced by a satellite located at 69.5 degrees east. An orbital position at the crossroads of four continents – Europe, Africa, Central and Southeast Asia, and Australia. Most severe areas affected are Indonesia, Philippines, Thailand and Australia where the television coverage is supplied to more than six hundred million inhabitants.'

John McCord whistled. 'Bet that makes the satellite owners popular.'

Geoff continued reading the text and précised it for them.

'Yes, the company that owns the satellite is one of the largest in the world. Has about sixty geo-stationary satellites supplying everything from broadband to professional data networks. Worrying thing is that 69.5E also transmits secure government communications in Central Asia. Can't imagine the havoc it's causing.'

'Dents our theory about astronomy wars,' muttered Harry reaching for his own mobile phone. 'But at least this time we have someone monitoring the situation.'

'The Rutherford?' asked Nathalie.

'The Rutherford,' echoed Harry. 'I asked them to put a tracker on the signal coming from that stud farm in Kazakhstan. We should soon know if they have anything to do with it.'

The answers took a little longer than they had expected.

The computing section at the Rutherford laboratory wanted to recheck their calculations and make contact with the Joint Space Operations Centre in the United States before they would disclose any of the results.

John McCord tried to give Nathalie further tips on handling the camera but she was too distracted to concentrate. Harry too was agitated. Phoning Trevor at Cosmat to check on their own satellite and continually re-phoning the Rutherford to the extent that they had stopped taking his calls. It was nearly noon before he got a call back. Everyone in the boardroom kept silent as he put the mobile on speaker.

'Right, we have the official report,' said Adam Brookes. 'For the time being, this is to be for your ears only and not published or disseminated in any way until you have written permission from this laboratory.'

'Accepted,' said Harry quietly.

'We have been in communication with JSpOC. They have confirmed that satellite 69.5E collided with a large piece of space junk, possibly from the debris of that old Boeing communications satellite, at exactly 9.53 GMT today. They reported the collision course to the satellite owners EtherSat, who attempted to avert the disaster by using the satellite's thrusters. Unfortunately, and by an unknown source, the satellite was repositioned onto the original collision course at the last moment. EtherSat had no time in which to re-correct the orbit.'

'Unknown source?' queried Harry.

'Unknown to JSpOC and EtherSat,' said Adam.

Harry's next words were patiently spoken, 'And our tracking measures?'

'Again, not for immediate publication,' replied Adam. 'It seems as if, and I stress *seems* that, at exactly 9.52 GMT an extra-terrestrial signal was transmitted from the coordinates we have been observing, approximately fifty kilometres due west of the Baikonur Cosmodrome.'

'And this extra-terrestrial signal could have taken down the satellite?' asked Harry, again patiently.

'Entirely supposition,' said Adam and, after a short pause, 'but the times are close.'

Nathalie shook her head. 'Scientists,' she hissed quietly.

'Nothing wrong with being circumspect,' said Harry overhearing her. 'Now, if we are going to empirically prove or disprove our theory, you should pack that camera away and call a cab or we are going to miss our flight.'

Jenny had agreed to meet Zikri in the bar at six, just before the barman's normal shift. Zikri had complained that he wasn't getting a good WiFi signal from his room and needed somewhere he could talk to his office. She had spent most of the morning in bed recovering from the trauma of the night before. After lunch she had avoided her companion by going for a walk around the hotel. Now she had to face him again. The bar was empty, most of the tourists still yet to return from their day trip to the Cosmodrome. Zikri was waiting for her at the corner table they had met at before, laptop open and mobile telephone in hand.

'Oh good,' he said, 'you're just in time.'

Jenny sat in the chair he had placed alongside so that she could see the screen of the laptop.

'Good evening,' she said, trying to disguise her unease.

'Perhaps,' he said, 'if he has done what we asked.'

Jenny was going to say it wasn't 'we' but thought better of it.

Zikri was accessing some of the live international television feeds, with the sound down. Lurid images of chat shows and quiz programmes were displayed on his screen.

'WiFi is a lot better down here,' he said, almost to himself.

Jenny waited patiently. Zikri pulled a Moleskine notebook from his top pocket and flicked through the pages.

'Well Mr WCMB let's see if you have done your magic.'

The screen suddenly turned to black with a white caption, presumably in Kazakh or Russian.

'Ah, perfect,' said Zikri. He looked down at his notebook again and pressed another key. 'Let's try another one.'

The action produced the same result. A black screen with a simple caption.

'Adi will be pleased,' he said looking at his watch and pressing a redial button on his telephone. 'Eight in the evening there,' he said as a means of explanation.

Jenny sat there staring at the laptop screen. A blank screen – perfect. Perfect for who and why? Zikri seemed so pleased with the results that he made no effort to disguise his telephone call. It was as if he wanted Jenny to share in his triumph.

'Adi, I expect you have already tuned in. Brilliant isn't it?'

Jenny could only catch part of the other side of the conversation. The chief technical officer of MalaySat was obviously ecstatic, heaping praise on Zikri and complimenting him on his success. '

'How's it going your end?' asked Zikri. 'Have you opened up negotiations yet?'

It was slowly dawning on Jenny what these two were talking about. They had crashed a major communication's satellite and were now filling the void with their own. She couldn't hear everything that Adi was saying but she could deduce the missing lines. It had been set-up from day one. MalaySat had launched a satellite with a similar orbit to that of one carrying television, data and vital communications to four continents. Now that the commercial satellite had been destroyed they had a captive audience. Television and broadband companies, along with certain Central Asian governments, were clamouring to reinstate their networks. For some time the MalaySat marketing teams had been seeding rumours about the unreliability of EtherSat and trying to woo these clients. Today they were pushing against open doors; potential clients in their droves were seeking satellite time.

'The phone hasn't stopped ringing, Amin,' said the voice down the phone. 'Well done, you deserve a break. Take a few days off, visit the Cosmodrome. We'll expect you back early next week.'

Zikri snapped the laptop shut and put away his phone. He sat there for a while smiling to himself.

'Well, Miss Kang, a successful operation all round.' He looked around the bar; it had begun to fill with the tourists returning from their outing.

'That deserves a drink, don't you think?'

Jenny heard the sound of the metal blind being rolled up to open the bar. Her barman nodded towards her and then to someone or some people sitting at the table behind. Jenny turned around to see the two large East-Asian men she had encountered a few days ago. The faint whiff of eau de cologne hit her nostrils. How long had they been sitting there she wondered?

Twenty-eight

It was baking hot and the interior of the taxi was stifling. They could hear the whir of the aircon fan but it was only circulating warm air. Nathalie wound down the window and watched the parched desert steppes crawl by. The driver and the Kazakh guide sat silently in the front seats. Harry was beside her in the back, lurching onto her shoulder now and again, in a deep slumber. The journey the day before had been exhausting – economy class international flight, an internal flight and then a six-hour coach drive, cramped in with twenty other tourists. They were given a basic meal at the hotel and everyone had an early night. Space Tours had predicted the toll on its clientele and had allocated today as a free day before the scheduled trip to the Cosmodrome tomorrow. Nathalie had approached the guide for a private tour. The woman was reluctant at first but a few US dollars soon made her change her mind. Nathalie explained that her blind uncle had little opportunity to travel and she wanted to give him the sounds and smells of the area; a once-in-a-lifetime trip she had said. The guide was less interested in her uncle than the money and a local taxi had soon pulled up at the Central Hotel. Nathalie made it clear that they didn't want to go far and pointed to the river on the map. The Syr Darya was the only interesting feature in the area, besides the miles and miles of flat grassland, so it didn't seem a strange choice. She kept checking her phone for the GPS coordinates and calculated that the turnoff to the stud farm would appear in the next few minutes. She nudged Harry awake.

'Plan A in two minutes,' she whispered.

Harry sat up and moved his neck from side to side to ease the stiffness. 'Ready when you are. Just give me a prod.'

Nathalie watched her phone map closely and as they approached the area she elbowed Harry.

'Bit hard,' said Harry softly, leaning forward in his seat. He tapped the guide on the shoulder.

'Excuse me, I'm afraid I have to take a toilet break. Could you ask him to pull over for a moment please?'

The guide said something to the driver who snapped a reply.

'He says this is not a good place,' she translated.

'Well that's too bad,' said Harry. 'It's this place or you are going to tell the cab driver that there's going to be an accident back here.'

The guide turned to the driver once more and rattled off another few sentences in Kazakh. The driver shook his head but pulled off the road anyway.

'He asks you to be as quick as you can,' said the guide.

But Harry and Nathalie were already halfway out of the doors.

'I'll help him get to the trees,' called Nathalie over her shoulder, pulling Harry towards the river.

The guide started to shout something back but by then they were almost out of earshot.

'Is she following?' asked Harry.

'No, she started to get out of the car but the taxi driver pulled her back. I don't think he wants to get involved.'

They followed the tarmac road until it turned into a rutted track. Ahead of them was an old stone bridge over the tree-lined river. Harry made for the undergrowth.

'Unless you really want to go, you can forget that,' said Nathalie 'We are out of sight now.'

Harry pulled up his zip. 'Just trying to be authentic,' he chuckled. 'Can you see the house?'

'Yes, it's the other side of the bridge. If I stand on the parapet here I could get a better look. We'll do the old spy trick. You stand there and I'll pretend to take pictures of you. It'll look like I'm pointing the camera away from the house, but I've cut a hole in the back of the case and am getting quite a good view.' Nathalie started moving her old tartan camera case around.

'A few dishes and aerials poking up behind the house,' she muttered to herself, peering through the zoom lens, and pressing 'record'.

Harry heard the man before Nathalie could see him.

'Wonderful day,' he shouted indicating that there was someone behind her.

Nathalie spun around to see a large man in khaki brandishing a PKM machine gun.

'Oh hello,' she said, quickly putting a broad smile on her face. 'We are tourists, just taking a few pictures of my uncle.'

The man strode up to her and said something gruffly which sounded Turkish but was most likely Kazakh.

Nathalie thought quickly on her feet, pulled her mobile phone from her pocket and pointed at it so the man could see what she was doing. She typed into Google Translate and made a calculated guess. English to Kazakh. She thrust the screen in front of the guard.

Tourist. Taking photos of my blind old uncle to show to his family at home. Will you photograph the two of us?

Турист. Үйде туыстарына көрсету үшін менің кәрі ағамның суреттерін түсіру. Екеуімізді суретке түсіресіз бе?

The guard peered at the screen looking nonplussed. Nathalie was wearing her sweetest smile and Harry had produced his white telescopic stick as she read out the text. She was now proffering the guard the phone and making gesticulations pointing first at herself and then at Harry. He took the phone from her, shrugged his shoulders, and looked through the viewfinder. Nathalie stood beside Harry and he put his arm around her shoulders. The guard said 'Күлімсіреу', which they took to mean 'smile', and pressed the button. Before he could question the situation further Nathalie took back the camera, thanked him effusively and, taking Harry by the arm, strolled back in the direction they had come from.

'Brilliant,' said Harry as they reached the taxi, 'but next time, less of the old blind uncle.'

The day had dragged. Jenny sat at the bar of the Sputnik Hotel and drained her third ice-cold lager. The afternoon sun had been blistering and the first beer was to quench her thirst, now the third was to dull her senses. Yesterday – the day after what Zikri was now calling EtherSat's satellite malfunction – he had gleefully dragged her around the Cosmodrome smarming up to Bykov. MalaySat were now prepared to put money behind quite a few new launches apparently. Today she had feigned a headache and refused to go with him. Now in the late afternoon she'd given up on the barman's ability to master eloquent English and ordered beers by pointing at her empty glass.

'Someone want to buy you drink,' the barman said in stuttering English, pointing over her shoulder as she pushed the glass towards him.

Jenny looked around to see the two large Asian men sitting at their corner table. One of them had his right arm raised miming drinking, the other was pointing at Jenny.

Jenny gave a grudging smile and said 'Spasibo', which she had learned was acceptable phonetic Russian for thank you.

'They North Korean,' said the barman.

Jenny swivelled on her barstool to turn back to the bar. 'Well, I'm damned if I'm going to learn Korean just to get a beer,' said Jenny with a slight slur in her voice.

The barman had no idea what she was saying and simply filled her glass.

She was feeling quite drunk by dinnertime. Zikri had insisted she meet him in the restaurant so he could boast about his successes of the day. This was the last thing she wanted but anything to keep him on her side. She had planned to ask him for a reference; best for all of them if she got a job elsewhere. But when she tried to broach the subject he pretended not to understand and continued to excitedly describe his negotiations at the Cosmodrome. As the coffee arrived his phone vibrated on the table. He covered the mouthpiece and spoke softly so that Jenny couldn't hear the conversation. At the end of the call he made his excuses and told her that he would see her at breakfast in the morning. Jenny watched him leave the restaurant and noticed, out of the corner of her eye, that the two Koreans, who were eating at a nearby table, also got up to follow him.

Jenny ordered a second coffee, trying to clear her head. She was feeling really down. She had done everything that Zikri had asked her, even to the extent of being complicit with blackmail. Her attempt at resigning with honours had been ignored. Surely now they had what they had set out to achieve they would let her go. She had mused about contacting her old boyfriend, the one with the satellite start-up company in China, maybe there was an opening there. Perhaps she would have better luck tomorrow. The people at MalaySat were so excited about their new contracts that they had almost forgotten about her. When things had settled down they might have time to consider her options. Even a golden handshake for helping them out. She stayed at the table for about an hour, her mood swings up one moment and down the next. The waiters were now clearing the tables around her and setting them for the next morning's breakfast. She took the hint, picked up her mobile phone and headed for her room. She had had enough of the bar for one day.

As she stepped out of the elevator and into her corridor she checked the room numbers for it seemed dimmer than usual. No, she was on the right floor. The route was now familiar, second turning on the right and third door on the left. She put the card key into the slot. A sudden pain in the ribs and she was pushed through the opening door. Her phone was flung across the room and she ended up sprawled across the floor. Dazed, she looked up to see the door closing behind her.

'Good evening, Miss Kang,' said the large North Korean, looming over her. 'Sorry about the rough intrusion, but my friend and I would like to ask you a small favour.'

There was no sign of the WCMB team at the Central Hotel. Harry and Nathalie were not surprised, the hotel had nearly two hundred rooms. They had waited until the last serving at dinner but they hadn't spotted anyone. A late night, working at the Cosmodrome perhaps. They tried to be as convivial as possible with the members of their tour so as not to stand out from the crowd but, after a while, the conversations about the exotic places everyone had visited became wearing and Nathalie suggested to Harry that they go up to their rooms.

'Doesn't look like they're going to turn up tonight,' she said. 'Why don't I review and describe the footage I took today.'

'Good idea,' said Harry. 'Your room or mine?'

'Let's take the nearest,' said Nathalie. 'Mine is on the first floor, yours is on the third I think. Why they couldn't put us next to each other I'll never know. First thing we do when arranging a shoot is to make sure the film crew are all close together on the ground floor.'

'Ground floor?'

'Yes, to get the kit in. Don't want to be dragging a dozen metal boxes up ten flights of stairs.'

'Good job you've got a pocket camera then,' said Harry. 'How did you avoid showing it to that guy by the way?'

Nathalie took Harry's arm, guided him into the elevator and pressed the button for the first floor. 'Quickly slung it over my shoulder and thrust my phone under his nose. Probably looked like an old tartan handbag. Anyway he was so shocked at being asked to take selfies that I don't think he realised that I switched the cameras.'

'Quick thinking,' said Harry.

'Had to be, a bullet-headed brute brandishing a machine gun.'

'Machine gun! You didn't tell me about that.'

'Thought it best not to pay attention to it, Harry. On a need-to-know basis.'

'I would have thought that...' began Harry, '...on the other hand...'

'Exactly,' said Nathalie stepping out of the lift. 'No need for both of us to panic.'

She took out her room key from her bag. It was the old-fashioned type, a small flat key on a huge metal fob shaped as a rocket.

'Here we are,' she said. 'Now let's take a closer look at those pictures.'

The images were incredibly sharp and detailed. Nathalie described them to Harry. Gold sandstone weathered walls with large gates fronted by signs, obviously displaying words like 'keep out'. She was quite pleased with the zoom. Keep it steady and slow, John had said. First timers always want to wave it about. Beyond the walls the camera had picked out roofs with enormous satellite dishes and aerials. Quite a nest of technology.

'Well Mr Director,' said Nathalie, 'we're both novices and I think we are doing a pretty good job. Obviously something to hide in there.'

'All we need now is to find out who from WCMB are here and how much they know about their billionaire sponsor,' said Harry. 'I suggest we grab an early breakfast, before the tour guide whips us all to the Cosmodrome; see if we can identify anyone we know.'

※

Jenny Kang was in a state of shock. The two Koreans had manhandled her onto the bed and were standing alongside. One bent over to pick up her smart phone from the floor.

'Code!' he barked.

Jenny tried to speak but she was terrified.

'Code or I break your fingers,' said the man, cracking his knuckles.

Jenny stuttered out the numbers.

He typed them in and scrolled through her messages. Looking up to his accomplice he shook his head and pocketed the phone.

'Catch,' said the other man throwing something towards Jenny.

She caught the object instinctively in her left hand. It was a semi-transparent amber-coloured bottle of pills.

'Return it please,' said the man holding out his palm.

Jenny did so and only then did she note that he was wearing some sort of latex gloves. Her eyes widened as he pocketed the pills and pulled out a serrated kitchen knife. She flinched backwards as he moved towards her. At the last moment he deftly swivelled the knife in his hands so that the handle pointed at Jenny.

'Take,' he ordered brusquely.

She nervously put out her hand.

'No the other,' he said.

She did as she was told and held the handle.

'Good,' said the man. 'Now return it.'

Jenny's hand was shaking so much that she dropped the knife on the bed. The second man scooped it up immediately. He said something in his native tongue and went towards the door, opened it and looked up and down the corridor. There was obviously no one there as he nodded to his friend, closed the door quietly and stood against it, arms folded.

'We just need a small favour, Miss Kang,' said the man standing next to the bed. 'Once you have done that, you will forget all about us and go home unharmed.'

Jenny was trying to recompose her senses. Keep calm, she was saying to herself, you have got out of scrapes like this before.

'How do you know my name?' she asked, trying to make light conversation. 'We've not met before have we?'

'Oh we know more than your name, Jenny Kang. And we have met, but at a distance. For a moment I thought you had seen us at the substation.'

Jenny suddenly remembered the flash of light. So it *was* binoculars.

The man sat down on the bed beside her. 'You'll be interested to know that we have been after the same thing.'

Jenny made a slight shuffle away from him. 'The same thing?'

'Don't pretend you don't understand, Miss Kang. The genius who has the ability to play with satellites. We thought we may have found him. Boasting about the substation on Facebook. Sadly he was just a bucolic farmer. I believe you were caught up in the aftermath. Messy business.'

Jenny closed her eyes. The nightmare was continuing.

The Korean pulled out a large mobile phone from his pocket. 'Now we believe you really have found him for us. Very clever of you.'

'What do you mean, for *you*?' asked Jenny. 'We were just trying to find out who took down our satellite.'

'So that is why you asked him to take down another is it?' asked the Korean, pointing the telephone towards her and pressing the 'on' button.

Zikri's voice emerged. They had obviously somehow captured his conversation in the restaurant.

'*Ah perfect, let's try another one...*' came the tinny voice from the speaker.

The recording was an indictment of Jenny and Zikri's actions.

'What do you want from us?' asked Jenny resignedly.

'As I said, a little favour.'

Jenny waited with dread as the man moved closer towards her on the bed.

'You seem to have a nice rapport with our satellite hacker,' he handed Jenny a piece of paper. 'All we are asking is that you ask him to move one more satellite, orbital path enclosed.'

Jenny looked at the piece of paper. She instantly recognised the numbers as a satellite orbital path and trajectory.

'Why should I do that?' she said.

Her bedfellow turned the screen of his mobile phone towards her and pressed another button.

'Because if you don't, I don't think your Mr Zikri is going to like it,' he said.

The screen came to life with a video – a room, looking like Jenny's but with different coloured wallpaper. The camera panned to a man bound and gagged sitting in a chair. It was Zikri, eyes wide open, looking terrified. The cameraman's accomplice was toying with Zikri's fingers with a pair of pincers. The gag, which was a sock being pushed into her boss's mouth, was stifling his screams.

Jenny took a deep breath. 'What makes you think I care about him?' she said desperately.

'Oh we know you don't,' said her tormentor. 'We are depending on that.' He held up the knife and the amber bottle in his gloved hands. 'If you don't comply, we simply make him swallow these sleeping pills and slit his throat. Your prints are all over them.'

Twenty-nine

The street lights were dim but there was still plenty of activity on Korolov Avenue. It was the main street in Baikonur and even this late at night the restaurants were selling street-food and some grocery stores were displaying their wares. By car it had only taken Zikri and Jenny a few minutes from the Sputnik to the Central Hotel, but this time she had to walk. She felt conspicuous carrying the large holdall so she took a detour via the quieter Gorkily Street. It would take her longer but she was in no hurry and she wanted to get her thoughts together. The 'small favour' was going to be difficult. They had asked her to persuade the hacker to take down another satellite. Tell him you were so pleased with his results that you would like him to do it again. Just one more, the last time. Simple. But it wasn't simple, Jenny had pleaded. He had taken a lot of persuading, and it was Zikri who was doing the talking not her. She had tried to pull the feminine card. She was small, physically weak, why would he listen to her? They had given her the answer in the large canvas bag she was holding. Half a million dollars.

She had considered trying to run away. Half a million dollars would go a long way. But they had thought about that. Wanted for Zikri's murder she would be on every television set in the country. She wouldn't even get to the airport. There was nothing else for it but to try to persuade the guy. It wouldn't be hurting anyone, just another media satellite, at least that's what the Koreans were telling her. And half a million dollars was not to be sniffed at.

Jenny turned the last corner to face the hotel. There were several coaches in the car park. Must be for the new bunch of Cosmodrome tourists that arrived yesterday. Most of the bedroom windows in the front of the hotel were lit up, they were probably turning in for the night. She was trying to spot the room where they had been the night before but was distracted by a large black limousine sweeping up the drive. She held back in the shadows and watched as the members of the WCMB delegation got out of the car. They were holding briefcases and talking loudly. They must have just returned from a late-night session at the Cosmodrome. She followed them into the lobby and held back as, in turn, they asked for their keys. To the side of the reception was a shelf full of travel brochures. She picked one up and, hiding her face, pretended to look through it. The men were still in animated conversation but following some hearty backslapping and 'good night's' they disappeared down the corridor. After a few minutes she took a deep breath, grabbed the handle of the holdall tightly and made her way to the elevator.

The next morning was as hot as the last. The members of the Space Tours trip filtered into the breakfast room in twos and threes. Nathalie and Harry were already ensconced at a corner table behind a pillar sipping their coffees and pretending to read a newspaper each.

'It's a good job they haven't got professional surveillance,' whispered Nathalie. 'The newspapers are in Kazakh and, even if they weren't, you couldn't read them anyway.'

Harry chuckled. 'Glad you've not lost your sense of humour.' He shook open the broadsheet and turned a page pretending to be engrossed in it. 'Have you spotted them yet?'

'No, oh wait, I think there's a group coming in now. They're not from our lot, wearing these terrible yellow Space Tours T-shirts.'

'Oh is that the colour? So they can't lose us I suppose; wondered why they wanted us to wear them.'

Nathalie peered around the side of her newspaper. She gasped, 'You're not going to believe this.'

'It's the WCMB team?'

'More than that, it's our Arizona friends. Sechenov, Rodin and Jacobs. They look really knackered.'

'Interesting. They weren't at dinner last night; must have been out on a jolly. Can they see us?'

'Not unless they can see through concrete pillars and these newspapers. Just a moment, I'll dig out the camera and take a few shots.'

'Hear what they're saying?'

'Unfortunately not, it's a pity that someone hasn't invented audio zoom to go with the pictures.'

'So do you think they're in league with this Usenov guy or just innocent bystanders?'

Nathalie zoomed in on the three characters, one by one. 'Not sure. There was a definite uncomfortable feeling between Rodin and Jacobs at the Mayall if you remember. The Rutherford tracking trace showed that the signal originated at a remote source. According to the correspondence in the file we discovered, Usenov has been in Kazakhstan all the time. So he has either instructed someone else to pull the trigger or they're doing it independently.'

The Tannoy system started to crackle followed by an almost incoherent announcement.

'I think that's us,' said Harry. 'The yellow shirt brigade being asked to board the coaches.'

'Right,' said Nathalie. 'Before you get up I'll just send the pictures we've got to Bagatelle – have to be lo-res at the moment, but we can patch in the original when we get back.'

'Patch it in?' asked Harry.

'Yes, Geoff's already got an editor working on the project. Rakesh is great, you'll like him. Wants to get ahead of the game, already sourcing archive from NASA. He'll put all this stuff in with our telescope shots and paste over the originals when he gets them.'

'Something else I'll have to learn,' said Harry. 'Let's hope we can get some nice video at the launch site.'

283

Much to the chagrin of Nathalie the whole coachload of yellow-shirted tourists started to sing 'Rocketman' on the road to the Cosmodrome. She closed her eyes and tried to ignore the sweat mingling with diesel that accompanied the song. Harry seemed completely oblivious to the situation and was typing frantically into his phone.

'This is the last time I'm going to join a group tour in an attempt to make a documentary film,' she said. 'Tell me when we've arrived, I'm going to try and take a nap.'

Harry, hearing some muttering next to him, pulled out his earphones.

'Sorry, what did you say?'

Nathalie opened her eyes, 'I said…' she stopped mid-sentence as she noticed a car speeding past the coach in a cloud of dust.

'That was a black limousine that's just overtaken us,' she added. 'I'm sure our three Arizona guys were inside.'

'Glad you told me that,' said Harry. 'I was just texting Adam to see if he could keep an eye on this area to watch out for any repeat of that signal. I'll now ask him to focus on the actual Cosmodrome.'

The 'actual' Cosmodrome gates loomed before them after a forty-minute uncomfortable coach ride. Their guide hopped out of the bus and gave the attendant their day passes. Nathalie was hoping to stroll around on her own but this was dashed when the tour guide held up a yellow flag on a stick and ordered them to follow like a crocodile of school children.

'How are we supposed to keep an eye on the WCMB lot when we are being dragooned around like this?' she complained to Harry.

Harry linked his arm with hers and walked meekly alongside. 'Probably for the best,' he said. 'They won't recognise us in these shirts mixed in with a bunch of tourists. As long as we know roughly where they are Adam should do the rest. A lot easier to track the signal now we know where we are looking.'

The guide was marching past the launch sites. They had had a spectacular launch the other day she was saying. A great success. Some of the group started muttering and complaining about why there wasn't one today. Nathalie used the opportunity to pan her camera around and take in the detail.

'Look towards me,' she suddenly instructed to Harry. 'I think I can see them, and the observation tower. They're not looking this way but we should obscure our faces.'

'Have you got some shots?' asked Harry.

'Zooming in now,' she replied. 'Got a big close-up of Rodin. They must be monitoring the satellite's progress from the control room.'

'Get the exact coordinates on your phone,' said Harry excitedly. 'Text them to me and I'll forward them to Adam to pinpoint the search. It's accurate within about ten metres. If the signal is sent from someone in that tower we will know.'

'Done,' said Nathalie. 'That's about all we can do for now. Let's see if we can break away from this group and do some exploring on our own. There's a cockpit of one of the old space rockets that you can sit in and play with the controls. Wouldn't mind having a go at that, just to see how cramped it is.'

'You're on,' said Harry. 'I've always read about this stuff; would be good to experience it, and I presume it will be out of sight from that viewing tower.'

Nathalie pulled a sweater from her bag and slipped it over her yellow T-shirt. Harry took his off to reveal a Pink Floyd Tour V-neck underneath.

'Trendy,' said Nathalie.

'I was once,' laughed Harry. 'Thought it suitable – "Dark Side of the Moon".'

They peeled off from the tour. The group was so engrossed in the guide giving her lecture on Yuri Gagarin that no one noticed. The rocket cockpit was even more cramped than Nathalie had anticipated. They had cut part of the machine in two, like an exploded diagram. It was possible for her to sit side-by-side with Harry, half leaning back like being in the dentist chair. She put the controls in his hands and told him how the machine was responding. A video of the receding Earth appeared on the screen in front of them. It was just a shame he couldn't see it.

Nathalie looked at the time. 'We're getting one more thing before we rejoin the group,' she said. 'Your pick.'

Harry eased himself out of the cockpit seat, 'Easy one that – Pad 41.'

Nathalie started rummaging through the brochure. 'What's that?'

'A sad story,' said Harry. 'The site of the Nedelin catastrophe.'

'I've not heard about that,' said Nathalie, eventually locating Pad 41 on her Cosmodrome brochure.

'Not many people have. In fact no one at all until 1985. The accident happened in 1960, all hushed up. If you lead me to the memorial I'll tell you about it on the way.'

There wasn't a cloud in the sky and very little topography to give any shelter so the walk was difficult in the unbearable heat. Nathalie described the buildings and artefacts on either side – large stone statues, pieces of rocket, technical buildings bearing satellite dishes – all very Eastern Bloc. In exchange Harry told her about the 1960s disaster – a short-circuit in a prototype rocket on the launch pad ignited its second stage on the ground. At least seventy-eight were killed including Chief Marshal Nedelin. The world didn't hear about it for another twenty-five years.

'It's surprising how much you could cover up in those days,' said Harry tracing his fingers across the raised names on the memorial as they stood by it.

Nathalie checked her phone. 'Well, someone is having a good job in covering up space flight today,' she said. 'Not a peep out of London. I suppose we had better rejoin the group and check-in when we get back to the hotel.'

Zikri Amin sat uncomfortably on the small stool peering into the dressing-table vanity mirror. The reflection was not a pretty sight. His mouth was bruised and swollen and his eyes were red from the sleepless night. He rubbed his wrists and inspected the cuts in his fingers that the pincers had made.

'We have to get out,' he said for the hundredth time.

Jenny had returned from her mission and found him in his room, alone, still bound to the chair. She had untied him and bathed his wounds. He was still in a state of shock and meekly let her manoeuvre him onto the bed. Neither of them had slept and they had spent the whole morning debating what to do next.

'They said if I did what I was told, they would disappear, leave us alone,' she said plaintively.

'Yes, but will *he* do as he is told,' said Zikri, addressing her image in the mirror.

'He's got half a million dollars,' she said. 'All he has to do is to move one more satellite.'

'Yes, but the coordinates they gave you, that's no media satellite. It's not even in geo-stationary orbit.'

'So what could it be?'

Zikri got up and paced up and down the hotel bedroom. 'No idea, but half a million dollars, it's got to be pretty important.'

'Well it's done now,' said Jenny in a huff. 'I don't know what he would have done to you if I hadn't gone.'

Zikri ignored her last remark. 'We've got to get out,' he said, sounding like a broken record. 'I tried to get flights this morning but the earliest is tomorrow, late afternoon. I've ordered a taxi.'

'You could have at least thanked me,' said Jenny forlornly.

The tour bus drew up at the Central Hotel and the bedraggled and tired troupe slowly made their way into the lobby. Most headed for their rooms and a cold shower. Harry and Nathalie aimed for the bar.

'Two cold beers,' ordered Harry. 'No, on second thoughts, make that four cold beers.'

The barman lined them up and watched as Harry and Nathalie downed their first in one.

'Good day?' he asked.

'Good but hot,' replied Harry picking up his second beer.

'Hotter tomorrow,' said the barman.

'In that case, I might give our last day's visit to the Cosmodrome a miss,' said Harry. 'Any chance this hotel has a swimming pool?'

The barman didn't have a chance to answer as Harry felt a vibration in his pocket. He put up his hand in apology and took out his phone.

'Sorry, I have to take this.'

He pressed the phone tightly to his ear and listened intently, only replying with the odd grunt or two. Nathalie sat on her barstool, next to him, waiting patiently. At last he put the phone away and indicated with his head that they should move somewhere more discreet. She guided him towards the corner of the bar and they sat at a quiet table.

'Yes?' she asked.

'They're doing it again.'

'What's it this time?'

'Very worrying, Adam says that JSpOC are on full alert. Some of the top brass in the States are very concerned. Reading between the lines I think someone's manipulating a military satellite.'

'That *is* worrying. Military you say. A spy sort of thing? Can't they just move it back again?'

'That's the problem, they've lost control of it completely. And Adam says it's worse than intelligence gathering, by the furore that it's causing; he thinks it could be carrying nuclear weapons.

'Shit!' exclaimed Nathalie. 'Have they traced the source?'

'As we suspected, triggered from the Cosmodrome. Exactly from the coordinates we gave them. It has to be one of those three guys.'

Nathalie's phone rang. She looked at the screen. It was Nick Coburn.

'Hi Nick, sorry but would you make it quick, we have a problem here.'

'I've heard. Panic stations everywhere. But I've got some news for you.'

Nick didn't sound his bantering self so Nathalie moved her phone over so Harry could hear.

'Go ahead Nick.'

'That video you sent Bagatelle. I viewed it with Geoff. Thought I recognised one of your WCMB guys. Couldn't pin him down at first. Then I remembered. Saw him in the Cambridge alumni magazine when I visited Jim Watts in the Battock Centre. First prize in computer science. Name of Terry Jacobs. Got a mate in the Secret Service to do some background checks. History of internet hacking as a teenager. Pretty clever stuff apparently. Some of it sensitive so didn't go to court, just a slapped wrist. Could be your guy.'

Thirty

The switchboard at JSpOC was incandescent. Silver-haired men in military uniforms were talking in small groups behind the array of monitors and keyboards. Although the aircon was turned on full the room was heating up and Carl Malczewski was getting more and more irritable.

'I'm a bloody tracker not a magician,' he muttered to his companion Ralph. 'One of those khaki geeks back there wanted me to move a piece of space junk in the way. I ask you. Move space junk! No idea these people.'

Ralph wheeled his chair a little closer to Carl so the top brass couldn't hear. 'Weird though isn't it? We've seen a black flag get into trouble before. Usually solved with a quick call from the hot phone. Moved within seconds.'

'Not this baby,' said Carl, running his finger across the mouse wheel to bring an image closer. 'They say it's been neutralised.'

'Neutralised? Sounds like a trip to the vet.'

'Army-speak for lost control of the bloody thing,' said Carl. 'Now we're getting the flak for not being able to move it back.'

Ralph was looking around the room. Some of these guys had more stripes on their arms than a zebra. 'Never seen a panic like this before. More than a spy job I think, don't you?'

Carl wasn't listening. He had suddenly spotted something on the monitors and was making lightning calculations on the computer that they had labelled 'the beast'. He gave out a low whistle.

Ralph leaned over to study the mass of numbers on the screen. 'What's up?'

'What's up is that these guys behind us are going to go so

ballistic that they might as well catch the fucking thing in a baseball glove.'

Ralph was still trying to get his head around the calculations. It slowly dawned on him that Carl had plotted the new trajectory of the incapacitated satellite for the next sixty minutes.

'Does that mean what I think it means?' he said with a worried look on his face.

'Sure does, buddy. Our friend here is on a collision course with another black flag. And this time it's not one of ours.'

It was getting late. Nathalie had checked the car park every half-hour. The WCMB limousine was yet to return.

'Perhaps they're all in it together,' said Nathalie. 'Done a runner.'

'None of this makes sense,' said Harry. 'From what Adam said this thing is military; why on earth would they be messing with that?'

The bar had closed ten minutes earlier and they had moved to the uncomfortable chairs in the lobby. There were windows but too high for them to see the driveway. Nathalie sat up as she saw a light strobe across the ceiling.

'Could be a car. I'll check it out. You duck into the gents. If it's them I'll keep out of sight and tap on the door when they've gone up.'

Her instinct was right. A sleek black Aurus was pulling into the forecourt. She slipped behind one of the tourist coaches and crouched down, peering from under the wheel arch. The three men got out, quite soberly she thought, and made their way to the lobby. Each one of them had a laptop case slung over their shoulder. A flicker of doubt passed through her mind. What if they were wrong about Jacobs? All they knew was that he was in the right place at the right time and had a history of hacking. But Rodin and Sechenov were there too. Both of them were scientists with highly developed computer skills. Terry Jacobs had wanted to talk about the satellites; it was Rodin who seemed so uncomfortable. Normally she would have needed to gather more sources, do further research. You couldn't go accusing people on broadcast television without absolute proof. That was Bagatelle's policy anyway. On this occasion, according to Harry, there was no time. Something catastrophic was going to happen. We have to confront him Nathalie, he had said.

She gave the men a few minutes to collect their keys and go to their rooms before tapping on the gents WC door. Harry appeared, telephone in hand.

'Worse than we thought. The Rutherford is getting leaked information. That satellite is not only military but has been aimed to intercept another. Massive alerts on both sides of the Atlantic. Adam thinks that JSpOc believe the target is Chinese. In the last hour the United States military's readiness has gone from DEFCON 5 to DEFCON 3. That's really serious. My guess is that both satellites could contain nuclear warheads. Internet chatter suggests that the Chinese are sabre-rattling and playing chicken. Probably don't believe that the thing is completely rudderless.'

Nathalie stood there mouth open. She had been involved in documentaries with dire consequences before but nothing remotely veering on World War Three. Harry was already making his way to the elevator.

She ran to catch up with him. 'What if it's not Terry?" she asked.

'Then we'll try one of the others,' said Harry. 'No time to be worried about people's sensitivities.'

Nathalie took him by the arm and stopped when they arrived at Terry Jacobs' room.

'Well, here we are,' she said. 'What's the plan?'

Harry softly knocked on the door. 'Fish out that camera of yours and surreptitiously film everything you see. Leave the rest to me.'

Terry Jacobs opened the door and gasped in surprise. 'Doctor Stones. What on earth are you doing here?'

'Same as you Terry. Have some business at the Cosmodrome. We are thinking of launching a new telescope satellite. Amazing coincidence, saw you in the lobby. Thought it rude not to come and say hello. Not too late for you is it?'

From behind Harry's shoulder Nathalie could see that Terry was trying to regain his composure.

'Not at all, not at all,' said Terry. 'Come in, I've got some cold beers in the minibar; would be good to catch up. A new telescope you say?'

Harry edged into the room and gestured to Nathalie standing behind him. 'You know Nathalie Thompson don't you. She's helping me get around.' He pointed to his eyes. 'Foreign environment you know, difficult to find my way.'

Terry nervously walked towards the minibar and pointed to the two small chairs by the bed.

'Yes of course, please sit down. That terrible accident – how are you by the way, Ms Thompson?'

'A lot better thank you,' said Nathalie, surveying the room and manoeuvring one of the chairs for Harry. The bedroom was identical to hers – faded green walls, cheap veneered furniture, old-fashioned concertina shades on the lamps. The minibar was the other side of the bed. There were only two of the spindly chairs. She calculated that if Harry was in one and she took the other Terry Jacobs would have to sit on the bed. The lighting wasn't great but this camera could cope with practically anything. Whilst Terry was bent down pulling out the cans of beer she lined up the shot. The camera was still in the shabby tartan case. If she put it on her lap no one would notice.

'Cheers,' said Terry putting the cold cans of beer into their hands. 'Here's to your new satellite.'

The hisses reverberated around the room as they pulled the rings. Harry took a long draught and, to Nathalie's delight, Terry placed himself on the corner of the bed.

'When did you arrive?' he asked them.

Harry leaned forward and carefully put his can on the floor.

'Just in time to discover that you had taken over another satellite,' he said calmly.

Terry's expression was priceless. Nathalie could see he was trying to interpret what Harry was saying.

'You mean, in time to see our launch, and control our new satellite,' stuttered Terry.

'Well, I wouldn't have been able to see it would I, Terry, but no, that's not what I meant. I meant control of someone else's satellite.'

'What are you talking about?' protested Terry. 'Someone else's?'

'I think you know what I'm talking about. The military satellite that you disabled. It's causing quite a bit of a problem you know.'

Terry looked like he had been shot. It took a while for him to answer. 'Military! Are you crazy?'

'It's not me that's crazy, Terry. Can you tell me why you did it? It's quite important.'

Nathalie glanced down at her viewfinder. Terry's face was going off the chroma scale. She couldn't help but admire Harry's composure. A classic documentary interview.

Terry was struggling for words.

'Let me help you,' said Harry hearing no response. 'At precisely 15:05 yesterday afternoon a United States military satellite was disabled from a signal sourced from the Baikonur control tower. The control tower where you were located, observing your own satellite.'

Terry's face had turned another colour. This time suitable for taking a white-balance, Nathalie thought.

'But there were other people there,' he was now hyperventilating. 'Doctor Rodin for instance. Yes, it must have been him.' The words were now coming out in a rush. 'I've been suspicious of his actions for some time. Moving satellites. We lost one of ours you know. He could be taking revenge.'

Harry leaned back in his chair. Nathalie had to move quickly to angle the camera to keep the shot.

'I don't think so Terry. You see the signal came from your computer. As you know the Cosmodrome have to scan them for viruses, and each computer has an individual footprint. Your boots are all over that satellite.'

Nathalie thought that Terry was about to faint. She was also wondering how on earth Harry had known about the computer identity.

Harry had repositioned himself once more. If he could have seen he would be boring his eyes into Terry's.

'Well, young Doctor Jacobs, PhD in astrophysics and computer science, I think we have very little time. I note your terror at the mention of the word military. Perhaps you didn't genuinely know that. Whether you did or you didn't I can tell you that the satellite you have disabled is on course to cause one of the biggest international incidents that this world has known. So, if we are to help you, I think we need you to tell us the whole story.'

Terry didn't give up easily. He obfuscated, pointed a finger elsewhere, said it was all a big mistake.

'I promise you, I promise you,' he eventually conceded, tears in his eyes. 'I really didn't know that satellite was military. They told me it was a media transmitter. You have to believe me.'

'That's a start,' said Harry steadily. 'So, before you tell us who *they* are, to keep me amused and to keep you out of a lifetime in jail, why don't you tell me how this all started. From the beginning.'

Terry was now shaking from head to toe. He had emotionally capitulated. Harry's mention of an international incident had obviously tweaked his imagination.

'As I told you, it was a mistake. New job at WCMB, wanted to prove myself. They were impressed with my computer skills and put me in charge of satellite navigation. The best trajectories and orbits for their observations, you know.'

Harry nodded.

Nathalie could now see that Terry's confession was being given with waves of relief.

'I made a mistake. Was playing with some of the orbits and smashed the thing into some space junk. Millions of dollars wasted into another few hundred bits of debris.'

'Did they know it was you?'

'Rodin did. Threatened me with a lawsuit and the sack.'

'So why didn't he carry out his threat? He seemed pretty keen to shelter you when we met in Arizona.'

'I found something on him. A real sleazebag. Kiddie porn on his computer.'

He paused so, to Nathalie's frustration, Harry filled in the gaps. She was imagining this interview on television.

'You blackmailed him and he kept quiet,' said Harry. 'Why didn't he spill the beans when you took down the next one?'

'I still had his files; no way was he going to go to jail as a paedophile for some media outfit.'

'Go on,' sighed Harry. 'You moved a few satellites in May and then bumped off *PhreeSat*. Why?'

'*PhreeSat*, is that what it was called? Just to see that I could do it. Became a bit of a game. You don't know how powerful it feels. Moving them about was fun but crashing one into thousands of pieces…'

'Caused a bit of problem to the viewers though.'

'I thought it was defunct. It was only when someone started moving it back I realised it was still operational.'

'So you returned it to the collision course to prove you were better.' Harry moved his audio watch to his ear. 'We're running out of time here, Terry. How did the *Diophantus* debacle come about?'

Terry put his face in his hands. 'That was terrible. I had no idea what the other satellite did. You were asking difficult questions in Arizona. I tried to cause a diversion, create confusion. FastTrack was connected to *Diophantus*. They were having difficulty in getting time on it. Annoyed with the operators. So I took it down. The navigation satellite was collateral damage. How was I to know it was crucial for shipping?'

Nathalie was now becoming anxious about the time. The shipping disaster was awful but would pale into insignificance if the current projected collision took place. She nudged Harry gently on the back.

Harry got the message. 'That leaves us with the last two, Terry. Be brief, please.'

A noise came from outside of the room. Someone was wheeling a trolley down the corridor. It stopped momentarily outside the door but took off again. Echoes of the real world seemed to break Terry's trance. He stood up from the bed.

'What do you intend to do? You have no proof. I'll deny all of it,' he spluttered.

Nathalie checked her bag and tilted the camera upwards until she had a full view of his face.

Harry remained passive. 'Difficult,' he said. 'I'm sure after we disclose the pornography on Doctor Rodin's computer he will be all too pleased to stand up in court, especially after we tell him you told us where to find it.'

Terry sat down. He opened his mouth as if to speak but shut it again.

'However,' said Harry slowly, 'all that will be chip paper if your actions have precipitated the largest nuclear fallout in history.'

Terry's eyes widened. 'Nuclear!'

'That's what we hear,' said Harry. 'Now, the last two.'

'I was blackmailed,' stuttered Terry. 'Two...two heavies from a media company broke into my room, threatened to expose my actions if I didn't take down one of their rival's satellite; said it was only carrying a few TV stations, would be up and running again in weeks.'

'And the last one?' asked Harry even more deliberately.

'The same.'

Nathalie noticed on camera that Terry flicked his eyes towards the corner of the room.

'How was it the same?' asked Harry.

'They returned, last night. Even more threatening. I was scared for my life. They said it would be the last one.'

'No mention of military,' said Harry.

'No, you have to believe me. They said it was another media thing, didn't even have to crash it, just disable the ground controls.'

'You weren't suspicious of the coordinates they gave you?'

'They looked odd, yes, but I panicked. Didn't have much time. Had to send the program from the Cosmodrome without anyone seeing.'

'And your sponsor, Usenov, has he anything to do with this?'

Terry went pale again. 'God no. He mustn't know about this, I'd rather take my chances in court. All WCMB's computers have access to his mainframe, one of the world's most sophisticated pieces of kit. If he knew I was using it to control satellites, I'd be good as dead.'

'Well we might all be that soon, Terry,' said Harry. 'Could you get back control of the thing?'

Terry shook his head, 'Completely disabled it. Instructions to keep it on the same course. Was even asked to put a remote program on it. If something tries to take it down or there's a piece of space junk in the way, it will automatically evade it.'

'Can the remote evasion program be disabled?'

Terry nodded forlornly.

'That's a yes, Harry,' intervened Nathalie.

'Terry, this is important,' said Harry with a new authority in his voice. 'Do you have the disabling codes together with the coordinates and orbital path the blackmailers gave you?'

Terry reached into the top pocket of his shirt and pulled out a piece of folded paper. Forgetting Harry was blind he held it out. Nathalie got up, switched the camera off and took the piece of paper from him.

'I would take the first flight back to the US and turn yourself in,' she said. 'I think you'll probably have more chance there than with either Usenov, or the authorities, here.'

She thrust the codes and coordinates into Harry's hand. 'If I know Harry, he has an idea. You had better start praying that it works. Otherwise I don't know if there will be anyone left to hear your story,' she said guiding her director to the door and slinging the camera over her shoulder.

Thirty-one

For such a large hotel the Central was eerily quiet. The restaurant had set-sittings and was now closed, as was the bar. With little else to do the clientele had retired to their rooms. Many of them had a busy schedule at the Cosmodrome the next day and no doubt were getting a well-earned sleep. Harry and Nathalie scurried down the poorly lit corridors and decided on Harry's room as the best meeting venue. Once inside he reached for the case beside his bed and pulled out his laptop and started typing.

'So you do have a plan?' asked Nathalie hopefully.

'Perhaps,' said Harry, 'but it depends on so many variables.'

Nathalie pulled up a chair. A small spindly thing just like the ones in Terry Jacobs's room. 'Shouldn't we call the police?'

Harry was now busy linking his phone to his laptop. 'About Terry you mean?'

'Of course. Criminal damage, manslaughter, precipitating World War Three. I think there are enough charges.'

'Fuck this cable,' said Harry, dropping his phone to the floor. 'I thought you told him to hand himself in back in the States.'

'Been having second thoughts.'

'You had the right idea the first time. We are in Russian jurisdiction. Report him and we will be sat here for hours under interrogation; not exactly a thing we've got time for at the moment. And, if the speculations are true about this American satellite hitting a Chinese one, the last thing we want to do is bring a third world power into the equation.'

'Good point,' said Nathalie picking up his phone. 'Can I help you with that?'

He took it from her and, with her aid, plugged it into the

computer. A few minutes later he had set up his mini office with his chair facing the laptop on the bed. Nathalie watched him as he flitted his fingers skilfully across the keys. He handed her the piece of paper from his pocket.

'Okay, read this out slowly and accurately, capital letters, spaces, special characters and so on. Look at my screen while you're doing so. Check that I've typed the correct thing.'

'Will you be able to manoeuvre the satellite with this?' asked Nathalie, studying the jumble of characters on the paper.

'Not a chance,' said Harry. 'He wasn't bluffing. He wouldn't even be able to take back control himself. No, we just hope that he was right when he said these codes would unlock the evasion program.'

Nathalie read the characters to him and checked them on the screen. Harry's typing was faultless.

'That's the easy bit,' said Harry, holding the phone to his ear. 'Now let's see if Adam has responded to my e-mail.'

'What e-mail?'

'Keep up, Nathalie, the one I sent as soon as we reached the room.'

Nathalie would normally have challenged this but, in the circumstances, she felt it best to leave everything to Harry. She had no understanding of the technology or how on earth he was going to prevent this disaster but he looked composed and appeared to know what he was doing.

Harry was listening to a message on his phone. His face betrayed no emotion and she was desperate to know what was happening.

'Harry, what's going on?'

Ignoring her Harry started typing again.

'Fuck!' he exclaimed.

'What's up?'

'Lost the internet connection. Fucking hotel WiFi.'

'Can you reconnect?'

'Trying, but using a lot of bites here.'

'What are you doing?'

'Connecting a three-way pathway – me, Cosmat and Joint Space Ops.'

'How…' began Nathalie.

'Bloody miracle,' said Harry rebooting his computer. 'Everyone on standby admittedly but to get access to JSpOC, now that's something.'

Now wasn't the time to ask about details, she could see he had enough on his plate. His computer flickered back into life.

'Any luck?'

'Not a squeak,' said Harry, 'and we've only got twenty minutes.'

'The lobby,' cried Nathalie.

Harry looked puzzled.

'It's always where the best WiFi reception is.'

'Brilliant,' said Harry snapping his laptop shut. 'Let's go.'

'Privacy will be difficult,' said Nathalie following him. 'There's a receptionist on even at this time of night.'

'Don't worry about that,' said Harry. 'I have an idea.'

The Ops Centre had gone quiet. In movies world-scale disasters are often portrayed by noise, clamour and the rushing about of staff screaming into telephones. In reality, the worse the situation the quieter it gets. Behind the scenes diplomats were trying to talk to the Chinese who were having nothing of it. In a nuclear bunker somewhere meetings were being held debating the criteria in raising DEFCON 3 to DEFCON 4; and in the Ops Centre, Carl Malczewski was planting an elbow on his desk with his hand on his forehead wondering why in the hell his screen had gone black.

Harry's 'bloody miracle' linking him to JSpOC and Cosmat had come about because of the freak chance that Adam Brookes, director of the Rutherford, had once worked for GCHQ. In that capacity he had forged relationships with JSpOC's controller. The controller had run out of options and, once the Kazakhstan situation was explained, it hadn't taken long for approval to be granted. All had been going well until five minutes ago.

'Jesus,' said Carl, almost under his breath, 'why now? Only ten minutes to impact. Even if those baby nukes aren't armed there's going to be one hell of a mess.'

'Not to mention a slight diplomatic hiccup with the Chinese,' said Ralph. 'Can't you do something with the remaining feed? The guy from Cosmat in Guildford is still there.'

'You don't pronounce the D,' chastised Carl. 'Even if you did, it's no use without the Stones guy. He's got all the data.'

'And the nearest satellite,' said Ralph. 'Let's prey he can get reconnected.'

The lobby gents was cramped, and not very sanitary Nathalie thought as she sniffed the air. The solitary receptionist had given them a strange look as they had entered the WC and locked the door behind them. Harry sat on the pan with his computer on his lap. Nathalie, not wanting to sit on the floor, stood pressed against the small hand basin. She suffered the resulting pain in her back as the lesser of two evils.

'Any luck?' she asked.

'Be patient, I've only just booted it up again.'

Nathalie hated the delay of computers at the best of times. From what Harry had said they only had five minutes to avert a worldwide crisis. Waiting for a bar to crawl across the screen in an edit was going to be a relative pleasure after this.

'Bingo,' he cried. 'You were right about the reception.'

'You've still not told me exactly what you're doing,' said Nathalie.

'Right, now I've got a connection, while we wait for these codes to download, I can tell you.' Harry pressed the 'send' key with aplomb. 'Now it's all up to Trevor and that Carl chap.' He swung the laptop so she could see. 'Is the little wheel still spinning?'

'Yep,' she said, 'spinning away. What's it doing?'

Harry leaned back against the cistern. 'The evasion codes have been sent to the Space Op Centre. If that worm Jacobs isn't lying, Carl will be able to stop their satellite from getting out of the way.'

Nathalie tried to rub her back, but there was little room to get a hand behind her. 'Getting out of the way of what?' she asked, wincing.

'My beloved space telescope,' said Harry. 'It happens to be in close proximity to the military one.'

Nathalie suddenly forgot the pain in her back. 'You're going to crash it into the nuclear satellite!'

'Well, Trevor is. I've given him Jacobs' coordinates. Trevor is a pain but he's highly skilled at manoeuvring satellites.' Harry put his audio watch to his ear. 'It should be hitting it in five, four, three, two, one – seconds.'

'But it's *nuclear*!' screamed Nathalie.

'Yes, but not armed. It will make a hell of a mess though.'

Nathalie watched as a large smile came across Harry's face.

'You've just lost your satellite,' she said. 'What's so amusing?'

'I was just thinking of the receptionist's face as we leave this toilet,' he said. 'Being in the gents together is one thing, you screaming *nuclear* is quite another.'

The forecasters had got it right. It was even hotter that day than yesterday. What had made it worse was that the Sputnik Hotel's air conditioning had collapsed under the strain. Jenny and Zikri had cowered in their rooms all morning ordering snacks and ice which never came. They communicated by the cheap pay-as-you-go phones that Zikri had supplied. Fat lot of use the covert security was now thought Jenny. Her bedroom window was stuck and she was trying to keep cool by splashing water over her face. She didn't dare step into the corridor in case she ran into those two North Korean brutes. In the hallucinogenic heat she was now repeating Zikri's mantra, 'We've got to get out.'

He had ordered the cab for noon. It had meant they would be at the airport early but a clinical air-conditioned waiting lounge seemed like nirvana at the moment. Her phone rang.

'Have you packed?'

Had she packed! She had packed the moment she had got up after that brief restless sleep. All she had to do was to be given the word and grab her bag.

'Of course, has the taxi arrived?'

'Take the back stairs, I'll meet you at the rear entrance. No need to check out, I'll pay by card on the phone when we get back to Kuala Lumpur.'

Kuala Lumpur. It sounded like the world's greatest holiday destination. What she would do to be there in her small apartment right now.

'Coming,' she said, snapping off the phone.

Her case was by the door. She took it in one hand and peered into the corridor. First one way, then the other. No one in sight. Only crazy people would be staying inside this oven on a day like this. The stairs were at the other end of the passage. She lifted the case rather than put it on its wheels to avoid the sound. A buzzing sound came from her pocket. She took out the phone, annoyed with herself for not putting it on silent and annoyed with Zikri for calling her again.

'It's a green Lada, driver by the name of Ahmed. Put your case in the trunk and get in the back, I'll be with you in two minutes.'

But there was no green Lada. In its place, a gleaming black Mercedes. A smart suited driver leaning on the wheel arch.

'Please, let me take bag,' he said in Russian accented English. 'Sorry, Ahmed called in sick today, I am replacement.'

Jenny looked nervously around for Zikri. Should she wait for him? Two minutes he had said. The sun was scorching and that Mercedes looked like it had efficient aircon. She handed the man her case and let him open the car door for her. The interior of the car was as cool as ice. For the first time in days Jenny sat back in the luxurious seats and relaxed. It felt like her nightmare was soon to be over.

Zikri was as good as his word and within minutes appeared from the rear entrance to the hotel, blinking in the sunshine. She wound down the window, a smooth glide at the press of a button, and shouted to him.

'The other driver's sick,' she said. 'Our luck, this luxury limousine was the only car left at their depot.'

The driver introduced himself to Zikri, took his bag, and insisted on holding the rear door open for him.

Zikri complied and slipped into the cool leather seats.

'It's so good to get out of that furnace,' he sighed. 'I never want to go through anything like that again.'

The chauffeur had closed the trunk and was getting into the driver's seat.

'I close the glass,' he said, 'very hot day, much cooler for you. Drinks in armrest.'

The glass divider slid between them with a low electronic hum. Jenny looked at the frosted bottles of mineral water, took one, unscrewed the cap and drank deeply. Zikri smiled at her, removed the other and did the same.

'The airport,' he said, 'but the driver, who hadn't been able to hear him through the glass, was already on his way.

The restaurant at the Central Hotel was only half full. Harry and Nathalie had been up all night and had not only missed breakfast but the tour group to the Cosmodrome. The lunch menu was a set-meal but, because Harry and Nathalie didn't have a voucher, no food was forthcoming. The Space Tours' arrangement was for a packed lunch and, no matter how much Nathalie ranted, they had all been put on the coach and there were none left. Eventually Harry sweet-talked the waitress into giving them a salad.

'I think the large tip helped,' he said forking a piece of tomato into his mouth. 'Probably tastes better than those stale sandwiches we had yesterday.'

'I'm almost glad we missed the trip,' said Nathalie, 'it's baking hot out there.'

'Well, we've got what we came for and averted a world crisis to boot,' said Harry. 'Got voicemails from Adam and my boss, Bernard, when I woke up. Cosmat are heroes apparently. Wanted to give us some sort of gold star. I sent a reply saying that I'd prefer a new telescope.'

'We still don't know who made Terry do it. Two thugs he said. I was itching for you to ask him more but the opportunity passed.'

'Yes, that was conscious. Just felt that what he was saying didn't ring true. Don't think he would have given us a photo fit anyway, more than his life was worth. The clock was ticking. The time was best spent getting the satellite data.'

There was a sudden commotion at the restaurant entrance. Nathalie turned to see their yellow shirted tour group spilling into the room. She explained to Harry what was happening and tried to get the attention of the nearest tourist.

'Hi, what's up? Thought the Cosmodrome trip was an all-day event.'

'I wish,' said the young man. 'Been shut down for the afternoon. The place is crawling with private security guards. Looking for a missing VIP or something.'

Nathalie waited until the man had re-joined his group before addressing Harry.

'Sounds like our Mr Jacobs has done a bunk. Wouldn't be surprised if those guards were Usenov's.'

'Agreed,' said Harry. 'Not much we can do about it now, but I think we've got enough for our film. We're on a group visa, best to keep to the tour schedule and go back to the UK with them tomorrow morning.'

'I don't think we've got any other option,' mused Nathalie. 'I reviewed some of the video interview, good stuff but it begged one question.'

'What's that?'

'How did you know that it was Terry's computer and not one of the others?'

'I didn't' said Harry, 'just made a guess.'

Nathalie shook her head with a smile. 'Perhaps you should give up your day job. Though while you're still working for Bagatelle we have a script to write. Suggest we leave this bunch of malcontents in the restaurant and retire to the bar.

She picked up her laptop, took Harry by the hand and led him out of the restaurant. To get to the bar they had to pass through the lobby. Nathalie winked at the receptionist on the way.

The Mercedes limousine drove smoothly out of the city. The nearest airport, Krayniy, was only twenty minutes away. The flights from there only went to a few destinations and it would mean a number of changes but Jenny could cope with that. Anything to get out of this godforsaken place. She turned to look at Zikri, his eyes were closed, she decided to follow suit and dozed in the back of the almost silent car.

She was woken with a jolt. The car had obviously hit rougher terrain. Looking at her watch she noticed that more than half an hour had passed. They should have been at the airport some time ago. She nudged Zikri awake. He must have been in a deep slumber for he jumped and made a sharp noise. Jenny looked out of the window, nothing but scrub and the odd bush.

'What airport did you book?'

Zikri was still rubbing his eyes. 'I told you, Krayniy. Why, are we nearly there?'

Jenny started tapping on the glass divider. 'I think he must have missed the turning, we should have been there ages ago.'

It was Zikri's turn to look out of the window. 'This isn't the way? Tell the guy to stop.'

But the driver either did not hear her or, as it was slowly dawning on Jenny, he was ignoring her.

She thumped on the partition with as much force as she could muster. No response. The shape in front of her behind the glass continued staring at the road in front. Jenny tried the door; handles. They were locked. That shouldn't have surprised her as many modern cars automatically lock in motion but it made her feel trapped. She stared out of the window again; the car was turning off into a smaller lane. What she saw next made her feel sick in her stomach. In the distance becoming remorselessly larger by the moment was an isolated farmhouse. She had seen it before. It had been with a man called Nikolai.

The Mercedes pulled into the yard. The driver switched off the ignition and got out. This time he did not offer to open the door; without even turning to look at them, he walked away and out of sight. Jenny's head was in a blur. Zikri was trying to ask something but the words made no sense. Suddenly the car doors flew open. Two large figures grabbed them both and roughly dragged them out of the car. Jenny instantly recognised the men and fainted.

When she came to she was sitting in a chair. The room had whitewashed walls and a large stone fireplace accompanied by a crude wooden settle. Her wrists and ankles were hurting. She stared at them to find they were tied tightly with electrical wire to the chair. The hulk of the man standing next to her must have guessed her thoughts.

'Shout out if you like, Miss Kang, there's no one to hear you.' He walked around the chair to face her. 'I must say we are very disappointed. It seems that your friend didn't take down that satellite after all.'

Jenny's eyes widened as she watched the man take out a pair of pincers from his pocket.

'Also, as your late colleague doesn't know, perhaps you might tell us what you have done with our half a million dollars.'

Only the pigs, feeding in the nearby barn, could hear Jenny's screams as the cold metal bit into her finger.

Thirty-two

A thin grey mist tumbled over the Soho streets. Solely the warmth of the air and the humid smell from the pavements suggested that it was early July. The media crowd, in their summer shorts, were wondering whether to pause in doorways or stride assertively to their darkened studios. It seemed set in for the day so Nathalie chose the latter and headed along Compton Street towards her destination. She hadn't seen Harry since their return. He had been locked in at Cosmat with some military types being debriefed, so she had got Geoff's permission to get some video interviews from the States and primed the editor on her own. Now she was on her way to one of the highlights of film-making – the viewing of the rushes. She had promised Harry she would wait for him, describe every shot in detail. He really did deserve the director's credit on this one. Without his heroics there wouldn't be a film.

The cutting-room chosen by Bagatelle was in Wardour Street behind an anonymous door concealing a set of narrow stairs. Geoff had hired this outfit before, not for the editing suite but for the editor, Rakesh. The guy didn't just have computer skills, he had rhythm, something you couldn't teach. Give him the pictures and a story and it would flow seamlessly through the ether. A talent acknowledged by four BAFTAs. She reached the landing and looked out for the door sign in the corridor, Cutting-Room 2. The words were nostalgic to Nathalie. In the recent past they really were cutting-rooms – places where editors manually spliced pieces of cut-up film together with tape. Today computers did the job, putting the images into electronic bins, rather than canvas ones, and joining them by touches on multi-coloured keyboards. She knocked and entered.

311

'Hi, Nathalie,' said Rakesh without turning around. 'Long time no see.'

'It's because you're always so busy,' said Nathalie, throwing her bag on the viewing sofa. 'And how did you know it was me?'

Rakesh pointed at a small monitor above his edit station. It showed the exterior of Wardour Street. 'Surveillance everywhere,' he grinned.

'Harry Stones been in yet?'

'Looks like he's just arrived,' said Rakesh, nodding at the screen again before turning back to his keyboard and entering some digits.

'Geoff's explained the situation,' said Nathalie.

'Yes, should be interesting. I've lined up the rushes in bins and put a few rough-cut scenes together. It's my scratch voice-over on the audio, so bit of a crap delivery, but gives some idea of timing. How do you want to play it?'

'From the beginning,' said Harry, entering the room. 'Describe the pictures to me and I'll stop you if you're going too fast.' He held his hand in the direction of the editor's voice. 'Harry Stones by the way.'

Rakesh got up from his chair and shook Harry's hand. 'Pleased to meet you, Harry. I'm, Rakesh, your editor.'

'Not the son of the famous…'

'Rakesh Roshan, no. Named after him though. My father is quite a fan.'

'Well if you make films as good as your namesake, we should get on fine,' said Harry. 'Now what have you got for us?'

Nathalie had never heard of Rakesh Roshan but, without letting on, she spent the next minutes describing the pictures to Harry. Many of the images he could visualise – he had been to the locations before – when sighted. The archive too was not difficult. Rocket launches, satellites and images of the Earth. Interestingly, where he wanted the video replayed was at Terry Jacobs' interview. The man's expressions were important to him.

'I think we've got a good story: the dangers of unsupervised space vehicles; the lack of security; territorial ownership; the millions of pieces of space junk up there, clouding our view for astronomical observations, and endangering critical communications. But what I like is Rakesh's idea of getting all this across with a personal narrative. And the problem with that is that we have a few pieces missing.'

Nathalie was amazed at how quickly Harry had grasped the idea of documentary filmmaking.

'You mean, what happened to Terry and, despite his denial, how far was Usenov involved?'

'If I might chip in here,' said Rakesh.

'By all means,' said Harry.

'I think it can be quite alluring to leave some of those questions for the viewer. Show them we don't have all the answers. Give them a chance to debate amongst themselves.'

'Good point,' said Harry, 'but I still feel we could give them some more clues.'

Nathalie checked her phone. 'Hopefully we might get some of those over lunch,' she said. 'Geoff just confirmed he's taking us out to the Ivy. I asked him to get a researcher onto the Kazakhstan newsfeeds. Sounds like he might have something for us.'

The Ivy was unusually quiet for a Wednesday afternoon. Harry and Nathalie were shown to Geoff's favourite table at the back of the restaurant. He had obviously been there for some time as the bottle of Meursault was already half empty. Papers were strewn across the table and he scooped them up as they joined him.

'Great to see you both. Glad to see your bruises have gone, Nathalie. Popped round the edit suite the other day. Rakesh thinks we've got a winner. Glass of wine?'

'Looking good,' said Nathalie. 'A lot of work to do yet though. Harry thinks we should tease out the story more.'

'I think I can help there,' said Geoff pushing one of the pieces of paper for Nathalie to read. 'She'll give you the details later, Harry, but our researcher has come up with dynamite.'

'The one you asked to check out the Kazakhstan news?' asked Harry.

'Too right' said Geoff. 'Though her job wasn't that difficult. It's been a media sensation over there. Lurid headlines in the papers and on all their main broadcast channels.'

Nathalie sipped her wine. 'Well, don't keep us in suspense.'

'In a nutshell, two people have been found tortured and butchered in a country farmhouse not far from Baikonur. Not much of them left. Fed to the pigs would you believe? Farmer, wife and sister also dead, in the house with their throats cut.'

'So what's that got to do with our film,' said Nathalie, suddenly feeling quite queasy.

'Your friend Terry Jacobs was picked up at the airport carrying a holdall containing half a million dollars. They found one of the poor girl's fingers behind a cupboard on the farmhouse floor. The prints match the ones on Jacobs' bag.' Geoff pointed to the article he had just given Nathalie. 'One of Moscow's top investigators, Nikolai Turgenev, is on the scene. The girl's mobile phone was found with the money. Jacobs has been arrested as a murder suspect.'

For a moment Harry and Nathalie sat in silence. The waiter came to take their order but they waved him away.

Harry was the first to speak. 'Do we know who the girl is, or should I say was?' he asked softly.

'They're not giving that away at the moment,' said Geoff. 'I've asked Stefanie to get someone onto it.'

Nathalie was reading the news article. 'A canvas bag it says.'

Geoff looked puzzled. 'So?'

Nathalie started to get up. 'Harry, do you mind if we skip lunch, there's something I'd like to check in the edit suite.'

'That was quick,' said Rakesh as Harry and Nathalie entered the cutting-room. 'I haven't even had chance to finish my sandwich.'

'You're the lucky one,' groaned Harry. 'This young woman has dragged me across Soho, through the rain, with an empty stomach.'

Nathalie ignored them both. 'Rakesh, spin through to the Jacobs interview and show it again.'

The editor spun round in his chair, pulled up the piece and pressed play. Terry's desperate voice came out of the speakers. Nathalie stared intently at the screen and, after a few minutes, rapped on the edit desk with her knuckles.

'That's it. Stop! Replay the last thirty seconds. Harry, listen carefully and tell me what you hear.'

Despite the recording being made through the camera's mic the audio was clear.

I was blackmailed. Two... Two heavies from a media company broke into my room. Threatened to expose my actions if I didn't take down one of their rival's satellite. Said it was only carrying a few TV stations, would be up and running again in weeks.

Harry's voice could be heard off mic.

And the last one?

After a short pause Terry gave his answer.

The same.

'Freeze there,' cried Nathalie. 'What did you get from that, Harry?'

'Not very convincing,' said Harry. 'I felt it then. His hesitation, something not ringing true.'

'I agree,' said Nathalie. 'Also, what you can't see is his body language. When you asked him about the last satellite his eyes glanced towards the corner of the room. I noticed it at the time. Now I think I know what he was looking at. Rakesh, can you blow up the image in the right-hand corner?'

Rakesh flipped a few controls which caused the picture to zoom in. There in the edge of frame was a large canvas holdall.

It had been raining all week. Another lousy summer. Geoff Sykes shook off his raincoat and threw it towards the coat stand. It missed. Leaving it on the floor, he switched on his monitor to show rolling twenty-four-hour news, turned it to mute and pressed the intercom button on his desk.

'Stefanie, did you give that stuff to Harry and Nathalie?'

'As soon as they arrived, Geoff. They're in the boardroom reading it now.'

'Could you ask them to step in,' said Geoff. 'I can't wait to see their faces.'

Within minutes his request was answered. Harry and Nathalie were bubbling.

'Where did you get this?' asked Nathalie, waving the report in excitement.

'Same researcher,' replied Geoff. 'Some good contacts in Kazakhstan. Who would have believed that the poor girl who was murdered was connected to that first satellite?'

'*PhreeSat*,' pondered Harry. 'The collision that started this whole thing off.'

'Makes our programme more interesting,' said Nathalie. 'Going to be difficult though, tying together all the loose ends.'

Geoff was now doing his traditional pacing around the room. 'Don't think you need to do that. Better to leave it in the air. By all means mention the connections – the people who had most vested interest in bringing these things down, MalaySat for one. Their shares are rocketing. And the military stuff? Any state who wanted to cause a problem between China and the US – let the audience have their own views.'

'That's just what Rakesh said,' ruminated Harry.

'Told you he was a good editor,' said Geoff.

Finally summer seemed to have won the day. The sunlight leaked through the murky clouds and started to light up the London streets.

For the first time in a week Rakesh had had to switch on the cutting-room aircon. The programme was all but finished, a final tweak here, a few frames there. He was pleased with the result. Not much to do now other than a professionally recorded voice-over and some titles and credits. The producer and the director were sitting on the viewing couch behind him waiting for the final run through.

'We'll do the same as before,' said Nathalie. 'Rakesh will run the movie and I'll whisper the picture changes.'

Harry nodded. 'Though you probably don't have to; I nearly know it off by heart we've played the rough-cuts so many times. Oh, and while we are waiting, I heard some interesting news this morning.'

'Which is?'

'Cosmat have had an application from Sechenov. Wants to join our Cold Dark Matter team.'

'He's leaving WCMB?'

'It's been disbanded. Rodin has disappeared and Usenov has pulled the plug on the funds.'

'Wow,' said Nathalie. 'Shouldn't be surprised though, the scandal I suppose.'

'Yes with their protégé Jacobs being secreted away in Russia and Rodin about to be exposed for child pornography, I don't expect the billionaire astronomer will get the plaudits he is looking for.'

They were interrupted by Geoff bursting into the room.

'What are you doing here, Mr Sykes,' exclaimed Nathalie. 'Don't you know it's the convention for us to have the first viewing of the director's cut?'

'Not interfering,' panted Geoff, who had obviously run up the stairs. 'Wanted to tell you in person. Broadcasters say we need to get this thing out this evening.'

'This evening!' said Nathalie in shock.

'Cooped up here you obviously haven't heard today's breaking news. The Russians have just brought down a Ukrainian satellite.'

'Not the one that's just been launched?' asked Harry. 'The one for the global air pollution study?'

'That's not what the Russians are saying, they allege it was being used for covert spying. They also claim that the Ukrainian technology was so poor that its orbit decayed and the thing burned up in the Earth's atmosphere.'

'Terry Jacobs,' said Harry, to no one in particular.

Geoff either didn't hear or pretended not to. 'The point is, we need to get this programme out now. Incredibly topical. Viewing figures should go through the roof. So, don't care what stage you're at, record the voice-over, slap on the music and bike it over to me by six o'clock.'

Without giving any of them time to object he left the room.

Nathalie took a deep breath. 'You heard what the man said. We better get this thing finished.'

'The title, we haven't got a title yet,' said Harry.

'Well, it's about a threat we can't see and it was conceived by a blind film director,' said Rakesh already typing in the title caption. 'There's only one thing it can be called.'

Also by Martin Granger

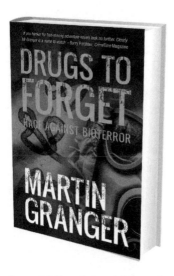

In a smoky hut in the middle of the African bush the eyes of the man in the mask stared into the camera. His threat was chilling. 'And if they don't,' he said, 'we will unleash hell by giving them a dose of African disease.'

Nathalie Thompson's film on bioterror takes her from the desolate interior of Zimbabwe to the Indonesian jungle. Posing as a Western activist and campaigner for the rights of Africans, Nathalie attempts to expose a Zimbabwean terrorist group and their possible involvement in an unusual outbreak of Ebola in Harare.

But when her new researcher Tom Finch unearths a laboratory in Eastern Java, which is suspected of producing biochemical weapons, they find themselves involved in a threat which may be closer to home than they realise. Can Nathalie unravel this dangerous plot in time to broadcast the facts and prevent the spread of a deadly disease?

DRUGS TO
FORGET

One

The explosion could be heard five blocks away. In the cafés of downtown Harare people steadied their spilling coffee. They were not the first to feel the blast. The German Ambassador was given a brief warning by a flash of light, then a muffled sound, and then silence. A few minutes later he slowly opened his eyes to see a cloud of dust swirling through a large hole in the once-tiled roof. He was on his back, legs pinned to the floor by some sort of concrete object with iron bars sticking out of it. A man in a flak jacket wearing a black beret shone a torch into his eyes and mouthed something. It took a while for him to realise the man was shouting, but he couldn't hear a thing.

The embassy was a small unassuming building with ornamental porticos and art deco styled bay windows. It had a yellow German plaque on the wall bearing the familiar black eagle. That was now all in the past tense. The plaque had disappeared along with half of the front wall. Special Forces climbed over the rubble to pick through the debris. Three members of the clerical staff, two of them African, were dead, buried under bricks and mortar. Those in the back offices had survived; some just covered in dust, others like the ambassador with broken bones. They carried him out on a stretcher.

Within hours a forensic team were picking over the details. A crude bomb, an effective one but crude nevertheless. Probably did more damage than intended. It had been placed under a structural pillar, one under investigation by the embassy's surveyor. A crack had been reported several weeks ago. But even if the bombers had not meant to bring down half the building, it was no consolation to the dead.

Lloyd Bamba showed his ID to a uniformed officer. Journalist, Zimbabwe Times. He was waved away with a threatening gesture of an M4 machine gun. After taking some surreptitious pictures with his phone he retreated and went back to his office. The files on bombings in Harare were sketchy. The mid-eighties, a huge explosion blamed on South African covert forces rumoured to be targeting the liberation movement in exile. The late nineties, a blast in the Sheraton, the venue for a Commonwealth summit. Closer to home, two attacks on his rival newspaper The Daily News in 2000 and 2001. Allegedly instigated by Zimbabwean security forces for its anti-presidential propaganda. Seemingly no connective thread with any of them. Lloyd turned to his editor.

'Can't seem to find a common lead, I'll have to go back when the dust has settled.' He suddenly realised the pun. 'I mean that metaphorically; when those twitchy guys with guns have relaxed a bit. Any ideas?'

The editor turned his screen towards Lloyd. 'Only this on WikiLeaks; from their Global Intelligence Files. Some sort of chatter about that bomb blast in Harare Central Police Station around election time. Police blamed the opposition party, others citing ZANU-PF. One common theme though.'

Lloyd peered at the text on the screen. 'Which is?'

'All of the authors, including the US Defence Intelligence Agency, agree that there are no active militant groups in Zimbabwe.'

Lloyd went back to his desk and started downloading the photographs from his phone. One caught his eye. He enlarged it and examined the image on his laptop.

'By the look of this, I think that might have just changed.'

Lloyd waited until dusk to make his way back to the embassy. This time he went via the grounds of the polytechnic. He entered the main building and climbed the staircase to the top floor. From here he had a view across Prince Edward Street and towards the roof of the damaged embassy. The area had been cordoned off and an armoured car sat at the entrance. He could see that if he approached the site from the girl's high school there was a small gap in the perimeter where he might gain access. He descended the stairs, strode across the street and through the high school as if he belonged. To a passer-by he would be taken as a teacher. Parts of the embassy were draped in orange striped tape, a few disinterested soldiers hovered around. Lloyd crossed one of the lawns confidently as if taking a short-cut home. No one seemed to notice. As he had anticipated the vigilance level had dropped and it was getting dark so he cast few shadows. He took out his phone, studied the picture and made his way to the spot. There it was. Under a piece of rubble a charred piece of paper. He was bending down to pick it up when he was startled by a shout.

'Halt, don't move. Put your hands on your head.'

Lloyd was wondering how he was going to put his hands on his head without moving when a steel barrel was thrust into his back.

'On your head, I said,' snapped the voice.

Lloyd slowly crumpled the paper into a ball and put his hands into the air.

'Turnaround!' The order was shouted.

Without lowering his arms Lloyd gradually rotated his body to face an intimidating soldier who was aiming his gun at him.

'Oh it's you,' barked the soldier. 'The journalist. I thought I told you to disappear.'

'Only doing my job,' said Lloyd quietly.

'And my job is to shoot intruders,' retorted the soldier.

'I'm sorry, I thought that…'

'I'm not interested in what you think. Get out, and if I see you here again I'll shoot first and ask questions afterwards.'

Lloyd deliberately lowered his arms, keeping his fist tightly closed. 'I'll go, but if there's anyone that can give me an interview...'

'You're pushing it son. Get out of my sight or the only interview you'll get is in a prison cell.' The soldier gestured to the exit with his weapon. 'Now!'

Lloyd picked his way across the masonry, the concrete and dust crunching underneath his feet. He didn't look back. He had what he had come for in his right hand. A leaflet left by the bombers. One of probably many that they had placed to promote their cause. The only problem for them was that the explosion had been so immense that the pamphlets had been scattered to the winds. A bombsite wasn't the place to read it so Lloyd made his way to the Book Café on the corner of Sixth Street. The café was a place for actors, musicians and writers. A space where artists liked to exchange ideas. It had been shut down for a while but now had relocated to a building near the Holiday Inn. It was the one place where Lloyd felt comfortable. There was a show on that night and people had started to gather in the bar. He ordered a beer and sat at a small table in the corner. The ball of paper in his hand was badly damaged. He slowly unwrapped it and smoothed it out on the table top. It was charred and torn but he could still make out the cheap printing. The grammar was poor but the message was clear. The West should stop exploiting African resources or they would get more of this. Lloyd assumed 'this' referred to the destruction by the bomb. The top portion of the pamphlet was missing but he could just about make out a logo. A capital E was followed by a large X, the strokes of which extended above the letters either side of it. Lloyd put two and two together and guessed at the acronym. WEXA; the Western Exploitation of Africa. The name was not unfamiliar to him. Despite the claims of WikiLeaks' Global Intelligence Files Lloyd had heard rumours about this group in this very café. The gossip was that this was neither a pro or anti-government lobby, but an extremist group with a grudge against Western involvement in African affairs. No clear-cut agenda apparently, just a small group of very angry young men. They were thought to be harmless malcontents. Well they weren't harmless now. Lloyd folded up the paper and made his way back to the office to write up his piece.

Three thousand kilometres away in Brazzaville a Zimbabwean nurse sat in her hotel room. To all intents and purposes she was a volunteer there to help the overloaded Congolese health service. She had travelled incognito and wished for no publicity. The Ebola outbreak was not meant to be talked about. But her experiences in Sierra Leone had made her the perfect candidate. She knew how to diagnose the disease and cope with the grieving relatives of the dead. Burying the contaminated bodies without contracting the virus was one of the keys to preventing it from spreading further. She had arrived a week ago and been through the local induction course. Now she was preparing for her first site visit away from the banks of the Congo. She was on the top floor and could see Kinshasa in the distance over the vast brown river. Many people confused the two regions: the Republic of the Congo on one side and the Democratic Republic on the other. Salina was not one of them. Her brief had been very clear. She turned away from the window and reached into her canvas medical bag. A smooth black object, something like a glasses' case, nestled in one of the pockets. The metal hinge creaked slightly as she opened it. Inside a glass vial and a plastic syringe. She screwed the long needle onto the syringe and inserted it into the rubber membrane of the vial. Slowly she pulled back the plunger and held it up to watch the liquid draw through. The needle was extricated, and with a flick of her finger the bubble dispersed. She rolled up her sleeve and gently pushed the needle into her arm. Insurance, that's all it was, but what she was about to do was far more dangerous than her normal practice. She replaced the equipment into the case and snapped it shut. Now for a shower and bed; it would be a long day tomorrow.

The health district vehicle turned up at 7.00 am. It had seen better days. Bald tyres, rusted wheel arches and a smashed-in headlight. Salina threw her bag in the back and sat beside the driver. The airconditioning wasn't working so she wound down the window. It was as hot outside as it was in but, as the car moved into the traffic, there was at least some breeze caused by the movement. The driver didn't have much to say for himself so she sat there in silence watching the crowded city. They passed the airport and drove away from the river along the N1 to Geula. It was humid as one would expect on the fringes of an equatorial river basin but at least it wasn't raining. It was the beginning of the wet season and Salina had already experienced one of the apocalyptic thunderstorms that threw water from the sky. The road had become impassable and her earlier visit had to be aborted. Now the road was clear, fringed by walls of red mud and the thick dark green vegetation beyond. The journey was only forty kilometres but the vehicle was so slow that it took nearly two hours to cover the distance. Salina reached for the water bottle in her bag; it was warm but she drank some anyway.

The driver pointed out of the window. 'There, just beyond those trees.'

She turned around to see a small clearing and a wooden house with two pitched roofs at right angles. It was constructed like a log cabin, only the logs were ten centimetres wide; despite this it was neat enough. The driver pulled off the road and stopped about a hundred metres from the house.

'That's as far as I go, I'll stay in the car.'

Salina threw him a disapproving glance before opening the door. He shrugged his shoulders as he passed her the bag. She slung it over her shoulder and marched towards the house. A young boy in ragged clothes ran out to meet her. She would have loved to have hugged him but she held up her hands for him to stop, took a mask and gloves from her bag and gestured for him to show the way. The interior was lit with kerosene lamps. A woman with tear-streaked cheeks greeted her and became effusive with thanks. Salina nodded politely and without taking the woman's hand moved towards the bed in the corner of the room. It was the last stages; she could tell that at a glance. She had already been told about the fever, diarrhoea and vomiting. Now she could see a rash and severe bruising around the man's face. He was moaning, doubled up with stomach pain. This was the nineteenth reported case, but the authorities wanted them to be kept quiet, or denied. Her job was to keep the patients comfortable and ensure as little contact as possible on burial. She despaired at the former; she had few drugs in her bag. As for the contact, the wife and little boy would take some persuading.

Salina placed her gloved hand on the man's forehead. It was dripping with sweat. A small stainless steel container with its vacuumed glass lining was in her pocket. It unscrewed easily. She placed a cotton bud into the patient's mouth, moved it around gently and then placed the tip into the container. A few turns and the rubber seal was tightened. Her work was done but the little boy looked up at her with pleading eyes and so she took off her gloves, reached into her bag and pressed some painkillers into his palms.

'Give these to him with plenty of water. Plenty of water, you hear me?'

He nodded. By his look he knew, as she did, that these ineffective tablets would be vomited out within minutes.

The return journey was as silent as the one on the way out. Salina was glad of it. She and the driver knew that the man would be dead within days. But it would be another nurse accompanying him for the burial. She would be flying back to Zimbabwe, a precious cargo in her hands.

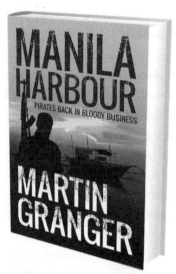

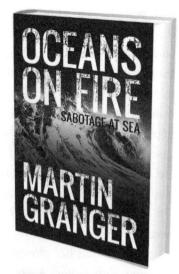

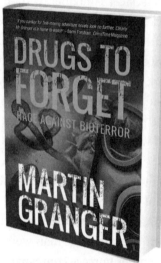

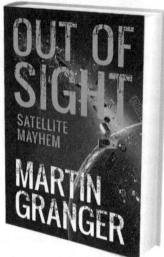

Whilst many books are made into films, Martin Granger's films have been made into books. The Nathalie Thompson series are inspired by a real film company and real events. The author has trodden Nathalie's path when making actual investigative television documentaries and many of the anecdotes and incidents are true. But what turns the plots into thrillers is the liberal sprinkling of crime amongst the pages.

Available in all good bookshops

About the author

Martin Granger has been making documentary films for thirty years. In that time he has won more than one hundred international film awards. His work has ranged from directing BBC's *Horizon* to producing a BAFTA nominated science series for Channel 4. His novels, although fiction, are based upon his experience in the film industry. He lives in Wimbledon with his wife Jacqueline.

www.martingrangerbooks.com

Find out more about RedDoor
Press and sign up to our
newsletter to hear about our
latest releases, author events,
exciting **competitions**
and more at

reddoorpress.co.uk

YOU CAN ALSO FOLLOW US:

 @RedDoorBooks

 Facebook.com/RedDoorPress

 @RedDoorBooks